I0654420

Love Addict

Caroline Olsen

Love Addict

Copyright © 2013 by Caroline Olsen

All rights reserved. No part of this book may be reproduced or transmitted in any form or by any means without written permission of the author.

ISBN: 978-82-998117-2-9

Very special thanks to Rora and Monica for proofing, for their continuous support, and their praise. Thanks for bothering with me all this time. ❤

Foreword

Dear reader,

Thank you for picking up this book, whether you have read my previous works or not. I want to extend special thanks in particular to all the fresh readers who might be picking this novel up on a whim, it means a lot.

'Love Addict' is the third installment in what has become known as the 'Jaded SNOW Project', and can be considered a spin-off to my previous novel, 'Jaded'. If you haven't already read it, I suggest you check it out if you want to understand this story to the fullest, as it did spring from the same story-line and runs parallel to the main events in 'Jaded'. I had a lot of fun with this script; exploring and inserting new views and angles on certain scenes that took place in 'Jaded', while at the same time developing an altogether new story, with a new main couple.

While 'Love Addict' is based on the JS-storyline, it is also perfectly able to stand on its own feet, so don't worry about reading this one first!

It's already been 4 years since the publication of SNOW, who knew this project would continue to live on and develop?

I certainly didn't. Not until Miya refused to let my mind go—I wondered what had really been going on with him in Jaded, and the wheels started turning. And now, here we are! I'm very excited to be able to bring this story to all of you, and to let you get to know Miya and his unlikely counterpart much better!

Compared to my other novels, "Love Addict" is a simpler story, a more clichéd BL story perhaps, but important nonetheless. Both to me, and to the characters at hand. Hopefully, this book can also mean something to you as a reader.

I would like to dedicate this book to everyone who loved my dear Miya, and to everyone who's had to fight for something.

I hope you will enjoy it.

1. One-Night Stand

He breathed shakily into another hot kiss as his body arched beneath the other man, trembling fingers digging into the man's sides, leaving little red, crescent-shaped markings on his flushed skin. His leg was extended, his knee resting against the other man's shoulder. His toes curled, calves tensed, and his entire body shook. The blood flow to his leg was gone, and the cry that emitted from his sore throat was raw and choked back.

They collapsed in a heap on the bed, heavy breaths and quiet laughter resounding in the stuffy bedroom.

Miya's leg tingled painfully as the blood trickled back into his veins and he regained the feeling in the rigid limb. He laughed softly, rolling over on his side. The little electric impulses still flickered through his intoxicated body.

It may be bad policy to go home with one's clients, but in his line of work, it was anything but uncommon.

Miya and his coworkers often reasoned that they were there for the patrons' pleasure, so why not pleasure them to the fullest?

He laughed again. The good-looking man at his side was propped up on his elbow, eyeing him quizzically beneath an arched eyebrow.

"It was just amazing, that's all." Miya leaned in closer, touching their lips together, smiling coyly at his lover for the night. A strong arm went around his torso, pulling him closer, engulfing him in warm kisses and the damp warmness of the sweat-soaked comforter. The familiarity of another's body against his, hot breath in his hair, and fingers stroking along his lean frame made him feel drowsy. His body was heavy with endorphins and alcohol, along with the fatigue of having worked until the wee hours of morning.

He fell asleep on the arm of this stranger with whom he'd gone home.

***

When he woke up, he was alone. Sunlight streamed through the dusty blinds. Confused, Miya blinked a couple of times. He must have slept long. The stranger was gone. Miya's body still felt the aftermath of last night's events though. He smiled. As handsome and intriguing as the young man had been, and as much as he wouldn't mind encountering him again, he was grateful that he'd left. Even if *he* had no problem with sharing an awkward cup of coffee with a one-night stand the morning after, that wasn't everyone's cup of tea. He stood, and without bothering to get dressed, he went out into the hall space between the bedroom and bathroom. Sneaking a quick glance into the combined living room/kitchen area, he figured his roommate was probably out of the house. The room was empty. He closed the bathroom door behind himself, squinting against the bright lights, and stepped into the shower.

Afterwards, he grabbed a quick bite to eat and headed out. The apartment was empty, as expected, and he didn't feel like being cooped up alone all day. Besides, his head hurt slightly, even after the shower, so he figured some fresh air wouldn't hurt. He got on a train and went to the district where the bar he worked at was located, but since they didn't open for hours, he ventured down to the *izakaya*-like establishment they all frequented, located in the dockside area. A fresh breeze blew in from the sea, strong enough to make him feel slightly chilled, but at the same time relieving his headache.

He pushed the door to the small shop open and uttered a soft, *"Ohayou"* as he came through the door.

"Good morning?" the man behind the counter shot back at him. "It's one in the afternoon!"

Miya grinned back at him, throwing himself down at a table by one of the windows next to a blond man who was reading the newspaper. He paid Miya no mind as he plopped down next to him.

"You hungry?" Maki, the bartender asked, throwing a glance

2

over his shoulder while stacking mugs and glasses into the shelves behind the bar counter.

Miya shook his head. "Already ate."

"I'm sure you did," the blond man next to him said, finally acknowledging his presence and glancing sidelong at him from beneath his glasses.

Miya grinned back, tugging at the man's hair. "Reading glasses? Really, Naru?"

"Do you mind?"

"Not at all," Miya replied, grabbing the newspaper, folding it and placing it aside on the table. "Tell me about last night."

"You can't remember it?" the bartender laughed towards him.

"Oh I remember it." The dark-haired man's lips curved upwards, and he nudged the blond man again. "Well?"

"What's there to say?" Naruse finally sighed, looking at him. "You left with the hottest one, and the rest of us were stuck with the leftovers."

The bartender laughed harder over by the counter.

"That is *not* true!" Miya retorted, trying to piece together what had actually happened after work the previous night. They'd gone out with a couple of friends and coworkers and ended up running into a group of guys who'd been frequenting their workplace for the past week or so. They'd been the ones who'd called Miya and his group over when they spotted them at the club they'd all been at, asking them if they were the waiters from the other bar. As if that hadn't been obvious; the three of them had been there enough to definitely recognize them, and especially as they'd been furiously flirting with them increasingly with every visit.

The guys had revealed that the three of them were just in Kobe for the week and had decided to make the best of it by checking out the nightclub scene in their district. The mood had been obvious right from the start, at least as far as Miya was concerned. He'd had a good tone with the short-haired man in the button-down shirt all week, and he was very appreciative of getting to talk to him in a different environment. Although he could barely hear what the other was shouting into his ear, and he wasn't really interested in *talking* to him. By the time he'd heard all about how the guy was a twenty-six-year-old journalism student, he was bored with the small talk. He only partially listened to what the man was saying while watching his two friends engrossed in conversation and laughter with Naruse and Hiiro at the table they'd been able to score. Naruse wasn't the type for dancing, and in any case, the floor was too crowded. He noted how one of the guys' hands was casually resting on the blond man's thigh though and smirked.

He'd considered asking the man to dance, precisely because the floor was crowded and would require the two of them getting close. But he couldn't stand the music they were playing, and his legs hurt—courtesy of his boots. Besides, the other man seemed to be under the belief that he had to *talk* Miya into being charmed with him. He sneered, emptying his drink, placing the glass on the nearest table and leaning in close to the student.

"Listen, Takahiro, is it?" He licked his lips, narrowing his dark-rimmed eyes. "What do you say we get out of here?" He spoke softly, gently gripping the man's wrist, caressing his underarm with two fingers, slipping them beneath the cuff of his shirt. "I'm sure your friends won't mind…?"

He glanced over at the group by the table; they'd been joined by some of Hiiro's friends, and Naruse and the other man still seemed to be hitting it off.

One of the definite upsides to the place where he worked was that you got used to cutting to the chase. Few of the guys he worked with beat around the bush if they saw someone they were interested in. They had no time to waste, and since most of the men that showed interest in them had no wish for a longer connection anyway, there was no need for pointless chitchat.

He exchanged glances with the man; he had deep, brown eyes, a little glazed over from the alcohol, but definitely interested.

Miya smiled at him, leaning even closer without letting go of the man's wrist, and kissed him lightly on the lips. "Good, let's go."

Dragging the student by the arm, Miya brushed past the table where the others were sitting. "We're out!" he called, grinning to his coworkers.

Hiiro offered half a wave, and Naruse shook his head laughing. "Not wasting time, are you?"

"We can't all be like *you*!" Miya retorted. "Good luck Naru!"

***

"So?" he nudged the other man in the arm.

"Don't get ahead of yourself," Naruse replied calmly, grabbing for his newspaper again. "We got along and all, but he shared a hotel room with his friend, and I didn't want to take him home."

"Are you kidding me?"

Naruse opened the paper on the same page as earlier.

"It was no strings attached though, and he seemed to be really into *you* at least! Plus, he was really cute!"

Miya groaned, thinking back to the young man in the red shirt. He'd had a contagious laugh and a very nice smile. Unlike Naruse, who was always composed, the guy had seemed really carefree and didn't seem like he'd mind going home with a stranger, even if it meant leaving his friend to go back to the hotel alone.

For that matter, the club had been packed; the third guy might have met someone anyway, assuming all three of them were gay. He sighed audibly. "Do you ever have *any* fun?"

Naruse sipped at his coffee, turning the page. A small smile played at the corner of his lips. "Did I say *nothing* happened?"

"I knew it!" Miya cheered. "Spill!"

"Yeah, thanks for helping with that," Naruse replied dryly. He'd been nudged hard enough to spill his coffee and looked mildly irritated. "How do you have so much energy when you're hung over?"

Maki came over to the table, handing them a few paper towels. He sat down, yawning. It was still really quiet, since most of his customers either came by during the breakfast hour or at night. "What is this, a high school? You two sound like a couple of students," he chuckled, lighting a cigarette.

"Speaking of," Miya replied, looking at the two of them, "I found myself abandoned this morning. Anyone seen Aki?"

The other two shrugged. "He's probably having a high school experience of his own."

Naruse crumpled the paper towels and placed them on his empty plate. Miya snickered.

"What about you?" the blond took another sip of his coffee. "What was it like with the journalist major?"

He said it with amusement, clearly aware that Miya had been annoyed with the small talk the night before.

"Thankfully, he was far less talkative and awkward once we made it home." Miya snagged a cigarette from the pack on the table, leaning across to light it on Maki's. "And he got quite *into* it."

He laughed hoarsely. His throat still felt scratchy. The two others exchanged glances.

"He was quite sweet as well." He smiled, exhaling a cloud of white smoke. "Generous with the compliments once he got over himself, and very handsy afterwards."

This kind of talk was common amongst his group. Not because they wanted to report their conquests to one another, but more because they were all so close—it was a very natural thing to do. None of them judged, and they were no better themselves. Maybe it was just a way of reassuring each other.

"He's probably going to make a great boyfriend for someone," Miya continued.

"Someone? Do you plan on seeing him again?" Naruse lifted his gaze from the paper.

Miya shrugged. "Nah, he left his number in the kitchen, but I don't think so. I'm not interested in a long-distance thing, but if he pays a visit, I wouldn't mind a reprise of last night."

"Of course not." It was flat, not without humor, but without being mean.

The door opened, and Maki stood, greeting the customers that came in. Miya and Naruse both glanced in their direction, but it wasn't anyone they knew.

They sat in silence, smoking and drinking coffee, waiting for time to pass so they could get to work. It was probably going to be another calm night, seeing as it was a weekday, but neither of them minded too much.

Takahiro had said that they weren't leaving Kobe until the next day, so there was a definite possibility they'd see the group again. Miya wasn't sure what he thought of that. The man had left his phone number, so he was probably interested, but Miya himself didn't feel much like giving him any hopes.

"Maybe I should offer him a proper good bye though..." he said out in the air, putting out his cigarette in the chipped ashtray on the table.

Naruse glanced at him but said nothing.

2. Routines

They did come by, fairly early in the evening on that same night. Miya was serving tables when they came in, acknowledging the three of them with a smile and a nod when they came through the door. He finished taking the order from the table he was working and made off to the bar. It was on purpose, as to make a point to the younger man that he wasn't overjoyed to see him, even though he had nothing against him either. He just wanted to establish a proper distance between them, although the man had tactfully left and probably didn't look for much more than a little fun while he was in town. The number he'd left might have just been to be courteous. He certainly seemed the type. Absentmindedly, Miya stacked drinks onto his tray, heading back to the table.

Scouting the club, he saw that the group was already seated and was being attended to by Ayase, one of the younger waiters at the bar. He was clearly charming them with his cheery disposition, and it didn't seem like they were waiting for either him or Naruse to show themselves. That was a relief.

He offered his table a wink and made sure to touch his fingers to the customer's as he placed the drinks on their table; keeping them enticed was half the point of the club. When his roommate had first showed up here for his job interview, Miya had told him it was a place where dreams came true. To a certain extent, it was. The waiters and bartenders were easy on the eyes, many of them hired for their looks; their unabashed flirting with the customers and each other was a sort of trademark for the club. And although it was frowned upon, the manager turned a blind eye when they took customers home—as long as they played it safe and made sure not to cause any trouble by getting too close and personal with them. Ironically, the manager didn't want any drama.

Most people who came here were usually pretty low-key though. Many of them were even married—to women—and many weren't openly gay either. And, as several of the guys had noted on numerous occasions, it was hard to be in a relationship with anyone working in a place like this, so for the most part, it all went pretty smoothly, at least as long as they picked their partners carefully.

His free hand stroked over Ayase's lower back as the younger man passed him on the floor.

"He's cute!" Ayase mouthed, having earlier heard all about the night before.

"Wanna share?" Miya smirked.

Ayase continued towards the back room, running his hand across Miya's chest in a brief caress, meant mostly for the customers who might be watching them.

***

"Back for more?" Miya lightly placed his hand on Takahiro's shoulder.

He'd waited about an hour before finally coming over to their table, making it look somewhat casual, asking them if they wanted anything else. He had no trouble acknowledging the other man and thought it polite to do so.

"It's our last night here, so we thought we'd come by again," one of the friends replied.

"Ah right." Miya nodded. "You're going back... We're so used to seeing you by now, I forgot that you're from out of town."

He put on the tone he used with clients—flirty and somewhat ditzy. They looked a tad embarrassed at his statement. Perhaps they didn't frequent these kinds of places in their everyday lives.

"Consider yourselves regulars." He smiled. "It's been a *pleasure* serving you."

He squeezed the younger man's shoulder a little.

"Likewise," Takahiro replied, smiling at him.

An image from the previous night flashed before Miya's

mind. "Any time," he replied. And he meant it. As long as it didn't occur too often, which was unlikely with the distance and all.

He took their orders for more drinks but sent Ayase back to their table to keep up some kind of distance still. When they were ready to leave, he was still on shift but pulled the student aside when they passed him.

"Come back if you're ever in the area," he said sweetly, kissing the corner of his mouth. "And thanks for the good time."

He allowed his hand to drop, lightly touching against Takahiro's lower stomach.

"Maybe I will," the other replied. He didn't look upset about leaving, but perhaps a little unwilling to leave for the time being.

"I'd send you off properly, but I'm at work till three, so I guess we'll have to take a rain check until next time, right?"

"Deal." Takahiro grinned. "I'll take you up on the offer."

"Come on, man!" His friends were getting impatient—with good reason. Miya needed to get back to work as well.

They parted ways without any more familiarities, and Miya made his way back towards the bar.

"Well, that was emotional."

Miya turned a deaf ear to his roommate, who'd appeared out of nowhere. He wasn't even scheduled to work tonight, so he was probably just there to waste time. Somehow, sleep didn't seem to be his top priority.

"It's called customer service." Miya brushed past him, yawning. *He* wanted to sleep at least. "You're the one to talk by the way!"

"I learned from the best!" the youngster replied snarkily, walking away.

"At least that's a compliment," Miya remarked dryly to himself, scratching his shoulder through the fishnet sleeves.

"I'm taking a break!" he said to the bartenders, heading out through the backroom and out into the back yard, lighting a cigarette.

There was always a chilly breeze blowing in from the sea in this part of the city, so even on relatively warm nights, the air would be cool. It nipped at his cheeks and exposed arms and thighs, where the skimpy outfits revealed pale skin.

He watched the clouds drifting past in the midnight sky above, and the white smoke that drifted upwards towards them. The fresh, crisp air felt good. The hangover from earlier was gone, and the fatigue he was feeling simply came from getting too little sleep and knowing that he still had a few more hours of work. He thought that he'd just head right home as soon as he was let off and get some proper sleep, maybe spend the next day lounging around the apartment.

"You look thoughtful." Naruse joined him, leaning against the fence.

"Dead tired," Miya yawned in response. He thrust the cigarette pack towards the man. "Cig?"

"You would be." Naruse shook his head. "No thanks. I just needed some air. It's stifling in there."

"Mmh." Miya nodded, tapping the cigarette, making ash fall to the ground. It was wet after the brief drizzle that had struck a short while ago. "You're driving, right?"

Naruse nodded. "Want me to give you a ride tonight?"

"Since you're offering..." Miya grinned. "I'm too tired to stay behind and drink, and I need to sleep."

"Wasn't it worth it though?" Naru smiled knowingly.

"Definitely." Miya revealed a dazzling smile. "I must admit, I was skeptical to begin with."

Naruse chuckled quietly. "You're so judgmental, even though *you* were the one who came on to *him*."

"Well, I had to try, right?" A mischievous grin crossed Miya's androgynous face. "He *was* really cute. You said so yourself!"

"Hey, not passing any judgment here." The other man held up the palms of his hands in a defensive manner. "After all..." He paused, looking away.

Miya's ears were on edge. "Yes? Are you *ever* gonna tell?"

"Gentlemen don't kiss and tell," came the calm reply. Naruse still wasn't looking at him. It was annoying. Naru was known as the big-brother type, the one who was responsible when the others weren't, the one who was sober when the rest were effectively killing their own livers, and the one who spoke least of his own private life. It wasn't like he was completely closed off and antisocial though—even Naruse was capable of losing himself to spontaneity, frivolity and intoxication. It was just that he was so damned responsible and respectful sometimes.

"Is this what you picked up in med-school?" Miya retorted a little sourly. "Confidentiality? Or are you just giving me the silent treatment because I took the hot one?"

His tone changed back to being joking just as quickly as he had snapped at the other man. Miya wasn't one to hold grudges. He was just naturally curious, that was all. Especially when it came to calm, composed ol' Naru. He knew for a fact, by *personal experience*, that Naruse was anything but chaste and frigid.

"Stupid," Naru laughed. "Let's go inside. I'm getting cold."

He started to cross the small graveled yard, skipping up the stairs to the back door. Just as he went inside he grinned. "He wasn't half bad though, if you have to know!"

"I knew it!" Miya shouted after him, following him inside the building.

***

The rest of the night was relatively calm. As there were very few guests, most of the waiters sat around for the remaining hours. The bartenders even had time to play a game of cards; that was how lively the place was in the middle of the week. Most of the clients had started leaving around midnight, most of them people who looked like they still had to get up the next morning.

"I don't envy them," Kyo said, fiddling with a black straw while leaning on the bar counter. "I wonder what possesses people to hang out here during the week."

"Aren't you glad they're so irresponsible?" Naru replied dryly. "They're the ones paying your salary."

"True."

They sat around chatting idly. Now and again, they'd take turns tending to the remaining clients while waiting for time to pass and for the manager to close the bar. For the time being, he was in his office and had barely been seen all night.

Hiiro yawned several times and seemed to be falling asleep where he sat, his eyes tired beneath the heavy make-up and his long, red bangs. He was currently working his ass off taking classes while working nights and barely got enough sleep as it was, but he still preferred the nightlife to going home to sleep on his days off. Lately, he'd been hunched over his books during breaks and after hours studying for a big exam, and now that it had passed, he was even more zombiefied than he'd been to begin with. Miya looked at him with concern. "Hiiro, aren't you going to take some time off?"

"The worst is over now," the other man sighed. "I just need to get my hours in order again."

It didn't really sound like he believed his own words, but Miya still couldn't help admiring him for trying to get his life back on track. Hiiro was still in his early twenties; there was no way things wouldn't work out for him, and all his hard work now would probably pay off later.

"Is it cruel to hope you never find a job?" he asked absentmindedly. "Or that you don't pass your exams?"

"Yes!" the red-haired male screeched. "I'm killing myself here!"

"But we love you so much," Miya cooed, stroking his hand over tousles of black and deep red.

"And after we lost Hiromu—"

"I saw him the other day by the way," Ayase shot in as he went behind the register to punch in the tab for someone. "He seemed to be doing really well. I hardly recognized him though; he looks very different in daylight!"

The others laughed. Hiromu had been working with them until fairly recently while saving up to pay for his university tuition. He had an irresistible charm but could be painfully shy sometimes. Regardless, he'd been very popular, and many clients still asked for him and were just as disappointed every time. Even though he'd thrived in the job itself, Hiromu had never been entirely comfortable with the way they dressed and wore make-up at the club, so it was probably a relief for him to be back in the real world again.

"He looked really good though." Ayase said, grinning. "Promised to come see him when the exam season is over."

"Did he miss us?" Hiiro wondered.

"Of course. How could he not?" Ayase replied, sauntering past them to deliver the tab and take the table's payment. Miya's eyes watched him as he walked, confidently striding through the room and feigning modesty as he "bumped into" Aki, who was coming from the opposite direction. "You think it's a little creepy?"

"What is?" The other three looked at him.

Miya shook his head. "Just... that perverse vibe some clients give off."

"I've had worse," Hiiro remarked dryly.

Miya shrugged. He loved his workplace, but sometimes he wondered if the manager was bonkers, hiring all these college kids and having them prance around in skimpy outfits acting out "types" that got the clientele going. It wasn't like they did anything illegal, but he knew very few people who'd think much of what went on inside of this establishment. He tried to shake off the thoughts. It was pointless thinking that way. Getting this job was probably one of the best things that had happened to him, and a couple of the others as well. But it wasn't really the way to go for someone who was seeking acceptance from others.

"Stop being such a helicopter-mom," Kyo interjected. "They're not kids."

"Obviously I know that," Miya shot back, looking in the general direction of his roommate. The raven-haired teenager was seemingly chatting up a rather intoxicated man. *Probably fishing for tips, the schemer.* The guy didn't look like his type at all.

Miya averted his eyes, glancing towards the clock visible on the wall in the back room. "I just want to go home—tonight *sucks*."

"You're the child here." Naruse stood, walking out into the club with a resigned smile on his lips.

A while later, the two of them left together, giving Hiiro a ride to the nearest station, while the others discussed where to go next. Neither of them had any intentions of going home it seemed, so they'd probably find somewhere to drink until it closed and then head on home, possibly with someone else.

Miya felt like he was constantly drifting off in the car seat next to Naruse on the way home. The quiet rumble of the engine and the assorted tunes playing on the radio were just about lulling him to sleep as they approached Higashinada.

When he made it inside the apartment and crept into his sheets, they still carried the musky scent of sex and sweat. He drifted off into pleasant, dreamless sleep.

3. Encounter

For the most part, Miya was content with the way things were. Even though he might seem like the fickle type to some, he really did like to have a sense of stability around him. He was happy in his two-bedroom apartment, which he got together with a friend a while after he first moved to Kobe. Tsuuji and he had known each other through mutual friends from high school and had hit it off pretty much instantly after meeting at a party. They didn't necessarily share the same opinions on everything and were far too different to ever be anything but friends—which seemed to have been the ulterior motive of their mutual friend, a girl Miya used to go to school with.

He'd told her he was sorry to disappoint her, but that he and Tsuuji would probably be miserable in a relationship with each other. It wasn't that they hadn't tried; they had in fact gone out a couple of times, and even been intimate on a few occasions. The chemistry hadn't been all that bad, but they didn't get along on many other levels. For instance, Tsuuji had been completely obsessed with baseball. The man used to play himself when he was in high school, and even when he went to university. He'd regularly played on an amateur team. His room had been plastered with posters of his favorite team, and he never missed a game, whereas Miya abhorred sports. He used to play a little, sure, when he was a kid growing up in the sticks and during sporting events in school. But he'd always hated it, and his classmates would never stand up an opportunity to tell him how much he sucked at anything from batting to pitching.

These days he'd laugh it off and retort with a snarky reply along the lines of "I'm a great catcher though!" or "Yeah well, handling *base*balls isn't really my thing."

They were probably vulgar jokes, and he knew more than a couple people who would have convulsed if they'd heard him say it, but Tsuuji had always laughed at them, even though he'd desperately tried to make Miya go to games with him back in the day. A futile mission.

Miya on his side didn't have any particular pastimes. He didn't especially care to have a specific hobby, but rather did whatever he felt like at the time. Sometimes he'd read magazines, or watch movies. He enjoyed fashion and actually quite liked the elaborate style he pulled off at work, but if he was at home, he was just as happy just lazing around in pajamas. If anything, Tsuuji would say that Miya's hobby was "drinking until morning with hot guys." He couldn't really deny it but wouldn't go as far as calling it a hobby.

"It's more a lifestyle," he'd occasionally replied.

He'd argue that his family was so uptight that he was having some kind of latent reaction in terms of wanting to just make the most out of life and living in the now. Tsuuji, however, had always claimed that Miya didn't really *do* anything. He was the type who needed to keep a full schedule: watch sports, play sports, work overtime... that kind of thing. The only thing Tsuuji *didn't* do was housework.

In the end, that's what it came down to; they'd become somewhat like an old married couple who fought over chores and placed the blame on each other until they finally realized that they couldn't keep living together.

Tsuuji had moved out a little over a year ago, and then Aki had moved in when Miya had heard that he was looking for a place. The two of them were more compatible, at least in the sense that they were more interested in the now than they were in trying to fill their days with much of anything. Miya didn't see the point in stressing and talking about how little time there was, or griping about all the things that people were always placing upon themselves and never managed to get out of the way.

He was twenty-eight years old, and his mother still scolded him for being irresponsible, for not getting "a proper job at least!" He generally turned a deaf ear to her preaching, since he felt content with the way things were.

Sometimes he talked to Tsuuji, who was now living on his own but supposedly seeing someone, at least for the time being. Another important flaw in the relationship that had almost been between the two of them was that neither was the type to commit. Miya didn't like to invest a lot of time and effort in something he didn't strongly feel was worth it. And Tsuuji just generally didn't like being tied down—another joke between the two of them.

They were on good terms now, although they hardly saw each other. But not living together anymore was probably an important factor in keeping their friendship from falling apart completely. If anything, Miya mused, it was the attachment he had to his friends that meant the most to him. When he'd moved to Kobe about eight or nine years earlier, he'd begun building this network, starting with Tsuuji and his old classmate, and then working at the nightclub, right from its early beginning. He'd grown to become very attached to his current group of friends. Although many of them had gone through more than what they wanted to share, there was a closeness in their group that was unrivaled by most things. Several of them had little to no contact with their families, so they'd all come to depend on each other as a kind of family.

Although he might have originally had a sort of idea that he was going to get some kind of education once he moved to Kobe, he'd more or less forgotten about those plans. His entire life had seemed to be staked out for him after he finished high school, and he resented it. It suited him better to take things as they came along and live for the moment rather than for the expectations society seemed to have for him.

His life as it currently was might be somewhat repetitious; working at the club almost every night, maybe going out or staying behind, drinking afterwards, picking up guys, or casually going home with someone when he felt like it, long mornings and little to fill his days off. But it was never entirely predictable, and he was never bored. Besides, living a standard life, working nine to five was every bit as repetitious and tedious, if not more so.

Presently, he was fairly certain that he didn't desire anything else. He was perfectly content with the way things were. Or so he thought.

***

It started on one of those days where everything seemed to be perfectly normal. He'd gone out together with Hiiro and his friend Yuura, who was still not out of the net Hiiro also used to be a part of. The two of them used to be friends as well as "competitors"—to put it that way. But Sho, the manager, had swept Hiiro off the street and given him a chance to redeem himself in society's eyes. Yuura, however, seemed to be fairly at ease with what he was doing for a living, even though it was hard for anyone to grasp that he'd willingly do what he did. Hustling was a term most associated with exploitation and the like, but even Miya had been surprised at how Yuura and some of his companions were living, voluntarily doing what they did when they didn't have to. At this point, he'd known them long enough not to pay it much mind. Yuura spent a lot of time with their group and was a frequent attendant at all their social events. Jokingly, he'd say that it was one of the main perks of deciding his own work hours, and then he'd laugh that hoarse laugh of his while covering his mouth slightly with his slim hand in an almost lady-like fashion.

They'd gone to Maki's for dinner and a round of beers before heading out on the town to have a good time. It hardly ever happened that they went out *looking* for guys to pick up; it was more that they didn't pass up opportunities when they came along and the time seemed right. That night had been completely unintentional from Miya's side though. And in retrospect, he wondered if he'd even considered it to be anything at all.

The evening in question took place a few weeks after the event with Takahiro, the journalism student, whom Miya hadn't heard from since their goodbye at the club. Naruse seemingly had some sort of sporadic contact with the guy who'd been wearing the red shirt, but that wasn't of the serious kind either. Apparently, they had something in common, causing them to keep in touch even now that the group had gone back to the city where they all lived and studied.

Miya, however, hadn't really been into meeting random guys out of their close circle lately. And he didn't have it in mind for this particular evening either. The place they'd gone to was a plain old bar, not being in the mood to go to any of the obnoxious clubs in the area. They'd sometimes go out to mainstream places just for the experience, especially if they weren't on the prowl, since theirs was one of the few gay establishments in their ward. But like their previous experience, those clubs were always loud, crowded and oozing with all kinds of stench and drama, so they'd chosen to keep it more down to earth.

It had been a night of casual chat and gossip, laughter bubbling between the clinking of glasses and pouring of neon-colored drinks.

"Did you hear that pouring liquid nitrogen in drinks is a thing?" Yuura emptied his glass, slamming it down on the table and looking at them with eager eyes.

"You mean that thing where they make them look all cool with the smoke and stuff?"

The other man nodded. "Yeah that. How come you don't do that over at your place? It would probably draw customers like crazy! It looks wicked."

Hiiro snorted. Miya shook his head laughing. It was clear that Yuura had already had too much. His alcohol tolerance didn't amount to much against stronger drinks.

"We don't need liquid nitrogen to draw customers," Miya replied, amused. "There's a sentence you don't say every day."

"And we're not really interested in killing our current clientele either," Hiiro replied, deadpan. "No matter how cool it looks."

The words came out wrong, and he laughed.

Miya leaned back in the booth, resting his neck against the smooth leather surface. He felt relaxed. The alcohol in his system calmed him, soothed his aching muscles and made a comfortable tingle spread all the way out to his fingertips.

He was halfway listening in on the other two talking. Hiiro drummed his painted fingernails against the frosted glass in the same rhythm of the bass beat filling the bar. "So, how's business?" he asked coyly, nudging his friend with his shoulder.

"Like you don't know?" Yuura gave a short bark of laughter, leaning back against Hiiro's shoulder. "Well, the other day I went with some guy to this really disgusting hotel. You could see the roaches in the lobby and—"

"Eeew!" Hiiro was grimacing, already laughing out loud at the most likely exaggerated story. Miya tuned them out. His gaze wandered around the bar from the lights blinking above the bar at the farthest wall to the group of what seemed to be university students playing pool in the corner. There was a girl in a pink top with caramel-colored hair and sparkling lips cheering loudly and laughing, although she kept yelling loud enough for half the bar to hear that she had no idea how to play the game. They seemed to be having fun, even though her friends were trying to shush her down. Maybe she'd had too much to drink as well.

Miya continued looking around at the people chatting and dancing; even though this wasn't really that kind of place, many people, girls in particular, were dancing where they stood, moving to the music—girlfriends grabbing each other and laughing loudly while they danced or couples being carried away by the atmosphere.

His eyes fell on the booth opposite from theirs across the floor. At first, he noticed the poster above it—a reproduction of a famous record cover. The bright colors were eye-catching against the dark background and bland wall.

In the booth below, he spotted several men and a couple of women. Their table was cluttered with drinks, glasses and handbags. He noticed one of the men in particular; a handsome-looking guy wearing a white button-up shirt—perfectly pressed without a crease in the fabric. The guy seemed to have a stick up his ass, as he was looking less and less amused the more Miya regarded him. He had a good face though—strong features, a nice jaw line, his hair was cut short but was still long enough to be ruffled. He didn't seem like the type to enjoy having his hair ruffled in the slightest though. In fact, he seemed to be wishing he was someplace far away. Now and again, he'd look at the woman seated next to him, seemingly feigning interest. Although she was a beautiful girl with long, chestnut hair and a lovely smile, he didn't seem to care much for her company.

Miya didn't really realize he was staring until he saw that the other man had noticed him. His expression had changed somewhat, his brow furrowing as if he was trying to figure out whether or not Miya was actually looking at *him* or something else. Miya pulled his gaze away, shifting focus back to his two friends, who were still engrossed in conversation about various disgusting situations they'd gotten themselves into at some point in their lives.

"Welcome back," Hiiro said, looking at him with something that resembled mild concern. "Have you had too much already? You seemed totally spaced out."

Miya cast him an unamused glare. "As if. I could drink you two under the table at any time."

"Oh." Red lips curved upwards. "Is that a challenge, Utsunomiya?"

"Would you like it to be?" he replied, grinning wolfishly.

"How about no?" Hiiro interjected. "I'm not taking the responsibility for you two drunkards all night."

"Then don't," Miya coaxed, reaching out across the table and placing his hand on top of the other man's. It was warm.

"Yeah," Yuura pressed himself closer to Hiiro, almost pushing him off the bench. "Drink with us."

The redhead laughed, sliding back into safety, tilting his head slightly to the side and kissing his friend on his bare shoulder. "Since it's *you*."

More laughter. They ordered another round of drinks as Miya remarked that as the oldest of the three, *he* really should be responsible enough not to get too carried away. The others argued that in that case, he was failing miserably for several reasons. He laughed at them—and with them. They lifted their glasses to a random but fitting toast.

"To irresponsibility!"

Miya's head was getting a little clouded, like it was starting to fill with cotton. Now and again, he'd turn his gaze towards the other booth and the morose man. He was still sitting with the same girl. Their ranks seemed to have thinned a little, as a couple of them had migrated over to the pool table. He peered at the man, who was absentmindedly nodding at whatever it was his companion was talking about over the rim of his glass.

Several times over the span of the night, he'd notice that his gaze wandered towards that table, and he was surprised to realize that the other man was looking in their direction a lot of the time as well. He couldn't be sure though, since they were seated fairly close to the exit. Maybe he was just wishing he was somewhere else.

"What's up?" Yuura came back from the bathroom, looking a little unsteady on his feet and swaying on his platform shoes. It looked suicidal. He leaned over Miya's shoulder, gawking obviously in the direction of the booth across from theirs. The other man's glance quickly shifted focus, averting from their general direction and fixing itself on the woman instead.

"Oh, is he checking you out?" Yuura chirped, gripping Miya's shoulder hard enough for his nails to pinch him through his shirt.

"Ouch." Miya shook him off. "Would you mind not staring so obviously?"

"Afraid I'll snatch him up before you do?" Yuura replied, scurrying back to his own seat. He grabbed a mug of beer from the table as he did and squeezed Hiiro further up against the wall as he sat on the outer part of the seat this time.

"He's not checking me out," Miya fended him off. "I looked at him first, okay?"

"So you're checking him out, and he caught you in the act?" Yuura clicked his tongue. Hiiro chuckled at his side.

Miya sighed, shaking his head. "Stop twisting my words, you moron. I just happened to notice that he must be having a bad time, so I was looking. That's it."

"Yeah, but you were probably thinking of several ways to make him enjoy himself, weren't you?" Yuura sniggered, wiping beer foam from his upper lip with the back of his hand.

"If I *did* have my eyes on him, I promise you I wouldn't want him to enjoy *himself*," Miya countered, smiling wryly at the other men. They burst out laughing.

"You're not gonna go talk to him though?" Hiiro asked. "It's not like you to stand up an opportunity."

"What opportunity?" Miya wasn't convinced that his friends were all that present at this point. "He's probably straight. We're the odd ones out here."

"So what if he is? It's not like you haven't jumped at the chance before."

Miya chuckled. It was true that picking up men outside of familiar territories was a gamble, and that it was a chance he usually didn't mind taking, but it wasn't like he had any kind of special interest in the other man. It had just happened to become a big deal when Tweedledum and Tweedledee across the table had meddled.

"He's with a girl," he simply said, hoping that would shut them up and turn them onto different subjects. "A really pretty one at that."

"Boring," Yuura replied, yawning demonstratively. "I'm tired of drinking; wanna do something else?"

Miya glanced at his wristwatch. He only ever wore it as an accessory, and since he wore it with the display side on the inside of his wrist, he tended to forget it wasn't just a leather bracelet. It was already close to four in the morning. The place was probably closing soon. Come to think of it, didn't it seem like the crowd had thinned over the last hour?

"Yeah," he said, rubbing his wrist and turning the watch slightly. "Just let me go to the bathroom first."

"Sure," Hiiro nodded. "Mind if we wait outside though? I need a smoke."

Miya knew what he was thinking; he didn't have to go outside to smoke a cigarette. He nodded in affirmation, emptying

24

the last of his drink.

He stood and strode through the bar, making his way towards the men's room.

There were no paper towels left by the sink. He shook his hands in annoyance, little droplets of water flying everywhere as he tried to air-dry them before finally wiping his palms on his thighs. When he exited the bathroom and came back out into the little alcove at the back of the bar, he nearly crashed into the man standing by the wall.

"I'm sorry!" he exclaimed, surprised to find someone standing there.

Their gazes met. It was the man in the starched shirt, looking just as unamused as before. "I didn't mean to... I didn't see you."

Miya cleared his throat, feeling an unfamiliar nervousness. It was unfamiliar because he was in reality a very confident person, but at the same time, he knew that because he was never willing to play himself down, he could easily become a victim of anyone who wanted to pick on him, especially in a place like this. For all he knew, the guy had been provoked by their little exchange of looks earlier.

"Why were you looking at me before?" the man asked him. His voice was quiet with a stern tone to it.

Miya shrugged. "You seemed to be having a bad time; it just happened to catch my eye."

That much was true at least. He looked back at the man, from the perfectly white shirt to his facial features— which were almost expressionless—and his general appearance. Everything had a certain authority to it, except for the hairstyle. He was probably a little younger than his persona led people to believe. And he was tall, probably taller than Miya if he wasn't wearing boots.

"I'm on a date," the man said somewhat unexpectedly. It sounded unconvincing and flat. Moreover, it wasn't a very natural thing to just say out of the blue, but it was four in the morning after all, and the other man was probably just as sober as Miya was.

"She's pretty," Miya replied, uncertain of why he was even having this conversation. He thought about Hiiro and Yuura outside smoking. Considering how careless those two were, they were likely to get arrested. His mind felt a little hazy.

"Which was why I was wondering why you looked so miserable."

"Excuse me?" The other man's blurry eyes glinted with confusion.

"Wouldn't most men grin from ear to ear in the company of a girl like her?" He pursed his lips, knowing that his tone carried a hint of condescendence. He wasn't really sure what he was doing at this point.

"Not if the company was forced," the man replied coolly.

"Oh?" Miya's lip quirked, and his voice changed slightly in his throat. His intoxicated mind was coming up with a theory. "She certainly seemed to be into you though."

"Well…" The man shrugged.

The conversation came to a halt. Starched-shirt guy looked uncomfortable. Come to think of it, they were standing outside of the men's room still, which basically could only mean two things, and Miya doubted that the man's intentions matched those of his usual crowd.

"In that case…" he allowed his voice to drop to the flirtatious tone he used with clients, smiling a little extra as he fished a card out from his back pocket, "…try this place. I can assure you there are no pesky, boring women over there."

He placed the card in the man's hesitantly outreached palm, gently caressing his fingertips at the same time, before walking away and taking aim at the front door.

He didn't know if he was being watched or not as he left.

4. Relative Happiness

The other two had been overly curious as to what took him so long, and it hadn't been unlikely, in their eyes, that Miya had encountered the man in the white shirt. The kind of encounter they imagined was way off, but Miya let them think what they wanted. Based on their mannerisms, they were already too wasted to be able to recall anything in detail the next day anyway. And if they did, at least it would be possible to talk to them then. He ushered them off the sidewalk, and the three of them left the bar to start on their respective ways home. Hiiro had decided to crash at Yuura's place, and since the trains had all stopped running, Miya decided to call Naruse.

"Naru?" he mumbled into the phone, hoping he didn't sound overly slurred. Naruse was the sweetest guy on the planet, but he could really tear you a new one if you called him in the middle of the night due to having had too much to drink and missing the last train.

"*Mmh, what do you want?*" the other man ground out over the line.

"Can I crash at your place? I'll walk over, but the trains—"

"*Sure. Be careful. Door's unlocked.*"

Naruse hung up just as quickly, going right back to sleep no doubt. His neighborhood wasn't far off though, so Miya didn't have any problem getting there on his own. Naruse had probably been at work until recently, as exhausted as he'd sounded on the phone.

If he hadn't been so numbed and exhausted himself, Miya would have felt bad about waking him up. Instead, he found his way to the man's building, locked the front door behind himself and stumbled over to the pull-out couch, where Naruse was already sleeping. He undressed partially and crawled in next to the sleeping blond.

"Idiot," Naruse muttered, throwing a limp arm around Miya's waist and pulling him closer. "You're freezing."

He breathed warmly against Miya's chilled skin in between unruly locks of midnight hair. Miya sighed with pleasure, allowed his shoulders to drop, and almost instantly fell asleep next to his friend, their bodies tightly pressed together on the couch.

***

The next morning, they had breakfast together while Miya retold the events of the previous night. There wasn't much to say though; it was just that the other two had blown everything out of proportion the night before.

"I just kind of wanted you to hear my story before you talk to Hiiro in case he actually remembers anything."

Naruse laughed, placing a plate of eggs and bacon in front of Miya before getting one for himself. His apartment was made up of only two rooms—a bathroom, and a combined kitchen/living room. Naruse's bed doubled as a regular couch in the daytime in the event that he should have visitors over and actually bother folding it up to an actual sofa. For the most part, he didn't.

"How come you live in this dump anyway?" Miya greedily helped himself to the bacon. "You could easily afford a bigger place."

"For what?" Naruse inquired, sliding down on the barstool on the other side of the counter and grabbing a fork. "I live alone anyway. This is plenty of room."

"I don't know about that," Miya said dryly while swallowing.

"What about *your* ramshackle building? It could be condemned at any given time. At least I'm guaranteed to still have a home next week."

"Earthquake of ninety-five," Miya shot back. "Nothing's for certain in this town."

"Funny."

"I need space," Miya continued. "Especially with my habit of finding roomies. Love him to death, but if we had any less space, I'm sure we'd rip each other's throats out."

Naruse nodded. "Probably helps a lot that you two are hardly ever at home."

"I'm just saying you should look into it; you could easily afford a bigger place. Or... a proper bed."

"It's quite convenient," Naruse defended.

"Tell that to my back," Miya groaned. "It hurts."

"That's because you sleep in ridiculous positions," the other man replied, smiling at him playfully. "It's not that bad."

"How can you even—"

"Did you ever stop to think," Naruse reached for the salt, "that it serves a purpose?"

"Hm?"

"Well, if I have guests, like your lovely self for example," there was a trace of sarcasm in his voice, "where will they sleep? Obviously not in the spare bed."

Miya caught on. "Because you don't have one."

"Precisely." The blond's pale lips curved upwards, his eyes gleaming.

"I *knew* you had it in you, you devil."

"Had what in me?" Naruse cocked an eyebrow, holding back a chuckle. It wasn't often he revealed this devious side of himself, so he had to be in a good mood, Miya mused, laughing out loud with the other man. He was glad he'd come there. Last night was still a bit of a blur, and the confusion still remained. He was unsure of why he'd struck up the conversation, but he also recognized that his drunken mind often did illogical things.

"Thanks for letting me stay over," he said, diverting his own thoughts.

"What?" Naruse stood up to make himself a cup of tea. "You think I'd let you roam the street in that state?"

"What state?"

"Don't play dumb; I know what you're like." Naruse grabbed a spoon from the kitchen drawer, placing it next to the cup on the counter. Miya watched him as he waited then slowly started to stir the hot tea. Naruse rarely drank anything but lemon tea, with sugar or preferably honey. It left his kitchen with a permanent scent of a mix between citrus and honey—today being no exception.

"I'm no worse than any of the rest of us," Miya defended himself, resting his chin on his knuckles. "Anyway, it's polite to say thanks."

"It was no problem. As long as I didn't need to pick your drunk ass up from somewhere." Naruse sipped at the hot beverage, licking his lips and then blowing gently at the steaming liquid, obviously deeming it too hot to drink still.

"And you love having me around. Let's not forget about that."

Naruse's smile curved along the rim of the porcelain cup. He didn't deny it, but he didn't confirm it either.

It was a perfectly serene morning. Miya was glad he'd had the wits about him to call the other man. Had he been back home at his own place, this morning wouldn't have been half as pleasant. He wouldn't have been served breakfast for one.

"Mind if I hang around for a while longer?" he asked, scratching his hair, which had turned into a bird's nest at some point during the night.

"Suit yourself," Naruse replied, shrugging, "I have the night off anyway, so I'm just going to take it easy today."

***

He remained at Naruse's place for most of the day. They didn't really talk much, just hung around in the apartment, watched an episode of a drama that was currently airing, and then Miya spent some time zapping through the channels while Naruse read a book. The blond man was leaning back on the wall, his knees pulled up against his body. Miya was leaning back on them, fiddling with the remote, irritated that daytime television was so pointless. He leaned back, resting the back of his head against Naruse's knees, looking up at the book's dust jacket.

"You're so intellectual," he said jokingly. "What's it about?"

"It's about a family who were exposed to the black rain after the Hiroshima bomb."

"Deep." Miya ran his finger along the spine of the book. "Sounds depressing."

"It's good though; you should try reading sometime." Naruse's voice was teasing.

"We learned about the black rain in school," Miya grumbled, "It was depressing enough then."

"Do you want something?" the other man wondered, peeking over the top of the novel.

Miya shook his head. "No, I'm comfortable like this. It's nice."

Naru's hand dropped from the book and came to rest on Miya's arm, stroking it gently. "Yeah, it is."

"Naru," Miya started again, "would you say that you're happy?"

"What do you mean?" Naruse turned a page. Evidently, he wasn't fully paying attention. Miya wasn't really sure what he'd meant himself. The words just came tumbling out of him.

"Well," he said, sitting up slightly, resting his elbow on his friend's knee. "Here we are. Two grown men..." he paused, and then smiled. "Two *attractive* grown men. And we're single. We don't have any education, and we're nowhere near settling down. Take your old class mates for instance; what are they doing these days?"

Naruse shrugged, folding the upper corner of the page he was on and placing the book up on the back of the sofa. "Most of them are married and raising families I guess."

"Precisely, and we're here, drinking every night, gossiping like teenagers."

"Are you saying you'd like to have a family?" Naruse's brow creased.

"Hell no!" Miya shuddered. "I have my folks and brother, that's enough. And with Aki and Ayase around, who needs kids?"

Naruse chuckled. "Ay-chan's not that young though. At least he's twenty."

"In any case, that's not what I meant." Miya ran little circles on Naruse's kneecap with his index finger. It seemed to tickle, as the man's leg twitched slightly. "We just don't seem to be matching that whole idea of what happiness is."

"That's just an ideal though," Naruse replied. "Based on expectations, upbringing and the whole reproductive instinct thing. To begin with, it's not like *we* can have families."

"Are you happy like that?"

Naruse shrugged again. "I haven't thought about it much. I don't think I'd want to have kids anyway… probably."

"Besides that though," Miya probed, "you failed med school, right? That must have been bitter."

"I could've gone back," Naru replied calmly, "but I'd already realized it wasn't for me. It was what was expected of me, not what I wanted to do."

"And is this what you wanted?"

He was acting like a child, asking question after question. They'd arisen in him after having had that conversation with the man in the white shirt the night before because he'd seemed so miserable. If he didn't want to be there, Miya had a hard time understanding why he'd waste time like that. The answer was probably expectations, just like Naru was saying.

"I don't know if I wanted it…" Naruse scratched his neck. "I sorta fell into it, I guess. But yeah, I think that at this point in my life, this is what I want."

Miya nodded slowly. "That's how I feel as well."

"Then why are you asking?"

"It just hit me, that's all," he replied thoughtfully. "I'm just glad we're on the same page. That I'm not the only one who thinks that the world is relative."

"Of course you're not," Naruse shook his head. "There's no way there's a right answer to how we should live in order to be happy."

"Exactly," Miya agreed with a nod. "Even if my life *is* superficial, this is what I want to do. At least right now, I can't picture my life any differently."

"Is that why you're being all philosophical?" Naruse

answered with another question. The man really liked conversations like these, so he was probably enjoying himself. "Because someone told you you're superficial?"

Miya snorted. "But I am. And so are the rest of you! No, it's just because... Never mind."

"It's a guy."

"It was just someone I talked to briefly last night, and he seemed unhappy. Got me thinking." Miya shrugged. "I mean, if he's miserable, why doesn't he do anything about it?"

"Maybe he can't. Some things are out of our hands, even when they're of direct concern to us." Naruse sounded like some sort of public service announcement.

"Obviously I know that." Miya felt exasperated. And guilty. He knew a lot of people who seemed happy on the surface, but if you just scraped a little at the top layer, it revealed scratches and dents, markings of the past and secrets they didn't want to uncover. He wasn't stupid. But something as trivial as being dragged out on a date with someone you didn't like should be an easily solved matter.

"But to a certain extent, it's oneself that is responsible for happiness," he stated more like he was thinking out loud.

"True." Naruse nodded. "I think that's why so many are unhappy even though they strive for what they are *told* means happiness."

"Maybe people should settle for being comfortable," Miya sighed. "It seems so much simpler. And then perhaps settle for something that's easier to obtain... like true friendship."

"Now you're just sucking up." Naruse prodded his hip with a naked toe. He leaned forward, touching their lips together.

"Hn." Miya grinned, kissing back. "Monogamy for instance, deprives you of so much fun."

Naruse chuckled, allowing Miya's arms to go up around his neck, caressing the nape and the hairline.

"You say that now..." he purred, biting softly down on Miya's lip. "Even you might change your mind one day."

It seemed unlikely, but Miya didn't feel like arguing. Happiness seemed to be within grasp at the present moment, so he didn't care to elaborate on the greater questions in life any more for the time being.

"Aren't sluts allowed to be happy?" he provoked, grinning against Naruse's soft lips.

"Idiot," the other replied, smacking him lovingly in the back of the head.

Later, he took a train back to Higashinada to find the apartment empty again. He changed and had a quick dinner consisting of leftovers from the fridge before running off to work. Inspired by the conversation he and Naruse had just had, he grabbed one of the pink post-its he currently used to mark his own food to draw a little smiley face with a red pen. Next to it, he jotted down one word: *"Smile,"* although he doubted his roommate would find it charming enough to actually do so.

A chilly draft blew in from the sea, rustling in the lofty, blossoming trees standing along the road; it was still fairly warm though. The sky was clear, but still tinted with grey. Miya walked briskly towards the subway station, feeling not at all like he'd been out drinking until four in the morning.

Too bad Naru failed, he would've made an excellent doctor, he thought to himself, making his way down the stairs to the platform.

Even if true happiness might have been a myth invented by lifestyle magazines, Miya was content. Truly happy with the way things were.

5. Nature of Man

Miya had more or less forgotten about the encounter with the man in the white shirt. Hiiro hadn't bugged him any more about that night either, having had enough with his own hangover, and then later new conquests. They hadn't gone out as much since then but mostly kept to the back room or their own apartments for the time being. So he was more than a little surprised one night when he was still getting ready in the back room, discussing loudly with Ayase as he showered his asymmetric tousles of ebony with hairspray from a silver canister.

"How can you even eat that crap?" He was referring to the pizza box on the small, outdated respatex table. The other man had arrived at work about twenty minutes earlier, carrying the pizza box, announcing that he'd had no time to eat earlier, and promptly sitting down to chow down. Miya regarded him from the corner of his smoky eye as if the presence of the anchovies offended him.

"You're the one to talk; you eat that disgusting yoghurt all the time."

"Fish does *not* belong on pizza," Miya declared. "And you're not gonna get any tips—or anything else for that matter—tonight smelling like fish. They'll think you've had a bad date recently."

Ayase stuffed a piece of crust into his mouth, glaring at the older man.

"Who smells like fish?" Tetsu stuck his head into the doorway.

"Anchovy-breath over there," Miya replied without looking at him. He tilted his head to the side, shaking it a little to see if the spray sufficed. "Apparently, he doesn't like attention."

"Oh shove it!" Ayase demonstratively grabbed another slice and turned to Tetsu. "Want some?"

"Please." The man came into the room, taking a slice off of

the cardboard. "Thanks! I'm starving."

Miya made a gagging noise in his throat.

"Grow up," Tetsu fired in his direction, chewing and swallowing. "And hurry up already. There's some guy out there asking for you."

"Huh?" He looked up from the mirror.

"I assume it's you he wants. He asked for some tall skinny guy with long black hair—must be you."

"Intriguing." Miya's lips curved upwards, something like anticipation igniting in his gut. "That's all he said?"

He adjusted his hair once more before standing and resolutely opening another button in his shirt. Showing some skin wouldn't hurt.

"Well, actually what he *said* was more a question of whether you worked here…"

"Same thing right?" Miya grinned, scurrying out into the club, scouting the area for anyone who looked familiar—or like his type anyway.

His gaze surveyed tables and groups of people before finally settling at one of the corner tables by the stage.

"Well I'll be damned." He inhaled sharply, smirking to himself as he saw *that man* sitting there by himself.

"Hm?" Hiiro approached, placing a hand lightly on Miya's shoulder, glancing in the same direction. "Oh!"

He flashed a fox-like grin. "I told you so!"

"Shut up." Miya pursed his lips, shaking him off. He was intrigued indeed. No wonder this guy had looked so sour next to the pretty girl. His hunch seemed to be spot on.

"Aren't you gonna talk to him?"

Miya glanced in the direction of the table again—it didn't seem like the man had noticed him yet. He planned to keep it that way while observing his behavior.

When he said that, Hiiro gave a bark of laughter. "You talk like this is a nature documentary or something."

Miya's lips curved. "It is… of sorts. Let's see what his nature is, shall we?"

"I don't get you." Hiiro rolled his eyes. "Since when are you all hard to get?"

Miya laughed quietly, and considering the fact that their argument was taking place in the midst of a crowded part of the bar, he leaned in, brushing his lips against Hiiro's bejeweled ear. "Wanna see how hard I can get?"

Hiiro strangled a laugh, pressing their bodies playfully together. "Later, babe."

He slipped away into the crowd, and Miya watched him disappear. He wondered how serious that remark had been; the lines between business and pleasure in this place were kind of blurred, so it was all about taking things as they came, so to speak.

Let's just see how this turns out, he thought to himself, gazing over towards the corner table a third time. Could it be that the man had actually come here to speak to him, or was his question just to confirm that he had the right place? The name of the bar was written on the card though, so it was unlikely that the latter was the case.

Over the next forty-five minutes or so, he kept an eye on the corner table. He never ventured close enough to actually make himself seem available for the man to talk to him but made sure to be visible still. He wanted to see if the guy was actually waiting for him, and how he acted. For the most part, he sat there, sipping at a mug of beer. He seemed almost as detached right now as he had done the other night. A couple of times, Miya saw people going over to the table trying to chat him up, and it seemed like they were all tastefully turned down. None of them were particularly bad-looking either, which puzzled him. Could it be he had been wrong after all?

"Aren't you going over there?" Naruse had been watching Miya the same way Miya had been watching the man at the table.

"Why do you care?"

"Hiiro's shooting off his mouth ab—"

"That little b-..." Miya hissed through gritted teeth. "I'm conducting an experiment if you must know."

"He's gonna leave you know."

"How do you know?"

"Ayase's bringing him his tab as we speak. You're really bad at paying attention." The blond man pet him lightly on the top of the head while turning it in the direction Ayase was walking.

"Ay-chan!" Miya called out in a somewhat surprisingly shrill tone. "Wait!"

He tore himself from Naru's grip and caught up to the younger man, taking the tab from him and smiling sweetly. "I'll take it from here."

Ayase looked at him from beneath a perfectly plucked and critically arched eyebrow. "Whatever you say." He shook his head, walking away.

Feigning nonchalance, Miya sauntered up to the table, slipping the tab across the smooth surface with two slim fingers. "Leaving so soon?"

He leaned down, still with his palm pressed against the tabletop, looking curiously into the man's eyes. The man's pupils were dilated because of the lack of light in this particular part of the club, so they seemed more black than brown this time around. Miya searched for a reaction in the man's face. He didn't even get a proper reply though, so he tried again. "I was told you asked for me."

"I didn't—" The man stopped himself, his voice still had that stern timbre to it but seemed hesitant at the same time. "You gave me the card, so I assumed you wanted to see me."

"I gave the card because I thought you might enjoy it here more than you did the other place," Miya replied, lips quirking. "But I seem to have been mistaken."

The other man looked thoughtful.

"It's... different," he finally said, looking around the club, his gaze casually sweeping over Miya's attire as well.

"Is different... bad?" Miya leaned even closer, pursing his lips, blinking slowly. The act was so embedded in him he didn't even have to strain for it to come forth. This flirtatiousness was part of his persona after having worked here more or less since the place was first established.

"Just... different," the other man replied just as tonelessly.

"I'm going to let that one count on the plus side then." Miya smiled sweetly at him, cocking his head to the side. No need to push things too far. This guy didn't seem to go much for the direct approaches, so he stuck to the sweet and polite side of things. It was oddly refreshing, considering how most of their clientele frequented the club purely for more lecherous reasons.

"If that's what you want." The man started to stand up.

Miya followed him with his gaze as he rose from the chair, his eyes tracing the contours of his lean frame through yet another white shirt and snugly fitting slacks.

"You're really leaving?" he blurted out.

The man placed the amount on the tab on Miya's tray along with a little extra. "Why else would I ask for the check?"

Miya gave him a crooked smile. "It's not often our clients leave this early... *alone*."

He was fishing for at least a hunch towards why Shirt-guy wasn't interested in his flirting, or the men who'd approached him over the course of the evening, purely out of his own curiosity.

The man uttered something like a cough and looked away.

"Better luck next time though," he offered.

"Next time?"

"That's the thing about fishing," Miya smirked. "If at first you don't succeed, try again."

"That's not how that expression goes."

Finally some sort of reply! Miya grinned. "Whatever. Keep in mind that when you're looking for me next time, the name is Miya."

Surprise was written on the other's face, but Miya wasn't sure why he was surprised.

He took the tray from the table and bowed politely. "Thanks for your business. Please come again."

Some customers really enjoyed this submissive, polite kind of service, so he threw it in for good measure. The man already carried a sense of authority with the stern way he spoke and dressed, so it was worth a shot.

"Thanks, I guess..."

The man didn't seem to be up for leaving though, so Miya decided to make it easier for him by shying away into the shadows and crowd and hoped that he'd enticed him enough to get another observation at a later time.

"What on earth are you doing?" Tetsu asked, leaning on the bar counter, taking the money from him.

"Playing," he grinned. "I found some entertainment."

"I think you've got it backwards. *You're* the entertainment."

"Precisely," he smirked. "I'm trying to find out if that's the case."

The bartender rolled his eyes. He wouldn't understand. Tetsu and Kyo had been attached at the hip for nearly as long as the managers and had probably forgotten all about the thrill of the hunt, and the exhilaration of having someone being interested in you. In this case though, Miya wasn't sure what he was going for. But he still enjoyed the process, even if it was all in his head. It was like a game of *Clue*, where he got to find out whether or not he was going to be right in his assumptions.

***

"Why am I paying you?" It was the manager, or well, *one* of them anyway. Kiyoshi, with the rusty hair, was more like an accountant than a real manager. He stood behind the bar for the most part when he wasn't working behind the scenes, and occasionally he served drinks. But his part in the actual running of the bar was as the guy laying down the numbers. It was his lover who owned the building and had opened the bar after his father had died and left the place to him. But Kiyoshi was the brains, or so they said. They'd been together since they were in their teens and were now both in their mid-twenties. Even so, Miya had no problem working for them. Kiyoshi hardly ever meddled with anything; he just kind of existed within the club. He wasn't very talkative, and although he was very attractive, he seemed to prefer remaining in the background. Regardless, he had quite the reputation, and though he was well liked among all of them, they'd given him the nickname "hime"—Princess.

"You're not, that would be your man's job," Miya replied.

"Without me, he wouldn't know *what* to pay you," Kiyoshi replied, somewhat snarkily. He seemed to be in a good mood. "He told me to go check on you guys, and what do I find?"

He looked around at the group of waiters at the bar, who'd been idly standing by as he came over. "A tea party."

"Anything for science." Miya beamed.

Tetsu sniggered. Kiyoshi merely looked at him. He looked like he was about to say something, but then his phone rang.

Sticking a finger in his ear, he answered without bothering to leave the room.

"Yeah? This weekend?" he looked a little surprised. "No that's fine."

Miya noted the smile crossing his face. It was rare to see the serious man smiling. It could only mean one thing. Tetsu also seemed to have caught on; he was smiling as well, inching closer to Kiyoshi like he wanted to listen in on the conversation.

"You'll make it here from the station okay?"

Kiyoshi's expression changed from the smile to something like resignation. "Yes, I know you're not ten."

Tetsu was now grinning behind the bar. Miya remained calm.

"Okay. See you." Kiyoshi hung up.

"Your brother's coming?"

"Don't try to talk yourself out of what we were just talking about," Kiyoshi warned, but his smile gave him away. "Yes, he is. Now go flirt with the customers—that's what we hired you for."

His tone was already lighter. Kiyoshi and his brother were really close, and the man always changed somewhat when the two of them talked. It was like he let go of his outward appearance or something and allowed himself to be more human. It suited him. Sho, the manager, could be stern, but he was also a genuinely good guy with a good portion of humor thrown in the mix, so it had always seemed strange that he and Kiyoshi were able to keep it together the way they did.

"Yes, Princess." Miya grinned, dodging the arm that shot out to push him gently.

He ventured back out into the crowd but couldn't help but feel like some of the amusement and excitement from earlier had faded.

He rarely thought much about his own family, and it wasn't like they had a bad relationship or anything. But… it was always a little too close for comfort when he saw Kiyoshi and his brother interacting. He sighed, taking aim for a party that was just coming through the doors. He plastered his usual smile on his face and pranced over to them, overbearingly tending to their needs.

6. Birds and Feathers

The feeling hadn't really subsided over the course of the next few weeks. It was summer vacation, and Kiyoshi's brother seemed to be intent on spending it all at his brother's place.

Miya had known Ryubi ever since the boy was small, and he was just as happy to see him as the others. They'd all been around to see him grow up, and each of them cared for him in their own way, so they were always thrilled when he came for a visit.

"You still aren't concerned?"

He was talking to Kiyoshi about it one day before opening time.

"Concerned?" Kiyoshi sipped at his latte.

Miya furrowed his brow. "You're the one pointing out how we're all lecherous vultures, and then you allow your little brother to come and go in this house of sin."

He said it jokingly, aiming to provoke.

Kiyoshi shook his head, showing no trace of amusement. "Well, there's that roommate of yours. Aside from that, I think the rest of you are respecting enough of the laws to stay away."

Kiyoshi was definitely scary. He flung what could only be described as threats out into the air so easily, and you never knew if he was being serious. Meanwhile, his brother was the exact opposite—always cheery and social.

"It was a joke." Miya stirred his glass with a straw, it was empty, save for some ice cubes that were already melting. "I was just thinking about how odd it is that you're both gay."

"He might turn out not to be—maybe he's just open-minded." Kiyoshi shrugged. "Seems like he's pretty serious about Lau though."

Miya grinned, unable to remain unaffected by the amused smirk on the elder brother's face.

The younger of the brothers had somehow gone and fallen for one of the kids in the neighborhood, and now they could often be found around the club, sneaking kisses when they thought nobody saw them. He knew first hand because Aki was constantly bitching about it. His teenage roommate had spent some time with them and wasn't impressed by their puppy love, as he put it. To top it off, he'd managed to stir up quite some trouble a little while ago when he'd stupidly decided to challenge their relationship.

"I'm glad they managed to work it out." He smiled, placing both of his elbows on the table. "Seriously, that kid…"

Kiyoshi's eyes darkened. "I don't want to hear more about that."

Miya shrugged. "Sure. I don't really care about it. I think he's learned his lesson though; he seems a little meek these days."

"Serves him right."

"How did your parents take it?" The words fell out of him.

"What?" Kiyoshi wondered. "About bro being gay as well? *If* he is."

"Yeah, were they upset? *My* parents would freak the hell out if there was no one to pass the family name on."

Not that there was any need to be concerned, he frowned, as his younger brother was straight as an arrow. Sharp as one as well.

The younger man shrugged, lifting his latte and bringing it to his mouth. "Our parents are really calm about it. They were a bit freaked when I came out, but it settled pretty quickly. Ryubi claims I paved the way for him; I guess there's something to that."

"No, you think?" Miya replied sarcastically, looking around the room, thinking about the secret world this place became in the late hours of the evening. They usually opened earlier in the day so people could come in and have some drinks, just coffee even, and chat. But then in the late afternoons, it started turning into something of a circus, with the skimpily dressed waiters, the flirtatious looks and words, the touches and bodies grinding on the floor. "How much do they know about this place?"

Kiyoshi's lip curled upwards on one side of his mouth. "Enough. Who do you think financed the revamp of this bar? It was a disaster when Sho's old man croaked."

"You're kidding! Weren't you like... *young* back then?" Miya sneered at his own statement. Kiyoshi was young *now* at twenty-five. One year younger than his lover, three full years younger than Miya himself.

"Yeah well." Kiyoshi shrugged again. "My dad's a businessman, so he believes in investments."

Miya narrowed his eyes, sending him a scrutinizing glare across the table. "And you're a rich kid to boot."

Kiyoshi chuckled softly. "Are you calling me spoiled?"

"*My* dad is also a businessman," Miya scratched his shoulder, "and if I wanted to open a gay bar, he'd write me out of his will."

Kiyoshi didn't get a chance to answer before his brother came through the doors with the Chinese kid, Lau, in tow.

"*Nii-chan!*" he called out, his voice resounding in the empty club. "We're gonna go see a movie. You got any money?"

The man with the messy hair turned towards his younger brother, resting his elbow on the back of the chair. "Excuse me?"

"I mean..." the teen forced a cutesy smile, "please?"

"I was just telling your brother what a rich kid he is." Miya smiled towards the boy. "That should apply to you as well, kiddo."

"He never has any money," Kiyoshi sighed. "Blows it on arcades and movies whenever he's got the chance."

"I do not!" Ryubi barked. "Obviously I spend it all to come here and see—"

He stopped himself, face flushing a deep red. Lau smiled shyly, still remaining a few paces behind him.

"Your beloved older brother, I'm sure." Kiyoshi sighed. "Fine. Come here then."

He waved the teen over, took out his wallet and pulled out a couple of notes. "Here, but spend them wisely, and tomorrow you're gonna work for them. Deal?"

The younger brother nodded several times. Miya smiled. The two of them were very different but had similar mannerisms, and there was something in their faces that was very reminiscent of each other, although he was unable to pinpoint it. Kiyoshi's face was refined and pale, whereas Ryubi's was rounder, his skin a healthy tan from being outside in the sun, and his ears were full of piercings. In his lip, the teen sported a brand-new lip ring. The elder brother had a pierced ear, but that was all. His hair was dyed, and Ryubi's was a natural pitch black.

"Deal." Ryubi grinned. "Thanks."

He was about to walk away but was grabbed by the shoulder. "Now give me a hug."

"Ew, no!"

Miya chuckled. No teen would want to hug his brother at this age, and certainly not in front of people. He was unable to fend off his stronger brother though, and was pulled into a reluctant embrace. Once he escaped, he wore a flustered expression on his face and ruffled his static hair. "Idiot," he muttered, striding out of the club. The other teen followed behind him, laughing quietly.

"You guys are really close, aren't you?" Miya was certain the envy in his voice was clear as day. He swallowed. "I mean…"

An odd smile crossed Kiyoshi's face. "Yeah well…"

He didn't seem to be interested in elaborating. Miya didn't blame him. He didn't particularly like talking about his own family affairs to anyone, so he let it slip. It didn't really matter anyway. He wouldn't get a better relationship with his own brother by listening to other people's stories. Sighing, he leaned back in the chair.

At least he had his roommate. Nine years separated them, yet they were still very similar to one another in certain ways, but then again, that wasn't entirely the way he wanted to look at their relationship. He didn't really consider Aki to be a kid in the proper sense of the word. That was impossible considering the way they knew each other. But they were really close. And a part of him wondered if the teenager had ever been a kid—those days seemed way past in any case.

His mind was just churning with thoughts lately. It was tiring.

The manager came into the room, walking over to them. He placed his hand on Kiyoshi's slim shoulder, squeezing it lovingly. "Your brother's up to no good?"

"Robbing me blind," the other man replied, feigning sadness. "What are you up to?"

"I was looking for you."

"Really?" he looked up at the taller man, his eyes glinting. "For what?"

There was a hint of flirtatiousness in his voice; his hand came up to run over Sho's. Public display of affection was nothing new in this place, but with these two, it was different. They'd been together for so long, it was as if they were attached to one another, and yet they managed to be so intimate and sweet with each other. He found it fascinating.

"I need you to look over some numbers; I can't make them add up."

"That's all? Now you're just using me for my brain," Kiyoshi teased. He definitely was in a great mood lately.

"If you'd like, I can use your body as well. Afterwards."

Miya shook his head, interrupting them. "Do you mind?"

"You work for us—deal with it," Sho reminded him, purposely running his hand further down the other man's chest.

"How do you do it anyway?" Miya demanded.

"What?" While Sho looked confused, a wry grin plastered itself on Kiyoshi's lips. This was how he became so popular, no doubt. He seemed to be very proper and composed, but his mind was probably in the gutter more often than not. It had to be for him to have been in on making this place what it was.

"Not *that*," he rolled his eyes. "I can imagine that already."

He offered the two of them a challenging look. "I meant, how do you still act all cozy after so many years? Especially being so young? How did that happen? I thought kids were supposed to tire easily."

Sho laughed. "Watch it, Miya, or we'll fire you for acting rude towards the management."

Miya waved his hand in an apologetic manner. "I'm just kidding. But I mean, it's kind of a feat, isn't it?"

Kiyoshi stood. "Part determination, part compatibility. Simple equation."

"And great sex."

The manager's interjection was overheard by his lover, who was already making his way back towards the office. Sho laughed still, following behind him, leaving Miya alone in the club.

He followed them with his eyes. They clearly seemed happy, but he didn't get how it was possible to be with someone for that long and not tire of them completely. They never seemed to argue, and although they were friendly and casual with everyone at work, they seemed to prefer each other's company to hanging around other people for the most part. Knowing himself, he'd probably go insane if he had to live that kind of life—no matter how secure it seemed.

Or maybe that was something he'd started thinking about after stacking up a fair amount of failed relationships. It was difficult to know whether these were legitimate feelings or if he was just protecting himself from the frightening thought that he might never find something genuine like what those two had.

But considering the freedom he had now... It would probably take a lot to make him want to give up on that. He was no saint. The relationships that had failed in the past weren't solely blamed on the other men he'd been with. He knew his own flaws, and his fickle mind, which made it far too easy for him to give in to stupid temptations and end up hurting himself more than he'd ever wanted; all the while stepping all over a person he initially had feelings for. It had been a while since he'd last attempted to even *try* being exclusive with someone, largely due to the way his relation with many of his friends worked. He couldn't really say he was unhappy with that either, but on the other hand, there was always the fear that should they find someone, he'd wind up alone somehow.

"Miya!" He was torn from his thoughts by the sound of Aki's voice. The teen was standing over by the door, looking annoyed.

"Jeez. I've been trying to get your attention forever. What are you doing?"

"Hm? Sorry, I guess I spaced out."

"Well get over here. A bulk of deliveries just came, and you need to help carry them!" His tone of voice was demanding.

He looked tired, Miya noted, even though he was only looking at him from afar. Come to think of it, he hadn't really been at home much lately. He thought that maybe he should talk the younger man into sleeping with him, just to make sure he got some rest for once.

He smiled to himself, getting up from his seat and grabbing his glass. The ice cubes had melted already, and he drank down the water before placing the glass in the tray with the others that were ready to be washed. It was things like that that made Aki refer to him as "mother" on occasion. It was always said in an irritated or teasing manner, but Miya liked to believe that it was evidence of the bond between them. He liked to think that there was a closeness between them that came from something other than their casual hookups.

He went after the younger man out into the back yard. It was raining heavily, and the delivery people had just dumped everything on the steps—like always.

"Let's get this stuff in here before it gets drenched." He frowned, picking up the first box—at least they were covered in plastic.

"You'd think they'd be more careful considering how it says *glass*." Aki sighed, picking up another one. "Where are the kids anyway? Isn't this the kind of thing they usually do for change?"

Miya turned and looked over his shoulder. "From what I heard earlier today, you're not to as much as *talk* to those two."

Aki laughed bitterly and then shrugged it off. "I have better things to do, so don't worry about that anymore."

"If you say so," Miya replied, skipping over the threshold as they came into the club, gently setting down the boxes on the bar counter. Tetsu had returned and immediately begun unpacking them.

"By the way, it's been ages since we hung out." Miya threw

it out there, allowing the other to interpret it whichever way he wanted. "Wanna do something tonight?"

His roommate shrugged. "Like what?"

"Order in junk food, watch bad movies and get drunk?"

"I don't have to hang out at home with you to do that."

"I miss you though." Miya cocked his head to the side, leaning it on the eighteen-year-old's shoulder and looking up at him with big, dark eyes.

Aki shrugged his shoulders in irritation. "Get off me."

"But fine if you don't want to."

"I didn't say that," the raven-haired teen replied. "Okay. Let's hang out."

"Yay!" Miya cheered.

Tetsu laughed at the two of them as Aki rolled his eyes. Miya's over-the-top attitude was part feigned for the gallery and part genuine traits of his personality. And he really was looking forward to spending some time with his roommate again for the first time in a while. For the most part, the two of them were always together when the rest of the group were also present and rarely had a night in together. It wasn't a given that they should, of course, but Miya enjoyed having the opportunity. There was also that little voice in him that told him to look after the younger man a little extra. Aki was the youngest of the group, so it was difficult not to feel a certain kind of responsibility for him. It wasn't always simple to look at him as a teenager and someone younger than them, however. Even though he sometimes actively went to great lengths to prove to them how much of an adult he was. Miya had to admit that even if he was a kid legally still... he was mature for his age, Sho wouldn't have hired him if he wasn't—dubious as it might all seem. Aki was no worse off than any of the others working here. The school of hard knocks had given most of them some harsh lessons, that much was certain. In that sense, it was better that he spent time with them rather than getting mixed up with all kinds of terrible crowds.

On the other hand... wouldn't most people say we're *a terrible crowd?* he mused, going out to get another box of deliveries to bring it inside.

***

Both of them had worked early shifts, meaning they got back home before one in the morning for once. The plus side of having many employees despite the fairly small size of the establishment was that they could split the hours if they wanted to as long as there was someone who could cover for them. He had found that Aki didn't really like being idle though; he seemed to enjoy working himself to death. And even when he wasn't working lately, there would be no trace of him anywhere half the time.

It wasn't any of Miya's business, so he didn't stick his nose into it. He was just happy once they both collapsed on the tattered old couch in their living room, a heap of junk food adorning the coffee table.

"What do you want to drink?" He ventured into the kitchen area, getting some regular glasses out of the cupboard.

"Whatever," came the reply, almost drowned out by the sound of paper rustling as he fished out his food from the paper bags.

"Why do we have wine?" Miya picked up a deep green bottle, ogling it in light confusion.

"Wine and hamburgers? Classy."

"Yeah, I didn't think so. Maybe someone left it here." He put it back on the counter and took out some of the random bottles they had sitting around, as well as some beers out of the fridge.

"Since when do you sleep with people who are classy enough to drink wine?" Aki snorted.

"What are you saying?" Miya squeezed himself down into the couch, purposely pushing Aki out of his seat and further against the middle.

"Just that there's no need to get classy with you—your standards aren't very high."

"Excuse me?" He grabbed Aki's thigh, squeezing it hard enough to make the younger man convulse on the couch. He writhed against the prickly fabric, a strangled laugh escaping his tightly pressed together lips. "Ow! I'm just s-saying!"

"Saying what?" Miya gripped a little harder.

"Why buy the cow when you can get the milk for free? OW!"

"I'll strangle you, you little brat!" But the laugh rolling out into the room gave him away and revealed that Miya wasn't upset at all. It was true, wasn't it? There was no need to charm him with wine; if he liked something, he usually took it. It was that simple.

"You're the one to talk." He let go of Aki's thigh but continued to press him down on the couch by placing his arm across his stomach, pushing him back against the cushions. "You're no saint yourself."

"Yeah, but nobody brings me wine either."

Miya shook his head. "Even if I'm a cheap date, I don't *mind* if they want to be sweet."

"What good does it do though," his roommate replied, forcing himself up in a sitting position, his abs tightening underneath Miya's underarm, "when you can't remember who you got it from?"

He chuckled. "Good point. Maybe I have a stalker."

"Only you would be aroused by that thought," the dry reply came back.

"Who's aroused?" Miya replied quizzically, purposely slipping his arm a little further down towards Aki's hips, fingertips stroking gently over his shirt.

The younger man sneered in response, pulling himself up to a completely sitting position. "I rest my case," he said, grabbing for his fries.

Miya smiled, pulling back as well and turning the television on. There was an old gore film on. He'd seen it before and found it disgusting, but Aki liked this kind of film, or rather, didn't *dislike* them, so he left it on. What else was there to watch in the middle of the night anyway?

He leaned back on the sofa, starting on his chicken nuggets. There was a limit to the availability of proper food at this time of the day, so they'd had to make do with some *real* junk for tonight. It tasted heavenly, even if the film they were mindlessly watching was incredibly gross.

He reached for his glass, finding that the sweet drink wasn't half bad with the deep-fried meal. He watched his roommate in the corner of his eye. He didn't seem to be paying too much attention to the film himself. He briefly wondered what it was like for Aki, being surrounded by everyone at the club all the time. It didn't seem like he hung around very many others, not that any of *them* did either, but for someone his age, wouldn't it be natural to have some friends his own age? The closest one to him in age at the club was Ayase, and he'd already turned twenty. Then, of course, there was Kiyoshi's brother, and his boyfriend, but well...

"You don't have any siblings, do you?" he asked absentmindedly, reaching for his glass again.

"Huh?"

"Siblings. You have any?"

They'd been living together for a year, but he knew little to nothing about Aki's family.

"Nah."

"Only child, eh? That explains some things." Aki merely stared at him. "An only child often becomes spoiled and self-centered."

The stare turned into a glare.

"But you can also become very self-reliant, since you have to carry everything yourself."

"Like?" Aki furrowed his brow, looking unamused.

"Like... if your parents got a divorce, speaking to adults might be difficult, but siblings would share their thoughts."

"Here are my thoughts," Aki shot back. "Watch the movie and shut up."

He really wasn't one for this kind of conversation. Miya thought he remembered hearing him say something about his parents having had a messy divorce though, so maybe he was avoiding the topic for that reason. In any case, it didn't really matter.

There seemed to be a movie marathon on because as soon as the gore-fest ended, another one began.

"How can you watch this crap?"

"How can you?" Aki countered. "You turned it on."

"That's because you're so delightful to make conversation with."

Aki's nutmeg gaze moved from the screen and met with Miya's own. It was slightly swimming, but the younger man wasn't drunk—not at all. He was probably mostly tired. "Maybe I didn't want to talk."

He knew that tone of voice. Miya smirked. "Then what *do* you want?"

As far as roommates went, they were probably a little unconventional. That was probably the case with their entire group to be honest. But neither of them was tied down, so it wasn't like it mattered. Their whole relationship was built on this flirtatious undertone that could easily spark a fire between them at any given point.

Miya met Aki's lips with his own, leaning into him and accepting the teasing bites to his bottom lip, the teeth on the light pink flesh and the tongue that traced over it. He was a hypocrite. Probably the greatest hypocrite in the world, at least that's what it felt like when he played the concerned elder card as soon as he got the chance, only to allow himself to be carried away by instinct and desire as soon as the younger man decided that he wanted to play.

A responsible person would have pushed him away instead of indulging him, but Miya wasn't responsible. And this wasn't by far the first time.

"Fuck responsibility," he smirked into the kiss, kissing back just as hard and wanton.

There had been a time when he'd been slightly taken aback—surprised—at the way Aki acted, at his directness and ability to get precisely what he had wanted. To begin with, Miya had stated that he was never going to hit on him, but finding a loophole had been simple enough when Aki had decided to prove himself by coming onto *Miya*, most likely just to show him how independent and self-aware he was. Miya had willingly walked into the trap. As far as he was concerned, there was nothing wrong with what they were doing, even if it had distorted the younger man's perspective of the world.

He felt teeth sinking into the soft flesh of his neck and moaned. Definitely nothing wrong. Despite being the older of the two, he had no problem giving up control, allowing Aki to run the show; he knew that was how he liked it, and Miya himself didn't mind in the slightest. Rather, one could say he got off on being controlled; pressed down on the couch, with hard, determined kisses showering the visible patches of skin, here and there substituted by swift licks and gentle nips.

And then their mouths clashed again as Aki hoisted himself on top of the older man, pressing their bodies together. Trying to remain relatively calm, Miya responded by placing a softer, more chaste-like kiss on the youngster's lips, kissing along his jaw, and down to the teen's neck. He shook slightly, Miya noted, continuing to kiss and nibble at his throat while running his hands down Aki's tense body, up underneath his shirt, and then down to his jeans, popping the buttons open without trouble.

"No need to rush," he cooed, licking a metal-adorned ear lobe, smirking a little to himself at the way Aki was trying to remain stoic, as if not wanting to give himself over. It was as if it was some sort of game to see who could hang in there longer.

It never was, and it always ended in the same way, with rushed motions, mind-blowing kisses and loud, throaty moans as their bodies connected—usually with the younger of the two in control. Tonight was no different. He lifted himself slightly from the cushions, allowing the younger man to remove his slacks. At the same time, placing his leg up on the sofa, giving better access when he reached down between their bodies, guiding his roommate in the right direction, sighing with anticipation as their flesh came into contact. It was rough, that was so. But he liked it that way.

Aki sneered, leaning down to kiss him. "You're so masochistic…"

"Shut up, brat." He grabbed the younger man by the neck,

kissing back even harder and pressing himself upwards, accepting the intrusion.

From there on, it was all playfulness—sounds, scents and the chase for pleasure.

Afterwards, he'd been able to talk Aki into sleeping with him, which hadn't been as difficult as expected. He was told not to be clingy but fell asleep with his arm casually thrown around the younger male.

When he woke up the following morning, he was alone again.

7. Summer Nights

Summer vacation came to an end. The charmer from Kagawa went back home, and his brother returned to his usual, reserved persona. At the same time, one could already tell that business was getting a little calmer—and less exciting. During the weeks of summer break, there were always a lot of younger men frequenting the club, not only on the weekends, as opposed to the usual routines. During summer, more students would take the chance on living a little outside of their bubbles and would liven up the place for the glorious months of July and August. In their wake, the same old clients were left—most of them deteriorating old alcoholics who were hiding from the world in this underground bar. They frequented the place during weekdays, no doubt telling their unfortunate wives that they'd been out drinking with their coworkers after hours.

Miya wondered if this was what Sho had had in mind when he and Kiyoshi opened the place up; that it would become a breeding ground for those who were slowly drinking themselves to death while hating the way their lives had been shaped by the norm. He wondered how ethical it was to keep up the business knowing that, but then again, the club had rescued many of its workers off of the streets, and for the younger clientele, it offered something that was sorely needed in the heteronormative society.

He rarely deep-dived into such thoughts, but what else was there to do on a dreadfully slow Tuesday night when there were hardly enough customers to serve, with three guys already working the floor, and working up the few guests purely by being themselves—flirtatious and overbearing, and affectionate with their colleagues.

He'd taken a break a couple of minutes ago, since there was nothing to do, and it didn't seem necessary for him to meddle with the entertainment that went on out on the floor, so he was looking on from the bar, giving his boot-clad legs a well-deserved break. Even when the place was virtually empty, they did a lot of running around. On top of that, it was far too hot, despite the air-conditioning. Miya preferred autumn to summer and its stifling climate; hot and humid really wasn't his thing, regardless of how lightly people were dressing. When it was too hot to do any kind of physical activity anyway, it didn't really matter if the guys were playing shirtless basketball on the court, or if they wore sexy, button-down shirts or tank tops. He liked autumn, when it was still warm enough for people not to be covered up by down jackets and woolen coats, but maybe a cute scarf over a cardigan—something like that. He wasn't a big fan of the cold either, but on days like this, Miya easily picked winter over the terrible summer heat.

He was sipping at a glass of water, gazing out at the room when he saw a familiar face insecurely entering the club.

White-shirt guy was back.

How many of these shirts does this guy own?

He jumped down from the barstool and crossed the room.

"Hey there," he said, grinning.

The man looked startled. Perhaps because the last time he had been here, which was back in July, Miya had purposely stayed away, and now here he was, appearing right off the bat.

Miya chewed on his lip; he didn't know for sure that this guy was actually here because of him. It didn't seem like he enjoyed coming here.

"I'm glad to see you again," he offered. "Feel free to sit anywhere. We're kinda slow tonight. I'm sorry about that, but at least we still serve the best drinks in town."

He didn't bother with the details. Rumor had it the best drinks in Kobe were in a more trendy part of the city, but whatever. People didn't come here for the drinks anyway unless they were drinking themselves up to the courage of taking someone home.

The man in the shirt nodded. "Anywhere is fine?"

"Anywhere you want." Miya smirked, gesticulating out into

the air. "Someone will be with you in a moment if you'd like to order something."

"Why can't you do it?"

The response startled Miya. He regarded the man, placing his hands on his hips. "Good point, I'm free after all... Usually the clients like to settle down a little before they order, but if you know what you'd like, then I can bring it to you right away."

"I'll just have a beer." The man cleared his throat and aimed his legs towards a nearby table—a little, secluded one, over by a wall. Just like last time.

Miya wondered what the deal with this one was. Lots of people who came here had the intention of keeping a low profile, but they rarely had people coming back who still seemed uncomfortable. As much as it puzzled him, it also amused him.

He left and returned with the foaming beverage in a tall, frosted glass. He'd brought a small bowl of pretzels with it, placing it on the table next to the glass. "On the house," he smiled sweetly.

"Thanks."

At that moment, Aki brushed past them, reaching out to run his hand over Miya's back and waist as he did. Automatically, Miya turned his smile towards him, running his hand lovingly across his shoulder, tugging gently at his hair—simple gestures that were highly regarded in this place. It was just as popular to only barely be in contact with someone as it was to engage in a full-fledged kiss on top of the stage. Well... almost anyway.

One gaze cast back at the man in the white shirt showed that it didn't seem to sit right with him though, which was strange since this wasn't his first visit. Miya shrugged. "Enjoy it," he said, picking up his tray again. "Don't hesitate to let us know if there's anything else you'd like."

He thought it looked like the man wanted to say something, but nothing came. He offered a polite bow and went to the next table, where a couple of already overly handsy and intoxicated men wanted to pay.

"Certainly." Miya nodded, running off to fix the check. It irked him that the system functioned in this way still, that they didn't pay when they ordered. Sho was lucky so few people ran out on the check. If a patron came up to the bar, he'd pay instantly, but as soon as someone was seated, they didn't pay until they requested a check. Kiyoshi had also mentioned that it was a bad arrangement, but nothing was ever done about it.

When he returned, he found to his surprise that the table by the wall was empty.

He turned to Hiiro, who strode past him, cash in hand. "He left?"

"Hm?" Hiiro looked at him, confused. "Who?"

"The man in the corner."

"Yeah, he left the exact amount on the table. One beer, right?" Hiiro showed the coins in his palm. "Didn't even finish it. Maybe he scored."

It wasn't a rare thing that people threw their payments on the table and left with a conquest, but it seemed unlikely.

"He just got here fifteen minutes ago though." Miya furrowed his brow.

"Wait." Hiiro searched Miya with his eyes. He was wearing fake lashes, Miya noted, and they were framing his dark eyes in a surprisingly fitting way. "That was *him* wasn't it? From that night!"

"Yeah." Miya didn't bother putting up a front. "He came back, but he doesn't seem to like it here."

"Maybe he likes you." Hiiro nudged him, making sure that clients were watching as he did.

Miya leaned in, brushing a lock of dyed red out of Hiiro's face. "If he did, he wouldn't have left, now would he?"

Hiiro shrugged. "Maybe he was in a hurry."

Miya sighed. "Who knows."

***

Miya wasn't any less surprised when he found the man appearing again the next day to request the same table, and the same order, only to leave again.

The following night was a day off, but the day after, the same thing happened—corner table, beer, snacks and slipping out quietly without anyone noticing whether he left with someone or not.

Miya was uncertain if he was the only one noticing this pattern—although he *knew* Hiiro was paying attention. It was really strange though. He'd heard about people who'd go to the same place night after night, sitting in the same spot, ordering the same things... but at least those kinds of people, as far as he knew, *enjoyed* the place they went to.

On the fourth night, he didn't come. Miya didn't even work that night. He'd originally requested the night off but found himself coming in anyway. He camouflaged it as wanting to hang out with the others since there was nothing to do anyway, and he volunteered to work behind the bar for a couple of hours during the evening rush. He waited. It was with a slight sense of resignation that he threw in the towel when he realized there was no way the man was going to show; he'd been so particular with the time the previous nights, there was little to no chance he'd show up in the later hours of the night.

He quickly forgot about his strange case of disappointment though, as he was pulled into the lounge after a couple of the guys went off their shifts and sat in the back room drinking. He suspected that a couple of them had done more than just pour some drinks by the time he joined them, but he wasn't interested in asking them to share.

Aki was there as well but disappeared as some point and didn't come home until the following morning. Miya didn't ask him where he'd been. The day passed slowly, with Miya on the sofa nursing his hangover, sipping water until it was time to go to work again.

It was a slow night, as expected on a Sunday. Just a couple of regulars and some dimwitted students who complained about how stupid it was to go out drinking on a school night while still ordering refills—they tipped well though.

Monday came. Miya worked the early shift and was absentmindedly cleaning tables when he heard Ayase saying,

"No, that's fine. Nobody's reserved it, so you can sit down. I'll get you the beer."

Miya snapped his head around to see the man taking his seat. Remarkable. He was back! For a while, he'd been convinced it was his and Aki's little affectionate touch that had offended the man. Maybe he just *had* been called out, like Hiiro had suggested.

Why do you even care though? he thought to himself. It was like he'd become obsessed with this man's strange habits, forgetting about how he'd been a little worried when they'd been face to face in that other nightclub that time, that he'd been worried the man might turn out to be hostile.

This time though, he stayed longer. He ordered another beer, and then a third.

Miya brought it to him, along with the complimentary dish of snacks. "Welcome back," he purred, daring to brush the man's fingertips as he placed the little bowl on the table. "You left so suddenly last time."

More like every time, he added in his mind.

"Thank you," the man's voice said, but he wasn't looking at him. Miya frowned. What was the point of trying to court the customers when they showed no interest?

He smiled, moving away from the table. As much as this person irritated him, he had to admit that he was enjoying whatever this was. He wondered if the man was doing it on purpose, or if he was just a flake.

***

"All right, see you guys tomorrow!" Miya called out as he was leaving.

"Bye!" Naruse waved at him. He'd just come in for his shift and was getting ready in the back room when Miya was on his way out.

The air felt a little chilly, but at least it wasn't raining, like it had seemed like it was about to earlier. Miya wished he'd brought a jacket though. The weather was so unpredictable in this part of town, since it was so close to the sea. Even warm days could bring very chilly evenings, and it was already past midnight.

He wrapped his arms around himself, walking out of the back yard and around the building, emerging near the front door.

He walked with hurried steps and winced when someone called out, "Hey!"

He turned around slowly. It was dark, but he saw the shape of a person standing near the streetlight outside the club.

He hesitantly walked closer. It *was* shirt-man.

"So," he said, relaxing his shoulders a little, "it *is* you."

The man continued to stare at him. Miya wasn't sure if he should be worried. He vaguely remembered Aki's comment from earlier. Weren't there all these horror stories about stalkers turned killers out there? He'd always laughed as such tales, and said that the people who were victims of them had probably brought it upon themselves, but now he felt a little tinge of worry again. Who was to say that this man wasn't mentally unstable? He didn't *seem* to be entirely at ease.

"What do you want?" he asked hesitantly. "I thought you'd already left."

"I did, but I decided to wait."

"Wait?" Miya pursed his lips, narrowing his painted eyes. "For me?"

"I heard you saying that your shift was almost over."

Maybe he should just get his ass back inside, as this was a little... Miya was a creature of impulse and challenge though, so he asked, "Why? You're always leaving so early in the evenings."

"You didn't have an early shift until now."

Miya blinked. "A-are you saying you *are* only coming here because of me?"

The other man looked away. It was dark, even in the sheen from the street lamp, but it seemed like his face was flushing. "Because of that night?"

He shook his head. "No... Yes..."

Miya cocked his head to the side. He felt drops of rain

starting to fall on his bare shoulders. Was he angry because Miya had been rude? Or was it…?

Was it possible that…?

"Would you mind…" the man took a deep breath, "…grabbing a cup of coffee some time?"

Miya couldn't stop himself from bursting out laughing. The other man seemed discouraged.

"No!" Miya fended him off, still laughing. "I'm not laughing *at* you. I thought… Never mind…"

He sobered, moving in closer. "Let me look at you…" he said, stepping into the light of the lamp. The man's face was most definitely flushed. His hair was damp, so it must have rained earlier after all. He felt a tinge of something in his chest. He noticed that the man was wearing a light, grey coat over his white shirt. And he was undeniably handsome.

"Sure," he nodded. "Let's go for coffee. I'm free right now."

The other man shook his head. "I have work in the morning. Wednesday?"

"I don't work until late then, so that's okay." Miya smiled. "Do you have a pen or something?"

He pulled a business card out of his pocket and wasn't very surprised to see the man pulling a pen out from his pocket and handing it over. He did seem like the type. Miya scribbled his name and number on the back of the card, along with a coffee shop in a different part of the city. "Call me if you can't make it. I'll be there at seven."

He moved in close, dropped the pen in the man's shirt pocket, and pulled back. "By the way," he said. "Isn't it common tact to introduce oneself before asking someone out?"

The man looked apologetic. "I'm sorry. I'm… Miura."

Miya grinned. "Nice to meet you, Miura-san. I'll see you on Wednesday!"

He turned on his heel and walked off with a strange feeling in his gut. Anticipation. Excitement. And… something else. When had he last been on a *date*?

8. Testing the Waters

Miya purposely arrived early that Wednesday. Since it was he who'd suggested the place to meet, and had picked the time, he figured it was appropriate. Not to mention how he'd purposely dragged out coming over to the man's table even though he'd asked for him. He'd made sure to charge his phone properly in advance for once, as he was still not sure he was entirely charmed by the way he'd been approached. It was just a precaution. But more importantly, he was early because he was actually excited.

When was the last time he'd been on an actual date? It must have been years ago, he mused. At some point, that kind of thing had just started to seem pointless to him. He was surrounded by loyal friends who did everything together and for each other, including sexual matters, if that was an issue. He was so used to the whole laid-back and loving relationship he had with most of his friends, he hadn't really been missing the company of a significant other. If he wanted to experience thrill and excitement, he just picked up some good-looking guy while out on the town, or went home with some guy from the club. His last relationship had been an absolute disaster and had probably been the trigger for his current outlook on the world.

He was getting ahead of himself though; this was nothing more than a date.

Miya had to admit he was a little nervous. The other man, Miura, had seemed so awkward when they'd talked earlier, he didn't think the prospects for the date were the most promising. But it could always be that the man was nervous. After all, it would bear fruits to Miya's theory that this man was new to the gay scene. Maybe it was the first time he'd even tried asking another man out. That thought did entice him.

It did nothing to soothe his own nerves though. A waitress

came up to him as he sat waiting at a small round table. He'd purposely picked one further into the café, close to the wall, as that seemed to be something Miura preferred. Albeit fairly secluded, it was still apparent enough for the man to notice him when he came in.

"Would you like to place an order?" the waitress asked, nodding politely at him.

"I'm waiting for someone—" Miya broke himself off. "Actually, you know what? I'll have a coffee while I wait."

He needed something to occupy himself with. The nerves that had become apparent were unfamiliar. He never felt nervous; he was confident and witty, never one to back down from a challenge, but this position was so out of his comfort zone that he had no idea how to deal with it. Just getting dressed had been somewhat of a challenge.

His friends usually said that Miya had two modes: "slut", and "slob." The former referred to the clothes he'd wear at work, or out, while the latter was his casual way of dressing when just lounging around at the house—usually sweats, or pajama pants and a tank top, and even then he'd have some sort of make-up on. It was so common in their circles, he didn't even think about it usually, but this morning... Miura had searched him out based on his nightlife persona and had never seen him in the light of day, so he was probably assuming that... Or maybe he thought that it *was* just because of Miya's line of work that he looked the way he did? Plus, he didn't think it was very appropriate dressing in his usual fashion when going out to a trendy coffee shop. So he'd played it down a bit, wearing a pair of simple, stone-washed jeans, two tanks over one another, and a black, button-up shirt thrown over those, without buttoning it. The style was casual enough to make it seem like he hadn't *tried* to dress up but still looked very flattering on him. As for hair and make-up, he'd coated his hair with a limited layer of spray and only wore some eyeliner; compared to the arsenal he owned, it wasn't half-bad. At least he didn't look dead.

The waitress came back with his coffee, along with those little packets of sugar and cream on the side. He took it black though, blowing gently on the hot beverage while keeping an eye on the front door.

A short while later, he spotted Miura coming through the door. The man looked around and came towards him shortly after.

Should he stand up? How did this work?

He remained seated, keenly watching the man as he came over. He smiled. "Hi, I already ordered something. I hope you don't mind."

"Not at all. Sorry I'm late."

Out of habit, Miya gestured towards the opposite chair. "Go on, sit."

The other man smiled. He was dressed as always: a white shirt, black pants, and a blazer. But his hair was just as unruly, his face just as unreadable. But his smile was nice. Miya wondered how old he was. Early thirties perhaps?

His own age was debatable. He often got surprised looks when the rare event occurred that he actually told people his age. Going on twenty-nine wasn't obvious based on his appearance.

Miura slipped down on the chair, and they regarded each other. Miya smiled a little. He might not have been the one who had initiated this, but it seemed like he was the one who would have to keep it afloat.

"Well," he said, lifting his coffee cup with both hands. "Here we are."

"I'm glad you could make it..." the other man said, still smiling. It suited him.

"Me too," he replied. It was a flirtatious answer, but his tone was calm and sober. "To be honest, I'm a little nervous."

Maybe disclosing that information would help.

"Nervous?"

"It's been a while since someone asked me out." Miya's lips curled up. He regarded Miura from underneath his dark fringe. If he played his cards carefully, he might be able to draw some proper pointers on what was going on out of the other man without him noticing that he was prodding.

"How can that be? You probably get offers all the time."

Miya snickered.

"No, not offers but…"

Miya shook his head, strands of ebony dancing around his shoulders. "Offers are one thing. Offers are well… *nice*. But nobody asks me *out*."

"I don't understand that," Miura replied, looking flustered still. "Why wouldn't they?"

Miya thought about what Aki had said but kept his mouth shut. No need to sabotage this for himself this early on in the game.

The waitress came back. Miura ordered tea, and she asked them if he'd like something to eat. The waitress suggested a variety of cakes and other sweets.

"Cake for dinner?" Miya smirked. "Why the hell not? Do you have those… lemon things?"

He'd come here a while back and had a kind of soft tea cake with lemon flavor and felt a sudden urge to eat it again. Miura asked for the same, and the waitress left, coming back moments later with their orders. Her interruption had saved Miya from having to reply to that awkward question, but now what?

"I don't go out much either," Miura said.

No really.

"So I'm sorry if this is a little awkward."

Miya shook his head, plunging his spoon into the cake slice. "How could it not be? Here we are, two people who know nothing about each other, and we're having… dinner?" He eyed their plates, lip curving softly. He grinned. "How about this then? We start out by getting to know each other? Presentations are in order, don't you think?"

"Of course. What do you want to know?"

Everything. His curious nature almost had him saying that out loud, but the little piece of lemony heaven in his mouth prevented him from it. He shrugged. "Whatever it is you think is important."

"Well… I'm a teacher," Miura started.

Miya arched an eyebrow. That would definitely explain the authority and the way he dressed, but not what he was doing hanging around that sleazy club. Then again, teachers probably needed to have social lives as well. He didn't seem all that social though. Miya felt himself smiling and grabbed his cup so the other man wouldn't notice.

"What do you teach?" he swallowed, directing his gaze on Miura.

"I'm a homeroom teacher, middle school, class three."

"Huh," Miya nodded. "Do all teachers run around outside at night?"

He couldn't help it, and for a moment, he thought he'd offended the other man.

"Why do you think I'm always leaving so early?" the man countered.

Miya sucked on his spoon, taking a moment to prevent himself from blurting his thoughts about Miura being afraid of taking the plunge.

"I think that… maybe you're a very disciplined man." Miya grinned at him. "As a teacher should be. What else?"

"What else?" Miura shrugged. "I'm a teacher. My life consists of grading tests, preparing assignments, lectures and conferences."

How different from his own life. How… boring in comparison. Miya licked his lips.

"You definitely deserve to go out and have some fun once in a while then," he replied.

Though, you don't seem to be having fun.

He was relieved that the conversation flowed easier now.

"Yeah well, nightclubs aren't exactly my scene."

"I noticed," Miya replied, still smiling sweetly and crossing his legs.

"Am I that obvious?"

He decided not to tear his new acquaintance too far down. He shook his head. "I've been working in this business forever. I'm good with people."

"I can tell." Miura smiled at him, almost a little shyly, like he was afraid of coming on too strong. That was almost a little heartwarming to Miya's surprise.

He cocked his head to the side. "You're not half bad yourself."

"What else?" Miura repeated his earlier statement. "What do you do when you're not up all night working?"

Sleep, drink, fuck...

What was he supposed to say? To an outsider, Miya's habits were probably unnerving.

"The lifestyle is sort of all-consuming." He smiled crookedly. "So there's a lot of after parties. A lot of sleeping it off."

That was a nicer way of saying it at least. This was *why* he didn't go on dates. He frowned. He wasn't of that caliber.

"So this is new to you too then."

"Hmm?" he was pulled from his thoughts.

"Neither of us seems to get out much, not in this way at least."

Miya laughed heartily. "You're right about that!"

"To hectic lives." Miura jokingly lifted his cup as if to a toast. Miya played along, lifting his coffee cup, which was practically empty at this point.

He ordered a refill. And they talked, keeping it to rather safe subjects—thoughts on various things, talk about being busy. No confessions about personal lives or families or any of that stuff. Both of them probably deemed it too early; they didn't know each other. And to a certain extent, they didn't know what they were doing.

They probably spent around two hours in the café talking about various topics. Overall, Miya got a really good feeling from the other man, despite his earlier hesitation. He found that he enjoyed talking to him, even about mundane things, and his open-minded nature made it no problem for him that they didn't really touch on subjects like age, politics or relationships. He was always afraid that his vanity and lack of interest in society would be a bad trait to present to a potential love interest. And when it came to his frivolity... that was usually the hook on the door. He didn't want to get into those things. Not yet. And it was probably way too early to consider Miura a love interest, or anything of the sort.

But still, he wasn't able to hide his excitement when they left the café.

"This was really nice," he said as they stood on the sidewalk outside of the building.

"I'm glad you think so."

Miya regarded him, searching for any hints that the man might be interested in something more; like going out for a drink, or maybe just any kind of hint that he'd want to do this again.

"I'm glad you asked. It was fun getting to know you a little better." He ran his hand swiftly through his long, black tresses, grinning. "Would you—"

"Can I ask—"

They spoke at the same time, awkwardly interrupting each other, both of them laughing a little nervously.

"What were you saying?"

"I wondered if you wanted to go somewhere else, or do you have plans?"

Miura frowned. "Unfortunately, I have some math tests to grade, so I need to get back. I've already been here longer than intended." He glanced at his wristwatch.

"Oh," Miya nodded. "I see."

It probably came out sounding a little more disappointed than he'd intended. He had no idea how to do this. He was so used to hitting it off with someone and taking them straight home, it hadn't occurred to him that a situation like this might come around, where they would have to decide whether or not they wanted to see each other.

"Not that I *want* to. But I should. So I was hoping…"

"Yes?" he waited, probably answering a little too soon.

"Can I see you again?"

Miya confidently placed a hand on his hip, grinning. "You can see me whenever you want."

Miura smiled. Genuinely so.

"Next time though," Miya continued, "should we go for a drink? Not at my workplace of course, somewhere else. Your call."

"I'll find a place," the other man said. "And then I'll give you a call. Sounds good?"

He was warming up it seemed. Miya was relieved. He'd been dreading this somewhat, thinking it might become awkward and strained. *He'd* had a good time, even if it was different from what he was used to. And he had no issues with tricky situations usually, but now he felt like he needed to step carefully.

So he wasn't surprised when he casually stepped forward, towards the other man, and he instinctively backed up. It wasn't an obvious move on Miya's part, and it was probably just reflexive for Miura. So then that was established—too soon for any kind of physical contact.

"You do that." He smiled instead, falling back on his heels. "I'll be looking forward to it."

"Me too."

They parted ways. Miya stuffed his hands in his pockets, walking in a sort of daze the entire way to the station. This was far too strange. He decided that it was probably best he kept it to himself for a while. Miura hadn't defined anything. Even if they'd agreed that they'd both had a good time and wanted to see each other again, there had been nothing indicating that he'd actually seen it as a date. Or maybe he had. Miya had to smile at how clueless they both seemed. In any case, he didn't want to involve any of his friends in this yet. Hiiro maybe, since he already knew something. But that seemed like a particularly bad idea, as the redhead had an unusually big mouth. He could probably tell Aki, if he wanted to tell *someone*. His roommate was hardly interested in anything anyway, so maybe that was the way to go, but then of course he'd get no response, and the fun in talking about it would be gone.

In the end, it was probably better to just keep quiet—until they'd had that drink at least.

He felt excited at the thought.

Rushing back home, he changed his clothes and headed straight to work.

9. Headway

He was surprised when Miura called. He hadn't expected to hear from him again so soon. He called him on Friday while Miya was working. Luckily, he'd been free at that moment, so he was able to pop out back and answer it.

"Hello?" he wondered if he was able to sound casual. The truth was that he'd assumed he'd be the one calling in the end.

"It's Miura, how are you?"

Miya smiled, clutching the phone a little tighter. "I'm good. Working right now."

"Sorry. You must be busy."

Miya laughed softly. "Not at all. We have recess here as well you know."

He thought he heard a short laugh on the other end. He liked the sound of it and was almost a little taken aback by how easily he'd become attracted to this person. Physical attraction was one thing but…

"That's good. It's important to take breaks now and again."

"Yeah, I'd say so. Are you calling about that drink?" He cut to the chase.

"I was… but I can't this weekend. I just thought I'd schedule with you in advance to make sure you had the time."

"I'm off on Tuesday," he said. "But since I'm at work now, why don't you come over?"

"I'm sorry, but I was on my way to bed. I just thought I'd ask you which day was good."

Usually Miya would have made a half-joking comment in response, but he just nodded. "Well, Tuesday sounds great. Where do you want to go?"

"I was thinking eight-ish, there's this bar…" He gave Miya the address.

Miya had heard of the place and knew the area, so he agreed.

It probably wasn't a flashy, noisy place, which suited him fine. "Sounds good," he replied. "I'm looking forward to it."

"Me too." Miura coughed on the other end. *"You should probably get back to work."*

"Shouldn't I be the judge of that?" Miya chirped back. "But yeah, I guess so. I'll see you Tuesday?"

"Tuesday it is."

"All right. Bye."

He hung up the phone and exhaled. His heart was beating surprisingly fast. Not because his feelings were getting carried away—after all, he didn't know what to feel—but the thought was still so absurd, and it was really nice to hear that someone was looking forward to spending time with him.

He reached into his pocket, getting out a pack of cigarettes. At that moment, Hiiro came out through the back door.

"What's up?"

"Needed a cigarette." Miya dug into his pocket, cigarette snugly tucked in between his lips.

"Sure you did." Hiiro held up a small, square item. "Your lighter was left inside though."

He tossed it over. Miya caught it in midair and quickly lit his cigarette. "That explains it."

"So what are you really doing out here?"

Miya shrugged. "Phone call."

"From?"

"Why are you so nosy?" He attempted a glare, but it fell through; he failed to contain the smile.

"Who?" Hiiro had already caught on. "Do I know him?"

"Know? *I* don't *know* him."

"It's that guy, isn't it? You're kidding me? He really *did* come here to get to you?"

Miya laughed out loud. "What do you mean *get to me*. He came here a couple of times, yeah. And then we got to talking, and he asked me out."

"And?"

Miya shrugged. "That's what I'm trying to find out."

Hiiro grinned, lighting a cigarette of his own. "I saw it

coming."

"No, you didn't." Miya rolled his eyes.

"Okay, maybe not like *that*. He doesn't seem like your type."

"Shut up, he's good looking."

"Is that enough?" Hiiro smirked.

Miya sent him a challenging glance. "Isn't it? *You're* good looking, aren't you?"

"Ouch!" Hiiro grinned, licking his lips. He came closer, placing his arm around Miya's waist. "Does that mean you're not gonna want to play with us anymore?"

Miya frowned.

"Idiot," he said. "It's not like we're going out or anything. We're having coffee. Last time I checked, that wasn't the same as being exclusive."

"And coffee means…?"

"Just coffee!" Miya pursed his lips, brushing them against the corner of the man's mouth. "Until Tuesday at least. We're having drinks then."

Hiiro said nothing and just grinned knowingly at him.

Miya nudged him in the side, sniggering. "Shut up. I don't think he's that kind of guy… He seems kind of held back."

"But you're not." the redhead countered, taking a deep drag of his cigarette. "Maybe you can guide him a little."

"We'll *see*," Miya hissed back, exhaling a cloud of smoke. That was precisely what he was going to do—see where this led.

The two of them went back inside. It was already chock full of people, enough to get the adrenaline pumping. As tiring as weekend nights could be in this place during what they called the rush hours, there was something special about it, at least compared to serving the same customers day after day on weekdays. Weekends were lively and fun—flirtatious customers, loud music, loud singing, dancing, and tension. That characteristic, heavy tension that arose when so many people were assembled in one place, looking for the same thing; sexual tension that could be cut with a knife, which the waiters helped rouse by egging on the clients, peeling away any level of shyness and withdrawnness.

And, of course, the tension rose when the waiters had been offered a few drinks by the customers and their touches had gone from playful to anticipating. Then they started looking forward to the after parties and the release of said tension... Tonight wasn't really an exception. He wasn't against a bit of heavy flirting or kissing to please the clients, or reeling up a coworker with promises of fulfilling what they'd started later on. It did cross his mind that Miura probably wasn't the kind of guy who approved of this kind of activity, but they barely knew each other. At the rate this was going, they might never get to the point of actually talking about whether they were going to turn this into a relationship or not.

At present, the thought was ludicrous. Miya was up for the fun; he'd gladly get to know the teacher to find out what he liked and didn't like, maybe get to know him on a more intimate level, but he didn't think that was within reach at this point. And in his world, you had to say the words out loud if you wanted to be exclusive.

He thought that to himself, and then allowed himself to go with the regular flow of the evening until it ended at his place—with Ayase. It was relatively innocent, on a somewhat adolescent level of drinking more and fooling around on the sofa, but in the end they were both really tired, and really drunk, and ended up falling asleep until the next morning when Aki came home, his hair a mess, he too looking exhausted and hung over. He collapsed on the couch next to them, stirring them both awake.

"Move over," he yawned, crawling in between the two of them.

Miya yawned. "Where have you been?"

"Out," Aki mumbled in response.

"Obviously," Miya replied, scratching his hair. His entire body ached. "Ay-chan? What time is it?"

Ayase peered at the clock with a red eye. "Ten. Jesus, my back hurts. Tell me why we didn't move to the bed?"

"Who knows," Miya replied. He threw an arm around Aki, pulling him close. "Did you have fun though? You disappeared last night. I was worried."

"Sure you were." The younger man rolled his eyes. "I could see that, the way you two were going at it. I kinda checked out so you could be alone."

"There was plenty of room you know." Ayase attempted a grin, but his lips were too dry and his face too stiff yet, so it came off sort of strained. "If you wanted to join."

"And I can tell you got so much out of it," came the dry reply.

"It was fun while it lasted." Miya pretended to pout, lovingly stroking Ayase's inner thigh. "Right?"

"A little PG is underrated," the other man replied with laughter in his voice.

"You're so juvenile," the eighteen-year-old sighed.

"And you're a grouch."

"Kids, don't fight." Miya attempted to mediate between them in a playful manner and earned himself an annoyed glance from his roommate. He also noticed several red marks on Aki's neck. "You definitely got some though."

He touched his hand to Aki's shoulder, stroking it gently, and received something as rare as a gentle kiss on the hand. Maybe the younger man was still a little drunk. He resisted the urge to coddle him just for the heck of it but turned his attention to Ayase instead. "Are you hungry?"

"A little, but I don't really feel like eating," he replied. "Besides, you never have food."

"Why would he have food?" Aki shot in. "He never cooks."

"Like you do?"

Aki shrugged, standing from the couch. "I'm gonna sleep. See ya."

The teen disappeared into his room, slamming the door shut. They could hear him shuffling around for a while before it went completely silent.

"Isn't he sweet though?" Miya commented dryly, leaning back on the couch.

"Yeah." Ayase's voice was flat. "So about food... What do we do? Wanna go to Maki's?"

"Mmh." Miya stretched. "Maybe. I wanna shower first though—I feel awful."

Slim, playful fingers intertwined with his own. "Shall I join you?"

"You're eager to finish what we started?" He smirked crookedly.

"Aren't you?"

Their lips met in a chaste kiss. It was still only Saturday. It didn't matter. He dragged the other man up from the couch, leading him into the bathroom.

***

By the time Tuesday came around, Miya had forgotten about any kind of guilt he might have been feeling regarding the weekend. He was excited about the second date, still without being entirely sure of if that was what it actually was. Maybe Miura was just after his friendship. Hiiro had snorted loudly at that theory, as well as the highly unlikely chance that this man was actually just trying to figure out his sexuality and wanted to try to get a proper idea of how to act.

"Miya!" Hiiro grabbed him by the shoulders, staring into his eyes, holding his gaze as if in a vice. "Stop with all the excuses already. He likes you, and he's too scared to make a move."

Miya groaned. "I know."

"Then what's the problem?"

"Do you remember the last time I attempted to date someone?"

"Yeah well." Hiiro shook his head. "That was a disaster waiting to happen. The guy was an idiot. This guy might be flaky, but I don't think they should be compared."

It was strange being talked to in this way. Miya felt like he was a kid again, needing reassurance that he wasn't completely off the map.

"What's going on with you anyway?" His friend looked exasperated. "Weren't you all excited this weekend?"

"I *am* excited!"

"Great, then shut up and be happy. Some hot guy wants to buy you drinks tonight, and that's great. Meanwhile, I'll be working my ass off for some ungrateful old geezers who keep asking me home with them." Hiiro grimaced. "Think of me when he takes you home, okay?"

"Freak." Miya chuckled. "Didn't I tell you he moves at the same pace as the middle-school kids he teaches?"

He sighed and turned his gaze back to Hiiro. "We're *not* gonna sleep together, I'll bet you that. And even if we did, I don't think that it would be appropriate to think of you during."

"It's for *my* sake!" Hiiro groaned. "For my sanity. Ugh. I'm so envious."

Maki slid a glass quarter-filled with a golden-brown liquid across the bar counter, aiming for Hiiro's outstretched hand.

"Stop complaining. If you didn't spend all your time here, maybe you could go on a date some time as well." The shopkeeper frowned. "And, Miya, I'm really happy for you. Don't worry so much; just go for it and let him decide the pace."

"Don't act like I've never dated before," he moped. "I'm just out of practice."

"And you're afraid, right?" Maki sighed. "That's not like you at all. Get over it already. The past is the past."

"Yeah, well, that's great, but what about the *present*?" Miya enquired. "How am I supposed to go out with someone who wants to take things slow while…"

He groaned loudly.

Although he didn't feel any guilt about the events that had taken place over the weekend, he was already over-thinking things and wondering what life would be like if he *did* get into a relationship. He knew it was possible; Tetsu and Kyo, or Sho and Kiyoshi, were examples that it was possible to be perfectly monogamous even though they were part of this crazy group. But the question was whether he *wanted* it now that he'd gotten used to this kind of freedom.

"If it doesn't work for you, then that sucks, but he'll have to accept that. You can pull out whenever you don't want to do it anymore," Hiiro advised, a mischievous smirk dancing on his painted lips.

"And I don't want to hear another word," Maki demanded. "Try to have a good time first and foremost. It's your second date, not a marriage proposal."

It was Miya's turn to grimace. He regretted having voiced his thoughts to these two. He and Hiiro had gone to Maki's to eat. Afterwards, his friend was going to work while Miya went to meet Miura. Hiiro had opened his stupid mouth, and Maki had gotten involved with well-meaning advice. The man was the oldest in their group, and if this was how it felt to be the youngest, he understood Aki's pissy attitude. He hadn't wanted any kind of reassurance; he just wanted to vent about how strange it was to be going out on a date—with someone who was actually a resident of the real world at that. He didn't know who found this more frightening, him or Miura.

***

Luckily, those thoughts vanished fairly quickly. The thing about insecurities was that they were often blown way out of proportion, and when it came down to it, things weren't half as bad as expected. Because of the hype that had arisen after he talked to Hiiro, he'd forgotten about how nice it had been last time. And although Miura still seemed a little guarded, Miya felt at ease in the other man's company. Perhaps it was the feeling of authority he still managed to give off.

The bar where they met was, as expected, a very low-key place. It was similar to the one where they'd first met, with dim lights and warm wooden panels on the floor. There were small, secluded tables, snack and drink menus on the table next to little red lanterns with tea lights inside giving off a warm glow through the red glass. There were pool tables, dartboards and a television—very similar to the kind of western-style bars you saw in the movies. And not overly crowded either. Miya assumed that Miura had picked it solely because of the low frequency of visitors.

He didn't mind though, as the lack of disturbances and loud

noises made it easier to have a proper conversation.

"How have you been?" Miya asked, swirling the ice cubes in his drink with his straw. "The kids treating you all right?"

"For the most part," Miura chuckled. "Every class has its bad seeds I guess, but they're good kids I'd say."

"That's good to hear. I've heard that teachers get no respect these days. I grew up in the sticks, so our teacher was really old-fashioned and threatened to hit us if we did something wrong." Miya said, laughing.

Miura didn't seem to find it funny though. His brow creased.

"Don't worry, they were empty threats, but they worked like a charm." Miya fended him off. "Somehow, we all turned into relatively respectable people. Imagine that."

He purposely laid out bait to check the terrain. He wasn't exactly regarded as respectable among his peers, especially those he used to go to school with.

Miura didn't seem to care though, as expected.

"Where are you from?" he asked instead.

"Kamigōri," Miya replied.

"I'm not sure I'd call that the sticks…"

"Where are you from then, somewhere even more deserted?" Miya tried him.

"I'm from Kobe actually. Just a different part of town from where I live now."

"See, you're a city kid. I'm from the sticks."

"I'm hardly a kid." Miura shook his head, and that unruly hair of his danced.

"No, which is why you're polite enough not to insult me for being a country bumpkin," Miya teased, flashing him a grin. "Though, when I go back to visit my folks, they pick on me for having become a vain city kid."

"I suppose you do stand out."

"I do, thank god." Miya frowned. "Everyone is the same where I used to live. They expect everyone else to be the same way. It's boring and wasteful. Maybe I am vain though…"

"I don't think you're vain."

"That's okay. I am." He laughed again. "But there's more

than that to me. Just because I'm particular about my looks, it doesn't mean I'm stupid."

"Why would anyone ever call you that?" Miura looked surprised.

Miya shrugged carelessly. "Judgementality you know. It's not very charming, but it's everywhere." He noticed Miura's eyes wandering, averting themselves from him for a second. "I don't care though. Not unless the person is very close to me."

The conversation reached an odd stop. Miya called a waiter over and ordered more drinks. He didn't want to have too much, but he figured if they both had a few, then things would loosen up more.

"I don't think I can drink any more," the teacher announced.

"Lightweight, are we?" Miya teased, hiding a smile behind his glass.

"I think you're already getting forgetful," came the quick retort. "I'm a teacher; it doesn't suit me very well to drink on school nights. I would like to keep my job."

"Hmm," Miya sighed. "But you're always going out on school nights. Alone at that."

"And I never get drunk," Miura reminded him, "I'm surprised you're still standing actually."

Miya chuckled. "I'm sitting down."

He was far from drunk, but definitely intoxicated. He made a mental note to be careful from here on. He didn't want to start revealing his less than charming sides at this point. "Don't worry about me," he added. "I might not look like it, but I'm no lightweight. It's quite the upside to working where I do."

"It's quite the… establishment."

"I know." Miya laughed at the man's overbearing expression. "It seems really sleazy, but you should see it during the weekends! It's much livelier and more diverse then, and a lot more fun."

"I don't think it's quite my scene…"

Miya supported himself on his elbow, leaning over the tabletop. "What *is* your scene then?"

The man's hand went up to loosen his collar slightly. He was dressed in the same way as always. "May I suggest dinner and a show?"

Miya said it with a mischievous glint in his eye and a playful smile. "You're a teacher, right? So you're probably more into literature and theatre and stuff, am I right?"

Miura smiled. "I hardly ever go to the theatre. But I read a lot, yeah."

"I have a friend who reads." Miya realized how dumb that sounded. "I mean... He might in fact be the *only* guy I know who actually reads regularly. But he sometimes reads out loud to us."

That probably sounded even dumber. He frowned. It was definitely time to stop drinking. He sipped at the glass of water that had been brought with the drinks. When Naruse read out loud, it was usually passages he felt were relevant to their lifestyle, maybe meant as critique or a poignant observation. Miya laughed softly. "I *can* read, in case you're wondering."

To his surprise, Miura laughed with him. "I get that. But I couldn't invite you to a library; you can't talk in libraries, so I asked you out to eat."

"Cake." Miya smirked. "How rebellious."

"It was good though."

Their eyes met, and Miya licked his lips. "Yeah, it was. Let them eat cake, isn't that a saying?"

"A false rumor." The teacher grinned. "See, you are pretty smart."

"I didn't know it was a false rumor."

"Does it matter?"

"I don't know... does it?" Miya shot back.

"Can I ask you something?" Miura changed the subject. "Is Miya your real name?"

Miya stared at him, surprised. Usually nobody questioned his name. A lot of the time, people didn't even know that he was known as Miya. Names became less important in his world, at least during casual encounters. And even those who were really close to him and knew him well referred to him by the nickname that had derived from his surname. He shook his head. "I usually don't disclose it to customers."

"Am I a customer?"

Miya gave a little jeer. "That sounded... No. You're not."

He stretched out a lean, pale arm across the table, giving Miura his hand. "Hi, I'm Utsunomiya, nice to meet you."

"Miura," Miura said. "Nice to meet you."

"That's cheating," Miya said, trying to look insulted. "I already know *your* surname."

The man in the white shirt chuckled quietly, gripping his hand a little tighter. "Shunsuke."

Miya allowed his thumb to casually stroke along the man's hand without breaching eye contact. "Satoru."

"Didn't I say that you were smart?" Miura Shunsuke smiled, referring to the way his name was spelled with the kanji for 'enlightenment.'

"I guess you were right," Miya replied warmly.

Their hands were still adjoined across the tabletop. Miura must have realized that as well because he let go shortly after. It got surprisingly cold once the handshake was broken and that warm hand let go of his.

"What about you?" Miya asked, his tone light but his gaze curiously searching the other man beneath dark eyelids and long lashes. "*Shun* means excellent. Right?"

"In this case, yes..."

"So..." Miya swirled two fingers around on the rim of his empty glass. "Are you?"

Based on the expression on Miura's face, he hadn't been prepared for that kind of question. Rather than looking surprised, he had no idea what to answer it seemed.

"I'm sorry." Miya shook his head in amusement. "That was too soon, wasn't it?"

"A tad abrupt maybe?"

"Like I said, I'm not used to this..." he excused himself. "Just let me know if I go too far sometimes."

"I thought the point of this was to get to know each other," Miura replied calmly. "Don't filter yourself for my sake."

It's more for my own sake, Miya thought but didn't answer.

"Then," he said, the corner of his lip twitching slightly, "can I ask you something?"

"Ask away."

"Are you…" he started, but then clamped his mouth shut. It wasn't the right place for it. Not here. This bar was new to both of them and not very crowded; he didn't want to risk upsetting the man in a place like this. "Why did you come to the club if it's not your scene?"

"I thought that's what you wanted."

"Who, me?" Miya looked back at him, his dark eyes widening.

"When you gave me that card, I assumed you wanted me to meet you there or something."

"But you didn't know I worked there."

"No." He shook his head. "I obviously figured that out though."

Miya almost felt bad. He hadn't thought of the possibility that the man would misunderstand the card he'd given him. And then he'd purposely ignored him that night when he'd first come to the nightclub. But he felt flattered all the same, getting it confirmed that it *was* in fact for his sake that Miura had come there night after night.

"I'm sorry if you… felt like I was rude."

Miura shook his head. "When you came over that time, I understood. You were at work, so you couldn't just drop everything."

Miya shrugged, reaching for what was left of his drink and gulping it down.

"I must admit I was… disappointed I guess."

Miya felt his body tensing up. "Why?"

"Well, when you gave me that card, I thought maybe it was an indirect approach…"

"Perhaps it was." Miya shrugged. "It worked, didn't it?"

"No, it wasn't." Miura shook his head. "You'd be more direct than that."

Miya grinned knowingly. "Maybe. I asked you out for a drink though. Even though I guess you were the one who initiated it. But that's okay."

He was relieved and anxious at the same time. He caught Miura looking at his watch. It was probably getting late—by his standards anyway. Miya hadn't paid attention to the time, but they must have been here a couple of hours at least.

"Don't take this the wrong way," he said apologetically, offering a concerned look.

"It's a school night," Miya finished for him. "Don't worry about it."

They paid for their last round of drinks and got up, ready to leave.

On their way out, they walked in silence. Miya was used to feeling eyes watching him when he went out, but tonight he was perceiving it differently. Maybe because he was so aware of the fact that Miura wasn't used to being looked at, if not for any other reason than being good-looking. A small smile forced its way onto his lips. He knew he stood out, and he just didn't want the man to feel uncomfortable. But then... he didn't want to have to tone himself down for the sake of someone else either. That was going too far into things though, he thought. For now, it was better to play it safe and see where this led. Although he was already getting impatient.

"Next time," he said, walking alongside the man towards the nearest subway, "should we go somewhere else?"

"Next time?"

"What," he dared to gently nudge the other man's arm, "you don't want to see me again?"

"You say these things so easily..." Miura stopped abruptly.

"Yes?" Miya blinked up at him; he wasn't wearing boots for once, and the man was a little taller than him. "Because I'm very direct, like you said. Is that... Does it put you off?"

His tone was probably a little sharper than he'd intended.

"I don't intend to hide anything." Miya shrugged, beginning to walk slowly ahead again.

"Hey—"

His arm was grabbed from behind, that firm grip from earlier grasping his wrist, pulling him back.

"What are yo—" His eyes met with Miura's. His pupils were dilated, like he was afraid or something, or maybe excited? Miura's lips trembled slightly as he pulled him a little closer, towards the corner of the building they were passing by.

"C-Can I kiss you?"

Miya thought his mouth would drop open. He wasn't used to this kind of abrupt physical contact leading to such a meek question. He was baffled.

And when the other man tentatively leaned forward to brush their lips together, he found his heart pounding preposterously as he grabbed the taller man by the neck and pressed their lips together, kissing him back intensely.

"Yes," he whispered breathlessly, touching their lips together again.

10. Dating for Dummies

He'd been more than a little surprised that his date had actually dared to kiss him in the middle of the street. All right, it had been an empty street corner, and it had been dark but... he was still perplexed by it. At that moment, when their lips had first met, he'd completely forgotten how to hold back. He'd forgotten about his fear of scaring off the man. But he'd been rewarded, not rejected. He hadn't been pushed away, but rather kissed back just as enthusiastically.

And then, Miura had pulled away, smiling. He'd run his thumb across Miya's cheek, just looking at him for a while. But he didn't say anything. Miya's heart had been pounding the whole time, which was incredibly surreal to him. Part of him was hoping it wouldn't end there. He wasn't convinced that Miura was the kind of person who'd just go from the first kiss to... something more. But a part of him was waiting for the question that never came.

Instead, he smiled back at him, genuinely, his cheeks flushing. "Next time, can we go out on the weekend?"

"Why?"

Miya grabbed the man's shirt, leaning close enough for him to hear his whisper. "That would give us more time."

"What would you like to do?"

Miya shook his head. "It doesn't really matter. Do you have anything in mind?"

In fact, he knew *exactly* what he'd like to do next, but he kept that to himself.

"We'll figure something out, okay?" He smiled, and although he looked so flustered from the sudden turn of events, and his parted lips revealed that his teeth were slightly crooked, he made Miya ache just by looking at him. This was so new and so nostalgic at the same time; he hadn't felt like this in ages. This was different than just wanting to go home with someone to get laid. It was thrilling, possibly more so than the prospect of taking some stranger home for the night and seeing where that led. After all, that would only conclude in more or less decent sex and an awkward morning after. *This* could probably go anywhere. Or nowhere... But he didn't want to think about that.

"Okay." He smiled, letting go of Miura's shirt. "No matter what, I'm sure I'll be looking forward to it all the same."

"That's good."

A slight awkward silence lowered itself between the two of them again. Miya wanted to kiss it away but remained standing still. He was going to play the ball over to the other man and take it from there.

"I'll be going then," Miura said without making any attempt at moving from where he stood. "Will you be all right on your own?"

"Don't worry." Miya waved his hand at him. "I'll be fine. I'll get home from here no problem."

Wasn't it sort of sweet how the teacher seemed to think that *this* was a bad state to be in at eleven o'clock on a weeknight? If he only knew... Miya bit down on his lip. That would be a fun discussion.

"Okay. I'll call you later."

"Please do," he replied, waving as the other man finally turned to walk down to the subway station. Miya had decided to walk. Although he didn't usually come to this part of the city, it wasn't a very long walk away from Higashinada. Taking the train would have been more comfortable, but he felt like walking, and it was a nice evening. He lit a cigarette as he walked, thinking about how strange this all was and absentmindedly touching his fingertips to his lips.

When he got home that night, he barely noticed that the apartment was empty again. He'd also forgotten that it was his turn to go shopping, but he was too wound up to go back out to the *conbini*, so he decided to just postpone it. Despite his exhilaration, he wound up going straight to bed. After playing with the thought for a while, he picked up his phone and texted;

"Thanks for tonight. Made it home safely, so don't worry, okay?" Then he fell asleep, drawing out his confusion in dreams about the past and the present.

***

He woke up the next morning feeling surprisingly refreshed, at least until he was met by Aki's sour expression when he came into the kitchen.

"You didn't buy food yesterday, did you?"

"Sorry, I forgot." He rubbed the back of his neck, yawning. "I'll do it later today."

"That's great and all, but what am I supposed to eat now?" The teenager was in a foul mood.

"What's the matter, sweetie?" Miya retorted in a provocative voice. "Hormones bothering you?"

Aki snorted. "You're the one to talk."

Miya smiled at him and came over to ruffle the boy's hair. "I am. Where were you last night?"

"I could ask you the same question. We were all getting together after hours, but you never showed."

Miya ignored the latter part of that statement. "And *who* did you get together with?"

The raven-haired teen glared, annoyed at him. "None of your business."

"Oh oh," Miya chuckled. "So it was an outsider then. Well right back at you."

Aki rolled his eyes. "Skank."

Miya laughed, ruffling his hair some more before his hand was slapped away. "How about you just hang out for a bit while I shower, and then we go out together and grab something? My treat."

Aki shrugged. "Fine. Be quick! No jerking off or whatever."

"Do you kiss your mother with that mouth?" Miya crossed his arms over his chest, teasing the younger man.

"No." Aki grinned. "I kiss *you* with that mouth."

Shaking his head, Miya left the obstinate teenager in the

living room and went to take a shower. He still felt that strange tingle in his chest. He felt happy, not that he hadn't been happy before, it was just... a different kind of cheerfulness?

He had a quick shower and blow-dried his hair only halfway before dragging Aki down to the usual place, where they as by default found several of their coworkers, and Yuura. A couple of them were looking slightly ashen and tired after a long night out; others were eating while reading a newspaper or chatting with each other.

"*Ohayou!*" Maki grinned at them as they came in.

Aki muttered something at him and threw himself down by a table. Miya nodded in the man's direction and shook his head in exasperation about his friend. "What do you wanna eat?"

Aki shrugged. "Whatever."

"You have any breakfast?" Miya called over to Maki.

The man smiled. "Coming up. You guys want coffee?"

"I'd love some."

Aki didn't reply. He didn't need to—everyone knew he hated coffee.

"Juice for you then."

There were no objections from the youngest of the group. Maki came over with a tray holding scrambled eggs, coffee and juice. "Honestly, you two should take better care of yourselves." he said, stroking Aki's head. He pulled away, looking irritated. No wonder with so many people patronizing him all morning. "Thanks for the food," he muttered, grabbing a fork.

"Thanks." Miya smiled at Maki, whose brown hair was tied back in a loose ponytail for once rather than being elaborately put up the way he usually did it. "It's my fault for forgetting to shop. By the way, what's with the hair? Could it be...?" He allowed the sentence to hang in the air while watching the smirk spreading over Maki's lips.

"Good for you!" Miya grinned, reaching for his cup.

"Don't make it sound like I never get any," Maki replied with laughter in his voice.

"But you don't," Aki mumbled with his mouth full of food. Maki smacked him over the shoulder.

"And why is that you think, huh? I spend all my time in this place, slaving away for you!"

Miya laughed. "You should hire someone. A nice young guy you can flirt with all day!"

"Good idea," Maki grinned. "But you know, mixing business and pleasure is…" He looked around at his clients, sighing. "You know what? Never mind."

A low collective laugh went through the shop.

"As long as there's no drama, there's nothing to worry about," Miya replied calmly while wondering how drama-free his life would be if he got further involved with the relatively conservative-seeming Miura.

"Said the drama queen," Maki replied dryly.

"How am I a drama queen?" Miya demanded, pouring ketchup on his eggs, noticing the way Aki grimaced across the table from him.

"Remember that time when you kicked Tsuuji out for being a messy person? I'd say that was pretty dramatic."

"Are you trying to start something?" Miya narrowed his eyes. "There was more to it than that."

"I should hope so." Yuura came over to their table, sitting down next to him, snatching Miya's fork to scoop some eggs into his own mouth. "You're not exactly the tidiest person on the block."

"Oh shove it!" Miya grabbed his fork back. "Tsuuji and I couldn't keep living together for several reasons."

"Didn't you go out with him for a brief time by the way?" Maki looked thoughtful. "Or am I imagining things?"

"Must be the Alzheimer's."

Aki earned himself another smack. "You're so charming this morning. What have you been doing? Bad night?"

"Not at all," Aki smirked.

"I don't get you at all," Maki rolled his eyes, turning his attention back to Miya.

"No, you're right; we did try to date but…" Miya chewed thoughtfully. Why did this come up now? "We were too different, simple as that. He was… nice and all," he stifled a snigger, "but we never agreed on anything. And that baseball thing... drove me crazy."

Maki nodded. "I know what you mean. I was with the same guy for over a year, even though we were polar opposites. One day I just *snapped* over nothing. It was just a stupid thing, like him forgetting to buy dinner or something... I don't know. I just went insane."

"One year?" Yuura gawked at him. "That's....a long time. At least for someone like you."

"Pardon?" the man crossed his arms over his chest. "I'll have you know it wasn't my longest relationship. But it sucked when it ended; as in, it was so bad at the end—it just had to be put out of its misery."

"My condolences." Yuura smiled crookedly. Miya glanced over at Aki, who didn't seem to be paying attention to their conversation anymore. Why should he? He was probably too young to bother with proper relationships, having just recently discovered this kind of frivolous lifestyle.

"Don't worry about it." Maki shook his head. "It was like ten years ago, and I've more or less been a free spirit since then."

He laughed that hoarse laugh of his.

"Don't you get tired of it though?" Miya blurted. Three pairs of eyes turned to him. "I mean, not that you're old, but... don't you want to find someone eventually?"

Maki shrugged. "If it so happens that I find someone I want to stay with, maybe I'll go for it. But at this point in my life, I've kissed enough frogs to feel like the chase is sort of futile."

"Hn." Miya sipped at his coffee, which was already starting to cool down. "I'm just looking at Tetsu and Kyo for instance. They seem happy."

"Yeah, but being single isn't the same as being unhappy either." Yuura helped himself to more of Miya's eggs. He looked tired, Miya noted. Maybe he'd been working all night. He was still wearing make-up and a relatively revealing outfit, but it was just as likely he could have spent the night out partying. It was hard to tell.

"Are you saying you're unhappy?" Maki looked a little

concerned.

"Not at all." Miya curled his fingers around the coffee mug. "I'm very content actually; it was just a thought."

"How could he be unhappy?" Yuura commented. "He's got hordes of men at his feet; I'd say that's reason enough to be happy."

"You're eating my eggs, and *that* makes me unhappy." Miya looked over at the other.

"I'm hungry!"

"Order your own food, freeloader."

"Children!" Maki laughed hoarsely, placing his hands on his hips.

"We're sorry, Mother." Yuura pretended to shamefully look down at his feet but just as quickly looked back up at the shopkeeper, "By the way, where's last night's conquest?"

"Sleeping upstairs. So hurry up and finish, so I can run upstairs and check on him."

Amused glances were exchanged.

"Speaking of," Yuura nudged Aki in the side, "did you find out what he's been up to?"

Aki shrugged. "That's not a very hard guess, is it?"

"We missed you last night," Yuura moped. "Didn't hear from you all night."

"Well, I was busy."

"Getting busy?"

Typical Yuura; always so nosy. If it hadn't been for their notorious licentiousness, Hiiro and Yuura could have married each other he thought.

"It didn't get to that point, actually," he replied matter-of-factly, annoyed at this cross-examination.

Aki looked up from the plate he'd been scraping. Disbelief was written on his pale face. "Are you sick?"

Miya ignored him and finished his meal without answering any more questions. He was perfectly happy with the way last night had turned out. Moreover, he was surprised at what he considered to be far quicker progress than he'd expected, and he wasn't going to let these two rain on his parade. Not today.

He was anxiously waiting for the man's call so they could meet again and see what that would lead to.

"Are you done?" He gulped down his nearly cold coffee and glanced over at his roommate.

"Pretty much." Aki pushed the plate away, stretching.

"Wanna come shopping with me? I'll still pay for everything; I just don't wanna go by myself."

The younger man shrugged. "Sure."

Miya turned his head, calling over his shoulder; "*Nee-san!* We're done here, so you can take my money and go see your toyboy now!"

Maki came over, gently nudging him in the shoulder. "Careful there, *Satoru*, or I might charge you a little extra for slurring the manager."

Miya slipped some cash into the man's hand, chuckling. "Bribe for you. Thanks for the food, it was great."

"Of course it was. Now get out." Maki smiled happily at them, picking up the plates and rolling his eyes at Yuura, who was still there. "And you?"

"I'll just stick around."

Aki and Miya exchanged glances. *"Cockblock,"* Aki mouthed.

Miya snickered, throwing his arm around the younger man's shoulder.

Laughing quietly, they made their way to the nearest convenience store, stocking up on mostly instant and frozen foods, before getting on the train home to Higashinada, where most of the day was spent doing absolutely nothing. Miya made a futile attempt at cleaning but gave it up pretty quickly. They ended up watching mindless television until dinnertime, again without talking much.

"Hey." Miya prodded Aki's side with his toe. The younger man looked like he was half-asleep.

"Hn?" Aki grunted, looking over at him.

"You feel like cutting my hair?"

"What, now?" Aki yawned.

"It's not like you've got anything better to do, is it?" Miya crawled over to the teen's side of the couch, looking up at him as he rested his chin on Aki's thigh.

"Are those supposed to be puppy eyes?" A faint grin crossed Aki's face as he reached down to ruffle Miya's silky, ebony tousles.

"Are they working?" Miya grinned, brushing his lips against the fabric of Aki's pants as he spoke.

"Not at all, but I'll do it anyway. Split ends bothering you?" He added the last bit with a slight sneer, stabbing at Miya's vanity.

"They *will*," Miya replied, taking a fistful of hair and regarding it in a critical manner, "at this rate."

Aki shrugged. "Get off. I'll do it now then. I'm going out later."

"Where?"

"None of your business." The teen disappeared into the bathroom, returning with a pair of silver scissors. He wasn't a great hairstylist or anything, but Aki had been cutting his own hair since he was young, so Miya had decided to start trusting him near his hair as well; at least if it was for something as simple as a trim.

He took the towel Aki threw him and wrapped it around his shoulders, sitting down on a chair in the middle of the living room floor.

"Isn't it strange?" he said, as Aki started snipping carefully at his split ends.

"What is?" Aki's voice was muffled, like he had something in his mouth. Hairpins probably.

"As *close* as we are," he grinned a little, "it's still more difficult for me to trust you with my hair, than with other parts of my body."

He thought he heard a quiet laugh in the depth of Aki's throat.

"Your hair has nothing to do with you being easy," came the flat reply. There was a light tug at the hair in the back of his neck as a confirmation that Aki was just joking around.

There was another tug on his hair, and then Aki swore

quietly. "Oh Sh—"

"What?"

The young man burst out laughing. "I'm *kidding*."

"You almost gave me a heart attack!" Miya smacked his hand dramatically to his chest.

"I was just making a point," Aki said calmly, running his hand through Miya's hair, continuing to snip carefully at the ends.

"Which point was that?"

"You don't trust me with your hair at all."

Miya was about to reply, when Aki continued, "Which, by the way, is turning grey."

"Funny," Miya snorted. "What if I rearrange that pretty face of yours a little?"

"Go on, threaten me, I dare you," the teen teased, coming around to stand in front of Miya, holding up the scissors in front of his face. "Maybe I'll give you a nice little side-cut."

"Don't you dare!"

"Ah, but you would be so pretty," Aki snickered, running the scissors along the shorter-length hair framing Miya's face. "Totally edgy, no?"

"Yeah, how about no," Miya countered. He winced slightly at the feeling of having hair pulled out as the scissors shaved off old, brittle hair on its way down.

Aki finished up what he was doing and reached for Miya's bangs, which were actually in need of some shortening anyway.

Before he managed to start though, Miya leaned forward, touching his forehead to Aki's stomach. "I *do* trust you."

"Don't get mushy on me," the teen replied coolly. "Not unless you plan on getting something out of it."

Miya kissed the younger man's flat stomach through the shirt he was wearing and looked up at him. "Just finish, okay?"

There wasn't any kind of promise in the words he spoke, even if they could be interpreted as such. He was just talking to his roommate in the habitual flirty tone he always used.

"Sit still," the teen replied, beginning to snip carefully at Miya's bangs. "I don't want to scalp you by accident."

"Please don't," Miya chuckled in response. "I don't think it would be quite my look."

"In that case, the side-cut is better."

A few short minutes later, his bangs were prettied up and his view of the world had literally changed in the sense that he could actually see compared to earlier.

"Thanks." He stood, dropping the towel onto the floor, which was covered with black hair. "Jeez, how much did you cut?"

"You're bald," Aki joked dryly. "Clean it up yourself, okay? I'm going out."

"Have fun!" Miya went to get the hoover whilst the younger man put his shoes on and left.

***

Aki didn't come home that night, which was okay by Miya, as the call he'd been waiting for finally came.

"How are you?" Miura's voice came through the phone, sounding more confident than it had last time.

"Really good, you?"

"Tired. But I'm All right."

Miya threw himself down on the couch, running his hand through his hair—it felt lighter somehow after getting that dead weight off.

"That's good."

"Are you going into work soon?"

Miya glanced at the clock on the kitchen wall. "Yeah, in a while. I've got time to chat though. Why? Were you thinking of coming to see me?"

"You know I can't do that."

Did he really? Miura had already come to see him several times, and he didn't even know him at that point. But maybe it was for the better. Considering the turn of events the night before, it was probably best that they avoided seeing each other during work hours.

"Then why are you calling?"

"About next time: Have you thought about something you

want to do?"

"It's only been a day, so... not really."

"I really have no idea what to do." Miura sounded like he was vexing. *"Today in class I overheard a couple of my students talking about dates. They're fourteen years old. Is this normal?"*

Miya chuckled, sitting upright on the sofa. "I don't know. I don't really know what kids are like these days. And I can't recall what it was like when I was young."

"You're still young."

Miya's lips curled into a smile. "I guess they go to see the new *Pokèmon* movie and have burgers afterwards."

"And so what would a grown-up date be like?"

"In your world or in mine?" Miya retorted quizzically. "My friends don't really go on dates either. We just drink a lot."

"Believe it or not, but that seems to be the norm among us office-rat people as well. That or dinner."

Miya curled his toes against the rough couch fabric. "I don't really like going out to eat all that much. Most places are so pretentious and expensive."

*"Me neither; I might eat at a ramen-*ya *on occasion but..."*

"Are you asking me to join you for dinner at a ramen-*ya*?" He laughed quietly into the phone.

"Not at all. Are you asking me to get mindlessly drunk?"

"No, I wouldn't dream of it. You're a figure of authority after all, isn't that true?"

"And still my coworkers go out drinking every pay day."

"Miura-san," Miya said softly into the phone, "I don't really care what we do—honestly. If you want to go for ramen, that's cool. If you want to take me to the movies... that would be nostalgic."

He hadn't been to a movie theater in ages. The last film he'd seen in the cinema had already been out on DVD for years. And he hadn't really paid much attention to it when he had seen it, even though the ticket had been pricey. He coughed nervously.

"Well... when are you free?"

Miya chewed his lip and told a white lie. "All weekend actually."

That wasn't true. He had Friday off—for a change—but he was sure that someone wouldn't mind stepping in for him if he asked them nicely for the rest of the weekend.

"There's a flea market in Meriken Park on Saturday..."

"Flea market?"

"Is that... no good?"

"Well, are you taking me there to look at... old stuff that people are selling?"

"They have lots of other things going on as well, and there'll be street vendors and fireworks at night. Kind of like a festival. We could have... a picnic."

"A picnic?" Miya found himself repeating virtually everything the man said. "That's... cute."

He hoped it didn't sound like he was making fun of him. That wasn't the intention at all.

"We don't have to—"

"Miura-san," Miya said just as softly but confidently, "I would love to. We go there, we eat and watch fireworks. It sounds nice, okay?"

"Are you sure?"

"Stop worrying so much. I love street food, okay? And I've never actually been to a flea market before. It'll be exotic."

What he was actually curious about was seeing how it would be to be out in the open with Miura—in daylight. Usually, it seemed like he was the type to lay low about these things and not expose himself too much. Miya wondered if that would be the case now as well. Probably, since they'd be in public. He wasn't sure if he liked the thought of hiding but decided to let go of that thought for the time being and focus on it when the time came.

"Exotic? I don't know about that."

"I think it'll be fun," Miya decided then and there. "I'll meet you at Motomachi Station on Saturday then?"

"Sounds good."

They exchanged some thoughts on when to meet and decided to meet up sometime in the afternoon, around five, and then see what they felt like doing. The fireworks wouldn't start until eight in the evening, so they'd have a few hours to walk around.

Miya was a little apprehensive, seeing as he'd hoped this time would be more serious... as in meeting somewhere and having a proper evening together. Now they were meeting early again, but he definitely saw prospects of dragging it out. And he really did feel excited about the idea of having a picnic for some reason.

11. Fireworks

After some coercing, Miya was able to talk Ayase into covering his shift without saying why, although he could tell Hiiro was listening in on their conversation, smiling knowingly in the background.

When Saturday came around, he'd tried several outfits before deciding on what to wear. He had no idea what people wore to these kinds of events, and once again, he discovered that he had very little clothing suited for a casual day out; most of his clothes were either too flashy or revealing, or they were too worn and slobbish to wear in public. In the end, he went for another look like last time with a tank top, black shirt and jeans. And just like last time, he played down the make-up, just a little, not to stick out too much among the crowd.

He grabbed his keys, phone and a jacket and went out about an hour earlier than he needed to. He ran into Aki, who was on his way in just as Miya left the building.

"Where are you going?" the teen asked.

"I'm going out for a while—not sure when I'll be home."

"Does it look like I'm gonna wait up?"

The truth was Aki looked like he could fall asleep where he stood; his eyes were lined with dark circles and his skin gusty.

"Not really, no. Get some rest before you go into work, okay? I got Ay-chan to cover for me, so I won't be coming."

"That's rare of you? You love Saturdays," the younger man sneered.

"Yeah well, I've got other plans." He didn't want to say anything else about that, but luckily Aki didn't bother asking. He probably made up his own mind, and Miya was fine with that.

"I left my keys at work," Aki said instead. "Did you lock?"

"Of course!" Miya tossed him his keys. "Take mine. But don't lose them anywhere. If I can, I'll come by work and pick them up later. If not, just take care of them for me."

Aki clenched the keychain in his fist. "Sure. Have *fun*."

Miya grinned. "I *will*!"

They parted ways, and Miya walked down the street towards the nearest shopping district. Miura hadn't said anything about whether or not he would be bringing anything, so to be on the safe side, Miya decided to shop before catching the train to Motomachi. There would be street vendors, so food was probably easy enough to get a hold of, but he still went into a grocery store, picking up some things—snacks and alcohol for the most part. Not a lot, but it seemed appropriate for watching fireworks.

"Thanks for your business!" the girl behind the counter called after him.

He caught a glance of himself in the store window as he exited, the little bell over the door ringing again as he did. He didn't look half-bad, he mused, even though he didn't feel all that comfortable going out in this kind of outfit. His hair blew slightly in the wind as he rushed towards the station, and he wondered if it would completely mess it up. Maybe he should have styled it more after all.

Miura didn't seem to mind though when they met up at the station a little later. As expected, *he* looked pretty much the same, although his shirt was open at the collar, and he looked more relaxed than usual. This time around, he was the first one to arrive.

"Sorry I'm late!" Miya walked briskly towards Miura, smiling apologetically.

"Don't worry about it; I actually live nearby, so I came here earlier than planned."

"Oh," Miya replied, looking around. He hadn't been here for a while, and as expected, the station was crowded and loud. Meriken Park was a popular attraction, and coming here on a Saturday was perhaps not the best decision.

"There are so many people here!" he exclaimed.

"Yeah, even more than usual, probably because there's so much happening here today. Would you like to do something else?"

"Nah." Miya shook his head, ebony strands dancing around his shoulders. "You promised me an exotic flea market experience, and I'm here to claim it!"

Miura laughed. "All right, come on."

They headed for the station's exit. Miya already felt the other man's eyes on him and smiled to himself. Maybe the initial awkwardness of their relation was coming to an end after all. He hoped so.

"Did you cut your hair?"

"I'm surprised you noticed!" He looked at Miura, astounded. "My roommate cut it for me. He didn't do half bad, did he?"

"You have a roommate?"

Miya nodded. "Yeah, we work together, so it's convenient like that."

"I see."

Miya wondered what that meant. "What about you? Do you live alone?"

He wanted to take the focus away from Aki. Their friendship was perhaps a little too intimate for most people's tastes, but that wasn't something he wanted to get into—certainly not here. And he was curious to learn more about Miura.

"Yeah, it's a dump of an apartment though," the teacher replied. "But I'm hardly ever at home, so I suppose it suffices."

"Yeah, well, our building is likely to be condemned at any given time," Miya shrugged, "so I'm sure yours is decent enough."

Miura laughed. "'Decent' is all you can afford on a teacher's salary. At least if you want to live alone."

Miya replied that he understood and added that that was part of the convenience about living with someone. "Plus, we're rarely home at the same time, so we get lots of privacy."

It was odd, like he was trying to smooth over his lifestyle to accommodate his fairly restrained companion. Wasn't this the kind of thing he resented in others? It felt fake, but... he couldn't quite shake the way Miura had looked at them in the club that time when he'd been talking to Hiiro and just playfully flirted with him for the sake of the club's audience. And then there were the other times people had decided to judge him based on his lifestyle rather than his character. It still didn't feel right, but he forced the thoughts aside, focusing on having a good time as they left the station and went out onto the street.

First, they just walked around the area, casually talking about things they saw, and when they'd last been at the park. Miya confessed that he was rarely ever outside of his usual districts, and that he couldn't remember the last time he'd been there, while Miura seemed to at least pass by frequently, as it was close to home.

As it turned out, he sometimes went jogging in the area. "When I run out of excuses that is," the man chuckled.

"You must be doing *something* right though," Miya replied, daring to nudge him briefly in the stomach while walking close to him because of the crowd. "You're quite fit."

"I walk a lot."

"Well, there you go."

That was largely how the conversation flowed as they walked around the park—quasi-flirtatious statements, and exchanging of words that slowly gave them more of an idea of what the other was like. The sun was warm on their backs, and the breeze was fresh but not cold.

As for the flea market, Miya was genuinely surprised at it. He'd expected tons of old junk but was surprised to find everything from electronics to students selling things they'd made themselves. He found himself letting go a little, allowing his excitement to show as they zigzagged in between the tables and blankets on the ground.

"I thought people only sold porcelain dogs and dusty old furniture at these places!" he confessed. "There were some flea markets arranged by the local elementary school when I grew up, but I think they mostly sold old clothes and boring things like that. From *Jusco*, I'm sure. But this is pretty amazing."

He was looking at a rack of clothes hand-sewn by a girl with curly, almost silvery hair.

Miura looked amused at his childlike excitement.

"I guess you see a lot of these, huh? Teachers help arrange tons of these things, don't they?"

"Well... it's been a while since *my* class did something like that. We had one once to raise money for a class trip, but like you said, there wasn't a lot of interest in the kind of things most people donated. We didn't get further away than Nara."

Miya excused himself to the girl, finding that he couldn't afford to buy anything at this point, but he happily accepted a cute, handwritten card she gave him with information about how to contact her. "Kids love Nara though, don't they?" he asked Miura.

"I suppose. It's a lovely city, and of course, feeding the deer is the greatest thing ever."

Miya shuddered. "I'm not big on animals," he disclosed. "Not wild ones anyway. I think it looks really scary being surrounded by them. And they're crazy about that food people give them, right? Scary!"

Miura laughed out loud, and Miya scowled at him. "I'm serious here."

"You should come with next time." Miura smiled. "You'll see that they're not dangerous. If a class full of thirteen-year-olds can feed the deer, then so can you."

"Will you hold my hand when I do it?" he asked curiously, turning his gaze to Miura.

The other man averted his eyes, looking a little embarrassed. "If that's what it takes to cure your phobia."

"Since when is it a phobia?"

The tension lightened, and they continued to walk the flea market grounds. Miya kept seeing things he liked, or stuff people he knew would love.

"Are you really that fascinated?"

"Yeah. It's really cool that people can make stuff like this!" Miya grinned. "When I was in school, my teachers used to get upset with me for having absolutely no patience to finish any creative projects. And I tried out different kinds of clubs, but nothing really suited me, so I think it's really fascinating to see what people can create just from their own imagination."

Miura chuckled again. "I'm the same way," he said. "I was never really good at anything in school either—at least nothing like this."

"I bet you were in the student council."

"I wasn't. I wasn't even nominated for class rep."

"Really? You seem the type." They were gravitating towards the area where the food vendors were located. "All smart and handsome-looking."

He thought he saw the man blushing. It was odd to see a grown and composed man responding in this way. He decided he'd investigate further at a more appropriate time—later, when they were in a more private place maybe.

"Well, I was smart. I guess you could say I was a bit of a *gariben*."

"Really!" It was Miya's turn to bark out with laughter. "I can sorta see that. But... not in a bad way; I just think it makes sense that you'd be the studious type."

"Because I'm a teacher?"

"Because you're... kind of held back and shy," he admitted. "But that's okay. I like that."

"In that case, you were probably a social butterfly in your years."

Miya shook his head, denying that statement. "I was social, but more of a caterpillar."

"I will *never* believe that!"

"No but..." Miya grinned, "I was, I don't know... There's not a lot of cool stuff in Kamigōri you know. So I was basically just another high school kid—just a really loud one."

"Now *that* I can believe."

They came to a row of provisory food stands. "Are you hungry? I'll treat you to something."

"Hmm..." Miya looked around, his mouth watering at the various kind of street food. "I must warn you. I can really pig out on this stuff, so don't blame me if it gets expensive. I *love* everything unhealthy that's served in paper trays."

"I'll keep that in mind." Miura looked at the time. "There's still a while before the fireworks, so do you wanna eat here?"

"Yeah sure. There are benches over there." Miya pointed to some wooden structures in the distance. "How about we get two things each and then we share? Sounds like a plan?"

He was excited. This was going really well. It was so… plain and innocent, and he couldn't remember the last time he'd gone out and done something like this. Sometimes the group would go out together for town festivals or something, but they'd always end up drinking and smoking while the whole atmosphere shrouding them tended to come with them wherever they went.

"Sounds good to me. I'll have the *soba* and *yakitori* then." Miura pointed to the booths next to one another further down the path.

"I need *takoyaki*," Miya announced. "Does *dango* count as food? I really want some."

"It's a Saturday, *dango* absolutely counts as food. Odd choice to go with *takoyaki* though," Miura commented.

"Yeah well, I'm known for my schizophrenic eating habits," Miya replied, dragging the man towards the booths.

They ordered and balanced the trays of food over to a free bench, where they sat down to eat. They didn't have anything to drink apart from the alcohol Miya had brought, but he didn't want to start taking that out here in the middle of the crowd. It was too early anyway.

"Would you like a drink?" Miura asked, standing up. "I saw a vending machine over there; I can get you something."

"Anything with lemon flavor please." Miya smiled thankfully. Miura returned shortly after with green tea for himself and Miya's lemon juice.

"Thank you! You're so nice, spoiling me like this."

"Well, you spend all your time waiting on everyone else; I thought maybe it was your turn to be pampered for a while."

Miya popped the can open, licking the drops of clear liquid from his fingertips before lifting the can into the air. "Cheers to that!"

Miura smiled, clinking their cans together. They sat facing each other on the bench, with the food in between them and eating off of all plates at once. It was an absolutely disastrous meal as far as collision of tastes went, but that was how days like these were supposed to be Miya thought, eating happily.

"This reminds me of festivals back home," he said thoughtfully, devouring the last piece of *dango* off of one of the skewers. "They were the same way—in terms of stuffing one's face anyway."

Miura agreed. "Festivals are like that, aren't they?"

"But this is somehow… nicer." Miya cocked his head to the side. "I'm looking forward to watching the fireworks. I brought snacks and everything!"

"*More* food?"

"Well of course. I brought drinks as well."

"Maybe we should've gotten a blanket or something."

"You didn't bring one?" Miya sent the man an accusing glare. "I thought you were the one who was taking me on a picnic."

"We're at a flea market though," Miura calmed him. "We'll see if we can find one. And then you'll get your exotic experience, okay?"

"I should certainly hope so!" Miya's eyes glinted dangerously beneath his fringe. It was about time to start turning up the charm. They were in public, but he was still hoping for some sort of physical contact soon. They'd already shared those incredible kisses. And now, looking at Miura's lips when he spoke, and at the way his hands moved when he excitedly talked about something… He swallowed. He definitely wanted more.

Miura lifted his can to his lips, drinking again, as if trying to avoid answering.

"You can have the rest if you want." Miya pushed the *dango* that was left over towards him. "I'm stuffed."

"Me too." Miura sighed, leaning back on the bench. "Maybe we went overboard."

"You can never have too much of a good thing, right?" Miya mused, looking over at the other, smiling suggestively.

"That's what they say," Miura admitted.

The sun was still blazing above them. Although they were in the shade, it was hot. Miya longed for that fresh breeze that had blown in when they were closer to the pier. Now the sunlight was playing in Miura's hair in its place. It highlighted it, making it appear more dark brown than black. He swallowed again.

He was definitely attracted to this man. He wanted to be close to him.

After eating and taking their time to recover from the food frenzy, they went back to the market, where Miura finally succumbed to a table full of old books. He ended up getting a few by foreign authors that Miya hadn't heard of. He seemed really excited about them as well. Miya observed him with a smile plastered on his face the whole time.

"What?" Miura asked.

"Nothing." He shook his head. "I was just thinking that this is so weird."

"Weird?"

"Yeah, going out like this. Having a good time even though we're not doing anything in particular."

"I'm glad you think so, even if it's nothing in particular." Miura winked at him.

Miya didn't act on the impulse of dragging the flirt on. Instead, he looked around the area and successfully spotted what he was after. "Look, I think they have blankets over there. I'll go check it out."

He left Miura to finish paying for his books and headed for the table he'd spotted. The lady behind it was middle-aged and sold all kinds of pillows and blankets it seemed.

When Miya got to talking to her, he learned that she too made them herself.

Again, he was stunned.

"I need one that's suitable for a picnic," he said. "We're going to watch the fireworks later, but we didn't bring one. Though, if you made these, maybe it's not very nice to put it down on the ground."

"Nonsense, young man," the woman jeered. "I partially come here for events like these because people buy lots of blankets during the firework season, or *hanami*. Just pick whichever you like—they all cost the same."

He picked one with a plaid pattern. Picnic blankets should be plaid, he thought, based on what he'd seen in movies. He paid and returned to Miura.

"I got one!" he announced. "Should we go see the fireworks now?"

"They won't start for a while, but I guess we could find a nice place to sit before everyone else gets the same idea."

"Yeah, that's what I was thinking too."

With the blanket under Miya's arm, and Miura carrying their bags, they walked away from the flea market and through the more crowded part of the park where all the attractions were. The fireworks were to be set off at the very edge of the park, where there was a large, open, grassy plain. Some people had already settled down, but not many as of yet, so they could pick and choose pretty much wherever they wanted.

Miya aimed for somewhere that had a view but was still secluded from most of the crowd so they could have some privacy.

"Here's good," he announced, throwing the blanket down in between two trees that sort of hid the sport somewhat from the general view.

"Won't it be better to sit in a more open space?"

"That depends," Miya replied promptly. "On what you're aiming for."

He was straightforward. As much as he was enjoying himself and didn't want to push this, he wanted Miura to know that he wasn't in this solely for the books and the food. He was there because he wanted to get to know the other man, and he didn't want to do that with the entire world looking on. Not the real world anyway; it would have been different had it been in *his* world, where everything was out in the open anyway.

"All right then, here's good," Miura finally agreed. His expression was unreadable.

Miya sat down cross-legged on the blanket and rustled around inside the plastic bag, starting to take out the snacks and drinks.

"I brought supplies," he chuckled when he saw the other

man's face.

"Are you planning on getting me drunk?" The way he said it was so casual that it was hard to know if it was a joke or not, but it was, no doubt.

Miya grinned. "That's exactly my plan."

Isn't it though?

Miura sat next to him. "And all the snacks; I'm not sure that was necessary."

"You should have snacks for these events," Miya responded. "It's tradition."

"In other words, fireworks aren't exotic to you."

"Well, no, I lived in the sticks, so there wasn't much else going on, so when there were festivals and fireworks, the entire town would go. It was either that or staying at home counting *tatami* mats." Miya grinned, popping open one of the beer cans. He passed it to Miura. "Here."

"Thank you." Miura's hand closed around the aluminum can.

"Of course, sometimes it was so crowded, you wished you'd stayed home anyway."

Miura drank and swallowed, looking thoughtful.

"How about now?"

Miya shook his head, "I'm right where I want to be."

"That's good to hear."

"And yet..." Miya smiled uncertainly, "we don't seem to know each other all that well still."

"Isn't that what we're here for?"

Miya wondered. What did it really mean to get to know someone? He could say that he knew his colleagues and friends better than he knew his own family, and yet he didn't know much about some of them. Like Aki for instance; he didn't really know him at all. He'd been in this circle for so long, where the familiarity came naturally with the bonding they did over their common interests outweighed the one they'd get if they got personal about their lives and the likes. But was that usually something you just blurted to your friends, or was it like in fiction, where it was something you spilled to a love interests on the first date?

He didn't really know how to approach someone with the objective of getting to know them unless it was to do so intimately. It was conflicting. He fiddled with the metal splint in the beer can. "I guess..." he said, "but we only seem to talk about current things. I know that you teach, and like to read. I don't think you like going out too much, not to drink anyway, and you like cake."

I don't even know if you like me... The thought was sudden, maybe not entirely correct. They'd already kissed, and Miura had initiated it, but throughout the day, there had been more of a friendly tone between them, aside from the flirting, which came from his side. Maybe Miura just wasn't susceptible to that kind of thing. Miya wondered if dating was his thing at all, seeing as he seemed to get mildly paranoid about it.

"I don't know much about you either, but I'm willing to learn."

Miya grinned. "Then shall we play a little game?"

"Game?"

"I know you're not into drinking too much, but how about we get to know each other in a more creative way?"

The teacher still looked perplexed.

"For instance, I will make a statement about you. Like... you're not a morning person. If I'm right, you drink. If I'm wrong, you get to make a statement about me."

He'd be more in his element this way, but only if Miura was willing to play along. He wasn't interested in pushing him into something he didn't want and risk driving them further apart, but Miura seemed amused by his idea.

"Of course, when the fireworks start, we'll stop the game. Deal?"

"All right, deal. Do you want to go first?"

Miya grinned. "All right. I'm sure you're an only child."

The man shook his head, smiling. "I have a brother. One year older. He's a teacher as well."

Miya lifted the can to his lips and drank a few gulps of the beverage. "I see where *this* is going." He laughed. "Good thing I'm such a charming drunk."

"Are you?"

"I don't know." He cocked an eyebrow. "Am I?"

"I suppose that is subjective," Miura replied, grinning. "But I'll say yes."

"And since it's subjective, I guess that means I lose either way." He gulped down another mouthful.

"At this rate, you really will get drunk."

"Mmh, I'll just have to drag you down with me," he cackled, placing the can on the patterned blanket. "You get along with your brother, right? Because you're so close in age."

Again, he touched upon that feeling of jealousy, even though the man had said nothing.

"Well..." Miura's expression wasn't entirely convincing, but he drank anyhow. "Brothers will never agree on everything I guess, but yeah, we're close. And *you*," he paused for a moment, as if trying to figure out what to say, "are probably a sibling as well, but there's an age difference."

Miya shrugged, drinking.

They kept going at it for a while, finding themselves becoming more loose lipped and playful with each gulp. The alcohol seemed to have relaxed even the high-strung teacher.

"You're a control freak," Miya stated, leaning towards the other man, reaching out with two slim fingers to pop the second button from the top open in Miura's shirt.

"I'm *organized*," he replied but lifted his plastic cup nonetheless. They'd finished their beers and had moved on to the bottle he'd brought. The liquor wasn't strong, but it was sweet tasting, not bitter, and that was probably not a very good idea. At this rate, they wouldn't get much out of the night at all.

He felt the man's breath on his skin as he spoke, with their faces so close, but he didn't act on his impulse. "And you're the opposite." Miura smiled erratically, Miya pulling away. "You knew that though," he replied, licking his lips. "So I'm not gonna drink to that."

He'd learned that Miura's favorite movie was *Violent Cop,* that he was thirty-two years old, that he'd never been abroad, and tons of other trivial things.

Miura now probably didn't know anything about Miya that was either relevant or not very obvious just by observing him for a while, although he'd learned that Miya's favorite food was *sukiyaki*, that he was the black sheep of the family, that he was a Gemini and that he couldn't remember the last time he'd read a book.

"In other words," Miya jittered, "we're not very compatible, are we?""

Miura looked back at him with eyes that were slightly more swimming by now. "Differences aren't necessarily the same as incapability."

"Opposites attract, isn't that so?" Miya pursed his lightly pink lips. "Which reminds me... you've dated a woman before, haven't you?"

He noticed that Miura was very hesitant to lift his glass and kept a nervous eye on Miya before emptying what was left of it.

Calmly, Miya refilled the plastic cup, offering a disarming smile. "Don't worry. I've been with straight guys before. Or... guys who claimed to be straight. Not that..." He stopped pouring the alcohol, taking a sip directly from the bottle—his composure was starting to slip.

They should start the fireworks already.

"It's quite easy to tell, you have a very... can I say *straight* approach to the whole dating thing." he furrowed his brow, waiting for a response, or a reaction. "Not that gay guys don't date. They probably do. My group doesn't, not really... But it's something about the approach."

He paused, continuing to regard the other man.

"Sorry, I'm rambling."

Miura slowly put down his cup. "Yes. I have," he finally said, "And you're probably right."

"You're only doing those things because they're expected of you though, right?" Miya's voice dropped to a low husk.

Miura just looked at him.

"That's okay though. I get that you're unfamiliar with everything." Miya placed his hand over the other man's. "And maybe I'm way out of line here, but..." He moved in even closer, looking into Miura's dark eyes, his own glinting curiously as he whispered, "You want to ask me to go home with you... Right?"

Flustered, Miura stood.

"Miura-san!"

"S-Sorry, I think perhaps I've had too much to drink. I need a moment." Miura started walking away with brisk steps between the trees and down a small slope towards where the crowd was at its thinnest due to the lack of view. The trees were blocking most of the sky from down there, so most people were seated further up the hill.

Miya got to his feet, leaving everything behind as he chased him down on the green.

"Miura-san!"

It was just like him to not be able to contain himself and let things take their natural course just because he was so impatient. Because he was so interested.

"Miura-san!" He caught up to him and ended up standing right before the other man gasping for air, hunched forward with his hands on his knees. "Please don't run, I can't... I've had too much to drink, so I can't run."

He coughed, forced himself to catch his breath as he stood up, looking the man right in the eyes. "I'm sorry... I didn't mean to be so abrupt again..."

"How can you say that so easily?" Miura replied, looking mildly disturbed. "I didn't mean to leave; it was just so..."

"Because I don't think sex is that big of a deal." Miya placed his hands on his hips, glaring accusingly at the teacher. "It's nothing to be ashamed of."

"But we're in a public place. It's not an appropriate discussion." Miura was lowering his voice even more, becoming aware of what he himself was saying. "Moreover, we're—"

"If you pull that idiotic crap about how we're both guys, I'll punch you in the face," Miya snapped back. He brushed his fringe aggressively out of his face. "*You're* the one who kissed me last time. And I totally get it if you're nervous and unfamiliar with this, but I'm not going to get pulled into some web where I can't be true to who I am just because you don't feel comfortable."

He was spitting the words, and he didn't get why he was so angry, or why this hurt so badly. They hardly knew each other. And he'd been drinking. Maybe that was it. Stress and alcohol. He felt sick. This wasn't how he'd intended the day to turn out— not in the slightest.

"I'm sorry," Miura finally replied, his voice thick. "I didn't mean to... I was just so surprised."

Miya looked away angrily. He was shaking. "Yeah, me too."

At that moment, the fireworks started exploding above them, filling the darkening sky with vibrant colors of red, gold and green, bathing their faces in the same warm colors as they rained down towards the ground.

"I get it..." Miya mumbled, looking down at the ground. "I get that you're not used to this, and that I'm probably way too abrupt. But if you don't want this to go any further then—"

"That's not it!" Miura almost shouted at him. "I'm not used to this, and I didn't know what to say... I had to go cool my head."

"Miura-san," Miya softened, his expression sad, "I know I can be rash sometimes, but I thought we were on the same page. We *were* having a good time, right?"

The fireworks above them seemed deafening. And his heart was beating so fast. They could have been sitting on the blanket right now, watching the sky erupting in all kinds of bright colors, maybe moving closer to one another, and now everything was confusing and painful. And he remembered why he never did things like this in the first place. Was it really worth it if you started fighting before there was even a proper relationship established?

Maybe he was in the wrong for getting so upset this early on, but he'd been hurt before, and he didn't want to bother with something similar.

"Even if you were a woman, I wouldn't be discussing such things in public. I'm a teacher for God's sake!"

"You're only human."

"There's a time and a place for everything."

"Yeah, there is." Miya sucked in his breath as he added, "I don't mean to pressure you, but this is a good time for us to decide what happens from here on—figure out what this means. If we're not going to see each other anymore, then I'd rather just know it right away."

He was being harsh, and he knew it. He didn't have the right to demand something like this on the third date. And maybe he was going overboard, demanding too much too soon. Heck, a part of him probably *wanted* to scare Miura away so he could return to the life he knew. But then moments ago, before the stupid argument had broken out, it had all felt so right.

"Don't go." Miura's voice was quiet, firm somehow. "Please. I don't want this to… I really do want to get to know you."

The hard front crumbled, and Miya felt incredibly small and exposed. He didn't want to leave either. He smiled weakly. "It's a good thing you're so charming or I'd never let this fly."

Their gazes met, and awkward smiles were exchanged.

"I'll try to be more patient," he mumbled.

"And I'll do my best to relax, all right?"

Miya nodded. "Let's just… take it slow for now. And then we'll see where it takes us."

He felt sobered up by the whole stupid argument. The comfortable buzz of intoxication was subsiding. He just felt tired and overwhelmed.

"We're missing the fireworks," Miura said, daring to step closer to Miya at last. "Want to go back? If I ruined it, I understand."

Miya shook his head. "*I* ruined it. And besides, I bounce back easily, so… can we just pretend like this didn't happen and we had a good time after all?"

Miura reached out, brushing his hand gently across Miya's flushing cheeks, smiling. "Let's do that."

They walked close together back to their blanket and watched the rest of the fireworks together in silence. At some point, Miura's hand tentatively came to rest on top of Miya's, thumb stroking carefully back and forth across it. Miya smiled, swallowing. He'd lean against the man's shoulder if he hadn't been worried that it would be too much for one night, and besides, there *were* a lot of people in the park. He did sort of understand where Miura was coming from in regards to public display of affections, but at the same time, that hand on his was so warm and gentle.

He watched the man out of the corner of his eye, wondering how this would all turn out in the end. Tonight had proven that he didn't know anything about taking it slow after all. Miura might be out of his comfort zone, but then so was he—majorly so.

***

He couldn't deny how awkward everything felt afterwards. Once the fireworks died down, and everyone started getting up to leave, they packed up their stuff, and then it was all so quiet. Even if he'd just told Miura that he bounced back easily, he had no idea what to do in this situation. In other cases like this one, he'd always up and left. Now that wasn't an option, so he remained seated on the ground for a while.

"Miura-san," he stated. "I know this might not be a great idea, but do you know how one cures this kind of awkward mood?"

The other man shook his head.

Miya lifted the bottle of alcohol in the air. "Like this!" He shook it so the contents that remained splashed around loudly inside of the bottle.

"You know what," the teacher dropped down next to him, taking the bottle from him, "I actually have to agree with you."

He put the bottle to his lips and drank. He handed it back to Miya and watched him drink as well, wiping his mouth with his sleeve.

"Rinse and repeat," Miya muttered, gazing out into the emptying park towards the crowd scurrying to the exits.

As the contents of the bottle had lessened and their minds gradually grew hazier, the two of them had started warming up again. Both felt stupid, neither knew how to act, and so they found a sort of common ground in their embarrassment.

"Forget what I said earlier. We suit each other," Miya finally said.

"How so?" Miura asked him, his voice sounding a little weird.

"We're both no good at this. You're not used to dating men, and I'm not used to dating…" He smiled crookedly.

"Well, you know, whenever my students come crying to me about how they don't get this or that, I always pat them on the shoulder and tell them they should practice more, and then they'll gradually come to understand."

"Is that the case here as well?" Miya smirked. "Should we keep practicing?"

"Would you like to?"

"Are you stupid?" Miya sneered. "If I didn't, I wouldn't be here still. In that case, I'd have left when you freaked out."

"*I* wasn't the angry one."

"Would you like to start another fight?" Miya asked sourly.

Miura took Miya's hand in his, pulling him to his feet. "No, not at all."

Surprisingly, he didn't let go. He stood still, holding Miya's hand in his own, and then he kissed it, ever so gently touching his lips to the thin skin on the back of his hand.

Their gazes met. "Let's just take it slow, okay?"

Miya nodded, squeezing Miura's hand. "Yeah. Slow."

"As nice as this is though, isn't it time we left?" Miura asked. "Your hand is cold."

"Mmh." Miya nodded. "We probably should get going."

He didn't know where though. They left the park, and although their hands were no longer joined, they walked closely together along the sidewalk. The mood that reigned between them was odd, but he was glad that they'd gotten through whatever it was that had just happened. Or rather, that they'd consumed enough liquor not to care about it anymore. He didn't care where they went, and he wasn't paying attention.

"This is my building," Miura finally said, coming to a stop in front of a perfectly plain-looking apartment building.

"So you *do* live that close after all. I thought maybe you just said that to make me feel less bad for being late," Miya rambled, smiling a little. He thought back on the afternoon and thought it felt like an eternity since the man had greeted him with a smile and complimented his hair.

"Heh, no, not exactly." Miura shook his head. "This is it. The glorious building. About the only thing it's good for is how close it is to the park and the station and everything."

Why did you bring me here?

"It's getting late."

That was probably Miura's most used line in conversation. And it wasn't that late. Probably. Miya had no idea. He felt drunk, tired and confused. "Maybe we should call it a night?"

"Maybe that's wise."

"You know, regardless of whatever that was all about..." Miya started, "I really enjoyed myself today. So... thanks for that."

"Are you going home?"

Their eyes met, gazes trembling.

"Why?"

"I mean... you don't *have* to." Miura fiddled with his collar. The button Miya had undone was still open. "You're drunk, and it's already this time..."

Like Miya wasn't used to this kind of situation. He said nothing, held his breath and waited.

"I don't have a lot of room, but... if you want to..." The teacher rubbed his neck nervously, gesticulating towards the front door. "I wouldn't mind..."

Miya smiled. "Do you think that's a good idea though based on what happened?"

"Didn't we agree to put that behind us?" Miura offered a half-smile. "Miya... stay?"

Miya opened his mouth, but no words came out. His lips felt dry. He nodded. "Okay..."

12. Give in to Me

There was no elevator. Miya was used to that though, and Miura only lived on the fifth floor, so it wasn't all that bad. He waited while the man fought with the lock; Miya wondered if it was just an old building or if Miura was too intoxicated or too nervous to properly unlock the door. He said nothing.

"I'm so sorry about what you're about to see," Miura apologized. "I live alone, so… well, I don't usually have people over."

Miya shrugged. "I'm not judging. My house is a total mess."

"All right, come on in." Miura slid the door open.

They removed their shoes in the itty-bitty hall space, and Miya could see pretty much all there was to the apartment from there—a living room with a kitchen nook, a hot plate and a miniature fridge on top of a small counter, some shelves above where various foodstuffs and utensils were stashed. The living area held bookshelves on all the walls, save for the two windows. There was a small television set and a traditional table. The floor was coated in *tatami* mats, which were covered in books and papers. From where he stood, Miya could even see into the bathroom and bedroom. Both seemed modest, but the place, despite its messy state, was cozy.

"Would you like anything?" Miura went over to the fridge, sighing heavily as he opened it. "I don't have anything but water though."

Miya chuckled. "That's okay. I don't need more to drink. How responsible by the way—a teacher who can't take care of himself."

The man scowled over at him. He took two bottles of Volvic out of the fridge and threw one to Miya. He had a sip, but put it away just as quickly, placing it on the small table then came over to Miura.

They were alone now, so he dared moving in closer. "Miura-san..." he said, his voice dropping, "do you remember what I said earlier?"

"About taking it slow?"

"If that's what you wanted, you wouldn't have brought me here, right?" He spoke quietly, slowly and in a velvety tone.

Miura swallowed. "You're..."

"Drunk? So are you. And that's okay, you can blame it on that." Miya smiled, leaning closer to brush his lips against the man's ear. "I don't mind."

Miura's hand found Miya's waist, and he regarded him with a curious, tense expression.

His fingers curled against the fabric of Miya's shirt.

"I don't want to," the man leaned in close, "blame it on anything."

His breath was hot and sweet. His unruly fringe brushed against Miya's forehead as he leaned in and kissed him. Miya kissed back, almost desperately.

Finally.

After that dreary afternoon, he was glad this could still happen. He didn't care if it was intoxication and lack of impulse control. People were at their most honest when they were drunk, right? He couldn't resist, even if he'd intended to. He returned the kiss with all that he had, closing his eyes and feeling like he was drifting away somewhere.

When he finally looked up again, Miura was gazing at him through half-lidded eyes, smiling. That was a relief. He licked his lips, aching for more.

"Hey," Miura murmured, stringing a long lock of black around his finger, "can I call you by your first name?"

He hesitated. The only people who used that name were his family. But everything was hazy and felt so right, despite the chaos he'd experienced earlier. He didn't know what to think of the question, but he nodded.

"Yes." He nodded, bringing their lips together in a lighter kiss. "If you'd like to, then please."

"Thank you for today, Satoru."

It definitely sounded weird, but nice the way the other man spoke his name, softly rolling it off his tongue as if he was caressing it when he spoke.

"How's it working for you?" Miya inquired, slowly running his arms up around the man's neck.

"I like it." Miura smiled. "Satoru."

Miya was okay with it. He didn't prefer it to his nickname, which he'd gotten so used to, but if it was Miura, then it was fine.

Their lips met once more, tongues searching one another out, brushing against one another, mouths clashing. He pulled the other man closer, pressing himself harder against him. "Nnh..."

A strangled sound in his throat made Miura grip Miya harder by the waist.

The lip lock was so intense, like there was years of pent-up frustration behind it. Maybe there was. Miya nibbled on surprisingly skilled lips, stroking his fingertips along the man's tense neck. And then there was the suspense and tension from earlier, evaporating and melting away in this embrace.

His legs were shaking, as if they were threatening to give in, tired as he was from walking around all day, and weakened by this sudden surge of passion.

He didn't know how far he could take this without causing another situation like earlier. This was nothing at all like taking it slow, but it seemed like Miura was changing his mind on that.

He decided to try his luck, running his hands down the other man's torso, opening one button, breaking the kiss, and looking hesitantly up at Miura as he undid the next one.

There were no protests. He undid another, ran his hand further down, up underneath the trim of his shirt, and upwards, pressing his palm against a toned, flat stomach. He swallowed.

Somehow, he was nervous, afraid that he'd cause a reaction again, afraid of being rejected. At this point, that would be nothing less than hurtful even if the alcohol had numbed him.

He pressed his lips to Miura chest whilst undoing the final couple of buttons but didn't make any attempt at taking Miura's shirt off completely at this point, just kissed softly along his collarbones up his neck.

"Kiss me..." he mouthed, trembling all over when Miura did as told, warmth shooting through him, his skin flushing. While their lips met and broke apart, only interrupted by the occasional sigh of pleasure, Miya discarded his own shirt, leaving him in the low-cut tank he was wearing underneath it.

"Miura-san..." he whispered into the kiss, "would you mind if we moved?"

It seemed like Miura was tired of standing upright as well, as he didn't protest when Miya started pulling him backwards through the room, still kissing him, enticing him with encouraging noises of approval and soft, intoxicating kisses.

But Miya left it up to Miura to push him onto the bed; actually, they sort of fell onto it, laughing as they landed in a heap.

"I'm sorry, am I heavy?"

Miya shook his head, looking up at Miura, touching his hand to the man's cheek. "Relax."

He lifted his head from the mattress, kissing Miura chastely on the lips. Scooting himself further up towards the headboard, he pulled Miura more on top of himself, still smiling reassuringly. He trusted that if he moved too fast, there would be a clear order to stop. As long as there wasn't, he allowed himself to dive into one kiss and the next, carefully beginning to grind their bodies together.

"Miura-san..." he breathed hard against the other man's mouth.

"You can say my name, as well you know," Miura chuckled, kissing him on the corner of the lips, and they curved upwards at the man's growing enthusiasm.

"Shunsuke,?" he tried, blushing furiously without understanding why. Miya didn't feel like himself; he felt hot, flustered, completely at Miura's mercy, even though he was the one running the show. "Touch me..." he whispered, placing the man's hand on his own chest, urging him to caress him.

He sighed happily at the sensation of warm, strong hands running down his torso, over and eventually underneath his tank top, inching towards his jeans but never reaching inside. More kisses—hard, needy this time.

His fingers curled against the man's back, against his neck, in his hair. Kisses burned against his skin and on his lips.

Then it all started calming down a little because Miura seemed to grow more hesitant as it became increasingly obvious where this was going to end. Miya looked up at him, running his hand down the man's neck and down his back.

"Shunsuke," he said with a small, shy smile, "this isn't your first time with a man, is it?"

The other man averted his eyes. "No..." he said, clearing his throat, "but like this..."

"Hn," Miya chuckled softly. So he *did* have some experience then. One night stands probably. Men he didn't know. No wonder he was so awkward.

"If you want to stop, we can go on taking it slow," Miya cooed, slipping his hand in between their bodies, placing it on the front of the man's jeans and pressing gently. "But if you want to continue, then don't worry about anything. I'll..." he leaned closer to the man's ear, lips brushing the lobe as he whispered breathlessly, "take care of you."

He pressed down harder and bit on Miura's ear. He swallowed. The man was hard. He ached for more, craved it. And he worried about what would happen if they weren't on the same page. But he needn't worry; Miura's lips found his once more, capturing them in one deep kiss that said it all and went on and on and on.

They undressed each other as if they'd never done anything else. Miya was surprised at the lack of hesitation and at the dominance the man was beginning to show. He moaned quietly, feeling lips and teeth engulfing his nipple while a hand ran down his tense, impatient body. Lips on his collarbones, tongue flicking over his jugular, his ear, a hand reaching and stroking along his inner thigh.

More hot, demanding kisses. Miya flexed against the warm body on top of his; he pulled one leg up to make more room in between his thighs and scooted closer.

A hand went in between his legs, stroking him gently. He shuddered, gasping.

Exhaling shakily, Miya looked up into Miura's face for the first time since the kisses had been initiated; he looked intoxicated with lust—and somewhat apologetic again.

"I'm sorry, I don't have any..."

"Protection?" Miya interrupted. "My pocket."

Miura rolled off the bed and dug through Miya's jeans pockets. "What about... lotion?"

Miya didn't mind the awkwardness. He shook his head. "If you have some. I'm not made of glass though." He smirked, but the man didn't seem to believe him and rummaged around in the small drawer next to the bed. He found something resembling hand lotion.

"That'll do," Miya assured him, knowing the brand to be non-toxic and acceptable for the purpose. He was impatient and pulled the other man back on top. Their lengths ground together and caused them to emit a unison hiss.

It was Miya who grabbed for the lotion, reaching down in between their bodies once more to grip both of their erections at once, stroking gently with one slick hand. He felt Miura shivering above him, kissed him hard and moved his hand slowly.

He'd go crazy. Miya was sure of it. Maybe it was the aggression from earlier, but he couldn't remember the last time anything had felt this intense. He let go, poured more lotion in his palm and led his hand in between his legs, moistening himself. He was already ready, trembling as his fingers brushed against his entrance.

He arched back, clenching his teeth. It didn't hurt much, but the intrusion was sudden due to the excess of lotion and their mutually shared excitement.

It felt like they lay like that for the longest time, just looking at each other, exchanging kisses, while their bodies connected. And then they moved—together. Gently at first, then getting lost in the kisses, their motions quickened—hips bucking, chests lowering and rising as they thrust into one another. He pulled his leg closer to his own chest, allowing the man to go deeper, moaning loudly. He was silenced by a kiss, but the waves of pleasure were too intense; their focus wasn't strong enough to keep either of them silent. Miya trembled, writhed and pressed himself closer and closer to Miura body, feeling his breath on his neck, his voice whispering and moaning into his ear.

"M-Miura-san!" He forgot that they were on first name basis, forgot where he was, and that they'd argued earlier. It was just the two of them; Shunsuke's hands on his body, his fists clenching the unfamiliar sheets, and his voice filling the apartment when he couldn't hold back anymore.

***

"Do you mind if I smoke?" Miya was wrapped in the sheets, still recovering from the intense pleasure.

"Actually," Miura looked apologetic, "I would prefer if you didn't in the house, but I don't want to ask you to smoke out the window."

Miya regarded the man; his hair was in complete disarray after his own hands had repeatedly run through and ruffled it, the way he'd imagined when they first met. The man was sweaty, skin flushing, Miya's markings visible here and there.

"Don't worry about it," Miya smirked. "I can handle it."

"How am I supposed to turn you down when you look like this?" Miura sighed, smiling playfully.

Miya just grinned at him. "You don't. You're not doing a very good job at resisting me at all, are you?"

He crawled over to him, touching their lips together, dragging out the kiss. "I'm glad."

"I'm glad you're so persistent."

Miya pulled the sheets tighter around himself as he stood from the bed, taking the smallest steps over towards the window. His lower back and the area around his hips hurt slightly, but he liked it. Even if it made him bruise and feel slight discomfort for a little while, he wouldn't be without the evidence of what they'd just done.

"Me too," he said, cracking open the window. He leaned on the windowsill as he lit his cigarette and stood smoking while regarding the street below. It was relatively empty, since it was nighttime and this was a residential area.

"And I was trying so hard not to smoke all day," he chuckled.

"How come?"

"I thought maybe it would put you off if I did. So I decided to not light up until we'd parted ways." Miya exhaled and turned looking over his shoulder at the man on the bed. "But you know. It was worth it."

Miura laughed. "Smoke all you want. It's dangerous though."

"Trust me, I am aware." Miya turned back to look out at the night sky. "Maybe I'll quit someday."

In the distance, he heard something like a scuffle—a girl yelling loudly and a guy yelling back. A car drove past on the street below; only one of its front lights was working. But apart from that, it was relatively quiet. He saw a television flickering in the window of the apartment across the street.

"You're not going to tell me to quit?" He put the cigarette back to his lips without turning to look back into the room.

"You're so opinionated." Miura stood, also wrapped in sheets. "I don't think I want to get into another discussion with you."

Miya tapped the cigarette, ash falling towards the ground. "You deserved that," he said, turning his head halfway as Miura came to stand behind him with one arm on either side and his palms resting on the sill. Miya kissed him on the corner of his mouth. "I'm sorry I got so angry though…"

"I understand," Miura sighed. "I'm sorry too. But we're not talking about that anymore, remember?"

"Thank God." Miya inhaled, exhaled and put the cigarette out against the outside of the windowsill. "You know, that wasn't very clever."

He closed the window and remained standing where he was. "If you don't want to attract attention, starting a fight in public during a crowded firework event isn't the best idea."

"You're right." Miura wrapped his arms around Miya, pulling him closer. "Let's keep our fights private from here on."

"I say we don't fight at all." Miya offered a kiss as a peace negotiation.

"Make love not war. Isn't that what they say?"

"Is it?" Miura cooed against his ear. "I can't remember."

"Shall I remind you then?" Miya snickered, driving the other man back through the room, the sheet he was wearing falling to the floor as he crawled onto the bed.

"Would you mind if I stayed the night?" Asking was probably the polite thing to do even though he doubted the man would be opposed to the suggestion. It didn't seem that way at least. He allowed himself to be lost in another bout of kisses and gentle touches, pressing his frame close against that of the elder man, moaning softly against his lips.

***

They slept very little. Even after doing it a second time, Miya didn't feel particularly tired. He was fueled by adrenaline and exhilaration rather than being sedated by the pheromones and endorphins.

"I'm surprised," he said on a whim.

"At?"

"Don't take this the wrong way, but I didn't think you had much experience."

"I don't." The teacher propped himself up on the elbow, stroking Miya's hair. "You were right about that."

"So you're some kind of natural?" the ebony-haired man grinned teasingly.

"You did a pretty good job guiding me?"

Miya shook his head. "Listen. When someone is bragging about your sexual feats, don't be humble about it. You don't want to talk yourself down in bed."

Miura laughed. "Sorry. But while we're being honest here, I did tell you that I'm not the most experienced with other men."

"I heard you the first time." Miya frowned. "Something about having been with women before. So... which is it? If you don't mind me asking?"

Miura looked uncomfortable. "I've always dated women."

Miya thought he felt his heart sinking a little.

"It seemed like the right thing to do, you know?"

"Not really." Miya smiled crookedly.

"Well, it was that way for me. And then I didn't get the big deal. Even when I was younger, I didn't get excited like my buddies would over being the subject of some woman's affection."

"But you dated them anyway?" Miya had a hard time understanding. For him, it had been much simpler. He didn't see how someone could date someone they weren't attracted to without getting that something was up.

"I did, again because I was brought up to think that was the right thing to do."

Miya grimaced. "Trust me, that's how we were all brought up, but it didn't result in me screwing around with women."

"I could never picture that either." Miura tugged on his hair.

He went on to share that he'd probably been suspicious for a while but didn't want to act on it. And then he had experienced his first contact with a man on a whim. It had been at a conference, and he'd been drinking. So his judgment had been way off, and the other man had been the aggressor.

"Is that why you don't like drinking?" Miya questioned, "Because you lose your impulse control and allow yourself to follow your heart or..." He grinned crookedly.

"Maybe." Miura furrowed his brow. "Plus, I'm a teacher, so I always feel like I should put forth a good example and control myself."

Miya didn't know if he was referring to the alcohol or the men in this case.

"But yes, every time I was with another man, there was alcohol in the mix."

"Believe it or not, that's pretty common." Miya shrugged. He kept smiling to disarm the other man, to keep him talking. He was curious, and he needed to know whether it was wise of him to keep up this relationship. He wasn't interested in getting hurt over something like guilt or shame.

"You're the first one I've approached on my own though." Miura smiled crookedly, glancing over at Miya.

"Wasn't I the one who spoke to *you*?"

"But I followed you, and then you walked into me!"

"Romantic," Miya teased. "You basically stalked me, and you were totally hostile!"

"I was a nervous wreck!"

Miya nuzzled closer to him. "It didn't seem that way."

"I'm just… really not good at this."

"Sure you are." Miya planted a kiss on his exposed shoulder. "All you need is some more practice. We've all been new at this once. Some of us take longer than others."

"And you?"

Miya shrugged. "I was born this way." He laughed. "I mean, there wasn't much of a question really, but we're completely different people." He failed to hold back a sneer. "You were on a date when we first met though. With a woman."

"Yes, against my will." Shunsuke sighed. "Try being over thirty when all your friends are settling down and getting married."

"No thanks." Miya rolled his eyes. "So they're all playing matchmaker in order to get you to step into their ranks then."

"Pretty much."

"But then… why can't you just say that you're not interested?" He reached his hand towards Miura, wanting to stroke him on the cheek, but Miura gripped his wrist and placed his hand back on the mattress.

"It's complicated. It doesn't work like that." His tone was uninviting. It was best to not pry any more for now. They were still at a very fragile point in their relationship, and too many questions at this point would ruin whatever it was that was developing between them.

"I'm sorry. I didn't mean to pry," Miya apologized. "I just want to get to know you better, that's all."

And while saying that, he hoped that Miura wouldn't pick up the thread and ask him the same questions because what would he say? That he had nothing but unsuccessful relationships behind him and had solved it by focusing solely on random and casual connections? There was no way that Miura thought he was some kind of saint, knowing where he worked and all, but he didn't think Miura had it in him to see the big picture of how Miya's world worked. At this point, he wasn't interested in pursuing that kind of discussion.

"And," he smiled disarmingly, eyes gleaming, "I'm honored to have been your first in some sense."

"I'm honored that you would even consider it!" Miura chuckled.

"There you go again, putting yourself down. Even though you're so hot." Miya pursed his lips.

"I'm just a regular guy. Nothing at all like the guys you hang out with. How do I know I even stand a chance against them?"

Was he being serious, or was it really intended as a joke?

"You know, just because we're all pretty feminine and vain down there, it doesn't mean we're all attracted to that type."

"What *is* your type then?"

"Right now?" Miya grinned wolfishly. "Sexy teachers with messy hair and low self-esteem that are unreasonably good in bed."

"Are you sucking up to me?"

"I don't think I have to," Miya purred, slipping his hand underneath the covers. "I'm already here after all. Game's up, and I won."

"I think we both won," the teacher laughed.

How could it already feel this comfortable? Or was it just his brain biting off more than he could chew already? It had been such a long time since he'd wanted to place his bet on one guy only, and he'd forgotten how things worked. He'd forgotten that someone could make him feel like he was fluttering.

He'd forgotten that sleeping together with someone for the first time could be this intimate and nice. And so, he drifted off, with Miura's arms around him, the man's breath on his neck, and their legs intertwined under the covers. Like in a fluffy chick-flick, except that this was real.

***

Reality smacked Miya in the face first thing by waking him up through his shrill cell phone going off some odd hours later. He stirred awake, looking around in the unfamiliar room. Slowly, the night before came back to him as he registered that Miura was no longer next to him, and that whoever was calling him wasn't about to give it up. Groaning loudly, he sat up, covering himself in the bed sheets as he reached for his phone. The name glaring towards him on the display didn't surprise him in the slightest.

"What do you want?" he yawned into the phone.

"Where are you?" Aki sounded annoyed on the other end.

"Secret."

"Ugh, save it. Listen, are you coming in today or what?"

Miya glanced at the clock on the nightstand. It was already early in the afternoon. Many of the guys went to work early on Sundays, and apparently, he was sorely missed. "I don't know. Not in a good while at least."

"You're kidding. What are you doing?"

"It's none of your business." He twirled his messy hair around his finger, grinning. "I'll be in; just cover for me until then, yeah?"

"Yeah sure."

"I promise!"

"Is he hot?" Aki sounded more amused.

"How do you know it's a guy?"

"What, it's not like you're ever gonna be with a woman. And you don't have any hobbies."

"Oh shut up," Miya chuckled. "But yeah. Okay."

"See, I thought so. I had a hunch."

"Yeah, well… How hard could it be?"

"You tell me."

"Okay, kiddo, you've had your fun. Just cover for me until I get there, okay?"

"Yeah fine. Have fun."

"I will! Bye, babe."

He heard Aki muttering on the other end as he hung up. The younger man hated it when he called him by pet names, but sometimes he just couldn't stop himself from purposely pushing his buttons—especially not if he was in a good mood.

He was on his way out of bed when the door to the bedroom opened and Shunsuke came in. The man had gotten dressed, at least partially; his shirt was undone, and he was wearing what appeared to be pajama pants. He was carrying a tray, and a mouthwatering scent filled the room.

"No way!" Miya curled his legs up against his body. "Breakfast in bed?"

"You're up!" Miura smiled. He came over to the bed, setting the tray down at the foot end.

"This is the first time I've ever had this happen to me after going home with someone."

"Well, I figured you would be hungry. There's nothing wrong with being a bit of a gentleman."

Miya looked at the tray—two cups of coffee, scrambled eggs, bacon, toast and even some fruit.

"Is this what they call an English breakfast?" He smiled.

"Well, not really. I just took what I could find in my kitchen. If you would rather like some tea I can—"

"Miu- Shunsuke," he corrected himself, "calm down. I like coffee in the morning just as much as the next person. I'm just really surprised."

For someone who seemed very uncertain about his own preferences and what he wanted out of his life, Shunsuke sure seemed very into making this a nice experience, and he certainly wasn't holding back. Although this couldn't be seen as a one-night stand, seeing as they'd already met several times, but he was still almost taken a little aback by the sudden turn of events. He'd gone home with enough people in his time, and none of them had made him breakfast. Not like this. It happened that he'd eat together with them, whether he was the one who offered to make something, or whether they had some leftovers or whatever, sometimes he'd even go out to eat with them the next morning, but this was special. Breakfast in bed, a very thought-through meal at that it seemed. Miya was stunned, and he felt all warm.

"I must say, you're quite the gentleman." He picked up one of the coffee mugs; the coffee was still steaming. He blew on it, warmth spreading from his fingertips to his flushing cheeks.

"You deserved that," the other man smiled, stroking him over the hand, "after being so patient."

"What?" Miya narrowed his eyes, putting his lips to the mug, "Because I waited a whooping three dates to sleep with you?"

He meant it to be humorous, but it still stung a little saying it like that.

"For keeping up with my held-back ways."

"I told you, I'm not that pushy. I don't necessarily rush into a good thing," Miya replied, putting down the cup—the coffee was still too hot. He grabbed a fork instead. "Although, you've got the looks and charm on your side, so my usual impatience doesn't apply to you." He grinned. "If you're gonna have tricks like these up your sleeve, I might actually keep you."

His heart skipped a beat as he uttered those words. Was that one of those abrupt things to say? He tried to look for a reaction, like immediate fear in the other man, but he only seemed to be mildly amused.

"Eggs are good," he changed the subject.

"They are. Who did you speak to on the phone earlier? I heard it ringing."

"Oh," Miya salted the eggs a little more, impaling a strip of bacon on his fork, "my roomie. He wondered if I was going to work today."

"Are you?"

"Not yet. I thought I'd keep you company for a bit longer. Though I need to leave at some point I guess. He didn't feel up to covering for me it seemed."

Shunsuke peered at him over his coffee mug, auburn eyes curiously regarding him.

"Is it that guy with the red hair? I keep seeing you together."

"Are you stalking me?" Miya laughed. "No, that guy's just a friend. Roomie's way younger. Hiiro's practically my age."

He'd already disclosed his age to Shunsuke, but still he avoided voicing the actual number.

Miura was older than him, but he was so used to appearing younger than he was, it was almost unnatural for him to talk about his age.

"How young?"

"Eighteen. How come?"

The teacher looked stunned. "Eighteen? He's just a few years older than my students. How is he even allowed to... isn't he in school?"

Miya shrugged. "Obviously not. He's really hard-working though, and very bright."

"Yeah but still..."

"I don't want to talk about him."

Miura shrugged, resigning. "Sure, then what do you want to talk about?"

"Whatever, anything but work and stuff. But we don't have to talk either—silence is a virtue."

"Isn't there something like if you can spend time in complete silence with someone, it means you're really comfortable with each other?" the teacher suggested.

Even so, they did end up chatting about various things while finishing their food. Afterwards, they spent some time just lying around before Miya finally, albeit regrettably, decided it was probably time to go do his share of work.

"Thanks for having me over," he said, slipping his shoes on.

"Thanks for staying."

Miya smiled. "So, are we seeing each other again?"

"Would you like to?"

Did you hear me last night?

"Can you ever have too much of a good time?" Miya suggestively arched an eyebrow.

"I'll give you a call."

"Great." Miya placed his hand against the man's cheek,

leaning in to kiss him softly on the lips. "I'll be looking forward to it."

"Me too," Miura whispered against his mouth. He smelled like coffee, and the scent of sex still remained on his skin. It was almost so he didn't want to leave.

But then, even though he'd just said that you could never get enough of a good thing, he did feel like it was possible to indulge himself too much early on and that maybe the wise thing would be to make a little distance between them. They could always see each other again. He didn't need to rush into something—not yet.

But the fuzzy feeling inside of him was nice to have. Although it started to drizzle as he walked to the train, he didn't really mind it. And although he hadn't slept all that much, he felt energized.

13. History

When he got into work that Sunday, there were some rather amused gazes meeting his. Aki clearly opened his mouth. Miya rolled his eyes towards the teen.

"Look what the cat dragged in." Hiiro threw his arm around Miya's shoulder, seemingly coming out of nowhere.

Miya shook him off, laughing. "You're the one to talk," he said, tugging on the collar of the man's shirt, red marks adorning his pale collarbones.

"At least I'm not trying to hide it," the redhead nudged him hard in the arm.

"Who's hiding anything?" Miya shoved him back. "I'm dressed in yesterday's clothes, I'm wearing old make-up, and my hair is a total rat's nest. What do you think could have happened?"

The others laughed. Come to think of it... "Pretty much everyone's here." He frowned. "What was so urgent?"

Aki sauntered up to him, smirking. "We missed you."

"Sure you did." Miya gripped the teen by the arm, squeezing slightly.

"Were you still with him when Aki called?" Hiiro was back.

Sometimes he was like one of those annoying little dogs that were always jumping and barking, desperately craving attention.

Miya ignored him, going into the back room to get a towel and dry off his hair. He came back out, still with the towel in hand. "I was, actually. He even made me breakfast; so typical of you lot to ruin everything. It's like you've got a radar."

"We're like superheroes." Hiiro laughed. "Cock Block Rangers. That's us!"

"Idiot!" Miya laughed out loud.

"Nice of you to join us." It was Kiyoshi, coming in from the office. He smiled crookedly, so even he was amused by this. "I hear you were doing the walk of shame to work this morning."

"*You're* in a good mood," Miya retorted. "Sure Mr. manager didn't get you a special wake-up call this morning?"

The rusty-haired male grinned back at him. "Get to work, idiots."

As soon as Miya turned his back, the others exchanged knowing glances. It seemed to be a good day for everyone. He felt so rejuvenated by the night before, despite the more unpleasant bits, which were now but distant memories. He took on any and every task he was given with gusto, which was unusual on a Sunday, especially with a hangover and everything.

And since the evening turned out to be fairly calm, they had plenty of time to take it slow and just enjoy themselves together with the crowd, which was mostly regulars.

After work ended, they all went down to Maki's for a couple of drinks before he and Aki went home together, for once.

***

It was definitely intriguing, Miya thought, the way this was developing. He wasn't used to getting text messages of the sort Miura would occasionally send him, with short little notices like "*Good morning*", or "*Hope you're having a good day.*"

It hadn't come out of nowhere of course. They'd met each other a couple of more times—for lunch when the opportunity arose, both of them on a weekend due to their work schedules, and then he'd gone over to the man's house for dinner at one point. He'd been surprised at the invitation, again not being used to this kind of companionship. Sure, he'd go over to dinner at, for instance, Naru's house on occasions, but even then, it was probably for something like a birthday celebration, and it was almost always guaranteed to end up out on the town or at least at Maki's afterwards. And, of course, he was keeping up that part of his life as well—going out with the others, shamelessly flirting, drinking and having a good time. And in that state, he'd sometimes initiate texts on his own, as if his intoxicated brain wasn't able to contain itself.

He was almost a little worried at what was happening. The thing was that he was starting to feel anticipation whenever the man's name glowed on the display of his phone, and he was even starting to enjoy it when Miura spoke his name in that peculiar tone that he used. It was almost as if...

He had been in love before—several times when he was younger. He'd actually already been quite fickle back then, but he'd fallen even easier than now, even though it mostly ended in disaster. But before he realized that that's how the world worked, cruel and cynical as it might seem, he'd been positive that at some point things would work out for him, and he'd find someone that he could actually be happy with at some point.

Growing up in Kamigōri, his chances of finding true love were probably a little farfetched, but that didn't mean he hadn't tried, vigorously, when he was young and naive.

Miya didn't really remember how he'd found out that he had no interest in women. It had just never been an option. For him, girls were classmates, even friends, but he'd never looked at one more than the rest. Likewise, when it had come to boys, he'd mostly just hung around the ones he shared similar interests with, that was of course until he entered high school and realized that several of his new classmates were catching his eye in a new way. Like for instance the freshman representative who sat on the front row, two places in front of his own seat, and had a surprisingly attractive neck. Up until that point, thinking someone's neck was attractive had sounded obscure. But this guy had a mole, a small one, to the left, near where his neck connected with his shoulder, right above the shirt collar. Once that had caught Miya's eye, he hadn't been able to stop looking at it whenever he'd been behind the other boy. And as a result, he'd discovered his fine lines, his perfect neck, being shown off beautifully by the fact that the representative wore his hair in a buzz cut.

Looking at the manager now, Miya sometimes thought about the boy in his freshman class; he remembered his neck, but he had a hard time making out his face in his mind whenever he thought back on those times. Then there was the son of the local optician, seated next to the window. He wore glasses that perfectly framed his face and brought out his intense eyes. He could have had a somewhat severe appearance if it hadn't been for the fact that he had a slightly pudgy face still at that point—a round, cute face, framed by those glasses, with dark hair falling down almost to the spectacles.

He wouldn't say he'd been in love with either of them, but he'd definitely been fascinated at that point, and it had pointed him towards the option that he was more unconventional than he'd first thought. But back then, at that age, even his friends had still been somewhat awkward and hesitant around the opposite sex, so they didn't talk much, at least not in-depth, about love and such at that point in their lives.

By summer that year, things had changed. He fell in love for the first time. It had been one-sided, a crush so to speak, on his friend's older brother.

His friend from class had introduced them during summer break, when the brother was home on vacation from university, where he lived in a dorm. When their eyes had first met, and the elder had presented himself to Miya, he'd been sold. It was impossible to pinpoint what it had been at that time that had made his heart pound like crazy when he'd first greeted him, but in retrospect, Miya suspected that it was the combination of this guy being older and more refined than they were, and the fact that he was a university student that had impressive advice and observations of the world to offer them, as high-schoolers. Of course, the elder man would always talk to them about what university life was like, and how important it was to study well in advance, because the hardest part was getting in, afterwards it was all fun and games supposedly. Then he'd talk about girls— always. He'd advise them on how to pick up girls, how to charm them, and sometimes, if he was certain that their mother wasn't listening at the door, he'd talk about things that he'd *done* with these girls. His younger brother and their friends had all been sitting there with flushing cheeks, gulping as he exaggerated what it was like to be with a girl. Miya on his side hadn't been cynical enough at that point to think that maybe the student was just overdoing it to impress them and seem like an experienced elder but had been listening eagerly, merely because it was *him* and because he was talking about sex with such enthusiasm. And then he'd go home and think about it, maybe even imagine it, the young man's naked form, the way his body would move, wondering what he sounded like, while touching himself.

But then his friend's brother had returned to university, and life had returned to normal. He still thought about him from time to time, but it wasn't the same, and soon the man's voice was just a faded memory, and new people took his place.

There had been many. At one point, when the hormones were at their worst, he'd thought that he'd end up crushing on the entire male population of the town. Luckily, that hadn't happened, though he'd continued being infatuated by random people, like the guy who worked the night shift at the *conbini* down the street, or the freshman class' substitute teacher.

And yet, despite his continuous spacing out and getting thrown off balance by these random guys floating in and out of his life, although barely being part of it, like extras in the back of a movie scene, it didn't seem like anyone was picking up on the vibe he was giving off.

Now, as an adult, he was almost ashamed to say he was relieved. Not because he felt like he'd deserved to be alienated for being different, but more because he was glad he never had to experience being bullied for who he was. It was different later, when everyone knew, and certain people would treat him differently. But by then, he'd gained enough insight and experience not to care. In high school, he couldn't have guaranteed that it wouldn't have gotten to him if people had decided to start ragging on him.

During his second year of high school he had his first relationship experience. His parents had insisted that he take up a part-time job in order to gain some "life experience," which he did. What they initially were aiming for was probably to get him to work more in their own shop, with the goal that he take over business at some point, since he was the eldest son, but Miya had refused. He insisted that if he was going to work, he wanted to get paid properly for it. His parents couldn't disagree with that, or with his argument that it didn't matter what kind of job he did, any experience would be good in some way or other, and he could easily apply it to the day when he had to start working properly for them.

At that point, they'd probably still thought that he was a reasonable and good kid with good insight.

It all seemed like a million years ago.

He and his friend Agata had ended up getting part-time jobs working for a small restaurant, only for the summer. The owner of the shop had a tight circle of regulars that always came in and ate, and the atmosphere was almost as great as the food they prepared. That summer had been stifling hot because they'd been working in the kitchen day in and day out even though every day was scorching hot thanks to the blazing sun. Another thing that was special about the job was that the owner of the shop was in the committee of a small festival that was held at the beginning of August. Because of this, he often asked the boys to stay a little while longer for extra pay to help make decorations or prepare food for the committee meetings.

It was there he'd met him—Nomura, the grandson of one of the committee members, an old woman who taught tea ceremony and sold *dango*. Nomura wore a moist towel around his head to shield himself from the heat and sleeveless tees that revealed his tan, muscular upper arms. Miya had been completely taken by him.

To Miya's surprise, the other teen had showed interest back. There had been a slight age difference, but not much. Nomura went to a different school and played for their baseball team. Miya had gone to see their games a few times that year after things had evolved the way they did. What had started in the committee meetings, where they'd been out in the kitchen talking or performing various tasks for the committee, had led to them sharing more private conversation; neither of them were particularly shy, but the conversations hadn't been entirely straightforward either. They'd just instinctively thrived in each other's company, maybe because they both knew.

Even now, his chest stung when he thought back on one particular evening in that kitchen; he'd been sweaty and exhausted from the heat, scrubbing plates when Nomura had come in.

"Are you alone?" he'd asked.

"Yeah, I told Agata to go ahead; we don't need two people to wash the dishes," he'd replied and added that it was so hot he almost regretted it. At that point, Nomura had gently dried Miya's sweaty forehead with his moist towel, smiling.

A brief silence had fallen between the two of them before Nomura spoke again.

"You're pretty," he said. It sounded awkward these days, but back then, it had been like a form of sorely needed confirmation. "Almost like a girl…"

He stared back at the other teenager, and when he took his hands out of the sink, he accidentally broke a plate by knocking it off the counter.

"Does that freak you out?" the other boy asked him.

He shook his head. "I-it just startled me," he replied, "because…"

Right then, the manager had come in to check on him and he explained that his soapy hand had slipped. "Be careful when you clean it up." The manager replied, and Miya immediately crouched down to pick up the pieces of porcelain, blushing furiously as if he felt like they'd been caught in the act. Nomura crouched down next to him and placed his hand on top of Miya's. Their hands gently took one another, and he whispered, "I like you, Utsunomiya."

He *had*, for a while. By the time of the festival, the two of them had snuck away time and time again to push boundaries and explore their sexualities. What had started with holding hands in secret under the table at lunch hour had evolved to kissing when they were by themselves and nobody was looking. Then it peaked at the night of the festival. Both had been dressed in traditional *yukata* and *hakama* for the occasion and had been running around like crazy hanging decorations and setting up stands and booths all day. When the evening finally came, they were kept on their toes for a while longer before finally being dismissed and told to come back and help out with the clean up the following morning.

While most of the teenagers that had spent their summer preparing for the festival went off to play and watch the fireworks, the two of them had snuck off to Nomura's grandmother's house, where he was staying for the summer. Since he went to a school in a different part of the prefecture, it had been easier for him to just stay the entire break with her, since he was to work anyway. His grandmother, of course, had been at the festival and would probably remain there for a while longer. Nomura had shown him to the room where he slept while he was visiting, a traditional room with *tatami* flooring and futons to sleep on.

They had no idea what they were doing; it was clumsy and rough and probably not a very successful first time for either of them. But Miya remembered the suspense, and the way his heart ran wild as their kisses grew intense in the way that only flustered teenagers could succumb to their raging hormones with their hands roaming everywhere—hormones and curiosity running the show. He remembered the room being badly lit by a small lamp, and himself shaking terribly, even though it was so hot, as he was laid down on the futon and partially undressed. He remembered the scent of *yakitori* and sweat, nervous hands on his body. He didn't remember much of the act itself, and it probably hadn't been much to talk about, but he remembered gaining confidence by looking at the elder teenager, his hands fumbling underneath Miya's partially undone *yukata*, and the way their kisses had tasted that night.

He'd been happy. They'd done it again, with more success, but looking back, in typical teenage fashion, they'd had no idea what they were doing, and in the end, it hadn't worked out. They'd kept in touch somewhat after school started again, mostly by phone, but then one day, Nomura had said that he didn't want to keep seeing him anymore.

"I've outgrown it," he'd said, and added that he'd heard it

was a phase some people went through at some point. Miya had never quite believed that. And for a while, he'd been bitter. Bitter that he'd thought that they felt the same way, and angry at himself for being stupid enough to fall for something like that. But then he'd somehow managed to get over it. Looking at it now, he still didn't fully believe that Nomura had just outgrown what they'd been up to, but rather that someone had found him out and lectured him. He sometimes wondered how that had worked out for him—if he was more comfortable with himself these days.

After that, he'd started up a futile relationship with a much older man. He'd been in his senior year, and rumors had started circulating. He'd never bothered to find out who had started them and for what reason, although he sometimes thought that it was pretty obvious; because he was feminine-looking, because he grew out his hair while the others were cutting theirs in the style that had been popular at that time, and because he turned down the girls who confessed to him, or asked him out. It was probably something as simple as that.

This had been at his more rebellious stage, where he'd tested limits and attempted driving his parents insane. He'd started talking about not wanting to go straight to university because he'd rather do other things first, like travel, or work a little to get a break from school. He was tired of teachers and homework, of studying and the constant pressure to be someone. Besides, he'd argued, he was supposed to go into the family business, so what use was going to university? It didn't seem important at all in that sense. He knew the business well; after all, he'd grown up in the shop. He was used to helping out and handling customers, even making phone calls on behalf of his father sometimes, so what did he have to worry about?

Apparently, this had been too much for his parents, who'd more or less started a crusade towards making him take some entrance exams and at least *attempt* to get in somewhere. In response, Miya had taken up smoking, started hanging out with his friends until late at night, and dyed his hair—relatively unsuccessfully. But at that time, the shocked expressions on his parents' faces when he came home with badly bleached hair had been sufficient enough for him to keep it that way for at least a few weeks.

It was during this ridiculous period of his life that he'd met a man whom he was fairly certain he didn't even know the real name of. He'd been a businessman—again, no personal details disclosed. To top it off, he'd turned out to be married. There had been absolutely no future in that disaster of a "relationship," but at seventeen, with a rebellious streak, all Miya had wanted was probably to do something that his parents would *never* approve of—even though they'd never find out about it.

He probably should have found it creepy when a grown man started hanging around him because of his frequenting a local *pachinko* parlor on several occasions. The man had started by asking him for a light and then made it clear that he was flirting with him. Miya, having been put off by Nomura's flaking out, had been uncertain but very easily charmed by this older man paying so much attention to him.

At twenty-eight, there were times where he wanted to bang his head against the wall when he thought about how utterly stupid he'd been ten years earlier. It was incredibly embarrassing that he'd somehow gotten into what he'd thought was a relationship, when in reality it was nothing more than a series of meetings at a trashy *love hotel,* where they'd drink cheap alcohol, and he'd allow every touch and accept every compliment he was given. He enjoyed being treated like an adult, and the fact that they could have proper conversations. But then, what did an adult businessman have in common with a teenager with dyed hair and a bad attitude?

To be honest, that stupid version of himself carried a hint of resemblance to the young man he was now sharing an apartment with, but he thought Aki was probably more cynical and thus smarter than he'd been himself.

Miya, being the country bumpkin he'd often refer to himself as, with a big heart and an open mind, would often just assume that everyone were what they passed themselves off as because he was such an honest person himself.

When he'd stupidly told this man that he was in love with him, he'd meant it and assumed that the compliments, the caresses and the long drives were all signs that they were on the same page.

At least until the day the other man stood him up, and he waited an entire night at that sleazy hotel, sitting on tasteless red satin sheets, waiting while drinking beer by himself, and then later finding that the man didn't answer any of his calls. Again, he'd been upset by it, and even more hurt than when Nomura had told him they shouldn't see each other anymore because this was supposed to be different, since his current lover was more mature.

The good thing about these events though was that although there was little Miya enjoyed as much as the fluttering butterflies of being in love with someone, or at least being infatuated with them, he was getting that life experience he'd been shouting so loudly at his parents about. When the affair with the good-for-nothing businessman had ended, he'd calmed down and started studying again. He still wasn't planning on taking any exams, but at least he'd decided to graduate high school, and matters had become calmer with his parents as well.

As for his relationships, he'd become more critical towards who he spent his time with. At that age, and even a while into his early twenties, Miya had been under the impression that the only way to be with someone was to be in an actual relationship with them, and so he'd started making more demands when he found someone he was interested in. He wasn't up for any low-key, hidden-away affairs anymore, and if the person he went out with seemed uninterested in him, he'd break it off before he was hurt. That was mostly after he'd graduated though. His last months in high school had been relatively eventless. He didn't care much for trying out anything, and considering how he needed to catch up on his school work, he ended up having little time for anything besides studying and working part time at the family shop.

But in the end, he'd decided to postpone university—something he obviously never got back into—and had moved to

Kobe "for a while." He'd originally moved there with a friend from high school who'd been accepted to a university there. She'd known about his sexuality, so she had no problem sharing a small two-room with him, but then she'd found herself a boyfriend and eventually moved in with him, which was when Miya had started laying low whenever she had him over, resulting in him going out a lot at night, and eventually getting to know Hiiro and Yuura.

In that time period, he'd met several people he'd gone out with for a while but didn't hit it off properly with anyone and didn't bother to try much at all to make it so after a while. Plus, he'd discovered the joys of being free and single, with the world as some sort of playroom where he could just pick off the shelves and play with whichever toy suited him best in the moment. Pretty soon, that had become habitual, and now it was standard.

But now, here he was again. And perhaps it wasn't love, but he definitely recognized that almost sickening excitement to see the other man whenever the opportunity came along. And part of him had seemingly missed this kind of excitement because he couldn't remember having felt this perky in a long time. But then there were other things, such as his dishonesty; the way he wasn't telling his friends about what was going on in his life out of fear that it would either jinx it or even that them finding out would somehow ruin something. And then of course he hadn't *defined* their relationship, so part of him was still carrying on like usual. Not that he necessarily slept with other people, but he still didn't see Miura that often, and when he did, they were mostly just brief meetings; he hadn't spent the night with him since after the fireworks display. So obviously, he didn't know how to classify their relation and so continued to keep his playful, characteristic game with his coworkers and friends.

"Utsunomiya!" He was torn from his thoughts.

"What?"

"Jesus Christ, you're impossible to talk to, do you know that?" Sho, the manager, looked at him with complete resignation written on his face.

"Sorry." Miya realized that he'd been wiping the same spot on the bar counter for at least ten minutes while cursing under his breath about his own stupidity and the conflicting emotions he was experiencing.

"Hey," he said, without bothering asking what it was Sho had wanted in the first place, "you and Kiyoshi have been together forever, right?"

"Forever is stretching it a bit," Sho replied, chuckling, "Why?"

"I was just wondering. I was reflecting a bit on my disastrous dating career, so I was wondering how you two are able to stand each other year after year."

The manager got a rare serious expression on his face, but a slight smile played on his thin lips. "Isn't it obvious?" he said. "He's the 'one.'"

Miya stared blankly at him. He'd never actually heard anyone use that expression before. Certainly not his playful boss, who was younger than him at that. Coming from him, those words were more than a little strange. Apparently, he wasn't the only one who thought so.

"Oh please." Aki brushed past them, looking incredibly annoyed. He'd been in a foul mood lately, and everything seemed to bother him.

"Hello to you too," Sho muttered. "Show some respect for your elders, will you?"

"Yeah sure," the younger man replied sourly, beginning to stack chairs on top of the tables.

It was past closing time, and they were all getting ready to go home.

"Anyway, I wanted to ask you if you could just mop the floors after you're done here?" the manager asked.

"Yeah sure." Miya nodded, sweeping the counter over once more with the wet rag. "Sorry about spacing out."

"No worries, just get a move on so we can all leave." Sho waved him off as he left the bar and headed for the office.

"Aki, are you going home after?"

"Nah, I thought I'd go out." The teen didn't elaborate. He

wasn't very talkative lately.

"Where?"

He received a dismissive shrug in response, and Miya gave up. "Fine, I'll go home by myself then," he mumbled.

Though, when he was finally ready to go home, he was struck by an idea. He wasn't sure if his head was screwed on right as he took the train to Motomachi rather than Higashinada. Not only did he decide to drop in unannounced, but it was a school night at that. Maybe this would be a direct sabotage of whatever it was he was doing with Miura, but he suddenly got the urge to go see him. He didn't feel up to spending the night alone.

Surprisingly, he was able to locate the correct building fairly quickly, and the front door wasn't locked, so he could go straight up to the fifth floor.

He rang the doorbell several times before he finally heard shuffling around on the other side of the door.

Satoru, you are an idiot, he told himself as the lock was turned and the door handle was pulled down. Soon he was face to face with a zombiefied teacher, whose features were drawn and gusty, his eyes barely open underneath a pair of heavy eyelids. The man peered at him, seemingly confused.

"Satoru…?"

"Surprise?" He grinned stupidly, leaning on the doorframe. "Can I stay with you?"

"You live on the other side of the city."

"Yeah, but I wanted to see you." He offered an apologetic smile, leaning a little closer to kiss Miura softly on the lips. "I'm sorry I woke you up."

For a second, he was afraid the other man would be so confused he'd deem it all a dream and lock the door again, but Miya was relieved when Miura just stepped aside, letting him into the apartment.

Miya had to smile at how tired the man was, like he was barely aware of Miya's presence, pattering back into the bedroom, collapsing on the bed again.

What exactly had he been thinking? Miya had to wonder as

he locked the door behind himself and went into the bedroom. He was the one who was hesitant about what kind of relation it was they had, and now what?

Hesitantly, he undressed himself down to his underwear and crept into bed next to the teacher, who already seemed to be fast asleep again.

He didn't think this was the smartest idea he'd ever had, but then Miura's arm coiled around his waist and pulled him close. He couldn't help but let out an audible gasp of surprise. He pulled the covers tighter around himself and enjoyed the warmth radiating from Miura. Even if he was sleeping, it didn't seem like he wasn't welcoming Miya to sleep next to him.

His smile morphed into a yawn, and pretty soon Miya was fast asleep as well.

14. Uncertainty

Miya was awoken by Miura's alarm clock. It carried a horrible howling sound that tore through his entire being, but he was too tired, having only slept a few short hours when it rang, so he didn't get up—not until a hand carefully shook him.

"Satoru."

"Nnh..." he mumbled, his voice muffled against the pillow he was burying his face in.

Miura shook him more persistently, and he turned around, looking sleepily at the man's puzzled face.

"Mmh, what time is it?"

"Six in the morning. Why are you...?" the man looked utterly confused. He *had* been completely asleep earlier then. Miya smiled at him, or attempted to anyway; his face felt stiff and tired and nothing really felt like it was functioning in his body at this point. He yawned. "Y-You... uh...let me in," he managed to force forth. "You don't remember?"

Miura narrowed his eyes, scratching his chin; there was a slight trace of stubble. Miya's lip twitched.

"Vaguely."

"I'm sorry. Maybe it wasn't the best..."

The teacher broke him off. "No, no, it's fine. I'm just a little surprised. I didn't say it wasn't a pleasant surprise."

Miya made a weak attempt to sit up. His body still felt fatigued. "I can make it better?"

He was so tired, but there was a slight excitement tingling in him. "If you have the time."

He reached underneath the covers, stroking his hand down the man's abdomen and brushing over the waistband of his pajama bottoms. "When do you usually leave?"

"Seven fifteen but—"

"That's plenty of time then..." Miya smirked, leaning over to kiss the teacher on the lips. He tasted like sleep and carried a faint scent of sweat. The room was hot. A bit taken aback, Miura returned the kiss. Miya nibbled on his bottom lip, his fingertips slipping beneath the waistband and into the pajama pants, brushing against rough, slightly curled hair. A surprised sigh escaped the other man's throat.

Miya smirked into the kiss, gripping the man's erection, stroking him carefully while continuing to kiss him on the lips, then on the chest, slowly moving downwards towards his target. Miura's breath grew quicker as he approached. He smiled against soft, tan skin, and encircled his target, feeling almost as excited as his partner evidently was.

***

"You are..." Miura sat on the bed, beginning to dress himself. His hair was wet from the quick shower he'd just taken, and his skin was still flushing from the hot water and the arousal. Miya still remained naked in his bed, playfully licking his lips and grinning.

"Crazy?" he suggested, fairly certain those would be the next words out of the man's mouth.

"More or less." Miura buttoned his shirt and grabbed for his pants.

"I just thought it seemed like a good start to your morning," Miya said, still smiling. "And it was, wasn't it?"

"What kind of question is that?" Miura shot back. "Weren't you convinced?"

"Hn," Miya grinned. "I just wanted to hear you say it."

"So, now what?" Miura stood from the bed and went back into the bathroom, seemingly trying to fix his hair. When he emerged, he looked a bit more respectable. "Are you staying here?"

"You'll be late, won't you?" Miya replied, shuffling his feet underneath the sheets.

"I won't be home until around five or six..."

"Well... would you *like* me to stay?"

"I suppose I wouldn't mind if you'll be okay here by yourself."

"S'okay." Miya smiled. "I'll just sleep. And I don't have work until eleven, so I can stay."

"Okay then. If that's what you want. Feel free to eat or whatever you want while I'm gone. If you go out, there's a spare key in the top kitchen drawer."

Miya yawned and nodded. "Noted," he said. "Now run along and get to work."

Miura smiled at him, an odd, awkward smile, shaking his head. He grabbed his briefcase and went out into the hallway. Miya watched him from the bed as he put on his shoes.

"All right, I'm off!" he called out.

"*Itterashai!*" Miya replied, his chest bubbling with something strange and familiar.

They regarded each other for a while longer, and then the elder man took his leave, locking the door from the outside. Miya was left wondering what on earth was going on, and if this was how proper relationships worked.

***

He woke up again around noon, feeling rested and content.

The warm sheets that engulfed him carried the teacher's scent, and created a distinct mood. For several minutes, he just laid in place, taking in the scents and views of the bedroom, the sheets rustling around him as he changed positions on the bed. While waking up in someone else's room was nothing new, this kind of awakening *was*, but it wasn't unwelcome. He felt calm and at home here, like he'd slept in this room forever. He looked at the white walls, adorned with framed posters of vintage prints—a black and white print from an old American movie, and a print in sepia tones that he wasn't familiar with.

He sat up and yawned, throwing the sheets aside at last, to lower himself onto the floor and walk into the bathroom, grabbing his clothes as he did. The bathroom was cramped, and probably not as clean as Miura would have liked it to be when having visitors over. It didn't matter to Miya though, since he wasn't very good at keeping his own apartment clean.

After a quick shower, he got dressed. In the kitchen he found some fruit, which he had for breakfast, mostly to make up for not having a toothbrush and wanting to feel a little more refreshed. He sank down in the sofa, watching some music channel until he got bored and started digging around the kitchen drawer for the spare key. He decided that since he had no real wish to hang around the apartment all day, he might as well head out to do some shopping.

In the end, he ended up tidying up a little and brought back some groceries before Miura came home.

***

"Is this the same house?" Miura exclaimed with surprise as he came home that afternoon. Miya was on the sofa, dressed in his clothes from the night before, watching television but paying only partial interest.

"Ah *okaeri!*" He sat up, grinning.

"Did you clean this place up?"

"Yeah well, I tidied a little, and did the dishes that were in the sink, mostly because I was bored. And I went shopping. I don't know if you like *gyūdon*, but I bought some meat and stuff. I'm terrible at cooking but…"

"You really didn't have to."

"Well, I did come in here and disrupt your sleep in the middle of the night, so I thought I'd redeem myself a little. Plus, I was bored sitting around here all day."

"Thanks in any case." Miura slipped down into the couch next to him. "I didn't expect this at all."

"Neither did I," Miya smiled, "but I couldn't very well just leave without paying you back, so…"

"Didn't you pay me back this morning?"

Miya laughed. "That was different. Spur of the moment, this was more… I don't know…"

"So, you're staying for dinner?"

"Will you make it?"

Miura laughed. "You bought me food so I could prepare it for you?"

"By all means," Miya grinned. "I can try, but I don't think you want to end up with food poisoning."

"You're not that bad, I'm sure."

"Ask my roommate," he replied, laughing even louder. "I'm horrible at cooking, honestly."

"To be honest…" Miura smiled crookedly, "so am I."

"So we starve."

They exchanged glances and then finally agreed to help each other out. The food came out fairly okay, not exactly a gourmet meal, but fairly edible at least. They ate at the small living room table, idly chatting, and then Miya took his leave.

"Thank you for letting me stay over," he said, smiling. "I really appreciate it."

"My pleasure."

"I'm sure it was." Miya smirked, winding his arms around Miura's neck, touching their lips together. "May I come over again?"

"You may. Although you might want to call first."

Miya nodded. "Yeah, I'll keep that in mind. Gotta go to work now… Have a good evening, 'kay?"

"You too," Miura's hand brushed Miya's upper arm as he showed him out.

***

On his way out of the building Miya picked up his phone and called Aki.

"Hey, you at work yet?"

"Not yet, what are you doing?"

"I thought I'd go in early, but then it's too early. Wanna hang out?"

"Nah, I'm tired."

"Please?" he begged. "We could go to Maki's or something."

"Go alone. I'm not up for anything."

"You sure? I'll buy you food."

"Can't you do anything by yourself?"

"I already ate though."

The teenager snarled on the other end. *"Then what's the point? I'm gonna come into work later, but I don't want to go out. Okay? Come home instead."*

"Too far," Miya rejected the offer. "I'll just go there myself then. See you later?"

"Yeah. Bye."

There was a click on the other end. To be honest, he'd mostly called to have something to do while walking, so he wouldn't be overrun by his own thoughts again. His mind had felt a little boggled after the crash-flashbacks of his teenage years earlier, but this had been a fairly good day. He hadn't intended for it to happen, but he was glad he'd spontaneously come over, although he hadn't expected to stay as long as he had, and certainly not to clean the place up. But he'd felt grateful. And then there was how he'd wanted to do it for his own sake, to make up for waking up Miura. He knew already based on their conversations that the man worked very hard, with all the grading he had to do, and the meetings and schedules he had to prepare, so he felt bad about intruding in the middle of the night.

Usually, he probably would have locked himself out using the spare key at some point during the day, but he'd really wanted to do something for the man and then see his face upon him returning. It had been almost just as enjoyable for him, he was sure of that, and it frightened him a little. So he'd wanted to get something more tangible and normal between his hands, which was why he'd called Aki.

"It can't be helped though," he said to himself, sighing as he walked down the street towards the station, passing people casting sidelong glances at him and the way he was dressed, still in his clothes from the night before—again. That certainly wouldn't go unnoticed by the other guys. He frowned. Perhaps going home to change was the better option after all, but it *was* a bit of a hassle. Nevertheless, he decided to do it for the sake of keeping his sanity around Hiiro.

Aki wasn't likely to question it any further than pointing it out, and perhaps offer a brief snicker. It was okay like that, to live with him, because while he could be snide, at least he was relatively uninterested in other people's business, and he wasn't very talkative. Although that was also somewhat of a downside, as Miya was a bit of a blabbermouth. He wondered if Miura disliked that about him. One thing was the rashness, but he was also fairly dominant in conversation, and really loud.

Well, he thought to himself, *that could count as a sort of confidence booster to be honest.*

***

Back in Higashinada, he found his roommate on the couch looking very tired. He came over, sitting next to him and glancing at him with slight concern.

"Are you okay?" he asked, wondering if perhaps Aki was just under the weather. He seemed almost a little feverish.

"Just tired. Couldn't sleep."

"Yeah?" He stroked the teen over the forehead. "You're hot though."

A sneer came as the response. "I'm aware."

"Idiot." Miya leaned forward, kissing the younger man on the temple. "I have some sleeping pills if you have real trouble sleeping."

"Ugh, no thanks. I just need some rest."

"Were you out last night?"

"Myeah, for a while." Aki shrugged. "Where have you been? You're dressed in the clothes you wore yesterday. *Again.*"

"Well, an opportunity came around, so I kinda went with it."

"Good for you." Aki turned on the couch, making more space for Miya to lie down next to him.

While they were like that, Aki seemed to grow less tense and eventually fell into something like a light sleep, breathing softly against Miya's bare arm.

Miya absentmindedly ran his fingers through stiff, wiry hair, and sighed. Sometimes he thought that this life was far too much for someone that young, but who was he to judge based on what *he* had been like at the same age? They weren't all that different, although he thought Aki was probably more skilled at fending for himself and less a victim to his own feelings compared to himself. He groaned, leaning his head back on the sofa.

***

That week he ended up going to Miura's house again twice more. Both times he'd gone there at night, and both times he'd been accepted in, even though he'd failed to call the first time. At that time, he'd been drinking after work and had decided that he wanted to re-experience the last incident. Both times had been enjoyable; creeping in next to the man, snuggling up against his warm body, and then starting the day off with sex—not the worst possible start to be honest. They'd left together at the time when Miura usually left for work, and Miya had tried to ignore that it seemed like the other man was nervous when they exited the apartment together, like he worried that people would see them together.

But then maybe that was just Miya being paranoid. Miya had never seen a single person aside from them in the building— neither coming in or going out—which could probably have to do with the timing of his visits.

Still, he decided to try to lay a little lower from there on, partially for Miura's sake, and partially for his own. He was still a little apprehensive about the man's lack of initiative.

One night he was discussing it with Hiiro as they tended to the bar; both Testu and Kyo had the night off, and pretty much everyone else were working the floor, so the two of them were talking in between mixing drinks and writing out tabs. It was a relief to have at least one friend to talk to, even if the redhead was a bit of a tease regarding the whole thing.

"Yeah, but do you want to like... *pursue* him?" Hiiro chewed on a painted nail, looking surprised.

"I'm not really sure what we're doing," Miya confessed.

"Which is why I'm gonna lay low for a while. I think maybe I'm coming on too strong."

"But he's not exactly the forward type, right?"

Miya shook his head, tucking a few loose strands of hair behind his ear.

Ayase came up to them, holding up two fingers. Miya dug out two cans of *Asahi* from the fridge below the counter and poured them into a couple of glasses.

"No, but he can't expect me to do everything." Miya bit his lip, turning back to his other colleague.

"I'm sure you don't do *everything*." Hiiro grinned, suggestively arching an eyebrow.

"I'm still the one *initiating* it." He didn't bother going along with the joke. "I need to see if he's willing to make an effort."

"Wait," Hiiro blinked, "are you saying you're going to go for it? Like, enter a relationship with this guy?"

Miya shrugged. "At this point, I'm not even defining it. As long as we're in this state, there's nothing to define."

"But you went to his house, right? Several times, and had dinner?"

"Yeah well, I have dinner at Naru's sometimes. And I sleep with Aki whenever we feel like it, but that doesn't mean we're in a relationship, even if we live together, you know? So I can't really say that that counts for anything."

"So basically you want to see if he makes a move."

"Yeah. *He* was the one who sought *me* out in the first place, so I want to see how far he's willing to go for this... whatever it is." He shrugged, making a hand gesture signaling resignation.

"Sounds complicated."

"Isn't that how this crazy little thing called love works?" Miya sighed, pouring a drink in accordance with an order that had just been slapped onto the bar.

"You're not in *love* with him?"

He clamped his lips together, drying off his hands with a piece of cloth. "Well... no. But—"

"Hey, Miya," Ayase interrupted the two of them. "Your lover boy's back."

A chill ran down his spine. "Lover boy?" he croaked, turning around to look at the younger man.

Hiiro hoisted himself up on his elbows, peeking over the bar counter and out into the club. "Ah, alas," he said, lowering himself back down on his feet, "wrong one."

"Who?" Miya swallowed dryly. Hadn't he hoped a little that it *would* be Miura? There was probably a part of him that wanted this tactic to work in the ways that the other man would miss him if he didn't show up again and then seek him out for once. But of course, that was ridiculous, as he'd only shown up at the ridiculous times of early morning, and in any case, this was a schoolteacher, not some party animal. If anything, it was probably more likely that he'd call.

"You know, that student?" Ayase grinned. "I remember your enthusiasm over *that* one..."

Miya grinned crookedly. It was true that he vividly remembered the night with Takahiro, the student, but it probably wasn't the best time to reminisce.

"What's he doing here? I thought he went back north?"

Ayase shrugged. "No idea. Maybe he came back here just to see you."

"Funny." Miya sneered. "Can you handle the bar, Hiiro? I wanna go see him for a bit."

"Sure thing." The redhead yawned. "Hey, if you don't want him, can I have him?"

He ignored the question and stepped around the counter onto the floor. "He's over by the stage," Ayase said, pointing.

Hands in pockets, Miya crossed the floor and made his way towards the table, grinning as he placed his hand lovingly on the other man's shoulder.

"Well hi," he said softly. "Long time no see!"

"Not that long," Takahiro smiled back, "surprisingly."

"Indeed." Miya smirked. "What's up? You missed me that much?"

"Heh," the younger man said, licking his lips. "More like I'm doing another study trip thing, and we're staying here overnight, taking the train to the real destination tomorrow morning. So I thought, when in Rome."

"Is that so?" Miya grinned, slipping down on the chair opposite the student. He turned his head, calling over his shoulder, "I'll take a short break—just saying!"

Naruse gestured in confirmation back to him. They were more than enough people working, so if someone disappeared for a bit, there was nothing wrong with that; the rest could manage fine on their own.

"So," he pursed his lips, regarding the younger man, "how have you been?"

"Good. We got the highest mark for our presentation."

"Great," Miya replied, just as softly. He was completely in work mode and his flirtatious persona effortlessly shone through. "Was I any help?"

"Not really. Many thanks to you, I lost sleep and passed out on the train rather than working on my notes," the man chuckled. He reached across the table, letting his fingertips brush against Miya's. "It was worth it though."

"I'm sure it was." He briefly returned the caress, and then retracted his fingers, leaning on his elbow instead, continuing to hold the other's gaze.

"So," Takahiro licked his lips, "are you working long tonight?"

"Mmh, until two," Miya replied. "I might hang around after that for some drinks."

The other man grinned. "May I join you?"

Miya crossed his legs underneath the table, drumming his fingers against his own thigh. His gaze wandered from the student's hand, up his sleeve and over his body. He was very attractive, and the memories from the night they'd spent together were welling up.

"I wouldn't mind if you did," he replied, swallowing nervously, "but…"

"But?" The other man looked surprised. He'd been confident then that this would be a repetition of the last time. Miya averted his eyes for a moment. He thought he spotted someone familiar by the entrance, but it was impossible. Not at this time of night.

It was probably his imagination, or guilty conscience, and he realized that this feeling he was having resembled guilt.

"Unfortunately, my dear Takahiro-kun, I can't play with you tonight," he sighed.

"I'm sorry, are you seeing someone?"

At least he understood. Miya smiled gratefully. "I guess you can say that," he replied apologetically. "Otherwise, I would have loved to."

The man shrugged. "It was worth a shot. He's a lucky man."

"Hn," Miya chuckled, "maybe he is."

He wasn't entirely sure of that with the way he was making himself seem so apologetic about seeing someone else.

Takahiro shrugged. "Let me know if you change your mind though."

"Oh, I will." Miya smirked, sending him a flirty look. "But if you're up for it, you can come with us for drinks later. We're basically friends by now."

"I'd say," the other man chuckled. "I might just take you up on that offer."

"You do that," Miya grinned, "and I'll introduce you to some other friends of mine if you'd like."

He cast a sidelong glance in Hiiro's direction, seeing the redhead seductively leaning over the shoulder of a good-looking client a couple of tables away, pointing out recommendations on the menu for him.

"Not sure how I feel about that though," Miya added, laughing quietly. "I did quite like you, you know."

Takahiro smirked, lifting his glass. "Yeah, me too."

"If it makes you feel any better, I'm not the best at relationships, so your chance might come again." He winked.

What are you even saying? He mentally frowned. There was the guilt again, no wonder he was seeing things.

"I'll hold you to that," the man chuckled.

"I need to get back to work though, but let me know if you're up for going out with us later, yeah?"

"Sure."

"Great, have a good time!" He stood from the table, offering a soft stroke along the man's upper arm as he headed for the next table, taking their check.

As it turned out, Takahiro didn't grieve very long over Miya's rejection, as he shortly after found a friend at the neighboring table and seemed to hit it off quite well with him.

Miya was slightly relieved. It wasn't that he was so attracted to the student that he'd be unable to resist if the chance should offer itself, or that he'd feel uncomfortable based on their previous meeting. It was more that he felt like he'd said too much earlier and cursed himself for not being able to hold his tongue. If he worried about hanging around other lovers while being somewhat bound to another person, he'd have to quit his job and find a new one, which was ridiculous. So that wasn't it. But he was still relieved that he didn't have to spend the night together with Takahiro later, even though he really liked the other man and wouldn't mind getting to know him as friends either. He was easygoing like that. But still...

"Damn, I missed out!" Hiiro interrupted his stream of thoughts.

They were in the lounge, changing after their shift ended. Hiiro came in, throwing his shirt away, glancing out into the club one last time.

"Did you ask him?"

"Yeah, and he seemed interested, but I guess he got a better offer." Miya shrugged, putting his jacket on.

"That's too bad; I was looking forward to checking if your claims about him were true."

Miya laughed. "Don't you trust me?"

Hiiro came up to him, putting his arms around Miya's waist and pulling him closer. "Body and soul." He grinned, his lips almost brushing over Miya's as he spoke.

"You're an idiot," Miya laughed, pushing him away. "Where do you wanna go?"

"I'm starving actually, so Maki's?"

"Sounds like a plan," Miya agreed. "Naru, wanna join us?"

The blond man was in the process of getting his boots on, patiently lacing them up, which seemingly took forever. "Mmh,

I was thinking of going home actually."

"Please, don't be such a bore! I haven't hung out with you in ages!" Miya groaned.

"Isn't that because you've been hanging out with someone else?" Hiiro smiled crookedly.

"Yeah, well. I'm here *now*. Join us, Naru!"

The blond sighed. "All right, for a short while. Is Aki coming?"

Miya shrugged. "I have no idea where he is actually."

"Does it matter?" Hiiro asked. "It's healthy for us adults to be by ourselves for once."

Miya snickered quietly. "That's mean!"

"Yeah, because I'm sure you'll miss him picking on you for being *old*."

"Okay, good point." He threw one arm around either companion and grinned. "Let's go out, just the three of us for once."

Naru poked him in the ribcage, freeing himself from his grip as soon as Miya doubled over. "Tickles!"

"I'm surprised, to be honest," he said. "What about Takahiro? It's not like you to pass up an opportunity like that."

"Ah that." Hiiro smirked, nudging Miya, receiving an annoyed glare in return. If the redhead kept doing things like this, he'd end up getting bruises from being nudged all the time.

"I just didn't feel up to it," he replied, shrugging. "You guys coming?"

He pushed open the door to the backyard and stepped out.

"Are you sick?" Naru called after him, grabbing his stuff and following him outside.

Hiiro laughed loudly, shutting the door behind the three of them.

"I'm just yanking your chain, you know that, right?" Naruse caught up to him, ruffling his hair.

"Yeah." Miya pushed him away, smiling crookedly. "It's just not the best day to do so."

"Is something wrong?"

Hiiro rolled his eyes as if Miya wouldn't notice.

"No, I'm just… I have a lot on my mind lately."

"Aha!" Naru nodded. "I won't bother you about it, but feel free to rant all you want, okay?"

He smiled again. Maybe he would—if he didn't hear anything. He didn't think it was very likely that Miura would call him up in the middle of the night if he didn't show up again, but was it too much to ask for, wanting Miura to call him in the morning, asking him about not having showed up?

"Why do I even bother?" he scolded himself, accidentally speaking the words out loud. There was no reason for him to act like this. None at all.

"Don't let it bother you," Naruse said softly, placing his arm around his shoulder, pulling him closer as they proceeded down the street. "Whatever it is, forget about it and let's have fun tonight, okay?"

"I'm glad you're firing up!" Hiiro slapped the blond man on the back, grinning. "It would really suck if you were both brooding all night."

Naruse laughed, and Miya felt his own lips quirking as well.

He was over-thinking things. It probably didn't help that people kept bothering him about it. If he got some time off from his own thoughts, then maybe he could relax. It wasn't the end of the world. He'd had casual relationships that had lasted longer than this, giving it time was naturally all he could do if he wanted to see what grew from there—*if* that was what he wanted.

It was important not to forget that he had some of the best friends around, and that he'd never complained about the state of his life, so he wasn't about to go and brood over something like this just yet. And so, he allowed himself to get carried away by the other two and their heightening spirits as they made their way down to the small drinking establishment by the docks, where several of their friends and acquaintances were already assembled.

"*Otsukaresama!*" Maki grinned at them from behind the counter, guessing that they were coming straight from work. "Hungry?"

"*Starving!*"

"I'll make you something. Have a seat," the androgynous man chirped, immediately starting to fry up something that smelled absolutely heavenly while Naruse got them some drinks—without any comments from the owner.

Not long after, there was nothing but golden drinks, laughter and excited jabbering. Miya felt incredibly relaxed, lifting his glass, leaning back against the windowsill. He was already starting to forget about what had become somewhat of a nightly ritual of his.

He ended up dragging Hiiro home with him, mostly because the other man was being clingy, but he didn't think much had happened between them. They'd both been tired and worn out by the time they entered the building in Higashinada and crashed on the sofa together.

***

They both woke up late the next afternoon, both with stiff necks and muscle cramps after sleeping on the ancient, worn-out sofa. Miya yawned, cracking his back as he sat upright.

"Morning," Hiiro grunted, scratching the unruly nest that was his hair.

"I'd say that was a successful evening." Miya clicked his tongue. His mouth felt like sandpaper. "I was out like a light."

"Mmh, me too. Maybe we did let it get sort of out of hand. Where's Naru?"

They hadn't intended to drink as much as they had, but the mood had just swept them away and carried them down the stream of alcohol once they'd finished their late meal. "I don't think he came home with us."

"Let's hope he went home with someone else then," Hiiro laughed, almost instantly breaking into a cough. "When was the last time you cleaned this place up? I think I inhaled something."

"I think you're developing COPD," Miya remarked dryly, standing up to patter across the room and fetch a bottle of water from the fridge.

"Could be," Hiiro groaned, taking the bottle offered to him. "You should get it first though. You've smoked longer than me."

Miya waited for him to gulp down almost half the bottle before taking it and putting it to his own lips. "I don't think fatal diseases use general logic," he remarked, wiping his mouth on his wrist.

"You mind if I shower?"

Miya shook his head. "Go right ahead. If you want to change, you can borrow some of my stuff. There should be something clean on the line."

"Okay, thanks." His friend sauntered into the bathroom, closing the door without locking it. There was no point in that anyway. They were all so used to one another in their group, seeing each other naked was hardly the end of the world.

Miya quietly stepped up to his roommate's door, listening for any sounds inside. He heard nothing and cracked the door slightly ajar. The room was empty. It almost looked abandoned, considering the naked walls and absolute minimum of furniture.

He shrugged, closing the door again.

Sinking down on the sofa, he fished out his phone and found that as expected there weren't any messages or missed calls. He sighed. What had he been hoping for anyway?

To be honest, he was tempted to slap himself in the face. Didn't he tell himself the night before to stop fretting?

Firstly, Miura couldn't *possibly* know that he was waiting to hear from him. Precisely because this was an experiment from his side to see how long it would take the other man to get in touch and initiate something again, so there was no point in letting him know about it. On the other hand, not knowing wouldn't exactly magically make the teacher start contacting him for no reason.

"You're an idiot," he muttered to himself. He fell back against the tattered old cushions, covering his eyes with a limp hand and sighing deeply.

Had being taken with someone always felt this frustrating?

The front door creaked, opening slowly and slamming against the wall as it was pushed open. He removed his hand, glancing towards the cramped hall space. His roommate was back. He kicked his shoes off, hitting the walls with a couple of low thumps. He looked just as tired as Miya felt.

"Morning," he said.

"Yeah hi," Aki grunted. "Who's here?"

He was referring to the sound of the shower running.

"Hiiro."

"Ah." He nodded, going into the bathroom and emerging minutes later, completely unaffected by the man already in there.

"Where were you?" Miya inquired, mostly to have something to say.

"All over," came the reply. Aki crossed the floor and shut himself in his room.

Miya had to smile. Sometimes he forgot about the age difference between them, but then on days like this, it was hard not to notice that the younger man was a teenager still. He yawned, grabbing for the bottle and drinking the rest of the water.

His phone was silent as death, and the only audible sounds were from the water trickling down the tiles and drain in the bathroom.

15. Punch Drunk

He hadn't heard anything. It had been three days since that night at work, and four since he'd last been at Miura's house. Irritation had given way to worry. Perhaps it was time to stop hoping that this would actually lead anywhere.

So he was more than a little surprised when the two of them ran into each other complete at random. He'd been in a part of the city he didn't usually frequent, but it was still not in the area where Miura lived, so he was surprised when he spotted the other man across the street. They were both standing on opposite sides of a crossing, and rather than crossing the street, Miya remained standing, watching as the teacher came closer, and finally all the way over the street.

"Satoru!" he exclaimed, surprise written all over his handsome, but tired-looking face.

"Hey," Miya said, feeling incredibly awkward all of a sudden.

"What are you doing in this part of the city?"

"Same goes for you. This isn't anywhere near your neighborhood."

"My school is nearby, so I always take this route home."

"Oh." Miya realized he knew nothing about where the guy worked, or maybe he'd been told but either he'd forgotten or it hadn't seemed relevant at that point. "I see."

"Are you busy?"

He shook his head. "Not really, I was just running some errands. Why?"

"Would you like to walk with me? We'll be obstructing traffic if we keep standing here." He gently grabbed Miya by the arm, leading him out of the way.

"Sure but..." He couldn't very well ask why Miura hadn't called him. He bit his tongue and silently walked next to the teacher, carefully distancing himself from him. As expected, there was no reaction to that.

"How have you been?"

"Fine I guess," he shrugged. "Been working a lot. Hung out with some friends."

Aren't you going to ask me why I haven't shown up?

"I was…"

"Yes?" He mentally cursed. Was he being too obvious?

"No, I'm surprised to see you. That's all. I'm glad you're okay."

Things were definitely awkward. It was like spending time apart had set them back in time. He didn't like it. He felt nervous.

"Have you eaten?" Miya tried.

"I was actually going to shop for groceries right now, for dinner."

"How about I treat you for once?" Miya urged, smiling hopefully up at the taller man.

He didn't have to look for the hesitation. It came before the excuse did; "I don't think I'm up for it. But how about you come back to my place? We'll prepare something together."

"I'm a lousy cook, remember?"

Miya was glad though. Glad that he was invited at least. "I can't stay over. But I'll take you up on that offer. I'm starving."

He said it all in one breath; as if to conceal that he was purposely mentioning the possibility of sleeping over while they were amongst people. He didn't see if Miura responded to it though, and he felt a little mean for inwardly testing him in this way.

"You will have to come shopping with me first though—do you want anything in particular?"

"What were you planning on making? I don't want to be a nuisance."

"Who said you would be?"

Wasn't the tone a bit more tense than usual?

"No, I was just… I don't want you to exhaust yourself."

"What do you want then?"

You. He almost said it out loud but stopped himself, and merely licked his lips, continuing to gaze at the man at his side as they walked towards the closest supermarket. Miya's body already craved for the other man's lips on his, for his gentle touches and warm embrace, as if he'd already gotten far too used to it. He tugged on his sleeves, forcing a smile. "Actually, I *really* want *sukiyaki*. It's almost winter."

"It's September."

"Almost winter."

"And there's only two of us."

"Shunsuke," he said, the name feeling strange on his tongue, "you've got to loosen up… *Live* a little."

"Fine," the teacher sighed. "We'll make *sukiyaki*. It's been a while since I've had it."

"Well of course if you only eat it in winter."

"You're so rebellious," Miura replied, his lips curving into a wry, becoming smile.

Going grocery-shopping together felt nice. Miya pushed the cart, leaning on it with his elbows, propelling it forwards between the aisles, while Miura picked out the ingredients. They didn't talk much as they shopped, but he didn't mind. He briefly wondered what people thought, seeing them together.

Miura was dressed in his usual way, looking respectable and completely like an adult. Meanwhile, Miya was dressed like some obscure teenager. Not thinking that he'd run into the man, he hadn't exactly dressed for the occasion, and so he was wearing a pair of Aki's pants, along with one of his standard tank tops, with an old tee thrown over. It was too big for him and was constantly slipping down his left shoulder, revealing his pale skin. He didn't feel ashamed, but he didn't think it looked right for the two of them to be together like this. It probably wouldn't be good news if this was close to the neighborhood where Miura worked; couldn't teachers get in trouble for this kind of thing? It was probably a lot like how students weren't supposed to loiter around after school or hang around delinquent types while wearing their uniforms.

Miya had never cared much about what others thought, and

he'd probably been rebellious in that sense ever since his youth, but it was different if it affected someone else in a really negative way. The bubble he resided within with his work and circle of friends made the outside world unfamiliar when it came to these kinds of things.

They were definitely an odd couple—he knew that. And although they weren't at the level of being an actual couple at this point, he could clearly see how their differences were in violation of those prospects.

He sighed audibly, and Miura turned to look at him, slight worry visible in his deep, auburn eyes.

"Are you okay?"

"It's fine," Miya said, shrugging. "I'm just really hungry. And the light in here is so bright. I'm nocturnal, remember?"

The other man chuckled softly. "I understand. We'll get out of here quickly. My back is killing me, so I really want to get home."

In any other situation a standard reply would have been *"Is that my fault?"* but he clamped his mouth shut and thought that in any case, two men shopping together already looked suspicious enough as it was. To be honest, he was really surprised at the way their meeting had turned out, but he wasn't going to complain.

They took the train to Motomachi, and due to the afternoon rush, there were no seats available, so they were forced to stand. The train cart was cramped, and they kept bumping into each other.

"Sorry," Miura would mouth, smiling awkwardly at him every time their bodies brushed in the throng. Miya wondered if he was the only one feeling a little excited by the whole ordeal— the eye contact and the way their bodies would grind lightly together when the train rumbled over the tracks. He probably wasn't, but he might be the only one who'd admit to it.

They exited, flushed and flustered, at the right station and made their way back to Miura's apartment complex.

It was as if the other man exhaled in relief as soon as they locked themselves in behind his front door. He dropped the plastic bags on the floor to remove his shoes.

Miya picked them up, going into the kitchen, proceeding to unpack everything.

"It's the least I can do," he said, "considering you'll have to do the actual cooking."

"Even you can put meat into the pot, I'm sure," Miura remarked dryly. "Just get the hotplate and pot out, okay? I'll go change."

He disappeared into the bedroom. Miya watched him out of corner of his eye while digging around in the cupboards. He saw traces of that muscular back, still adorned with light pink scratches. He swallowed. Part of him wanted to go over to the man, press his lips against that warm back and rest his forehead between his shoulder blades. But he couldn't. Not now.

What am I even doing here? he thought. He was confused. Miura was acting like nothing had happened—which by all means was true, but he must have noticed the awkward tension from before.

And why hadn't he said anything?

Miura came back wearing a surprisingly plain T-shirt. It was red, which was probably the first color he'd ever seen the man apart from plain white or black. Even his underwear had been black.

"Red looks good on you," he said, placing the hotplate and pot on the small table. "You should wear more colors."

"You think so?"

He nodded.

"What about you? You're always wearing black, aren't you?"

"It's just that you've only happened to see me in my work clothes." Miya tugged on the shirt. "See? This color is called white."

"White isn't a color though."

Miya rolled his eyes. And then a firm hand gripped him by the upper arm, pulling him closer, lips pressing against the top of his head.

And he completely melted. He felt like jelly. He looked up,

their gazes meeting.

"What are we doing?" he asked, breathlessly.

"Weren't we going to make dinner?" Miura smiled, stroking him over the hair. "I will teach you how."

Of course.

He didn't bother pursuing it further. It was too early. Or maybe too late?

Although he loved *sukiyaki*, and Miura really knew his way around the hotplate, it didn't taste as good as he'd wanted it to.

And things would continue in that bad direction in which his gut feeling was already headed.

"So," Miura said, slurping up the last of his noodles. "Can I ask how you ended up working in that place?"

It was a very sudden question, even more so coming from someone who was always so held back and composed. He'd only had one can of beer at that. It must have been on his mind for some time based on the resolute way he asked.

"Why this all of a sudden?"

"I'm curious; it can't be what you originally wanted to do."

"Why's that?" Miya replied sourly, drinking a gulp from his beer can.

"Well... I just thought that most people wanted something more than just to wait tables for a living."

Miya shrugged stubbornly. He'd heard this before. His last relationship had been with someone who'd wanted to change him. That man had sought him out because of what he did, and they'd met because of the club as well, and although it was ill advised to get involved with clients to the point of dating them, he'd allowed himself to fall victim to the pampering and the compliments. But then the man had changed, starting to act as if nothing he did was good enough anymore; he was too flirtatious, not ambitious enough, too vain and not attentive enough. Before the end of their relation, which hadn't been longer than about nine months, he'd been a complete mess of contradictive feelings and emotions and convinced that the other man was what society referred to as a psychopath. It had almost seemed that way. Luckily, he hadn't kept coming around the club, and if he had, the manager would have made sure to throw him out. It was especially thanks to this incident that he'd started getting defensive as soon as someone questioned his profession—that, and his parents' view on the whole thing.

"I used to want to study… something, but I never knew what. I never felt at home anywhere, but at the club I do." he replied, fighting to remain composed.

"You feel at home?"

"Don't you at your workplace?"

"I work at a school." Miura grabbed his chopsticks, fishing out more meat and vegetables from the pot. "Nothing there feels like home. It's nice, but it can be very stressful. I do thrive there, but I wouldn't go that far."

"I love my job," Miya said resolutely. "And my colleagues."

They regarded each other over the cluttered wooden table and the steaming pot of meat and vegetables.

"It might not be somewhere in high standards, and we're certainly not regarded as a contributor to society," he continued, allowing himself to ramble as if he was taking out all his confusion and frustration on this particular subject, "but we're all enjoying it down there. Every one of my colleagues, even the managers, are my friends. And I love them."

His words must have made some sort of impact. Miura looked genuinely surprised at the words that came tumbling from his lips like pearls on a string.

"You know, you teach for a living. Your job is to make sure others have a future, to teach kids valuable knowledge and also lessons for the future. School is a place for social skills and developing one's own persona," he said, swallowing. "But what we do is more than wait tables. We're company for those who can't be themselves anywhere else, and for each other when our families have written us off, or when our lovers have turned their backs on us. I guess you could say we're each other's family."

He felt incredibly emotional. It wasn't just about Miura. Not at all. It was about his own life, and his friends, and Aki, who didn't sleep properly at night, and Naruse, who had failed his medical exam.

"You call them your family." Miura wasn't following.

Miya nodded, placing his bowl on the table. "I guess you could think that's a little weird, after all... we're a bit incestuous." He laughed bitterly, picking up his beer to chug it completely. He didn't want to see Miura's face.

What are you saying, you idiot?

But it was out now. If Miura had had any suspicions that they were all sleeping with each other, the cat was out of the bag. It felt relieving somehow—liberating to have said it at long last. The first step in going into a relationship with anyone in his group would be for any outsider to accept the relationship they all shared.

"Incestuous?" The man's flat voice was like an echo.

Miya clenched his eyes shut.

"Is that why you're upset? Because you feel like I was stepping all over them?"

The way he spoke. It was probably the voice he used when he attempted to mediate between middle-schoolers who got in arguments with each other.

"Weren't you?"

"I didn't *mean* to. I just wanted to get to know you."

"Well, now you do," Miya sighed, still staring at the floor. He felt sick.

More than you'd ever want to know, I'm sure.

"Satoru..."

Miya shook his head. It was as if his own words had knocked the air out of him. If he had been drunk, then at least he could have defended this kind of outburst.

"Why didn't you call me?" Miya muttered.

"What?"

He didn't know if Miura hadn't heard him speak out loud, or if he was asking because he didn't understand what Miya meant.

"Never mind," he sighed. "I'm sorry. I'm not feeling very well... I think I'm going to head home and change. I've got work tonight."

He stood, and left Miura confused, sitting on the floor next to the table.

He hoped that Miura wouldn't get up and grab him. He needed air.

He left the apartment, already gasping for breath, trembling as he ran down the stairs and out into the fresh, cool air. He leaned against the brick wall, catching his breath again, swallowing several times in a row.

What are you doing, you idiot? Are you trying to ruin everything?

***

Luckily, he wasn't the only one with problems.

Coming into work that night, he felt sullen and worn out, but the friends he'd defended so fiercely just hours earlier were all there to cheer him up. Of course, they didn't know that, but the second he came in, he was met by loud voices and roaring laughter.

"It is *not* funny!" Ayase shrilled, sitting on the couch in the backroom, looking just as sullen as Miya felt.

"What's going on?" Miya asked, throwing himself down next to the other man.

Hiiro was doubled over from laughing. "Ay-chan had a little trip to the doctor's this morning."

"Shut up!" The youngster's pale cheeks were glowing with crimson.

"Oh no, you finally got yourself knocked up?" Miya nudged him playfully in the arm.

"Shut uuup," the younger groaned.

"He just had to get rid of a pesky little problem – didn't you?" Kyo was laughing as he spoke, covering his mouth with his hand, which was futile as long as he was practically choking on his own laughter.

"Ay-chan?" Miya grinned, casting an amused glance towards the younger man sitting next to him. "Care to elaborate?"

"It's an *infection*! Can we all calm down?"

More laughter. "So does this mean it's time for an outing downtown to the clinic?" Hiiro was blunt as always.

"Yay, fieldtrip!"

Only his friends would be this laid back about something like this.

"How stupid can you get?" Kiyoshi brushed past them on his way into the office, muttering under his breath. Miya snickered.

"Kiyoshi's got a point though." Naruse slid down next to them. "You should be more careful. Nobody knows what you might catch these days."

"I *was* careful! It was a one-time thing! And the only reason I'm telling these idiots is because it's required by the doctors that you inform other partners."

At that, they all burst out laughing.

"Somehow, I don't think *we* are what they had in mind when they said 'partners.'" Hiiro came around the back of the couch, gripping Ayase by the shoulder. "How was it?"

"Well you know, uncomfortable. But I got a prescription, so it should be fine." Ayase grimaced.

"In other words, you're quarantined?"

"Pretty much," he sighed. "I'll stay at the bar for safe measure."

"Thank you, Ay-chan." Miya tilted his head to the side, resting it on Ayase's shoulder.

"For what?"

"I thought *my* day sucked."

More stifled sniggers and suppressed laughter followed.

"Stop laughing! You should all get tested as well you know! Just in case!"

They laughed, dismissing him. At first glance, things might seem wild and risqué at the club, but even if they were all involved with each other, they were always careful and made sure to get tested frequently—just in case. Still, accidents happened and could easily affect all of them should one catch something. It was a little nerve-wracking to be honest, considering the big risks that were out there, and even though they knew better, it was easier to laugh out loud at situations like these than to take it all in and worry about more serious diseases.

His body slumped further. Wasn't this just peachy? As

hilarious as the thought of Ayase getting swabbed was, the notion of his conversation with the teacher earlier, or rather his "monologue," clearly stood out in his mind. Wasn't this kind of thing precisely what he'd wanted to defend himself and the rest of them against?

"What's up with you?" Naruse tugged on his hair. "Why does your day suck?"

"No reason," he shrugged, looking away. "I just got a bit ahead of myself and got upset with someone I didn't want to argue with."

"Why would you do that?" Ayase sighed, looking down at him as he tilted his head to the side, resting it against Miya's.

"Says you, who had unsafe sex like some stupid teenager," Miya replied gruffly.

"Miya, play nice." Naruse attempted to mediate, as was his role in the group.

Miya groaned. "I don't know. I got upset. It was stupid."

Was it though? Based on recent events, it was probably relevant; although he wasn't sure he remembered in the heat of the moment what had triggered the whole ordeal.

"In any case," Naruse said softly, stroking him over the hair, "there's nothing that can be done with that right now. What's done is done, right?"

Miya sighed. "Yeah…"

"How about this, we both get out early tonight, right? Let's go somewhere, have some fun."

He looked at the blond man. Naruse's idea of fun was often different from the others' perception of the word. He enjoyed drinking as much as the rest of them, but he was more held back, always composed. His calm temper was like a safe haven compared to how the rest of their group acted, and he seemed to almost always know what to say. Even though Miya was older than him, Naruse often seemed to be the eldest. It felt comforting to know that he'd be there to listen. Even if Hiiro would be the one who knew most about the situation at hand, he did feel more comfortable discussing it with Naruse.

"Okay," he nodded. "Let's go somewhere. But promise not

to be a total drag this time, okay?"

"What's that supposed to mean?"

"Let me drink you under the table." He grinned, nudging the blond.

"We'll see." Naruse shook his head, smirking.

He didn't seem opposed to it. Maybe he wasn't having the best day either.

They pulled themselves together and got to work, readying the club before opening time. After that, everything ran smoothly, with clients coming in, drinks and snacks being served and music playing louder than what was necessary for a Wednesday night with mostly only regulars coming in.

He and Naruse went out as soon as their shift ended, and Miya felt relieved that none of the others were able to come with them. In case he felt like spilling the beans about the recent events in his life, he didn't want to have the entire gang there listening in and turning it into some kind of circus.

***

"So, what's on your mind?" Naruse looked calmly at him from across the table. They'd gone to a bar nearby where their group rarely went. Since Maki's was close by, nobody ever went anywhere else, which was precisely why they'd gone here, to talk in peace.

"How do you know something's on my mind?"

"Don't be silly." Naruse smiled at him. "You told me you were upset earlier—isn't that what you wanted to talk about?"

"You were the one who asked me out though," Miya replied, waving a waitress over and asking her to bring a couple of drinks. He didn't feel like having any himself for once though; his mind was already clouded enough as it was. Plus, Naruse drove, so one of them had to stay sober. "It's my treat," he offered, when the drinks were brought. "I told you I'd—"

"Get me drunk?" Naruse smiled, sipping at one of the glasses already.

"Not really, just... You don't seem like you get to relax a

whole lot, with the rest of us being so clingy."

The other man chuckled quietly. "You're not clingy," he said. "And they depend just as much on you as they do on me. You *are* the oldest after all."

Miya frowned. "Can you please not remind me?"

Naru smiled tiredly.

"But yeah. Feel free to drop your guard a little. It's okay if you want to drink. I can drive afterwards."

Naruse eyed him suspiciously, well knowing that his driving wasn't the best. Then again, Naruse's car was a heap of junk. If he dented it, it wasn't like anyone would notice.

"It's rare for you to drink though," Miya said, watching the other man, his gaze curious. "At least like this."

"Said the one who treated me."

"You know what I mean... Are *you* okay?"

Naruse shrugged. "I'm okay, I just feel a little tense lately, lots of stuff going on in my family. Nothing to worry about."

Miya nodded slowly. He didn't know much about Naruse's family, or anything else really, but he knew that the man's parents were fairly old. They'd been pretty much middle-aged when he'd been born, and it was for their sake he had studied medicine—at least Miya thought so. It seemed like the kind of thing parents would want. He hoped nothing was wrong. He couldn't place all of his worries on Naruse's shoulders if the other man was already upset about something.

"Are you sure.?"

"It's just some minor things, but it's enough to give me a headache. But don't worry about me, it's nothing serious, or I'd be going home, wouldn't I?"

Miya nodded slowly. "Is... your relationship with them good?"

"I guess so." Naruse's slim, graceful fingers curled around the tall glass, nails tapping against the smooth surface. "I mean, we get along. No hard feelings, and I'm an only child so..."

"That's so odd though." Miya narrowed his eyes curiously. "Even though you're an only child, you're so dependable."

"For others you mean?"

Miya nodded, recalling the conversation Aki and he had had earlier about this topic, about that kids who grew up without siblings were often spoiled, or very self-sufficient. Naruse seemed to be the latter, but he was also a rock for his friends, and evidently his own family as well.

"You're always supporting the rest of us when we need something, and even now you're here even though you're worrying about your family."

"I didn't say I was worried. I said I had a headache," he corrected. "But yeah. Since they had me so late, I learned to fend for myself since I didn't want to be a burden to them. But they're also dependent on me now that they're older and need help with errands and such, although they're usually too proud to ask for help yet."

Naru laughed a little. There was a loving gleam in his eyes, but at the same time, it was also sad—a familiar sadness that Miya knew all too well.

"They don't know, do they?" he said.

Naruse gulped down the rest of his drink, reaching for the next. He seemed bothered by the question. Miya was about to tell him not to mind when he replied.

"No, they don't."

That was honestly surprising. Out of all of them, Naruse was the one who seemed to have his life the most together, who seemed to be in total control. He was so natural and honest; it was shocking to hear that he still kept something like this from his parents.

"How could I tell them?" he sighed. "I know how they feel on the subject, and I don't want to hurt them or upset them."

"But that's—" Miya gawked at him. "Aren't you in *pain?*"

It was the only word he could find to describe his immediate feeling.

The blond man shrugged. "You get used to it," he said. "Besides, I'm not ashamed. I'm not hiding myself away, am I? It's just that I don't want to involve them in this part of my life because I know it would just be a lot of trouble for everyone. They need me, and I want to be able to support them when they grow old."

He spoke so lightly, yet with so much clarity.

"So what do you tell them? What about medical school?"

Naruse shook his head, blond tousles dancing and swaying as he did. "It's true I wanted to do that for them—as well as for myself because I wanted it. But I realized I wasn't cut out for that kind of work. Maybe I could be like a pediatrician or something, a general practitioner, but the study itself is so wide, I had a hard time managing it. They understood when I dropped out. And they know that I'm working at a bar, so they don't ask much."

Miya wondered if it was because they didn't want to know, because they were ashamed, or if it was because they didn't think it mattered, since it was such a trivial job. His own parents never let go of the idea that he should get a *proper* occupation.

"I'm sorry," he swallowed. "I didn't mean to pry."

"You didn't," Naruse replied. "You asked, and I let you. And I'm glad you decided to buy me drinks; I think I needed the relaxation."

Miya regarded the attractive male across the table. He looked more relaxed indeed, his shoulders had dropped, and his neck seemed less tense. Plus, now that he was out of his work clothes, dressed in a plaid, red shirt and jeans, he looked more comfortable. Not that he didn't look stunning at work; he just seemed far too down to earth for a lot of the looks they demanded at the club.

He smiled. "No problem. I'll get you some more if you want."

"Let's just take it easy, shall we?" Naruse waved his hand dismissively. His cheeks were already carrying a telltale pink, and the night was still young. "I don't intend to go overboard tonight, but it's nice to be able to do this for once."

Miya nodded, tugging on a string in his hoodie, which he was wearing over the shirt he'd worn at work; he hadn't bothered changing.

"And now that you've tricked me into telling you about my issues, it's your turn."

"Tricked you?" Miya grinned crookedly. "You were the one who started rambling. Besides, you didn't tell me squat! Not about what's causing you the headache."

"Well, it's none of your business."

"Sure, but don't claim you told me everything then," he replied teasingly, sipping at the tea he'd ordered for himself. It burned the tip of his tongue, and felt unfamiliar and bitter to the taste compared to the sweet drinks he was used to consuming.

"Miya," Naruse cocked his head to the side, smiling that crooked, comforting smile of his, "what happened earlier today?"

Miya sighed deeply, placing both elbows on the table. He leaned forward, resting his head on his arms, looking down into the polished tabletop and exhaling slowly.

"There's..." he stopped himself, sighing deeper. "I don't know what I'm doing," he finally said, his voice hoarse in his throat. He coughed, rising back up into a sitting position. He felt exposed, and he hadn't even said anything yet.

"I don't even know how to talk about it because it's so obscure. Do you remember that guy I used to go out with?"

"The obsessive one?" Naruse seemed to have a clear recollection of the other man. A shudder ran through his body at the mention. "Is he bothering you again?"

"No, nothing like that..." Miya averted his eyes, shaking his head. "I just got to thinking about him earlier today because I was with this guy..."

"Guy?"

"Don't repeat things I say," he bit the other man off. "It's irritating."

"Sorry." Naruse leaned back in his seat, regarding him with golden brown eyes, a slightly concerned look running over his attractive face.

"I think I might... like this guy even..." He stared down into the table, feeling as if he was a teenager again, unable to put words on his own emotions, and feeling utterly embarrassed for exposing himself in this way, presenting his uncertainties to another person. But Naruse didn't say anything. He watched him in silence, waiting.

"Well, we were together this afternoon and we... *I* got into a heated discussion."

He noted the other man's lip quirking a little.

"I know. I know." Miya frowned, well aware of how he had a habit of reeling himself up and going off on some poor soul without warning. "And I don't know... I got really upset. And I think he was upset as well, and it's just really awkward."

"So you're bothered by it? That you went a little too far and think you might've scared him off?"

"Not so much scared him off..." He hesitated.

More like he didn't want to be with me in the first place?

"But more like..." he tried finding the words. "We're so different. And I didn't want to create more distance, you know? But I think I did, and then I panicked. So I just left."

"I think that's very common to do when you think you fucked up with someone you really like," Naruse said matter-of-factly.

Miya sighed heavily. "Yeah, I know, but I don't even know what I want."

"It's hard, isn't it?" Naruse sighed. "When something like that happens?"

"What about you? You're never in a relationship either."

"How do you know?" Naruse replied, smiling coyly.

"What, when?"

"Occasionally," the blond replied. "I don't convey everything to you guys you know. I guess for the same reason. If I get hurt, then I get to deal with it without getting others mixed up in it, or you know having everyone's nose in my business before it's serious. And it rarely gets serious."

"It doesn't, does it?" Miya frowned. "But you're not seeing anyone right now, are you?"

Naruse shook his head. "Obviously it's been a while, but I guess I'm hoping to find someone at some point. It's no rush though, especially not as long as I can't let on to my parents."

"That's true." Miya nodded, sipping at his tea. It had cooled down and tasted better as well. His mind felt refreshed, as if the herbs had cleared things up a little, or maybe it was the relief of being able to discuss his thoughts with someone, even though he wasn't fully letting Naruse know what was going on. It was too complicated, or rather too undetermined for the time being for him to be completely open.

"It's just... I love this life, you know?" he ran his fingertips against the porcelain cup, licking his lips. "Every time I'm in a relationship, I feel so obstructed; it's like I can't breathe sometimes. I need my freedom."

The other man nodded, listening.

"But then, it's like... I just want to spend time with this guy and see where it leads."

"Then do so; it won't hurt. Or are you afraid of something new?" Naruse questioned. "It's not like you to be opposed to a challenge."

"I know," Miya replied, "but it's not like me to place all my bets on one card either. I feel like this is something like messing with fire, knowing I'm going to get burned. But..." he sighed in frustration again, "I'm just really annoyed I allowed myself to get carried away earlier. At this rate, I'll sabotage myself before I even get anywhere."

"Maybe you do it because you're afraid of getting somewhere," Naruse suggested, looking thoughtful.

"I've never really wanted to... settle down." He almost whispered the words, and they felt alien on his tongue, completely new to him. "And I'm not thinking of it now either, but I mean... I just... If I fuck it up, I can always return to the way things are now, but in that case, will it even be worth it?"

"There's only one way to find out, isn't there?" Naruse challenged.

"I guess." Miya hesitated, wondering if he should keep going, air the thought that frightened him most of all. It was one thing to be fascinated or even infatuated with someone, but the moment those feelings were allowed to grow and prosper, they'd take on a life of their own, and everything could get so unbelievably painful.

"We haven't talked about it," he confessed. "About what we

are, or whatever. I'm okay like that, as it allows me to kind of keep my own life, you know?"

The other man nodded, understanding as always. Of course he did. He was the same way. Where they came from, monogamy wasn't a thing. Not unless it had been previously decided on. Even the bartenders were able to cut loose on occasion and invite a third party into their room—very rarely, but if the mood was right.

Why was he even thinking of that? It had nothing to do with that.

"I hate this," he mumbled. "I don't like being this uncertain about something."

Naruse looked sympathetic, standing up to come sit next to him on the other side of the table, wrapping his arm lovingly around Miya's shoulders.

"Of course you don't," Naruse replied softly. "I wouldn't either. Just don't panic."

"I'm trying," he mumbled. "But after today well... I accidentally mentioned... *us.*"

Not as in the two of them, but as in *all* of them.

"Oh." Naruse's voice sounded as if it was stuck in his throat.

"Yeah."

Gloom reigned over the two of them.

"What did he say?"

"Nothing. I kinda freaked out after that."

"So you don't know what he thinks?"

"Sure I do," he sighed. "I said it before, didn't I? How can anyone want to be with someone who sleeps with someone else on a regular basis? I'm not exactly marriage material."

"I thought you were just fooling around?"

"It's an expression," he said, deadpan. "But either way..."

"Miya," Naruse kissed him on the temple, "give yourself more credit. I think you're just really upset and confused, so you're over-thinking things. You wouldn't fall for someone who wasn't smarter than that."

"May I remind you of who just came up earlier? Or any of my other ex-disasters?"

"Those relations ended for other reasons. Try not to be so negative."

"Maybe that's what I want though," Miya sighed, leaning back against the blond man. "For it to fail, so I can go back to being myself."

"Then what are you afraid of?"

"Hn?"

"If the worst thing that can happen is that it fails and your life returns to normal, what else is there to worry about? If it works out, you'll be happy, and if it doesn't, then you'll be yourself again, like you say."

Maybe he was tired. Maybe he was just looking for an easy way out, for a sentence that could fix the chaos reigning inside of his head, but what Naruse said actually made some sort of sense.

"Maybe that's true..." he mused. "I think maybe you have a point."

He wanted there to be a point. He didn't want to deal with these idiotic conflicting feelings anymore, especially not when things could be worse.

He thought about how the day had turned out; he'd been upset that the other man hadn't called him, but when they met up, it was as if nothing had changed. Even with the awkwardness, but Miura had always had an awkward approach from the very beginning. Hadn't they had a good time over dinner until he'd exploded?

They had. And that had been on *his* account.

"Are you sure you're not older than me?" Miya smirked. "You're so wise, Naru."

He said the other's name playfully, rolling it off his tongue, whispering it into the man's ear, noting how the little hairs in his neck stood on end in reaction to the sensation.

"You wish!" Naruse shrugged him off, turning a dazzling smile towards him.

"You're drunk," Miya chuckled, touching their foreheads together. "You should have another. Just for the heck of it."

He waved for the waitress, placing another order.

"You're terrible," Naruse grinned, "but since you insist. I can't say I mind letting go of all kinds of responsibility for one night."

"So you say, but aren't you here playing hobby psychologist with me?" Miya countered, smirking. "Which I appreciate so much by the way."

"What are friends for?" Naruse shrugged. "Apart from getting you drunk on a Wednesday night of course."

Miya grinned. "I'm sorry though. I feel like a total idiot for spilling this all over you—for no reason at that. I was just being paranoid."

"Yeah well, it happens to the best of us," Naruse assured. "Besides, based on how Hiiro's been hinting left and right, he hasn't made this much easier for you, has he now?"

"Who needs enemies when you've got friends like him?" Miya remarked dryly, bursting into laughter. He felt much better now. Better because he was finally able to puncture the infected swelling in his chest and pour his worries onto someone who not only listened but made him see things in a more constructive light instead of just plowing around in his own mess constantly. Also, he really liked Miura, and he wanted to keep seeing him, at least for a while, no matter what that meant. He really did think so. Wasn't he the only one who'd been upset to begin with anyway? And with that realization clear in his mind, he felt his shoulders slump and his head lightening.

The next hour was spent just chatting with one another at the table in the bar before they got up and left around thirty minutes past midnight, when they got in the car. At first, Miya thought about crashing at Naru's place, but then he decided he didn't feel like it, so he asked to borrow the car until the next day, as he wanted to run some errands anyway. Naruse was okay with that, seeing as the club would be closed the next day, and he foresaw himself sleeping the night off, so it was okay by him.

"As long as you don't crash, okay? I can't afford to fix that old wreck."

Miya had agreed and promised infinitely, and got himself back home by one in the morning. The tea had cleared his mind, and he didn't feel sleepy just yet, so he plopped down on the couch, turning the TV on. Feeling inspired by the night's events, he even picked up his phone and wrote a quick text before he had time to regret it.

"I'm sorry about today. Don't know what got into me."

He sent it without looking and didn't expect a reply. It was too late for that, but he felt better in any case. He thought about Naru, feeling grateful as well as puzzled at his revelations. And then he thought about poor Ayase and his humiliation. He chuckled to himself. What a day this had been—truthfully.

***

He was on the sofa still when the door to the apartment opened.

He turned to look at his roommate, only to see that he wasn't alone. In the hallway, Aki was staggering next to a white-haired teen dressed in a school uniform.

"Welcome home..." he said as the teen stumbled over to greet him in form of a very demonstrative kiss. Miya allowed it for a while but was completely baffled at this turn of events.

The teenager in the hall looked completely taken aback as well. Understandably enough, being dragged here in the middle of the night and then being faced with the two of them and their usual antics. Miya pulled away and asked some probing questions.

To begin with, he was able to drag out of them that the kid with the dyed hair was seventeen, which was okay—better than fifteen, but still. Then he learned that he'd had absolutely no intention of coming here, and that he had no idea what to do from here on; now that he found himself in their house, obviously knowing nothing about Miya's existence, or their relationship, or how to get home.

Miya felt for him. And he felt a little annoyed at his roommate for being so careless. It wasn't odd at all that Aki might want to socialize with someone his own age for once, but this was hardly the way to do it. Moreover, he was profusely drunk, like so often lately. A slight worry came over Miya, and he stood from the sofa.

He tore his roommate away from the other teenager as he was embracing him from behind, clearly with ulterior motives.

"I'll go to bed with you," he said. "Come on."

He told the kid he could sleep in the living room and gestured towards the pull-out couch while taking Aki into his room.

Closing the door behind them, he glared furiously at the younger man. "What are you thinking?"

Aki shrugged.

"He could get in serious trouble for this, do you know that?"

"Calm down." Aki dropped down on the bed, looking tired. "He didn't mind."

"It doesn't seem to me like he even had a choice in the matter. Who is he anyway?"

"An acquaintance, okay?" Aki's lips curved mischievously. "Jealous?"

"Shut up, no." Miya sighed, sliding down next to him. "I don't need to add your antics to my list of concerns for the time being."

"Then don't," came the cool reply as the younger man pulled his shirt over his head, throwing it to the floor, revealing his thin, pale frame.

Miya looked away. He knew that body all too well, and it seemed wrong somehow.

"I worry about you, okay? And now I'm worrying about your sense of sanity," he sighed. "You can't bring schoolboys home in the middle of the night..."

"I told you—"

"It doesn't matter!" he stated, shaking his head. There was no point in arguing, especially not when Aki was in this state. He seemed exhausted and far too intoxicated to reason with. He didn't seem to be feeling too great either, pale and gusty as he was.

"Are you okay?" Miya asked instead.

"Don't bother with it," came the sour reply. The teen's

trousers pooled around his feet on the floor before he pulled his legs up into the bed and turned away from him, facing the wall. He was still wearing his socks and underwear. Miya sighed again.

Something was definitely bothering him, but he had no business sticking his nose into it. And he had enough on his mind as it was. He'd said that he'd take the younger teen, whom Aki had referred to as "Precious" to school in the morning, and figured he'd try to get some sleep.

The conversation with Naruse was still clear in his mind, but he wasn't able to process his own thoughts at this point. He'd thought he was done worrying for the day, and then this situation came along. And he wondered why his roommate seemed so miserable, and the boy he'd brought with him seemed to feel the exact same way. The way he'd looked at Miya... there had been real concern in his eyes, and likewise, the uncomfortable expression on his face when he and Aki had kissed each other. He wondered if Aki had noticed it as well, or if it was just that he was so perceptive of these things.

Miya lay down next to the raven-haired teen, still dressed in his pajama pants and the colorful top. Although he was certain the younger man disdained it, he reached out and touched him, resting his palm on Aki's upper arm, and nuzzling softly against the back of his neck. The teen reeked of alcohol and cigarettes, and something convulsed in him—how messed up this really was in some ways.

He felt how tense Aki was and wondered why. He softly kissed the boy's neck and thought that in many ways, Aki *was* still a boy. It wasn't so odd that he'd brought someone similar back home with him, even though they seemed very different merely on first-glance basis. Of course, he wasn't one to talk, considering how he was going out, or whatever it was to be called, with someone who was polar opposites of himself. He sighed loudly.

"You're not the only one, kiddo," he mumbled against stiff, hairspray-scented strands of midnight. "My day's been hard as well."

"Mmh, great for you." It sounded like the teenager was on his way to pass out.

He smiled against his neck, curling his fingers a little firmer around his thin upper arm.

"Sweet dreams," Miya whispered, noting how tired he himself was starting to feel, his body growing heavy.

He slowly nodded off next to the teenager, who was already breathing heavily in his sleep in that drunken way.

His dreams were noisy and confusing, and then Naru was there, and he relaxed, and a warmth spread inside of him, even though that might just be the heat created by their bodies as they lay pressed tightly together on the narrow bed.

***

The next morning, he got up before Aki was awake, noting that the teen still seemed to be completely out of it, sleeping with his mouth half-open and his darkly made-up eyes tightly clenched shut beneath a messy fringe.

He got up quietly, stating that he'd only gotten a couple of hours of sleep; the clock on the kitchen wall said six in the morning. The living room was bleakly illuminated by the sheen from the window and the lamps beneath the kitchen cupboards. The teenager on the sofa was fast asleep as well, looking peaceful, despite the events the night before. Miya smiled crookedly, turning on the coffee machine, trying to be as quiet as he could while preparing coffee and some kind of breakfast with what little they had of ingredients. He yawned, feeling incredibly tired still.

He wondered what Miura would have thought about this, and the realization made him put down the coffee mug he'd been taking out of the cupboard and go over to his phone, which had been left on the table since last night. He made sure not to disturb the serene teenager, having promised to wake him up at seven, as he reached for his phone. The display was blank, showing no sign of a reply. He wasn't all that surprised, but it was still a bit hurtful, since he'd apologized and all. But on the other hand, he was probably just being overly paranoid, and he'd decided yesterday that it was better to see where it went and accept whatever happened than endlessly fretting about it. Plus, it was still early. Teachers probably weren't all about checking their phones first thing in the morning.

"Aren't you just making up excuses for yourself?" a voice in his head asked him in a loud, annoying tone. He tuned it out. A quick glance over to the sleeping form on the sofa made him think of other things. It was, after all, better to be where he was than in the position this kid found himself in. He wondered what this kid's perception was, what he felt about Miya's connection with Aki, and how it had impacted him last night.

He couldn't help but feel curious.

The teen stirred slightly, and afraid of waking him, Miya moved away and went back into the kitchen, putting the coffee on. He went to the front door and picked up their newspaper. It was Tsuuji who'd subscribed to it to make sure he didn't miss out on any important sports news, but Miya had never bothered to cancel it, even though he rarely read it. But since he couldn't listen to music or watch the morning news, he decided it was a good way to make time pass.

Shortly after the door to Aki's room opened, the pale teenager came out into the living area, his hair a mess, his feet bare.

"Morning," Miya said dryly, clicking his tongue. He received something like a grunt in response.

The teen on the couch stirred as Aki strode over to him, looking utterly confused and annoyed. He asked rather rudely what the other teenager was doing there, and the tone between them was anything but friendly.

Miya bit his lip, grabbing a cup of coffee and going over to stop the fray.

"Here, take a shower." He shoved the mug into Aki's hands, well knowing that the younger man didn't like coffee but feeling the need to calm the situation down. He didn't want to witness too much of their private matters, and in any case, it was too early in the morning for this kind of thing.

Aki disappeared into the bathroom with a disgruntled sigh, slamming the door behind him. Miya offered an apologetic look to the white-haired teen, who was getting dressed, looking embarrassed.

While Aki was in the shower, they chatted a little. Miya thought it was awkward for the boy, being exposed like this, especially since he was so straightforward, asking about their relation, if Aki was using him. He could read both annoyance and hesitation in the other's young face, and it pained him.

What was with everyone and getting into these unhealthy relationships and twisted connections at such a young, crucial age? Didn't anyone try to pursue actual happiness anymore?

Still, he could tell that the boy, his name which fittingly turned out to be Yuuki, had guts. It didn't seem like he was unable to fend for himself or if he was so naive he didn't know what he was doing. If he was entirely on board with it was a different matter. He didn't want any coffee but accepted a glass of juice and conveyed to Miya which school he went to.

"Good thing I have a car today then," he said smiling. "I don't mind taking you, since I have to take it back anyway."

"I appreciate that," the teen replied, smiling slightly. He looked really tired, and his eyes were red and irritated from the contacts he was wearing. That probably wasn't healthy.

***

When he drove the boy to the school, they talked more, but he didn't want to impose too much. It was clear that Yuuki, much like his counterpart, to put it that way, wasn't very generous on details when it came to their connection, even though it was obvious that they were sleeping together. It was understandable though, based on how Aki had acted both last night and this morning, as if the other boy wasn't even there.

But still Miya couldn't find it in him to tell the boy that they were just friends—with certain benefits when the chance presented itself. Instead, they talked about random, less private things, and Yuuki apologized for having intruded the previous night.

"We're the ones who should be sorry," Miya replied, chuckling. "Or rather, *he*. I'm gonna apologize on his behalf because he's too moronic to do it himself. He's so selfish he doesn't really see the way his actions might affect others."

"That's okay, I don't really mind."

"Still, I'm glad you're able to argue with him. The kid needs some resistance. We tend to go soft on him because he's younger than us," Miya laughed.

Yuuki looked as if he wanted to ask a question but held it back, staring ahead at the road. Miya searched his face for any kind of emotion. He was often told he was a terrible driver, so fear was as good as any, but the kid's face was perfectly expressionless aside from looking very tired.

"By the way," he asked, the thought hitting him suddenly. "Which middle school did you go to?"

"Why?" Yuuki replied, looking at him with his reddening eyes.

"You should really take those out," Miya said, referring to the contacts, "No reason. I'm just curious."

Yuuki mentioned the school, and Miya chuckled. "Didn't think so."

"Hmm?"

He shook his head. "No, nothing. Left here, yeah?"

He made a hairpin turn, almost missing their exit, but making it at the last moment, someone behind them blaring their horn.

The teen looked a slight bit worried. "Are you sure you should be driving?"

"It's fine. Got my license, didn't I?" he grinned back at the boy.

"I wonder..." the teen replied quietly. Oh yes, definitely an acquaintance of Aki. Miya laughed quietly again.

"What?"

He shook his head, grinning. "Nothing. Listen, keep giving him a hard time, okay?"

Yuuki looked puzzled. That was okay. He didn't need to understand.

"But try not to let him drag you home anymore, at least not on a school night. I might not have a car next time." He winked as the car came to a stop outside the school gates.

"Yeah sure, I'll keep that in mind," the teen replied a little awkwardly. "Thank you for driving me."

"You're very welcome, sweetie." Miya smiled. He was almost tempted to give the teen a hug before letting him go but decided against it. "Now off you go," he said. "Study hard."

Yuuki got out of the car and ran over to the boy Miya recognized as Lau, the love interest of Kiyoshi's younger brother, who often did odd jobs for the managers.

So that's how they knew each other.

"What a mess," he mumbled to himself, turning the keys in the ignition. At least he wasn't young *and* confused anymore, that would probably be too much.

But he envied the confidence these two carried themselves with. He'd also been confident at their age, but much like Naru, there had also been a lot of concern in the way he'd carried himself—thinking about his family and their reputation, at least at first. He'd been uncertain of himself, why else would he have allowed those men to keep their relationships in the dark, hidden away from the world as if they were ashamed?

16. Drowning

Aki hadn't seemed keen on talking much about the schoolboy, and Miya hadn't bothered asking. He'd been preoccupied with his own thoughts. He'd returned the car to Naru, and although he'd been hoping that the blond would drive him back home, he was in no fit state. The poor guy looked even worse than Aki had done and was confined to his sofa. Taking partial responsibility for the state he was in, Miya had offered to run out and get him some junk food as a way of apologizing for talking him into downing all those drinks the night before. It was always odd to him that Naruse had such weak tolerance for alcohol even though he seemed so strong in other ways.

So he'd hung around for a while, nursing the patient, as he laughingly put it to the miserable blond on the sofa, earning himself a weak push but nothing more.

"How are you feeling today?" Naruse asked, propping himself up on a couple of pillows.

"You're asking me?"

"You look tired."

"Oh, that. That's Aki's fault." He smirked, but he didn't elaborate. He didn't care to bring other people into this.

"Really." Naruse rolled his eyes. It looked as if it hurt his eyes.

"But yeah, better. Thank you for listening to me last night."

Naruse shook his head gently. "You seemed to need it. I'm glad you're better."

"It's fine," Miya assured. "I'm just really sleepy today. Maybe I'll go home and rest afterwards."

"Sounds like a plan." Naruse smiled weakly. "How do you even do this as often as you do? I feel dead."

Miya shrugged. "Years of practice. You should start doing it more often—that'd make you feel better."

"You do realize that's a disturbing way of thinking?" Naruse asked, putting on his strict med-student face. "Not to mention completely backwards?"

"Oh just lay down before your head explodes," Miya replied grinning. "I'm gonna leave you alone, okay? Need to get myself some dinner as well."

"Sure." Naruse nodded, lovingly kissing the hand that rested against his cheek. "Thanks for nursing me back to health."

Miya laughed. "Anytime. Next time, I'll give you a sponge bath as well!"

The blond sniggered. "Just get out, idiot."

***

Miura had in fact texted him back later that same day, and they'd kept in touch, mostly via text messages and phone calls. As far as meetings went, there hadn't been a lot of them lately, save for a brief lunch at a café near the school where Miura taught. Apart from that, seeing each other in person had seemed almost impossible. Miura was busy at work and seemed to be bringing it back home with him more often than usual. Miya understood that and had allowed himself to let his shoulders drop slightly. Perhaps he still had a vague perception that something unsaid lingered between the two of them, but he hadn't allowed it to get to him. He'd decided that even though he was the one initiating contact, that didn't *have* to be a bad thing and shifted the focus to having fun with his friends while subconsciously longing to see Miura again. But he was patient, having taken Naruse's words to heart.

It seemed so strange.

Only days ago, he'd been joking around like that, happily thinking he had it all figured out. So then why was it that only days later he sat at Maki's drowning his sorrows in glass after glass of bitter, foul-tasting alcohol, ranting his guts out to the gentle, understanding bartender, who probably didn't get *anything* he was saying because he was just too drunk to make sense anymore?

What had happened was that he'd received a call from Miura, and he'd wondered if they could meet somewhere after his work was finished.

Miya, surprised to receive a call after the way things had been lately, had excitedly agreed. He was happy to hear the other man's voice, and to be asked out for the first time in a while. It had been as if they'd stagnated a little once he had started being on the offense. And after he'd started sleeping over at Miura's house, they hardly ever went out anywhere. Not that he minded staying in, having homemade meals and spending most of the time in bed, but he was partially convinced that it was a tactic the teacher used to hide their relationship from the outside world. He wasn't sure that he liked it, and now that they seemed to be communicating better again after his little meltdown; he was glad to hear that Miura wanted to take him out.

He had the day off, so meeting early in the evening worked out for him for once. Not that he cared much; usually he'd be able somehow to squeeze in a meeting if he really wanted to before work. It generally wasn't a problem.

They'd met in the same bar they'd gone to before, the secluded, cozy place where they didn't know anyone. And right from the start, Miura seemed distraught and concerned about something. He arrived late, even though he'd been the one who said it was a good time, and he was dressed in his work clothes, his leather briefcase underneath his arm, and hair even more unruly than usual, probably because of the wind. Apologetically, he smiled a rather stiff smile as he sank down in the seat opposite Miya in the booth where he was sitting, sipping at a cup of coffee to start with. "Sorry I'm late."

"No worries." Miya smiled towards him, eyes gleaming playfully. "I'm used to it."

Miura didn't smile back. He looked tired.

"Don't take that to heart," Miya reeled himself back in, "I was just joking. I'm the one to talk, right? Coming to your house at night and—"

"Do you have to say that so loudly?"

Miya was taken aback by the man's abrupt outspokenness.

"Is something wrong?" he tried, feeling a sneaking uncertainty creeping up inside of his body.

Miura shook his head. "No, I just... I've had a lot on my mind lately."

"You shouldn't work so hard," Miya replied softly. "What do you want to eat?"

Miura glanced at the table menu. "I actually haven't eaten yet," he replied, loosening his necktie, allowing himself to breathe more freely. He still looked tense though. "What are you having?"

Miya shrugged. "I'm drinking coffee, so I haven't really thought much further. Something deep-fried and simple I think."

The place didn't have the best selection of food, although it beat the beer snacks at his own workplace. In the end, he chose a serving of *yakitori*, while Miura went for the *kushiyaki*, as if he wanted to appear at least somewhat healthy. But he ordered beer on the side.

They mostly ate in silence, and Miya couldn't help but feel like the atmosphere around them was tense and uncomfortable, like there was something pressing down on them or surrounding them. He tried to ask questions once in a while, or engage the other man in conversation, but Miura seemed to be far away, lost in his own thoughts. He'd hardly touched his food, but he was already on his second beer of the evening, which was disturbing for this sober and composed man.

"Did you have a hard day at work?" Miya tried, feeling less and less like there was any point to this meeting. He was beginning to feel disappointed, having hoped that they'd share another nice evening together. This was nothing short of tense and oppressive.

"I was up all night grading papers," Miura replied, picking up a skewer of fried vegetables. He regarded it with heavy eyes, speaking as if his mind was on autopilot.

"You really shouldn't work that hard," Miya advised, concerned with the lethargy the teacher was displaying. He was a grown man, but being a teacher surely didn't seem like a walk in the park, and especially not for a class of middle-schoolers who more likely than not were a real handful. The fact that he had to take work home with him probably didn't help. Wasn't that why so many teachers, unless they were really passionate about what they did, gave up and got different jobs? Not only because of the workload and students, but for the sake of being nagged by stubborn parents all the time. And the pay was supposedly lousy. He'd heard reports of the sort from a former classmate and friend who'd worked as a teacher for a while before going on to build more on his education. He'd compared the hours of work and the dedication you had to display and decided it was hardly paid enough. Miya didn't doubt that in the slightest judging by Miura's modest living quarters.

"You're the one to talk," Miura sighed. "You work nights all the time."

"My job is less demanding," Miya replied, gesturing for the waitress to bring him another beer as well. "And I don't take it home with me. When I'm done with my shift, I go home and I sleep."

"Do you?"

Miya wrinkled his brow, automatically responding by sending a challenging glare across the table. "What's that supposed to mean?"

"Aren't you constantly going out after work?"

"Sure, but I also sleep half the day. Because I can."

"Is there much of a difference?" Miura countered. He seemed irritated, and Miya had no idea why, or what had brought it on other than the mood the other man had been in from the start.

"I'm sorry. Is there a problem?" Miya replied, pulling himself together enough to nod politely when the waitress came back with his order. He rested his elbows on the table, leaning forward. "I get that you're tired, but you seem really irritated."

"I was just implying that maybe you shouldn't talk too much about overworking myself and getting too little sleep when you're out drinking night after night."

"Yeah well," Miya snorted, "I don't think that's what's bothering you at all. And also, some of those nights were spent with you as well, remember?"

He purposely didn't lower his voice, and perhaps it was childish, but he had a sneaking fear of what was to come.

"Some of them," Miura replied.

That stung. Miya swallowed the pain and glared straight at the other man, firing, "Are you drunk?"

"Not really, no. I was just—"

"Yeah, you were implying something, right?" He knew how hurt he sounded.

"Now you're making assumptions," Miura replied, his voice cool.

Unease. That's what Miya was feeling. And he wasn't making assumptions; he was fairly sure he knew what the teacher had been close to spurting out. And he didn't like it. He'd heard it before.

"Then tell me I'm wrong," he said, his voice quieter. He looked down at his plate, finding that his appetite was lost, and he didn't feel like finishing any of it. Not his drink either. "You're angry about something."

"It's been a long day," Miura started, and for a while, Miya was hoping that he'd explain it all by blaming it on some brat in class, or having overslept, or anything trivial like that, but he didn't think it would come.

"Actually, it's been a long couple of weeks... And I've really enjoyed this time with you but—"

Miya turned ice cold. The room seemed to be askew, and the voices around them rose to a loud, deafening buzz in his ears.

The monologue the other man was sporting sounded almost as if it had been rehearsed and perfected. He was a teacher after all, and lectures probably came easily to him. He felt like zoning out, but he heard every single painful word.

"You're really something, Satoru," he said, and Miya shrunk in his seat. "But we're too different... I don't think I can do this."

Miya was a teenager again. Vulnerable and unguarded, stripped of wit and experience, down to his bare, shivering form, taking every word like an arrow to his fragile body.

"In other words..." he mouthed, his lips feeling dry all of a sudden, "we shouldn't see each other anymore."

It was true that he'd feared it. True that he'd somewhat expected it to come, or at least that something would come, something bad, and yet it was like a pool of ice cold water had been dropped over him—concrete floor and all.

He didn't think that it would be so sudden.

And he hadn't expected it to hurt in this way. It hadn't been that long that they'd known each other…

"Why?" he heard himself asking, but it was so quiet he wasn't sure he'd ever spoken out loud. And when he looked up from his plate, from his hands limply lying in his lap, he saw that Miura had left money on the table for his part of the tab and was already standing up.

He sprung to his feet, knocking his kneecap against the underside of the table as he did, but he held back the curse threatening to fall from his lips.

Their gazes locked, and Miya was certain his was one of desperation. He felt like his eyes were saucer-wide.

Why?

Nothing came out. His mouth was half-open, but he had no words. They just looked at each other. And people had started turning their attention to them, turning and looking over towards their table. Miya realized he'd knocked his glass over as he stood up, and that the same waitress from before was already heading right for them, a cloth in her hand. Helplessly, he looked towards the teacher, waiting for him to explain.

"I'm sorry."

That was all he got. Miura must have practiced acting this cold, as he simply turned on his heel and walked out of the bar without looking back at him, and Miya was left behind, barely noticing the girl already wiping their table, asking if he'd like a new drink.

He slumped back down into his seat and sat motionless, staring at the way she cleaned the table with circular motions, a trail of moisture left on the smooth surface.

A distinct bitterness welled up in him—familiar and cruel. It burned on his inside and made him grit his teeth, forcing himself to hold back.

He'd forgotten how painful this was. How much this kind of rejection hurt. Even though it had been such a short time, he couldn't remember when he'd last felt this lousy—out of the blue at that.

And it wasn't hard to understand *why* this sudden turn of events had come along. It was all in the way the other man had worded it, even though he'd been holding back. Miya wasn't stupid.

He watched the waitress pick up the partially beer-soaked money from the center of the table and mumbled something like an excuse.

When he left, he made sure to tip her generously for the trouble as well as to be remembered for something other than the scene it felt like they'd caused.

He stuffed his hands in his pockets and came to realize that he hadn't brought any keys. Aki had still been at home when he'd left, and the younger man had his key, having forgotten his own somewhere or other earlier. Since he didn't think he'd be returning home tonight anyway, he hadn't bothered asking for it back.

He glanced at his watch, which he'd now made a habit of wearing, starting to like the way it looked on his wrist. He figured it was probably a slim chance his roommate was at home at this hour.

He made a futile attempt to call him, but as expected, Aki didn't pick up his phone. He tried to remember if the younger man had work or if it was a day off but couldn't remember. And in any case, he didn't feel like going by the club in this state.

Instead, he resolutely walked towards the station, intending to head down to Maki's.

Hands in pockets, he made his way down the street, the cool air pinching at his cheeks, causing him to shiver.

He felt incredibly disappointed—sad even. It was frightening.

Sinking down on a seat inside the subway train, he felt like his being just slumped against the nearest wall, leaning his head on the window, watching the darkness outside. He didn't understand.

***

And so here he was, hanging listlessly over the bar at Maki's, blurting everything to anyone who cared to listen—or not.

"I'm so stupid," he muttered, emptying his glass, slamming it hard enough against the bar for the bartender to turn towards him, worried that he was damaging his property.

"Miya," he said softly, "don't you think you've had enough?"

Miya didn't know how many hours had passed since he got here after hopping on the train, but he could easily count the number of glasses in front of him on the bar. He groaned loudly. His throat felt like sandpaper from all the dry drinks and his head and eyes were swimming.

"What?" he murmured, resting his head against the bar as if it was too heavy for him to hold it up on his own—there was some truth to that. "Never seen a man drink away his sorrows before?"

"Too many times." Maki threw a rag across his shoulder, placing two martini glasses back onto a shelf, and then making his way over to Miya again. He ran his manicured hand over Miya's collapsed hairdo, stroking gently. "What did you say happened?"

"He dumped me."

"Who did?" Maki wasn't following in the slightest. He tried to sound patient and understanding, but it was probably a bit of a burden to him, playing psychologist when the place was as crowded as it was. Surprisingly, none of Miya's colleagues were there. None of them had probably ended their shifts yet, or perhaps they had but had decided not to pop in for a snack before going out or going home.

It was just as well. He didn't want to see any of them.

"Aki has my keys…" he muttered, running his hand through his catastrophic mess of hair. "And he dumped me."

"Aki did?"

Annoyed, Miya glared up into Maki's face, trying to form an insult.

"No you… Not him. I was going out with someone."

"This is new to me."

"Is it?" Miya felt like he'd been the worst person on the planet to keep his secret. He'd been sure anyone could read him like a book, as had been so common before. But everything was hazy, and he didn't know what he'd said and not said over the last few weeks.

Maki was gone again, having headed over towards a table, talking and laughing in the distance as he took someone's order. He returned, first to bring drinks for the same people, then to Miya's side.

"I'm gonna fry up some food for them." He jerked his head towards the table. Miya ignored it, not bothering to lift his head and look in the direction Maki was indicating. "You want some?"

"Nah. I ate earlier. I was on a date," Miya sighed bitterly. "At least I thought it was. But he was so… It wasn't all that surprising."

"Wait, are you saying you were actually *seeing* someone?"

"No really? Is that what I said?" He tasted the bitterness in his own voice. "Are you deaf?"

"You've definitely had enough." Maki frowned. "I'm cutting you off."

And then Hiiro was there. Miya wasn't sure he'd heard him come in. He thought Maki had mentioned the red-haired man, but his mind was so clouded that he wasn't really following.

"I'm gonna make you some coffee." Maki sighed. "You're way out of it."

"Aren't you the one responsible for that?" Miya countered.

Hiiro slid up next to him. "You look… awful," he blurted.

"Thanks."

"So, what's going on?"

Maki returned, placing a porcelain cup of steaming hot coffee in front of Miya before turning to Hiiro. "You want something?"

"Yeah, get me something to drink, and fries?"

"You guys should eat healthier," Maki chuckled. "All I do is make burgers and fries. Maybe we should try having one of those veggie-weeks."

"In that case, I'm out." The redhead grinned. "And so is he."

Miya noted that Hiiro was jerking his head in his direction.

"What's going on there?" Hiiro asked.

"I hoped you could tell me," Maki replied, sounding exasperated. "Supposedly it's about this guy he's been seeing, but I know nothing about that. You?"

"Yeah, you do. It's that same guy he mentioned earlier, remember? They're going out."

"Not anymore," Maki said quietly.

Hiiro and Maki exchanged glances across the counter.

"He's been dumped, apparently."

"Oh no, you broke up?" Hiiro turned his gaze towards Miya, looking apologetic. "How come?"

"You tell me," Miya groaned, looking with disdain at the coffee. "This isn't gonna make me feel any better you know."

"I thought you were doing good."

"Yeah well…" Miya sighed heavily, "so did I."

"Mi-chan," Hiiro smiled softly, pulling him close and resting their foreheads together, "I'm sorry…"

Miya slowly closed his eyes. It made him feel even dizzier when he couldn't see. Specks of light danced behind his eyelids. He felt empty, as if only the alcohol could fill the void. "Don't be," he mumbled. "It wasn't meant to be—obviously."

"What did he say though?" Hiiro almost whispered, leaning in closer. His breath felt warm on Miya's skin, gently caressing his ear, making his neck hair stand up.

Miya shrugged. "That we just didn't work out." He grinned bitterly, pulling out from the embrace. "He said he was sorry though."

"What a jerk," Hiiro growled. "I thought he was enjoying your company."

"Ah, but he's not the only one, is he?" Miya's shoulders

slumped. He'd meant for it to be a quick, witty comeback, but it came out sounding sad and hurt instead.

"Wait, was it because of that? Does he think you're—" Hiiro knit his brow, looking upset. "But you didn't go with anyone else while you were with him, right?"

"Does it matter?" he replied sourly. "It's not like he'll believe that."

"Maybe he misunderstood." Hiiro's expression softened, the angry furrow in his forehead smoothing out.

"Even if he did, does it seem likely to you that he'd trust me?"

"Stop pitying yourself," Hiiro scolded. "If some guy doesn't want to be with you over something stupid like that, then—"

"He's not worth you." Maki soothed the tension and sent a warning glare in Hiiro's direction, urging the other man to calm down a little as the other customers had started staring at them. Miya didn't care. He wasn't the first one to spill his heart out in this place, and he wouldn't be the last.

"I know he's not," he groaned, "but I think I really liked him."

He felt stupid and weak, showing this side of himself to his friends. Hiiro was younger than him and didn't know much about relationships. Perhaps that was why he had no problems talking to him about it in the first place; Hiiro himself had given up before he even started looking for someone. With his background, he didn't think it was likely he'd find someone who'd dare to trust him enough to settle down. But above everything else, Hiiro was young and *wanted* to be free. Miya didn't want to open up too much in this way to him, precisely because of that. Even though they had a shared outlook on these things, it was unlikely that Hiiro understood him to the fullest. And of course, he was younger. Miya didn't want to take advice from someone younger than him, except maybe Naru. In that case, Maki was different.

But it didn't matter. It wasn't like either of them could change anything after all.

The other two looked uncomfortable, unable to find the

words they were looking for it seemed.

"You don't have to comfort me," Miya mumbled. "I'll be fine. I'm just gonna focus on other things."

"Like alcohol?" Hiiro asked.

"I would. Maki cut me off though."

"You're cruel, *Nee-san*," Hiiro pouted in the bartender's direction.

"It's called caring."

"Care a little less, will you?" Miya replied. "I was feeling better there for a while."

"I'll make you feel better!" Hiiro slammed his fist down on Miya's back, almost knocking the breath out of him. "*Nee-san*, you don't mind if *I* drink, right?"

The effeminate man rolled his eyes and shoved a glass towards him. "What do you want?"

Hiiro named his drink of choice and started telling a story about some guy he'd hooked up with the other day and how it had been a complete disaster.

"At least *you* had the privilege of *good* sex while it lasted!" he finished, looking like he pitied himself endlessly for his choice in men.

"Really?" Maki arched an eyebrow, listening in on their conversation.

"What do you mean *really*?" Miya snapped. "I'm not interested in someone who can't keep me satisfied."

"Neither am I," Hiiro shot back. "But I seem to be cursed or something. Maybe it's karma."

"Didn't you enjoy what you did in your previous... job though?" Miya sniggered, feeling like the buzz, or rather the roar, of the alcohol in his body was finally beginning to pick him up a little.

"Yeah, hence the karma. I don't think that kind of employment gives a whole lot of points."

"I didn't know you were religious," Maki stated, smirking.

"Oh yeah he is." Miya grinned. "You should hear him crying out for God in ecstasy."

"Oh shut up." Hiiro nudged him hard with his shoulder,

laughing loudly.

Miya felt better. At least he thought so. He wasn't sure if he felt all that much anymore, but hearing Hiiro babbling on freed him somewhat of the gloom from earlier. The intoxication and the constant jabber of the other man's voice filled up his head and made it difficult to focus on much else. It was a welcome sensation.

Finally, after they'd been gossiping and laughing for what seemed to be hours, the door opened, and his roommate strode in.

Miya sprung to his feet, throwing himself at the teenager, who was still in possession of his key. After a stupid argument over whose fault that was, and bickering over who was more irresponsible, the younger man joined them, grabbing a quick bite to eat.

The topic of the other night, when Yuuki had been dragged to their place, came up, and the two others were more than a little curious to hear about that turn of events. Miya threw in his own comments here and there, but he was barely paying attention. He felt plastered and exhausted. And the other two, Hiiro in particular, having had quite a lot to drink at this point as well, filled Aki in on why *he* was here drinking himself to death. As expected, there was little empathy to spot in the aloof teenager, who seemed to disdain hearing about the situation altogether.

He had his own issues to deal with it seemed. It sounded like he and Yuuki had gotten into some sort of scuffle, and as expected, Aki wasn't exactly taking the high road. He commented on it and earned himself a snide remark about his own current state.

Just as quickly as he offended him, Aki touched their lips together and suggested they spend the night together.

Miya's mind was swimming. His thoughts were jumbled, and something from a short while back was pressing to be summoned forth but failed to make any sense.

He smirked back, shaking his head. It was his own fault, having said something that Aki could easily twist and use against him, but it was up to him if he wanted to go with the flow and succumb to his flirty and suggestive tone.

It wasn't like Miya needed to worry about the man who'd just rejected him, but on the other hand, it probably wasn't very classy to throw himself at the first offer that came along just to mend his broken heart. If it could even be described as such after such a short time. He was full of doubt. But at the same time, he also felt vengeful and obstinate.

Between the two of them, Aki was probably the less serious. Despite his young age, he was cynical and calculating, and not at all one for pillow talk or breakfast the morning after. Miya had always suspected it had something to do with his young age and his determination to fit in amongst them, and had to a certain extent found it cute, or at least charming. Tonight, he found it liberating.

It was okay to blame everything on the intoxication and the suggestive look in his roommate's dark eyes. Aki probably needed to blow off some steam as well to prove what they'd all been making a point of—him being cruel and inconsiderate, stepping all over the teenage boy he was screwing around with. Although Miya felt for the boy, having found him to be a good kid, he couldn't involve himself too much, and neither did he want to. For the time being, he just wanted to play around and forget about the distracting pain in his chest.

***

The two of them went home together, Aki partially supporting Miya's drunken form as they staggered up the stairs and into the apartment.

"Jeez," he commented, "how much did you have to drink?"

"And that comes from you? The crown prince of hangovers?" Miya slurred back, shooting Aki an accusing glare.

They ended up in his room, and what happened next had been a completely natural development—the kisses, the hands on each other's bodies, and hips grinding together while their lips met and broke apart over and over.

Although they were far apart in age, their chemistry never failed; they knew each other well by now, knew what made each other tick, and how to wind one another up.

Miya breathed into the kiss, allowing the younger man to flip him over on the side, his nimble fingers inching down his abdomen. He sighed, arching up to allow it; so close to letting go of himself and going with the impulses but then... In the back of his blurry mind, something was happening. He recalled the conversation he'd had with Miura over lunch a short while ago about Aki. It had been after he'd asked if the man had ever taught at a certain middle school. Miura had asked him why, and he'd mentioned that his roommate knew someone who'd gone there.

At that point, Miura's expression had changed, a shadow running over it.

"Wait, how old is your roommate again?" he'd asked. He could still hear that tone of voice, already judgmental, inside of his head.

"He's almost nineteen," Miya had replied, noting how different his own voice sounded, noting that he was purposely trying to make Aki sound older, to make himself look better.

"What you said earlier," Miura had followed up with after a while, "about your relationship..."

He'd swallowed dryly, sipping at his drink mostly to keep himself occupied as the discomfort grew and his heart pounded hard in his chest, pumping blood up to his pale cheeks, filling them with glowing splotches of crimson.

"What about that?" He'd tried to sound indifferent. He wasn't ashamed.

Have you slept with him as well?

Miura hadn't voiced the question, but Miya knew he'd wanted to ask. He could tell by the look on the man's face, and the way he was staring at Miya.

A man who taught kids only a few years younger wouldn't look with much understanding on a connection such as the one he and Aki had. Someone who lived in the "real" world wouldn't be able to distinguish the kind of mutual detachment the two of them shared and occasionally fed off of.

Miya abruptly pulled away from the younger man's lips, still tasting him as he opened his eyes and looked hazily up at him. Aki looked surprised. And then he realized Miya had stopped the hand from advancing further down.

"Miya?"

"I… don't feel so good…" he excused himself, beckoning Aki to move over.

"Your call," Aki replied, rolling himself off of him. He was so light that there was barely any sense of relief when his weight was lifted from Miya's own slim frame.

He thought Aki looked tired as well, seemingly not minding that they were putting a halt to their activities, even though he'd been quite excited just a few seconds ago.

He touched his hand to the teen's face, kissing him gently on the lips. "We'll pick up the thread again later, 'kay?"

"Whatever," Aki replied, unfazed.

It wasn't right. It all came back to him, crashing over him like waves of cold, painful feelings, sucking him under.

Nothing felt right. He sighed heavily, turning over on his side, throwing his arm across the pillow, gripping it tightly, and covering his face at the same time.

At his side, he heard Aki rustling, seemingly having decided to stay with him for the night regardless. He didn't mind.

Miya bit his own lip, thinking about how he shouldn't be thinking of anything. He hoped that the inebriated condition he had put himself in would lead him into silent, dreamless sleep.

Alas, he wasn't that lucky. As he finally nodded off, it was with the disapproving eyes of Miura looking down on him, his voice full of contempt as he asked, *"Did you sleep with him as well?"* And he'd try to reply that no, he'd stopped himself, and their relationship wasn't like that. But it was like he was screaming against the wind, and his voice was whisked away somewhere, screaming for deaf ears, screaming for nothing at all. He felt the cold sweat emerge on his forehead, and his gut wrenching in dread as he muttered, trying to express himself, tossing and turning in his sleep all night.

When he woke up, he felt even more tired than he had going

to bed. His eyes were florid and puffy, and he felt like he'd been run over by a truck. Aki was still fast asleep on his side next to him. He looked peaceful enough but was expressionless and barely even seemed to breathe.

Running his fingers gently over the teen's upper arm, Miya stood from the bed, carefully not to wake him, and left the room to have a quick shower.

It was already nine in the morning, but for all he cared, it could have been four a.m. with the way he was feeling—like he'd gotten no sleep whatsoever.

He got out of the shower, shaking himself like a dog, slipping into his most comfortable pair of sweats, throwing on a hoodie over an old T-shirt, blow-drying his hair sloppily, giving up before it was completely dry.

He felt restless, and nauseated. It could be due to the excess drinking the night before, but just as much it might have had to do with his nightmares and the way yesterday had turned out.

He'd almost forgotten about it all when he'd been with Aki, but then it had all come crashing down on him. In the same way that he'd forgotten how much it hurt to be told by someone that you just weren't good enough. Until that came crashing down as well. Maybe it was his fickle personality, his tendency to be ditzy and careless, that made him so prone to burning himself over and over. Sometimes, he felt like he was a child, never understanding that the same action would have the same consequence again and again. In the same sense that he knew Miura had turned him down because of his relation with Aki and everyone else, he'd still allowed himself to go along with it last night. Precisely like he'd remembered all his other disastrous attempts at going out with someone, and he'd still thought that this might be different somehow.

And he still didn't seem like he was able to learn anything, not even from the gash his feelings had torn in his own chest, as he soon found himself throwing on his boots and coat, making his way out.

Because he never learned.

17. History II

Miya was the eldest son in a family of four; he'd been an only child for several years before his younger brother, Shigeru, had finally been born. Both his parents were born and raised in Kamigōri. A couple of years separated them in age, and they'd gone to the same high school. After his father had graduated university, and while his mother was still enrolled, they'd gotten married. It was a classic story in their circuits—childhood acquaintances getting married, moving back home and taking over the family business or starting up a shop of their own, which was what his parents had done. Then they'd had him, a couple of years into their marriage, when his mother was also done with her education.

Miya had always disdained something about this perfect traditional imagery that his parents and their friends and family were all painting, about what growing up should be like, and what happiness meant.

He was part of the generation that was starting to see things differently—wanting something new. To him, taking the road that his family had paved for him wasn't the obvious answer. Even as a child, he'd been the one who took the shortcuts that always had him running in circles, getting lost in the scrubland enveloping their neighborhood, causing him to be late for school.

At the same time, he had tremendous respect for his parents, for what they'd been able to accomplish, and he loved them dearly, so he'd started wanting to please them from very early on. They'd waited for the perfect time to have a child, and when he was born, he was already a highly longed-for child. He'd always been aware of how precious he was to them, and maybe it was just because he never lacked love or attention that he wanted to give something back. Even when Shigeru had been born, he'd been patient and understanding, not at all jealous, which had surprised many in their family, having warned his parents endlessly about how jealous a long-time only child could become when a sibling threatened their spotlight. But Miya had felt nothing less than adoration for his brother from the first moment that he'd laid eyes on his wrinkly, scrunched-up little face. His mother had told him that it would be his job to protect his brother and look out for him, and being the responsible little kid that he'd been, Miya had been more than ready to take on the task.

He'd probably been happy growing up, he realized.

This was why it was so difficult once he realized that the person he'd become was not acceptable to many, certainly not to those who were more old-fashioned and bound by tradition. That kind was aplenty in his family. He wasn't sure of when his parents figured him out—if they'd been aware of his sexuality before he came out to them.

Coming out wasn't the right way to put it even. Getting caught red-handed was more like it, if not a little less dramatic. He never brought people home to his parents' house; when he was younger, he respected them too much and was afraid of what they'd say if they came home and found him with another guy. Even if he hadn't been gay, he was fairly certain being walked in on would have been just as traumatizing for him as it would have been for his parents. Not so much because of the guy-part, but more the whole teenage son having sex thing. They were fairly conservative people, and while perhaps not entirely tied up in the tradition of getting married before sleeping together, they certainly wouldn't have approved of his casual connections. As a teen, and later as a young adult, he'd been preoccupied with his relationships, but looking back at them now, he did see how casual and even destructive many of these were. As an adult, he didn't bring people home merely because he didn't feel like his family needed to know what he was doing. Even when he had strong feelings for someone, he didn't want to involve his family in anything, possibly because he was so insecure of how they'd take to it. Bringing home a boyfriend was one thing, but he'd never *dream* of taking some random guy home to his parents' house. That would undoubtedly end in a disaster.

In any case, he was certain they'd heard the rumors circulating about him from his time in high school. People talked in Kamigōri, especially in their neighborhood.

He didn't know if the rumors had spread because someone had known about him and Nomura, or him and the useless businessman, if they'd been seen together, or if it was just pure speculation based on his traits and personality, but he knew that word traveled fast, and that the adults knew almost just as much as the kids. It didn't bother him. He figured that even in Kamigōri he couldn't possibly be the only gay teenager and took it all with a grain of salt. Nobody had ever bullied him about it either, or given him a particularly rough time. His classmates were probably all wondering about it, but none of them asked, and nobody treated him any differently than before. He wondered though if they saw the glances he snuck after the student council president, or the first years' new homeroom teacher—fresh out of university. It wasn't particularly hard to notice if one knew where to look.

His parents had never asked him flat out during these years, not until he'd been seen with that older man by someone who'd found it suspicious. At that point, his mother had discreetly pulled him aside and asked if it was true. She didn't elaborate on what she'd heard, or what she'd meant, and Miya decided to refuse. At this point, he was still madly in love with this creep of a guy and wanted to protect him at all cost. So he'd said that it was true he'd been talking to an older man in the city but made up a lie that he was the parent of someone he knew from school and that he'd offered him a ride downtown. She seemed to have settled on that, but perhaps that was only for her own convenience.

He wondered about it now though; what kind of mother looked away when there was a possibility her teenage son was sleeping with a married man twice his own age?

Maybe she hadn't been able to swallow it. Maybe she was

hoping that he was doing it of his own will, or maybe she thought it was another one of his rebellious acts towards her and his father, in the same way that she'd demonstratively turn away whenever he lit up a cigarette anywhere near her, as if she didn't see it.

In retrospect, he was still a little relieved because if she'd reacted in the expected way and thrown a fit, he would easily have been exposed to even more gossip, and shame—not to mention all the trouble his lover would get into. He didn't think that statutory rape was all that likely, not with him having turned eighteen, but he'd been concerned that it would get out and ruin the man's reputation and position in his company. Another paradox was his worry that the man's wife would find out and have her life ruined.

After that incident, his sexuality hadn't been a subject to discuss in the Utsunomiya household for the longest time, but when he met Tsuuji, he'd brought him home. He didn't see any problem with it, as the two of them were just good friends at that time, even though they were still in the process of trying to see if they *could* function as a couple.

That year, when they were both in their early twenties, he'd brought Tsuuji home with him for Golden Week in May. The man had wanted to come after having heard so much about Miya's hometown. There wasn't much else to it. Tsuuji himself was from the big city, raised in an apartment complex, and had grown up with dusty lungs, as he put it. Miya's family lived in a moderately sized traditional house with their shop downstairs and a large back yard. The entire neighborhood was compiled of old-fashioned houses with large gardens and tall, wooden fences. It was a peaceful neighborhood. And precisely because of that, he'd been okay with bringing a friend, to have someone to talk to while he was home.

It was the closest he'd ever come to bringing a guy home to meet his parents, but he'd made nothing of it, and he hadn't thought that his parents would either.

The week passed relatively painlessly, and Miya had decided to stay a while longer after Tsuuji went back to Kobe. Shortly thereafter, an old aunt of his came by for a visit. She pinched Shigeru's cheek and told him he was growing up so quickly. At this point, the boy had been around twelve or so. Then she'd turned to him and said, "Satoru, how are you doing?"

"He's fine," his mother had replied, almost a little too quickly. She'd then more or less hurriedly ushered the ageing woman into the house. They'd been seated on the *tatami* mats around the small table, the adults dressed in traditional *yukatas*, as was common for older people, but Miya's parents also dressed traditionally at the shop. He and Shigeru were casually dressed in regular clothing. They'd been eating and drinking tea, the two brothers playfully nudging and insulting each other as if they were both little kids. He was often told to stop acting like such a child at his age, but Miya couldn't help it; he loved his little brother, and the way the kid's face lit up whenever he came down to his level and roused around with him.

Shigeru's laughter was possibly his favorite thing in the entire world and had been ever since the younger brother had been a baby.

"Are you still not going to university?" the old woman had asked, her tone both condescending and curious at the same time.

He shook his head. "Doesn't seem like it's in the cards."

He was just being honest, but his father sent him a warning glare across the table, and his mother hissed under her breath, "Satoru!"

"What?" he asked. "It's true. I'm not going to lie to the woman!"

Despite the respect he had for his parents, he wasn't about to tell lies for their sake. At that point, he'd long since realized that he didn't want to take up his education again. He'd started working at the club, and he was happy with the way things were.

He didn't want to make them look bad by being a bratty kid, so he turned his smiling face towards his brother and said, "Shigeru will go to university, right?"

"Yeah!" The young boy nodded his head vigorously. "I'm gonna go to a good school when I grow up and become something great!"

Miya smiled, ruffling the boy's hair. "Good boy."

He had to strangle a laugh; the words coming from his brother's mouth were planted there by adults, adults who wanted to make sure he didn't become as stubborn and confused as Miya was. It didn't bother him. He knew that Shigeru would be able to make his own decisions as well when the time came.

He knew the old aunt was far from pleased by the way he was carrying himself or the way he talked so freely about his *frivolous ways* as she put it. He had to force back a grin overhearing *that*. If only she knew how frivolous he could be! But it was for the best that she didn't. She was from an older generation. Even if his own parents agreed with her, they'd never force him into something, but it was definitely plausible that they'd try to coax him into changing his mind.

He took Shigeru out after the meal, and they were playing with a tattered old ball in the back yard, trying to shoot it into the makeshift goal that was really just a space between his mother's potted plants.

The sliding doors were open, and he could still hear the voices coming from inside.

"How can you allow him to act that way at his age? It's about time he started acting like an adult!" The old woman sounded upset.

Miya rolled his eyes, passing the ball to his brother, only so he could apprehend him in the next second and snatch it away from him.

"That's not fair!" Shigeru shrilled, chasing after him. Miya laughed teasingly and kicked the ball towards the goal, but he missed.

"The oldest kid makes the rules!" he called back.

"The oldest kid is a cheater!" his brother echoed, seemingly attempting to shoot the ball *at* him.

That moment was still vivid in his mind: Their laughter and the low thumping of their sneakers against the tattered leather and the ball bouncing against the clay pots or the wooden fence. Shigeru's exclamations and his own barks of amusement, and then the voices, fading in and out as he passed by the door.

"Isn't he already past twenty? He should be ready to settle down!"

He thought he heard his mother sounding somewhat sarcastic when she replied, "What do you suppose we do, *ba-san*? Arrange an *omiai*?"

"Of course not. You two managed to marry on your own. But you met in school! If that boy gets back into his education, I'm sure he'll find a nice girl that—"

He grimaced at the thought. Both the idea of finding some sweet girl and the insistence that he go to university disgusted him.

"That boy will never get married." It was his father's voice. And Miya felt the color drain from his face. Did they know?

Where did this come from? It was possible that they were only claiming he'd never marry out of spite to annoy them and go against their wishes, but… At that point, he was worried.

"Is it because of those rumors?" the aunt asked. "You know, old Suzuki told me that there were some people saying that Satoru—"

"Enough." It was his father's voice, stern this time. It sounded like he'd slammed his fists against the table. So he was upset. They definitely knew.

"Satoru! Hey! *Aniki!*" Shigeru was impatiently tugging at his sleeve, trying to get him to chase the ball again.

"Coming," he replied absentmindedly.

From that moment, he'd known that he'd have to talk to them about it in some way or another. But he didn't want to do it with the old hag in the house. And he suddenly felt like he wanted her to leave—or disappear.

He was past his teenage rebellion, regardless of what people thought, and he didn't want people to think that his parents had done a bad job; neither did he want them to have to deal with things they didn't want to talk about. He *knew* that it wasn't easy for them, dealing with the fact that he, their eldest, had given up the opportunity to get a proper education, and now there were these rumors. Obviously it was hard for them to talk about it, but he wasn't about to start living his life based on a lie. It was impossible. So that afternoon, he'd decided that he'd tell them. He didn't know how, or when, but it would have to come out somehow.

And it did. At complete random, his parents had shown up at his apartment. They never visited, and certainly not without letting him know first, but on this particular occasion, they'd been on a short trip to Kobe and had decided to drop in and check in on their somewhat estranged firstborn. The scenario he'd attempted to prevent from his teenage years had finally come, if not in a more toned-down version.

This event had taken place some months after their trip to Kamigōri, and at this point in time, his and Tsuuji's relationship had still been something intangible and messy.

When the doorbell rang on this particular Sunday, they'd been on the sofa together; nothing in particular had been going on, but if someone really wanted it to, it could look suspicious. Because it was a Sunday, and they weren't expecting any company, or rather because neither of them were all too particular about the cleaning, the place had been in a slight state of chaos—an ashtray that should have been emptied, and empty beer cans on the table, a pair of trousers thrown over one of the stools in the kitchen, and because it was a hot day, they were both shirtless. And who would ever have thought that it would be his own parents standing outside the door?

Tsuuji had opened it, and the color had drained from his face as he saw who was standing outside.

"Who is it?" Miya called from the sofa, not bothering to stand up. Either way it wouldn't have made much of a difference.

All too late, he heard Tsuuji's voice nervously sputtering, "U-Utsunomiya-san! Come in!"

Miya stood abruptly, gawking at his parents now coming into their cramped hall space, critically looking around the apartment, his mother's sharp eyes in particular resting on Tsuuji's exposed, lean body.

He swallowed.

Although they weren't a couple, and although he was certain they hadn't suspected much of the sort after their visit that summer, he didn't like the expression on her face.

"Sorry to be like this," his roommate said, trying to explain himself. "The aircon's broken, so we can't turn it up any higher…"

Miya came over to them and sent him a look, urging Tsuuji not to say anything else.

"What are you doing here?" he said instead. "I mean… what brings you to the city? If you needed me to come meet you, you should've—"

"We're just passing by," his mother cut him off. "Can't a mother see her son without being questioned?"

She gazed at him with a look that seemed more accusing than anything else and a complaining tone in her voice.

"Of course, I just… I would've cleaned this place up if I knew you were coming."

"Looks like you should have done that in the first place," his father had cut in.

Tsuuji lurked off at that point into his room, grabbing a shirt and coming back out, announcing that he'd go buy something to eat while they all caught up. Miya envied him; he wanted to get away from them as well.

***

"You look tired." His mother had darted about, picking up things and throwing them into a plastic bag she'd found in the kitchen while stopping once in a while to touch her hand to his cheek in a worried manner.

"It's nothing. We had some friends over last night—went to bed too late."

His father eyed him suspiciously at that point.

Miya swallowed, changing the subject as he grabbed for a discarded shirt on the floor and threw it on.

"Where's Shigeru?"

"He had a soccer match today, so he didn't want to come. Besides, he's old enough to be alone for a couple of days."

"It's that lifestyle of yours," his father interrupted.

Miya felt cold, despite the stifling heat. "What?"

"Staying up all night, working at a nightclub, no wonder you're tired. You should get a real job that pays enough for you to get proper housing."

Miya frowned back at the stern man. "Dad, there's nothing wrong with the apartment; it's just a bit messy. We—"

"You wouldn't have to live with someone if you got a proper job. You can still get—"

"I don't want an education." He knew how insolent he sounded. "I'm happy the way things are."

"As an older brother, you should set an example."

"As if Shigeru can't figure things out on his own?" His tone was harsher than intended. He felt violated; his parents ambushing him like this, coming into his home, criticizing and even cleaning, a blatant act of evidence that his mother wasn't impressed in the slightest. He knew that was only a fraction of it. He loved them, but he could feel something loosening. He knew there was something brewing beneath the surface that couldn't be ignored any longer, that would erupt at any given time.

"Besides, that's not what this is about, is it?"

Part of him actually believed that this sudden visit was solely to check up on him, to confirm any suspicions they might have had. Bracing himself, he stared at the two of them.

"What are you implying?" his father retorted, annoyance clear in his voice.

"Honey," his mother was more forward, "what did we walk in on... just now?"

"Huh?" he gawked. He didn't expect that kind of direct question, not after years of beating around the bush.

"Nothing? What... you're referring to Tsuuji?"

"Satoru, the village is talking..."

A shadow crossed his face, and he narrowed his eyes. "About me, right? You don't think I know that?"

"That time... did you lie?"

Miya continued to stare right at her. He didn't know what she'd told his father about the time when he'd denied the rumors about having been seen with the businessman. Although this might have been a good time to come clean, there were still some things he didn't want his parents to know about. He continued to deny that part of his past. "I didn't."

"Are you lying now?"

"I'm not," he denied.

He wasn't. There wasn't anything between him and Tsuuji, after all.

"But then why won't you get married?"

"Is *that* really what you want to ask me, Mother?" He used a more formal word, stressing it, as if wanting to pressure her into coming clean already about what it was she wanted to hear.

"I think you know." He turned his gaze towards his dad, noticing that his hair was getting a gray-ish sheen near the temples. "I heard you that time, Dad. When you told *obasan* that I would never marry. So why can't you say it to me?"

"Satoru!"

He was in his mid-twenties that sweltering day when he finally came out to his parents. Although the truth had probably been out as something vexing and ugly for a long time.

"You know, don't you? You've just chosen to ignore it, right?"

"Ignore what?"

"That you think Tsuuji and I are a couple?"

"Are you?" His mother looked aghast, and his father looked as if he didn't want to hear the answer.

"We're not."

A sigh of relief.

"Then why couldn't you just say—"

"But it's true." He didn't really care anymore. He was an adult. It was time. "I like men."

It looked as if they were about to faint. His father supported his mother, grabbing her by the arm.

"How could you l—"

"I've never lied about it," he shrugged. "You just never asked me directly. I didn't think it was that much of an issue to be honest."

"How is it not an issue?" His mother's face was white. "You're the eldest son, you're supposed to—"

"If I ever choose to carry on the family business, it doesn't matter who I sleep with," he replied. "And for the record, you didn't *walk in* on anything. Tsuuji and I are just friends."

That didn't seem to assure them one bit.

"What are we supposed to say to—"

"You don't have to tell anyone," he replied calmly. "People will believe what they want to regardless of what you say. I don't mind if you don't tell them anything. They talked about me before this too, for all kinds of reasons. It doesn't bother me, so why should it bother you?"

"We're your parents. That's why."

So they said. And he'd replied that he hoped they would continue to be, even if they looked at him as a failure and a disappointment. Although he'd turned self-reliant and strong over the years, he wanted to hear them say something like that as a reassurance that it wasn't that big of a deal. But the response was miniscule. He couldn't expect less of them. Or more for that matter.

In the end, they didn't respond to it. And they left shortly after.

In his family, it wasn't something that had been spoken about much since then. It wasn't as if they were ignoring what he'd told them that day, but it stood between them as an invisible barrier obstructing their relationship. Whenever he went home, the atmosphere felt colder somehow, certain words felt more probing, irritated. Regardless, it seemed like they weren't about to write him off because of it. It was more like they'd just chosen to disregard what he'd told them and carry on with their lives as if they never knew.

He was fine with this, despite the sting of rejection he felt once in a while when he couldn't tell them about things happening in his life the way others could. It hurt him, but not as much as Shigeru did.

The two brothers had always been close, ever since Shigeru was a baby. His first word had been something similar to

"Satoru," and everyone around them had been nothing but charmed by the way the little brother depended on him.

How Shigeru had come to know, Miya didn't know. He was certain their parents hadn't told him based on how they acted. He'd probably heard the rumors as well. By the time this incident occurred, Shigeru was a teenager, and maybe he was bothered by the thought that his brother was a target because wouldn't that make him one as well?

Still, it had come as a shock to Miya upon coming back for New Year's that year and finding that his brother showed a more aloof side towards him and often left the room if he came in. Finally, it had surfaced.

"Satoru," Shigeru had said, sitting a few paces away from him on the tatami. He used his name rather than the familiar *nii-san* or a teasing *aniki*. "Is it true?"

"Is what true?" he replied calmly, turning his gaze onto his younger brother, half-expecting what was to come.

"Everyone's acting so strange," Shigeru replied, "because you're a homo, right?"

Miya's mouth had literally dropped open at the abruptness of his brother's words and the complete disdain in his young voice.

He didn't ask who'd told him, and he didn't know what to say. He just stared blankly ahead before finally turning to look at Shigeru yet again and giving half a nod.

"Yeah, I am," he said.

"Did you fuck that guy you brought here?"

"Even if I did, that is not something you should ask," Miya replied coolly, trying to hide his shock at the crude words leaving his brother's lips. He briefly wondered if maybe he should just continue the denial. But being a big brother, he couldn't just allow his brother to ask that kind of question without any consequences.

Shigeru stared at him—*through* him. "That's disgusting," he said before standing up and leaving the room.

At that moment, Miya felt his heart breaking into a thousand little pieces.

For the rest of the New Year's visit, the two brothers had

231

barely spoken to each other, and Shigeru had refrained from seeing him off when Miya left for the first time since he'd left the city years before. And everything had hurt.

Even now their relationship was strained. He went home less and less often and saw less and less of his teenage brother. In the rare event that he called home, Shigeru would hardly talk to him on the phone. For someone who adored his younger brother, it was a harsh blow. And along with the hurt, Miya felt the bitterness seeping through, invading his very being, and threatening to tear him apart when he saw Kiyoshi and his brother getting along the way they did. He couldn't stand it.

And maybe even more so because of this than because his parents weren't all right with the way he lived and the people he fell in love with. He feared rejection beyond anything else.

***

Frightened, Miya realized, sitting in the apartment in Higashinada that morning, that the feeling he experienced now that Miura had rejected him was far too similar to the shock that had hit him when Shigeru had said those words and proceeded to ignore him.

It was similar to the despair he'd felt when he realized that the businessman had never loved him back, and the time when Nomura had told him that he'd *outgrown* their relation. He didn't understand it—none of it. But in the short time that they'd spent together, he'd apparently grown some rather strong feelings for the teacher, and he was overcome by the thought that he'd indeed wanted this to work out so badly.

Now all he wanted was to get drunk and sleep until the hurt all went away once more. Wasn't this precisely why he'd never wanted to be in another relationship? Because every single time he fell in love with someone, this happened? Maybe he fell too easily, but was it really necessary that it should hurt this badly every single time?

He felt miserable, and he had no idea how to handle it or acknowledge that it was somehow his own damned fault that these things kept happening.

If he'd kept his big mouth shut, then surely Miura wouldn't have turned around the way he had and suddenly changed his mind about everything.

Hadn't he known from the beginning that the other man was the more careful sort, that he didn't like rushing into anything and that he was insecure and new to this? Where did he come from, spouting the things that he'd done that night while they had been eating *sukiyaki*? Had it been absolutely necessary for him to just dump everything on the other man? And again, he absolutely resented every outspoken bone in his own body and wished he could be just the slightest bit conceited without any kind of need to tell people about his relationship with his friends and coworkers. His mother had accused him of lying. But even omitting the truth… If he never *said* anything, it couldn't be accounted as lying, could it? And it would be better for everyone in the long run if he just didn't say anything at all.

But it was too late now. And he absolutely hated it.

18. Callous

It was cold, his fingers already blue and purple even as he was stuffing them as deeply into his pockets as he could, balling them up and squeezing as hard as possible. He felt chilled to the bone as the wind gusted through his coat and the zip-up hoodie he was wearing with nothing underneath it.

He was standing outside the gate of a relatively normal-looking middle school, surprised that he remembered the name and had found his way there, as he wasn't usually one to pay attention to such details. Miura's work had just been a small detail in their so-called relationship, not at all relevant to Miya's interests, but it must have wedged itself in the back of his mind somehow.

His head was pounding, and unless he grit them hard together, his teeth would chatter in the sudden cold that had gripped the city so abruptly this morning.

He didn't know what he was doing here, much less if there was any point to it. Teachers were probably usually confined to the teachers' lounge during lunch, unless they had some kind of errand, especially when the weather was this bad.

He didn't even know when lunch hour started. It probably wasn't until eleven. Standing there until then was madness. It was over an hour until lunchtime, and by then he'd be frozen solid. Yet, he didn't move, and remained standing.

Finally someone seemed to notice him and made their way over to where Miya was standing. The person turned out to be a middle-aged man dressed in an expensive-looking coat. He had an overall respectable aura about him.

"Excuse me, sir?"

Sir. That was a new one.

"I'm sorry, does it appear suspicious that I'm standing here?" He suddenly realized he was dressed like a total slob, and he was standing outside a middle school, looking in through the gates. It probably didn't look very good. The news was always full of things like this, creepy old men gawking at kids, and parents being told to keep an eye on their teenagers at all times to make sure they weren't getting involved with any suspicious characters.

"I don't know about suspicious but... Are you waiting for someone?"

Miya inhaled sharply. "Miura Shunsuke." He bit his own lip. "I mean, I know him. He works here, doesn't he?"

"He does... He's got class at the moment though. Would you like me to pass on a message?"

"No... I just wanted to see if he was around. It's nothing important."

It wasn't a lie. After all, it *wasn't* important. He had no idea what he was doing here, or why. If Miura appeared, he wouldn't know what to say to him. And what *could* he say when everything had been said and determined already?

"So, are you a friend of Miura-sensei?"

Miya shrugged absentmindedly. "Something like that."

"I see. Well, he'll be off in about an hour for lunch. But I suppose that's a bit long to wait."

"That's okay," he replied again, just as flatly. "It's nothing important. I just happened to be passing by."

"Well then," the other man said, looking a little perplexed. "I should go back; it's time for my class."

The man in the coat walked away. Miya watched him as he disappeared through the large front doors to the building. The man had seemed like a serious kind of teacher, perhaps history or literature or something. Miya wondered if he'd sensed anything.

***

By the time the bell rang for lunch, Miya was so used to freezing that he didn't notice that his toes were curling reflexively in his boots, or that his hands were already entirely numb.

He'd long since passed the point where he wished he'd brought gloves with him, and he had absolutely no idea what he had been doing while standing in pretty much the same place, looking up at the school building. Perhaps he'd been trying to find out which floor Miura taught on, or which window was in his classroom. Perhaps he'd been asking himself the question of whether or not this bordered on stalking.

It probably did.

And it was probably stupid, and self-pitying, standing here in the cold, allowing himself to be numbed by the weather as he wished deep down to be noticed by someone who apparently didn't want anything to do with him anymore.

But then, all of a sudden, he found himself face to face with the teacher, and he wondered if he was starting to see things, having been so dazed for such a long time.

"Satoru, what are you doing here?"

Hearing his name spoken in that voice... it almost made him feel a little warmer. And he wondered how Miura could call him by that name when he'd made it clear that they were over. Didn't it signify a kind of affirmation?

"I..." he started, but his cold lips couldn't form the words, and they seemed to have wedged in his throat anyhow.

"What are you thinking?" Miura stepped out between the gates, pulling him aside, lowering his voice, "coming here like this?"

"I wasn't," he replied, honestly. "I just... What happened yesterday?"

"You know very well what happened."

It didn't appear like Miura wanted to go into detail in such a public place. Miya looked down at himself, at the baggy pants he was still wearing and the way they were sloppily tucked into his boots. His jacket was undone, and the hood of his sweater was sticking out in the back, looking ridiculous no doubt. He probably looked just about as horrible as he felt.

"But... I don't understand it. I thought things were good..."

Miura sighed heavily and didn't reply.

"Shuns-" he bit his own tongue, "Miura, I'm sorry if I did

236

something that—"

"It doesn't matter. You shouldn't be here."

Miya grit his teeth, forcing himself to hold back so the bitter disappointment wouldn't wash over him and show. Maybe he'd been hoping for a better conclusion—an explanation as to what had triggered the sudden rejection. And then perhaps an excuse and an apology from him as well for whatever it was he'd done that had triggered the event because it *had* to be his fault somehow. And in the end, maybe things would have worked out.

He could dream. But instead, he felt his cheeks growing hot as his body grew colder when he realized there was nothing more than cold dismissal in the other man's tone.

"This isn't the place to talk about this," he said in a stern way, and it reminded Miya of the first night they'd met, and how threatening Miura had seemed. Afterwards, he'd learned that it had been a shield to hide behind, and that he was really interested in getting to know him better. Apparently, that must have resulted in nothing but disdain; why else would he be pushing him away again, in the same cold way?

"Then let's go somewhere else." He reached for the man's hand, his mind still hazy and unclear.

Miura pulled away, looking just as sternly at him.

"I'm at work. Go home, Satoru." He averted his eyes.

So you can't even look at me.

He swallowed his wounded pride and just stared at the teacher, his eyes burning. He wanted it to be from the icy wind. It wasn't.

"Sorry," he said, looking down at his feet.

He felt defeated. There was nothing more to say. He wrapped his arms around himself and kicked a pebble that was on the ground. It partly rolled, partly skipped across the pavement before, finally landing with a quiet *plop* in a puddle nearby.

"I'll be going then." He gave something like a wave with two fingers and turned away without casting another glance at the man. He couldn't take it.

One more look at that cold, harsh face would be enough to throw him into feelings he didn't want to explore any further. He couldn't stand that the face that had smiled so brightly at him, the lips that had kissed him on the nose first thing in the morning or whispered sweet words into his ear during a moment of passion were now expressing nothing but disgust at him.

He lacked the words to describe the way it felt. So he turned away and left without saying another word.

***

Feeling even more discouraged than before, he found himself going down to Maki's.

"Morning," he said as he slammed the door open and staggered inside.

"Hey!" Maki barely turned his head to look at him; he was busy doing something or other over by the burners, and the place already smelled of delicious, fried, greasy food. "Aki came looking for you this morning."

"Yeah?"

"It was a few hours ago. He had breakfast here. Where were you?"

Miya slumped down on the barstool closest to where Maki stood, placing his arms on the bar, resting his chin on top of them and sighing heavily. "Nowhere."

"Miya..." Maki turned, and his expression immediately changed to one of concern. "You look terrible! What have you been up to?"

"You should know; you were the one serving me last night."

"I don't expect you to remember, but I cut you off."

"Thank you," Miya groaned. His headache hadn't exactly lessened after walking in the freezing cold wind they were blessed with in this part of the city at all times.

"I wasn't referring to that though," the bartender said, getting himself back on track and placing his hand on top of Miya's. "You're ice cold! Have you been out long?"

"A couple of hours," he admitted. "I went to see someone..."

"That guy?" Maki was way ahead of him, as expected. He was already preparing a cup of steaming hot coffee.

"Yeah." Miya accepted the mug, sipping at it before the beverage had even had time to cool down. It burned his lips and scorched his tongue, but he was thankful for the warmth slowly spreading inside of his frozen self.

"How did it go?"

"Uh..." Miya tried to smile, but it came off as something like a bitter grimace instead. His fingers clenched the porcelain cup harder, and his eyes darted around the room. He felt incredibly vulnerable and was afraid he might break down crying. Not only because of Miura, but the whole situation—feeling hung over, being ice cold, being tired and sleepy, and feeling so completely out of touch with the world and himself. "It didn't..."

"Oh sweetie." Maki resorted to the same words Miya used to comfort other people. And Miya had to admit it felt good when the other man came around the bar to stand behind him and wrap his arms around his chest, hugging him from behind. "I'm really sorry."

Maki rested his chin on Miya's shoulder, touching their cheeks together. He remained standing in that position for a while, just holding him. His body was warm against Miya's, helping with the cold as well as with his general feeling of discomfort.

"Thanks..." he whispered, sipping at the coffee. "I'm sure I'll get over it."

"Isn't that how it goes?" Maki spoke softly next to his ear. "We always get through it somehow, but it hurts like a bitch in the meantime, right?"

"Mhm." Miya nodded thoughtfully. "And yet we never seem to learn."

"So true," Maki sighed, exhaling soft, warm breath against his neck as he nuzzled into him one last time before pulling away. "Maybe we're all too optimistic."

"Maybe. Is it too much to ask for though?"

Maki shook his head. "I'm still trying to figure that one out myself."

Miya was grateful it was just the two of them in the shop so they could talk in peace. He didn't remember the night before in vivid detail but enough to feel a little ashamed of the way he had acted, not only in front of his own friends, but more because of the other customers. It wasn't the first time a scene like that had played out in the shop, but it still didn't sit right with him that it had been *his* private life on display for everyone.

"Mind if I remove my boots?" he asked. "My toes are freezing."

"Didn't you wear any socks?"

"I wasn't thinking clearly this morning…"

"Are you insane?" Maki exclaimed. "Wait there."

He disappeared through the door in the back and up the short flight of stairs to his two-room where he resided, returning with a pair of knitted woolen socks. "Here. Put those on. They should fit you."

"You knit?"

The elder man sent him a firm look. "No. I don't. They were a gift. Now put them on before you get gangrene."

"You're hilarious, you know that?" Miya grinned, heartfelt this time as he took the socks from the other man and put them on his benumbed feet. Almost instantly, he felt better. "Whatever happened to that guy anyway?"

"What guy?"

"Remember, that morning, you had that guy sleeping upstairs?"

"Oh *him*." Maki's eyes glazed over with something dreamy and nostalgic. "We saw each other a few times. Nothing serious."

"How come?"

"Since when are you so inquisitive?" the other man retorted. "I told you about the frogs of the past, did I not? Anyway, he's too young for me."

"How young?" Miya grinned.

"Says you, who sleeps with your teenage roomie."

A shadow washed over Miya's face. "He's practically an adult."

"Or so he thinks," Maki snorted. "I'm only teasing you. But no, he's not someone I'll be getting further involved with, though if he comes knocking, I suppose I have no other choice than to let him in."

There was a playful smirk on his painted lips. Miya felt out of place when looking down at himself in comparison to Maki's flawlessness. The man rarely looked anything less than respectable, sometimes even dressing in traditional *yukata* and putting up his hair, looking almost like a woman. It was frightening. Maki's beauty was something more classy and refined than the one the rest of them sported, with their heavy make-up and revealing clothing.

"I'm sure," he replied, shaking his head.

"You feel better now?"

"A little, I don't know. It helps talking to you I guess, or to Naru."

Maki nodded. "Yeah, you shouldn't keep things bottled up; it's not healthy. If you want to cry, then cry!" He said it with such determination, pumping his fist in the air, that Miya had to laugh at him. "I'm serious though!" the man exclaimed. "If you want to cry about it, then do. If you keep it in, it'll just eat you up from the inside. I should know."

"I'm tired of crying though," Miya replied, not inquiring about Maki's reasons for crying in the past. "I did that. Before. And it didn't really help."

"Didn't it?"

"Well, it got the emotions out all right until the next heartbreak came along. I found not falling in love to be more effective." He was referring to his younger, more vulnerable self.

"You're a love addict." Maki said it so matter-of-factly that it sounded like an actual condition. "Aren't you?"

"What?"

"You fall in love with the feeling of being in love."

"Something like that," Miya replied. "Can that be considered real love or is it just fascination?"

Maki shrugged. "I think perhaps scientists are still working on that. Meanwhile, we mortals are falling left and right for people that don't want to be with us. It's kinda sad."

"You're *making* me want to cry," Miya remarked dryly,

lifting the coffee mug to his lips again. It was cooling, and the taste was bitter. He dropped a couple of sugar cubes into it and stirred slowly with a spoon, staring right ahead as he did.

"Like I said—"

"Leave it," he said, rejecting the advice.

"So what are you going to do about it?" Maki asked.

"About what?"

"Him of course. What was his name?"

"Miura," Miya replied, noticing how impersonal, almost clinical that sounded when he'd been getting used to his given name. In the back of his mind, he could clearly hear the echo of himself whispering *"Shunsuke"* into the man's ear in a hoarse, strained voice. His cheeks felt warm, flushing with something that was part embarrassment, part something else.

"Whoever this Miura is," Maki continued, "he's making you blush. And he makes you want to cry. So which is it?"

"Which is what?" Miya felt a little irritated, having been too far off in his own thoughts to understand what the other man was trying to get at.

"You have two choices from here." Maki held up two fingers in front of himself. "Either you accept the rejection and move on with your life—in other words, you give up on him. Or you try to convince him into giving you another chance—as in, you're not willing to let him go."

Miya sighed. "I don't know. He said he didn't want to see me again."

"Were those his exact words?"

Perhaps not, but the tone of Miura's voice, the look in his eyes... Those had been enough. No more words were needed beyond that. It was more than enough to get his point across.

"Just remember that you're always free to change your mind, but it's easier one way than the other," Maki said solemnly, looking dead serious.

"This comes from you, the one who doesn't even look at a frog anymore?"

"I don't necessarily need to follow my own advice, do I?"

"Hmm," Miya grunted in response. "Can I get another cup of

coffee, please?"

"Sure. Are you getting any warmer over there?"

"Yeah," he smiled briefly, "thank you."

Miya remained sitting for a while longer, and shortly after, the lunch rush finally started—an odd number of guys he more or less recognized from various places coming in through the doors. He decided to leave, not wanting to be around people.

Maki talked him into keeping the socks for now as he sent him off with an encouraging smile. "Think about it, yeah?"

***

And he did. Maki's words churned around inside of his mind for the better part of the week. He didn't act on them because he still didn't know what to think, but he kept them close to heart, as they hit him over and over.

On the outside, he probably seemed like he was bouncing back. It wasn't so much that he felt better though, it was more the fact that he was so used to dealing with this kind of thing that once he got over the initial shock, he became a champion at ignoring it and pretending like nothing was wrong.

He played the feisty, flirty character that he was so used to portraying at work, and he had no problem laughing and joking with the others after hours, especially not after influences of various kinds had found their way inside of his system. And while it probably wasn't entirely right, he found himself occasionally taking the flirting to a higher level, fending off the little voice inside of him that told him he was doing exactly what he *shouldn't* be doing.

But more than Maki's words about making a proper choice stuck with him, it was something else Miya's mind was focusing on—the ghost of his past. Not only the victims of his implied addiction, but his own growing up as well.

A haunting or two from his teenage years was just as common in his dreams lately as a replay of the scene in the bar, or the one in front of the school.

19. Confrontation

Life had been dismal after the day at the bar with Miura, when they'd gone their separate ways, more than painful after their meeting outside the school when Miya had been so utterly rejected and crushed.

Miya didn't understand himself, and his friends weren't much help in the matter either. Hiiro kept telling him the same things Maki did—that he'd get new chances, and that it probably wasn't meant to be. Naru tried soothing him by talking about how he'd taken the plunge and nobody could expect more. But it didn't help. Not when Miya couldn't stop feeling like it was all his fault.

But then his sadness had turned to anger. He was angry because Miura had taken it upon himself to end their relation before it had even begun without explaining properly. He was angry that he had to figure it all out on his own, and that the man could fire such cheap shots at him. Like he was so high and mighty himself? The man who couldn't even go out with him in public without cautiously looking left and right! But that was stretching it too far—there was a reason their club was underground. *He* was the one who'd defended the club and his coworkers, talking about how they were supporting each other and the clientele in this cruel, callous world they all lived in. So why was he so sad? Everything pointed towards the other man being just another loser not worth fighting for, didn't it?

But Miya had always been like this. For him, not being able to separate his own stupidity from that of others just made his condition so much worse—the condition that he, despite trying to appear cynical, fell in love far too easily. Maki was probably right about him.

It didn't matter who he went home with, and what he did with them, or how drunk he was, and where he slept it off, spending yet another drunken stupor together with someone or on his own. What did it matter when all that came to mind constantly were pale, soft lips whispering arousing words into his ear only to turn treacherous and whisper cruel words in the next second? And when the hands he felt so vividly on his body still just as quickly turned cold and unfamiliar, almost as if they didn't want to touch him. He longed for it nonetheless. For this familiar, scary thing he'd experienced for some short weeks in his twenty-eighth year. The year he fell in love so unexpectedly with such force.

Yet again, he turned around and uprooted himself and everything he'd been determined to do.

He'd silently accepted that there were people out there who didn't accept him for who he was. He'd silently accepted that Shigeru hated him because of who he fell in love with. And that day in front of the school, he'd accepted that Miura had decided they weren't to see each other again without even attempting to put up a fight or asking if there was something he could do to prevent them from falling apart.

At the very least, he wanted to know for certain what had happened between the two of them, and why things had changed so suddenly. If possible, he hoped to make enough of an impact for Miura to reconsider, or at least hear him out properly. He was hurt, and he was sad, and he was terrified of being dragged even further down after having put himself through his own personal incarnation of hell over the past weeks.

But then he'd opened his eyes to look at Aki—even more than usual.

It was partially thanks to his roommate that he changed. From that night when he'd brought the other teenager home, Aki had changed as well. He seemed more bitter, less sociable. True, the teen had never been particularly cheerful or even polite, but it was as if the other teenager brought out the worst in him. And in the same way, Miya had noticed that the white-haired boy carried some sort of reminiscence of his own past: the acceptance, the hopeful gleam in his seemingly innocent eyes. Miya had observed them together and established that whatever it was that was developing between the two of them, there was definitely a certain sense of self-loathing and strangeness between them. He became more aware of Aki's miserable disposition and became increasingly worried—for him as well as for Yuuki.

And it made him consider how strange they all were, what they were willing to put up with, or give up for the sake of someone else. And how dishonest they all were.

He realized that the feelings he carried, albeit budding and immature still, were worth something. He didn't want them to wither away. He didn't want to *not* know, to carry on and wonder what potentially *could* have happened.

He regarded his younger friends, and upon seeing their destructive patterns, he wondered how happy he really was.

Had he been any happier before than he was now? Sure, he was heartbroken, and he'd been content before. But wasn't it all habitual? Defensive? Most likely a combination of everything. And perhaps he just wanted something new and exciting and someone who would love him, if only for a short period of time. But even so…

He decided that he had to take the chance and seek out Miura once more. Even though he would probably brush him off again, he needed to do this for his own sake—to get closure. He had things he wanted to say and impulses he desperately needed to follow.

In their world, happiness wasn't something to reckon with. Luck wasn't the same as getting lucky. He'd had the taste of something he thought he'd stopped longing for. And with a heavy heart and trembling fingers, he picked up his phone and called up Miura. It was a school day, and he was well aware that he was probably interrupting. He could only hope that the teacher would actually pick up the phone when he called, or at least call him back when he noticed the missed call.

If he didn't, or rather because he probably wouldn't, Miya dragged himself to the school district where the man worked, near the place where they'd gone shopping, found a café with grand windows facing the street, and called him from there. As expected, there was no response.

He ordered a large cup of coffee, to which he absentmindedly added extreme quantities of the sugar supplied on the side in small packages. He paid it no mind as he stirred the hot beverage slowly, the spoon clinking against the yellow porcelain while he sat at the counter by the window, waiting to see the familiar shape of that man walk past the window.

He hadn't even touched his coffee when it finally happened, and he nearly knocked the mug over as he sprung to his feet to apprehend him.

The ground was wet under the soles of his shoes as he stepped out of the café and rapidly carried on down the street, trailing the suit-clad man holding a generic, transparent umbrella, fending off the small drops of rain that fell from the light grey sky on this day that seemed to reflect his ambivalent mood. It looked like the sun could break through the clouds at any given moment, but it was impossible to tell whether it actually would. Miya felt the same way and was hesitant to speak up. His steps were quick, rapid strides, squelching sounds of wet shoes against the pavement, arms swinging nervously at his side. He was trailing the man, and it probably looked apparent to anyone passing them by. He bit his lip, inhaling sharply.

He heard his own voice calling out, "Miura!"

He was so afraid of calling him out that his voice cracked, and he was worried that the other man hadn't heard him, that his voice had been drowned out in the bustle of the street and the people coming to and fro, brushing past them at a steady pace. But the man carrying the umbrella stopped uncertainly and slowly turned around to look in his direction.

He seemed at a loss about what to do, and Miya understood him. After all, he had no idea what he was doing himself. Hesitantly, he came over, all the while hearing his own voice chanting inside of his mind, *"Don't go. Don't go. Please wait…"*

The teacher stayed put, standing in the same place. The drizzle fell on his umbrella and ran in slow streams from the curved plastic before dripping to the ground, turning into black splotches on the pavement.

Miya watched them intensely as he approached, staring at the ground as if all his bravado had seeped into the cracks in the pavement as well.

"What do you want, Satoru?"

The sound of his own name coming out from in between those lips again sent chills down his spine as he recalled a hoarser version of the same speech, breathed into his ear in a moment of passion, which seemed like a million years ago, but still so recent. Although it was cold outside, and Miya wasn't wearing anything more than a cardigan he'd thrown on before leaving the house, he felt like heat enveloped him as the thought crossed his mind.

"I tried calling you," he tried.

"I know."

So he'd seen it then, which also meant he'd chosen to ignore him. This was going to be hard, and he started to feel the sting of anger again.

"Why didn't you pick up?"

"You know why. There's nothing left to say."

"For you maybe," Miya replied stubbornly. "But regardless of what you want to call this—a relationship or whatever—we were two people going into it, and I think it's reasonable that you allow me to talk as well."

The words just streamed forwards without any kind of structure, and Miya felt incapable of stopping the flow of disappointment and accusation that forced its way out from between his lips.

"I think it was really unfair of you to just storm off without listening to me—*twice*." His voice was full of resentment, threatening to break at any moment. "So I'd like to talk to you. And preferably not here."

He noticed that people were already sneaking glances in their direction, and that Miura was nervously shifting his weight from one leg to the other, looking around fretfully. There was a high chance someone might come by and see them, someone who knew him. It didn't look right. And as much as the focus on outward appearance infuriated Miya as he stood feeling his hair grow damp from the drizzle trickling down between tousles of ebony, he did have enough tact to at least offer the man a chance to talk to him somewhere more private.

Although, to a certain extent, it felt like he was doing some kind of extortion, ambushing the man in the street like this and then demanding they talk somewhere else.

"I suppose that's fair," Miura finally sighed. "We should go somewhere else."

"Let's go to your house," Miya suggested.

He assumed that would be impossible given the situation and their history, but he was surprised when the man agreed.

"It's not ideal, but I suppose it's the best option," he said, beginning to walk down the sidewalk again. He made no gesture for Miya to follow, but he did so anyway, keeping a couple of paces behind, trying to appear calm.

He was surprised however when the other man turned a slightly uncertain gaze towards him and said, "You're getting wet."

Miya looked back at him, brushing his moist fringe out of his eyes, hoping that his make-up wasn't getting smeared.

"Come." Miura gestured for him to come closer and made a motion to the umbrella slightly as a signal that Miya should join him. It felt far too intimate. Miya's chest ached. It wasn't fair. How could he suggest something like that when the situation was what it was?

Miya came up to walk at his side. The space underneath the umbrella was limited, even though it was of the large kind. Nonetheless, their elbows occasionally brushed as they walked beneath the drumming of the raindrops on the umbrella. He felt his cheeks burning and concentrated on watching his own feet, swallowing over and over. He felt like crying. It was impossible to understand why this hurt so badly.

He thought to himself that he was pathetic, but it was pointless. He knew that guts were needed for him to do what he was doing at this moment, and he couldn't deny that his heart jumped a little every time they touched their elbows together, but he didn't dare look at the other man. He barely dared to breathe. But again, just like before, he was certain that the teacher could hear his heart pounding even over the sounds that filled the busy street.

He was relieved when they reached the teacher's small apartment. Even though he was so nervous it made him feel nauseous, and he considered giving up the whole thing for the umpteenth time, he removed his shoes in the entrance hall and tentatively stepped inside, remaining standing in the middle of the room so as to not seem too familiar with being here. Not that it mattered. He felt so awkward and insecure that he couldn't feel at home here even if he tried. And he purposely turned his back on the bed where he'd previously slept with the other man.

"I'm sorry," he said, "for doing this, but I really wanted to talk to you."

Miura stood over by the kitchen, regarding him with something indescribable in his dark eyes, which didn't seem to be entirely fixated on Miya at all. "Talk," he said gruffly.

The tension in the air was heavy, crushing. It was somewhat reminiscent of what things had been like that night when they had first met, but darker... gloomier. Miya felt like he was suffocating and a desperate need to open a window filled him, but he didn't move. His lips parted, but no words came out.

"Satoru."

He regarded the man in the kitchen and felt overcome with emotions at the sound of his own name yet again.

"Why do you keep saying that?" he whispered. "Satoru, Satoru..."

"That's your name, isn't it?" He was feigning aloofness.

"Yeah, but very few people use it."

"I couldn't call you 'Miya.'"

"How come?"

He was relieved that they were talking at least.

"Because...."

"Then why don't you call me by my last name instead?" he countered. "You don't have to say anything else."

It stung inside of him. Miya was the name *they* all used. Wasn't that why?

"It's too familiar," he said. "You can't call me by that name if you're going to…" He swallowed bitterly. The taste was salty.

He remembered that night when Miura had asked to call him by his first name and how odd he'd found it, but yet how willing he'd been to comply… And it bothered him that he himself was back to using the man's last name. He didn't dare say his given name out loud.

"What is it you wanted to talk about?"

"Us," Miya replied, the word coming as part of a nervous exhalation. "Whatever we used to be."

It was so recent but so distant. It wasn't very tangible either, and he even wondered if the events in this very room had ever even taken place. It had been like they'd been inside of a bubble, a world of their own whenever they met, especially on the drowsy mornings and late nights when he'd crawled into bed with the other man. Much of their relationship was no more than hazy memories, but Miya cherished them as something that was completely different from what he'd experienced in his other relations. The scent of the man everywhere in this room overpowered him.

"I just… I wanted to have the opportunity to talk to you too, if you don't mind," he pleaded and noticed his voice growing thicker.

Miura nodded, half a nod, still standing immobile over by the counter, his arms crossed over his chest. He really was defensive.

"So talk," the man said again.

Miya started hesitantly, mumbling about how he didn't know what he wanted to say, but that he felt it necessary to say *something*, and that he was sorry if the other saw this as some sort of waste of time, but he felt the need to express himself and how unfair he found it that he hadn't gotten a say in anything.

"And I need to know," he said, "what happened?"

"We're just too different," Miura replied.

"I don't buy into that."

The other man disregarded the statement. "I'm a teacher. I grade papers and wear ties every day. I hate my job on occasion, but I love it all the more when I feel like I'm doing the right thing, when I see their eyes light up as they understand something I'm explaining to them. I'm a role model. And you... your lifestyle is so different from mine."

Again with the lifestyle. Miya was certain that even if he'd been a straight man, he would have led the same kind of life and enjoyed a variety of the same things, like drinking and partying till the early hours. It wasn't uncommon for young people. Perhaps he was irresponsible, but was that enough of a reason to just give up on someone so suddenly? Obviously that wasn't the sole reason.

"Every time I went to your workplace, I felt so out of place. The music, and the outfits... and the way everyone acts." It looked as if it made his skin crawl. "The way *you* act with them."

That one hurt. It dug into his chest like a sharp dagger, carving through the flesh, and Miya vaguely recalled that night when Takahiro had returned. Hadn't he thought he saw...

"You were there," he said. "You were there that night when I was talking to Takahiro-kun!"

He remembered now. He'd thought he'd spotted Miura somewhere near the entrance, but at that point, he'd been very tired and because he'd been so infatuated already, it was no problem for him to easily imagine seeing the other man in places where he wasn't—if he saw someone dressed in a similar way, or with the same build. That night though, his colleagues had loudly been talking and teasing him about the last time the student had come to the club. He'd been flirty himself as well, but mostly because it was part of the job. Though he'd said some things that...

"I didn't mean—" he bit his own lip. "If you heard us talking... it was in bad taste, but I was only joking."

He didn't know whether or not Miura had stuck around long enough to hear him say that he was bad with relationships, as if he wasn't putting any kind of faith in the two of them. So he'd been the one to sabotage it from the very beginning after all?

He didn't at all feel like a grown man at this point but like a cowering child, trying to apologize for breaking something he shouldn't have played with in the first place.

"Nothing happened. I swear." It felt degrading that he had to defend himself in this way, but he knew it was necessary. He'd been open with what kind of background he had after all.

Miura said nothing. He felt the need to spill everything, about every single person he'd seen over the course of time they'd been an item. But what was the use? If Miura didn't believe him, or if he cut him off…

"I slept with him before," he said, "but that was before I met you… And nothing happened. But even if… if you thought so, why didn't you bring it up?"

"I never said that was the reason," Miura replied, still making no attempt at moving or appearing more animated.

"Then what *is* it?" Miya demanded, growing hot underneath his collar. "Because you don't really say anything! I didn't get any reasons."

The other man didn't say anything—as expected.

Miya let out a loud sigh, a scoff of frustration as he placed his hands angrily on his hips, glaring at him. "I didn't think so."

His insides were at war. He was so hurt and so full of questions, but the meek approach was waning, making room for the anger he was carrying, threatening to break loose.

"But I'm not stupid," he said, his teeth gnashing together as he spoke. "It's really sort of obvious."

"What are you talking about?"

Miya thought to himself that his way of bringing things up wasn't the best, and that he was somehow about to live up to his friends' idea of a drama queen, and that perhaps it had influenced him a bit too much to be living together with a teenager.

"I didn't do anything with Takahiro. I didn't do anything with anyone else when I thought we were together, but you're not the first one to do this to me."

Their gazes locked. Miya's lips trembled, but he continued to speak.

"You're too respectable to be with someone like me, right?"

He swallowed, tears burning behind his eyelids, while his tired gaze still refused to avert itself. "And it's not like I don't get it; that I'm not good enough for you. But you didn't have to lie about it! Why couldn't you just tell me right away?" His shoulders drooped in resignation. "It's not like I'm not already aware of what I am…"

He finally tore his eyes from the man standing stiffly before him, unable to look at his expressionless face and lack of reaction anymore.

He'd never fought for anything before in his life—not anything like this. He was used to falling in love, or falling in love with the emotion itself, only to be rejected. But he'd never fought for *someone* before. He'd never accepted rejection, but he still hadn't argued, just allowed himself to silently get hurt, crying his bitter tears at night when nobody saw. For once, he'd decided to try and get back something he wanted, only to realize that there wasn't much of a point to it, not with him being what he was. How was he ever supposed to get anything this way?

"After all," he muttered quietly, "I live my life this way because there's no other way for someone like me to live." He bitterly swallowed his tears. "Maybe I *am* a slut, but I still thought you were different. At least I thought you were man enough to tell me the truth when you ended it. Guess I was wrong."

That was it. There wasn't really much else to say. He felt empty and irritated with himself for having come all this way just to say that, like some overly dramatic kid. It didn't stop the pain in the slightest though.

"I should go," he said. "Sorry for wasting your time. I just wanted to say that."

He forced a sad smile as he started edging towards the hall and the front door. "And whether you choose to believe it or not, I do have some moral standards. Just thought I'd put that out there."

"Satoru…"

At the sound of his own name, he bit down on his lip hard, but he didn't turn around.

"It's fine," he said quietly. "I understand."

"No, you don't."

He wanted to leave, and he wanted Miura to stop him, to grab him by the arm and hold him back if he tried, but he didn't move an inch, and from the sound of it, neither did the other man. They just remained standing in the small apartment with an oppressive silence reigning.

"What?" he finally dared to speak. "What is it I don't understand?"

The words were heavy, like the feeling in his gut, falling quietly from his dry, pale lips.

"Or maybe I'm the clueless one," Miura muttered as if he was speaking to himself and not to Miya at all. "Maybe *I* didn't understand."

There was a pause. Was he waiting for him to turn around? Miya didn't in any case. He couldn't stand it—wouldn't be able to leave if he did.

"I was selfish and didn't think about your feelings. Maybe even purposely."

It didn't sound like any kind of apology... if Miya had been hoping for one.

"You're not really helping," he whispered hoarsely.

"Of course it might seem that way... And maybe I even was a bit put off by your lifestyle and everything that goes with it. That was why I left that night at the club! I'm a teacher, how am I supposed to stand by and look at your roommate, barely older than my own students acting like—"

Miya spun around. "Don't talk about him like that! You don't know the first thing about him, so don't you even dare!"

It was as if he was transferring all his anger into this, wanting to focus it on something else, as well as being fed up with the talk about teachers and students and all the excuses.

"He's a good kid," he mumbled, "even if he's in a lot of trouble. And he's got nothing to do with this."

"I know," Miura sighed. "Maybe I'm just making excuses. I

blamed you for my own shortcomings."

Miya let out a frustrated sigh. There wasn't much of a point apologizing or explaining now that it was over anyway. He just wanted to get out of there and get on with his heartbreak.

"Even if I don't condone a lot of the things that are normal for you guys, and maybe I don't understand the first thing about any of you... That's not relevant. I never thought you went behind my back or anything. I didn't leave that night because I saw you with that guy and assumed... You're not like that, Satoru."

"Sure I am," he smiled bitterly, "but not this time."

"Why are you making this so difficult?"

"Why are we doing this at all?" Miya retorted stubbornly, not wanting to show any more emotion. If he was going to be emotional, then he'd only express anger; he'd decided on that before going out.

"You aren't the problem here at all. I broke up with you because I was afraid."

"Afraid of what?" Miya struggled to hide his curiosity and to keep the coolness in his voice. "We don't have to do this."

"Yes, we do. Rather that than having you walking around taking all the blame, losing confidence over my mistakes."

"Shunsuke..." He accidentally called the man by his first name and turned away nervously for a moment, pulling himself together. "I *am* one of your mistakes."

"Stop it!"

The teacher had actually raised his voice for a moment, but then his gaze turned milder again, and he looked more forlorn than anything.

"Can you just listen to me please? I know it's not easy seeing how I acted earlier. I was afraid, Satoru. That's the truth. Maybe that's strange to you, but we're so different. That in itself is perhaps daunting, but for me, there have been a lot of things to take in in a very short time. You're not the type to be quiet and hold back, but I've been hiding myself for years. In comparison, we're not all that compatible."

Miya wanted to comment on him rubbing it in but kept his

mouth shut. It felt dry. He waited for the rest.

"I never meant to be cruel or hurt you the way I did. I guess I panicked. For you, maybe it's weird to hear a grown man say something like this, but I didn't know what to say when people asked, I didn't know what excuses to make when they wanted to set me up with women. What if I lost my job? I'm a middle school teacher—a role model! Those were the things I had on my mind. Maybe it's shallow, but this country..."

His words were poison arrows, and they etched into Miya's chest with each syllable. Miya grabbed the front of his shirt, nervously tugging on it. His eyes were turned down towards his feet. He felt incredibly small.

What was he supposed to say to something like that? That the man he was in love with had to make up excuses because they were together?

Hadn't he been through this enough times before?

"You don't have to do that anymore though," he said quietly, swallowing. "After all, we're not together anymore."

Those words stung just as much.

"But what if...." Miura took a step forward but stopped. He hesitated. "I know I'm worthless for putting you through this for such selfish reasons. I don't expect you to forgive or even understand that."

"That's fine." Miya shook his head slowly. "I just wanted to know what the reason was. Why you didn't want to be with me."

"Aren't you listening? I want to be with you!"

Miya's heart ached, jumped inside his ribcage.

He tilted his head upwards and noticed that the other man had come closer.

"Do you know how much it took," Miura asked, "keeping you at a distance? Pretending like I was completely unaffected? Not answering your calls? I saw you standing out there in the cold that day, and I had to leave the class for a moment to pull myself together. I've never felt so rotten before in my life."

"And yet you didn't really put a stop to it," Miya replied coolly. "You think you're the only one who's afraid? Do you know what it was like opening up to someone only to be pushed away like that? You think it gets any easier just because I'm used to it?"

He noticed the tremble in his own voice and wanted to give in to his shaking knees and drop to the floor.

"Nobody ever wants anything more from me," he whispered so quietly he was sure only he could hear it. "And it's not like I mind, but... I was happy, you know? What was I supposed to think?"

He sniffed hard, trying to hold himself together for a while longer. He felt ridiculous. He felt like that kid who'd cried for days because some middle-aged scumbag didn't love him. Or that kid who hurt so badly on the inside because the guy he'd been close with in school had excitedly bragged to him about his new girlfriend. He felt like that young man who had only himself to blame and continued sticking up for the lover who might as well have been a psychopath at heart. Here he was again. And this time it really hurt because this man was someone who'd been good to him, and honest—or so he'd thought.

"Satoru, the only reason I said those things was to push you away, so it would be easier. I'm not going to lie; it was easier because we had some fundamental differences to begin with. But I never suspected you of anything; I didn't blame you for being yourself. Even if it was way out of my comfort zone. I trusted you."

"And I trusted you," Miya replied, not daring to look up and see if the man had come even closer. He felt his presence off on his left side, and his heart beat faster.

"Do you know what a love addict is?" he blurted. "Someone who falls in love with the feeling of being in love? It's a person who loves easily and strongly. Regardless of time span. I might fall easily, but believe it or not, I'm faithful."

"Like I said, I never doubted that you—"

"Are you in love with me?"

Even in these situations, he'd always benefited from being able to ask direct questions.

"How can you ask—"

"Are you?"

He had to ask. Miura wasn't the kind to say things on his own or bring up things that weren't casually talked about. But he needed to know. And so he had to drag it out himself, although he wasn't sure what he'd do with the information once he'd obtained it.

"I've never…" the teacher started. "I don't have much to compare to. I guess I was."

Miya shifted his dark, watery eyes.

"I still am."

Miya felt the corner of his lip pulling slightly upwards in a small curve. He blinked several times.

"What about you?" The words were tentative and sounded strange, coming from somewhere deep inside Miura's throat.

Miya sighed heavily. "I'm in love with a man who doesn't know what he wants," he replied. "With a man who doesn't want to be seen in public with me. Who is threatened by the very idea of my persona." His voice softened. "And I'm afraid too. I'm never good with relationships. I'm too abrupt and intense. And I understand that I'm difficult to deal with. I fear rejection above all else, and this man rejected me. But I understand."

He felt a tinge of sadness, a different kind, washing over him. "I understand that you pulled away. After all, my own family despises me. I can see how you don't want that."

Miura stared at him, wordlessly, seemingly taking in the quiet flow of words as they came, stringing along effortlessly.

"You know why we're all so close? It's because we don't really have anyone else. But because we're so close, we scare away everyone else. So it's going to have to be their choice, *your* choice, if you want to deal with it or not. But at least it's easier to understand if you'd actually say something. It's natural to be scared I guess."

"I'm not threatened by you or any of your friends," the man defended himself. "I was threatened by the idea of being different, and the thought that others would have an opinion on it." Miura offered a consoling smile. "If anything, I admired you for being so open and straightforward. It's just that I'm not like that."

Miya sighed. He felt tired.

"But I could be."

"Could you?"

"If I tried."

"Why would you? Is it worth losing everything over?"

"In this day and age, losing everything sounds impossible," the teacher countered.

"Worst-case scenario, you'd be alone."

"Would I?"

"I don't know." Miya finally looked at him properly, regarding him with dark eyes from beneath the fringe he'd been hiding behind. "Would you?"

He was slipping. His intentions hadn't been to come over to fix things; he just wanted to speak his mind and get closure, but he hadn't expected this. He hadn't expected such honesty, even if it was too late.

"I made a mistake."

Miura's hand reached towards him. It landed on Miya's upper arm, palm tentatively resting on his exposed, cool skin. It was questioning. He allowed it to rest there.

Miura came closer, his hand gripping Miya's arm a little harder.

"I made tons of mistakes."

"How long are you going to keep apologizing?" Miya fired back, smiling crookedly. He grabbed the hand on his arm, took it in his own and lowered it, but he didn't let go.

"As long as I have to."

Miya shook his head and chuckled softly, surprising himself.

"Remember when I said you had a very straight approach to all of this? You're doing it again."

The man looked confused.

Miya felt calmer somehow. He was more in control of the situation, even though he felt his own impulse control slipping by the minute.

"I can forgive you," he continued honestly. "That's not the issue, but I can't be with you if you're not going to be honest. Least of all with yourself."

His fingers intertwined with Miura's. "You say you're in love with me, but if you can't be honest about it, if you can't see us being together as something acceptable, then you're right about us not being compatible."

It was funny. He'd come here for closure. Now he was giving an ultimatum. He wondered what the others would say if they knew what he was doing.

"So which is it?" he demanded. "Do you want me, or not?"

The grip on his hand tightened.

"Satoru. I want to be honest."

Miya inhaled sharply, waiting for the rest.

"With myself and everyone else. If that's what it takes."

"Will you?" They were in such dangerous territory. The ground seemed to be giving way underneath them. "Even if it costs you your family and your job?"

He saw the hesitation in the man's eyes.

"It won't, you know," he said without waiting for any kind of response. "People aren't that bad really. I'd rather be myself and live honestly."

"We all tell lies sometimes," Miya offered, softening again. "I don't care what you tell your family, but I don't want to be any kind of dirty secret."

"You never were. That's why I couldn't do it anymore. I couldn't stand hurting you."

"How ironic."

"I'm an idiot."

Miya's free hand found its way to Miura's shirt, tugging awkwardly at it. "Yeah, you kinda are. But so am I," he added, "for chasing someone who's so out of my league."

He looked into the teacher's face, reaching up to touch it briefly with the back of his hand. "You're this handsome, proper teacher. And it's kind of crazy that you'd even want me to begin with."

"Why do you say that?"

"Because I'm a big fake." Miya smiled crookedly. "I bleach my teeth. I lie about my age. I have no education. I work in a seedy club. My family is ashamed of me. And because I'm a slut."

"Don't talk about yourself like that."

And then Miura threw his arms around him and pulled him close. Miya was pressed against his chest, inhaling the scent of cologne and rain.

"It's true though." he whispered. Although he often joked about it, some of the discouragement from earlier came back. He didn't know how long they'd been standing in the apartment, but he was feeling emotionally fatigued.

"No, it isn't." Firm hands stroked him over his hair. "You're the most honest person I've ever met. And the most beautiful."

He tugged on strands of hair, and at Miya's heartstrings at the same time.

"And I won't allow that kind of talk about the man I'm in love with."

Miya melted. Despite himself, he clung to the man, and the tears he'd been holding back earlier spilled from his eyes—not many, but enough to form wet stains on the man's shirt.

"I want you," Miura cooed into his hair. "Fake or not. I want to be with you. I want to hold you. I want to be seen in public with you."

And so, Miya caved. He uttered an audible sob and didn't know whether he was laughing or crying anymore. But he allowed his head to be tilted upwards, for their lips to meet. He opened up, kissed back with all his might.

20. Suburban Bliss

Miya sat upright, knees pressed against his chest, pulling the sheets closer around himself. They smelled like detergent... like flowers in the spring. And spicy, of cologne, sweat and their individual scents blended together.

"I can't believe I let you sweet-talk me like that," he murmured, hiding his face behind his knees. He felt kind of dumb, but his body was heavy with satisfaction, his head light from the pleasure, and his heart starting to calm from the race.

Miura leaned in towards him, touching their foreheads together, running his thumb along his jaw line. He kissed him softly.

"Are you upset?"

Miya shook his head. "No. I forgive easily."

"I'm glad you feel better." He pulled him close. Miya closed his eyes, listening to the man's heart beating beneath his ear. He tried to summarize what exactly had gone down in the last few hours. He felt confused. But relieved.

"I missed you," he whispered, touching his lips to glistening, warm skin. "So much."

Fingers danced along his spine, palm gently brushing his back.

"But let's take it slow, okay? Let's see how it works out."

How many times had they said that before he wondered.

"You don't trust me?"

Miya smiled. "Trust takes time," he said. "We need to figure things out—together. I don't want to mess up again."

"I think that sounds wise."

The covers rustled as the man turned over to look directly at him.

"Are you sure you're okay?"

Miura's voice was full of concern, which wasn't hard to

understand. A lot of things had been said between them, not only today, but over the past weeks. So many feelings were still coursing between them. It was hard to grasp, and it would probably take a while for everything to stabilize.

"I'm fine," Miya kissed him on the shoulder. "I'm a pushover. But I'm okay."

***

For Miya, this was a completely new sensation, a new dimension. He'd been concerned, worried that they'd fail so miserably again, that their relationship wouldn't be able to withstand the aftermath of the storms that had shaken it so badly before.

But it seemed like he'd worried for no reason.

After their somewhat unexpected reconciliation, Miura seemed determined to show Miya that he was serious about him. It was surprising to say the least. Not that the man had turned one-eighty in a matter of one night; he was still hesitant about things like holding hands or kissing in public, and Miya wasn't expecting him to randomly jump out of the closet and call up his friends and colleagues, let alone his family, just like that.

Miya understood the need for taking it slow, which was why he had demanded that from the get-go this time around, without ulterior motives anyway. He wanted to wait and see, but the way they worked together for the time being was so unexpectedly good that he found it hard to contain himself.

Of course, the recent development hadn't gone the slightest bit unnoticed by Miya's friends.

There had been a general outrage of "You took him back?" and the like, although Maki had smiled knowingly at him from behind the bar as he explained to them that they were giving it another go, and that he was positively surprised by Miura—now reverting back to "Shunsuke"—and his determination to make it work between them this time. For the most part, the others were supportive. Naru had expressed slight concern but had still happily hugged him. Aki was sullen as always; he didn't seem to approve of relationships too much. Miya had to admit though that he was being slightly unfair, dumping his shifts on the teen and occasionally abandoning him to go on dates rather than spending a day or two in with him like they used to. He made a mental note to invite him to watch movies and get hammered as soon as they both had the time.

But finding the time for anything else was difficult to be honest when all he wanted was to spend as much time with his lover as possible. The symptoms of his addiction were starting to show once more. Similar to his tendencies of falling head over heels when he was younger, he was now unable to think of anything else but Miura and the way he'd wrap his arms around him after a long day—strong, protective arms, and warm, gentle lips pressing lovingly against his neck.

And as much as Miya wanted to be blinded by all the sudden attention and affection, he was still slightly skeptical, or at least trying to be, to protect himself. He'd never be able to be entirely reserved, or to play it cool, but he did have some thoughts in mind that he needed to air out at some point. It was just difficult to find an opening for it whenever they were together. He didn't want to bring up too much personal stuff on their dates, and as soon as they were behind closed doors, he had no interest in mundane talk. He was far too easy to seduce, figuratively and literally speaking.

To be honest, he was starting to feel surprisingly happy. As much as the others made fun of him for it, he was enjoying the fact that he now had his own key to the other man's apartment, even though they were hardly apart. He spent most of his nights there, and thus would be at home when Miura came back in the afternoons. Hiiro had bought him an apron as a joke, but even so, he'd decided to put it to good use and use what limited knowledge he had when it came to the culinary arts to whip up simple dinners for his lover whenever the chance offered itself.

The apron had been a huge hit. So he wasn't complaining at all.

***

November was approaching, and the cold winds blowing in from the sea were getting more and more unpleasant with each passing day. The sun poked out from between grey, heavy clouds on a rare basis as winter really started approaching.

Even so, Miya happily smiled from ear to ear as he strode up the street towards the apartment building where he was keeping his temporary residence.

He unlocked the door and called out the habitual greeting, *"Tadaima!"* Even though there was nobody at home. For a moment, he felt bad about not having been at his own place for a while, but he figured Aki was glad to be rid of him anyway. The two of them saw each other at work, and the teenager seemed fed up with his suburban bliss as it was. Plus, he had his own thing going with the infamous *Precious*, so Miya allowed him to have the space to himself for a while.

Because the outside world had turned into a cold, wet and generally unpleasant place, he decided to have a hot shower before getting started on dinner. When he got out, he grabbed a huge sweatshirt and pulled over his head. It was wide enough to fit two of him inside, and long enough to reach down to his knees. Not bothering to put anything else on, he went back into the kitchen.

He rolled up his sleeves, pinned his hair away from his face and put the apron on over the shirt, tying it with a sloppy, loose knot in the back, and started preparing the meal. Nothing fancy: rice, vegetables and thin slices of meat, no particular recipe or anything, just things he knew Miura liked. He hummed to himself, chopping the vegetables, and thought back to his childhood and how his mother would usually be all smiles while preparing dinner. When he asked why she was so happy, she would reply, "Because I'm grateful, being able to cook for the people I love the most."

Oftentimes, the sentence would be followed by a pinch to his cheek by hands that were soft and scented with vegetables and spices, or a ruffle of his hair.

He stopped for a moment, looking down at his own hands,

chopping up carrots on the plastic cutting board. They were slender, pale and almost ladylike. Maybe he resembled her more than he liked to remember. Something stung in him. When was the last time he'd called them? Usually it was such an unpleasant experience that he avoided it if necessary. But he still felt bad. He wished they could be happy for him now that he truly understood the meaning of those words she'd told him back then.

Turning on the rice cooker and placing the vegetables in a bowl, he started on the meat, dipping the thin slices in an instant marinade and shaking off the pointless thoughts. Whether they came around or not wasn't his job to worry about; he'd rather enjoy the present.

He cast a glance on the clock on the wall, wondering if Miura would be much longer. He was hoping to be able to spend at least some time with him before *he* had to go to work. The downside of their relationship was working at completely opposite hours of the day, which meant not having as much time to see each other as he'd have liked. On the other hand, it made for plenty of personal space and prevented any possible chance of getting sick of one another. Somehow, he thought the latter one would be impossible as far as he was concerned, but that was probably his endorphins talking.

He heard the footsteps approaching in the hallway outside and realized once again how little soundproofing there was in this apartment. If Miura had any intention of hiding their relationship, *that* cover was definitely blown ages ago.

"Welcome home!" he chirped the moment the door opened.

The teacher sighed, hanging up his drenched coat. "I'm home."

"It's raining again?" Miya asked, looking him up and down. "It was fine when I went shopping just now. Just a bit cold."

"Dressed like that?" Miura nodded in his general direction, placing his briefcase on a wooden chair next to the small hallway.

"Silly, of course not." Miya shook his head. "I showered."

He was hoping Miura would reply with a coy "Without me?"

or something of the sort, but Miura didn't seem to be in such a mood. He sighed again and strode over to the couch, slouching heavily between the pillows and blankets that had piled up there—Miya hadn't bothered cleaning. He didn't want to spoil the man after all.

A wry smile curled over his lips. "Indeed," he said to himself, rinsing his hands off in the sink.

"Did you say something?"

Miya shook his head, turning around to face the other man. "Nothing," he said, drying himself off on a kitchen towel, starting to make his way over to the sofa. "How was work?"

"Tedious. And all these people on the subway..." The man shuddered. "I don't know if the numbers have increased, or if it's just all the thick coats, but it's more cramped than usual. And I had to throw three students out of the classroom today for disturbing the class. Youths!"

He said the last word with such exasperation it made Miya chuckle softly.

"Poor dear, you had a hard day, huh?" he placed his hand gently on Miura's shoulder, and as he walked around to the front of the couch, he allowed the hand to wander.

"Awful." Miura's hand grabbed his wrist and pulled him swiftly down on his lap. "It's getting better though. Increasingly."

"Is that so?" Miya allowed his lips to be caught in a feathery kiss.

"That's only natural," the man replied, smiling and pulling Miya up into a sitting position, still on his lap. "I come home to you, looking all cute like this. Preparing food for me and everything."

"Cute?" Miya felt himself turning red. Being called something that innocent was a rarity for him to say the least. He bit down on his lip.

"Don't you think you'd make a good wife?" Miura teased him, stringing strands of ebony around his index finger.

"Well, I know my mother would be disappointed," he replied dryly, "considering how she wants *me* to find a wife."

"I must say that's rather hard to picture."

"Hn," Miya didn't want to think about it. He pressed himself down, rocking forwards to touch their foreheads together. "Weren't you just telling me about your hard day by the way?"

He grinned wickedly, kissing the man's temple. Strong, rough hands gripped his bare thighs, going up slightly underneath the sweatshirt he wore.

"You're not wearing any—"

"Ssh," Miya cooed against the shell of his ear. "Let's just focus on something less depressing, shall we? You had a rough day, right?"

He repeated the question from before while kissing his way down Miura's neck, loosening his tie and top buttons while he was at it. His hands moved steadily and determinately towards their goal, one reaching into the man's pocket, knowing full well that he carried protection. Meanwhile, the other hand popped open his trousers as well, reaching inside. He grinned at the reaction, a soft, almost relieved sigh as the man slid further back in the couch.

Nimbly, Miya tugged the man's pants down as far as he could and got back in the same position as before; straddling him, one leg on each side, still dressed in the hoodie. "*Sensei,*" he mumbled coyly, hiding his smile behind his sleeve, catching the man's eyes with his own, "Forget about the world for a while, okay?"

"S-Satoru..."

Perhaps he'd crossed a line, he mused. Even if the man was a teacher and that was his title, it was probably way out of his comfort zone after all.

He leaned forward, their lips met. He felt his own erection quivering against the sweatshirt, and his thighs were shaking from holding his body up in this position for so long, but he didn't want to rush it. He wanted to savor this moment, and every other moment with this man. He nibbled on his bottom lip and sighed audibly into the kiss. His body was already aching. It was as if he'd been constantly on fire ever since they got back together. The smallest of touches would set him off.

Breaking the kiss, he looked into Miura's gaze with his own half-lidded eyes. His tongue darted out to follow the contours of Miura's lips.

Slowly, he started letting himself down, supporting himself with one hand.

"You don't have to—"

"Ssh." He silenced the teacher with a determined kiss. "Stay still."

He kissed his jaw, the corner of his mouth. "Let me be good to you..."

Miura gave in, supporting him as Miya gradually, painfully slowly, lowered himself onto his shaft, inch by inch, in controlled little motions. It wasn't entirely painless, but he grit his teeth, placing his trust in his own patience and the want coursing inside of him. He gave himself time to accustom to the intrusion, pausing and focusing on his own breathing and Miura's expression, his control evidently slipping, his gaze glazing over. One of his hands found its way to Miya's cheek, resting gently against his flushing skin before venturing to his neck, pulling him in close so their lips could continue to meet and break apart. Meanwhile, they started moving together, carefully.

But Miya placed his hand firmly on Miura's shoulder and demanded that he kept still. "Let me do this for you," he whispered quietly. The elder man smiled at him, loosened his grip on Miya's neck and tugged on his hair, bringing the soft tousles to the front so they were draped over his shoulders.

"All right."

The hands that were tugging at his hair went down along the length of his torso and gripped the oversized sweater, pulling it up over Miya's head. The apron followed, before brushing his hair back the way it was, lovingly combing through silky tresses with his fingers.

The feelings that gripped Miya were overwhelming. He almost wanted to cry, being so overcome by how gentle and loving this man truly was, and by how much he ached to be with him, to be closer, and even closer.

His patience was running short, the slight pain becoming less relevant as his desire fueled him to start moving again; gentle and slow at first, lifting his hips up and lowering himself down, impaling himself over and over, accepting the man inside of himself, soon making way for a budding, prickling pleasure that grew to control his being.

His muscles tensed and relaxed, fingertips gripping and clawing at the man's shirt, legs trembling and his voice seeping through their kiss-sealed lips. His motions grew quicker, more determined, lifting himself up and slamming himself back down. Though the other man held him, he was remaining passive, only expressing himself through the way he squeezed him harder, moaning and whispering into Miya's ears.

Until they finally cried out almost in unison and sunk down on the sofa together, trembling, Miya collapsing almost face first into the man's chest, attempting to catch his breath.

"I really could get used to this," Miura mumbled into his hair, running his hand down Miya's back.

The younger man didn't reply, just smiled against the formerly freshly pressed shirt.

"I was actually late today because I spoke to a realtor," Miura suddenly said.

"Hn?" Miya jerked his head up in surprise. "You're moving?"

"I've been considering it for a while. Isn't this place too small?"

Miya's heart beat a little faster. "For what?"

Miura swallowed audibly, sitting up, despite being weighed down by the younger man. "I was thinking of moving anyway… It's just… I was thinking of how nice this is, and we're going to make it work anyway, why not try living together?"

"You're kidding!" Miya barked without thinking, sitting up straight. He grimaced.

"You don't want to?" The other man wrinkled his brow in a purely quizzical manner.

"It's not that I don't—" His face felt hot. "What happened to taking it slow?"

"It's just a question. You don't have to answer it now, but I thought I'd share the thought with you in any case."

The conversation from earlier came to mind, the jokes about him being a housewife. It wasn't that it wasn't tempting to be like this every day, but it was a huge step, and he didn't know what to make of it.

"You and I were never good at taking it slow," the teacher teased.

"Let me think about it," Miya finally replied, chewing on his lip. He stood, pulling the discarded sweater back on.

Miura regarded him, wearing a half smile on his face. "You do that."

He looked silly, halfway undressed, with that hopeful look on his face, and Miya felt his heart aching. "I forgot about dinner," he mumbled, scurrying into the kitchen area. His mind felt dizzy; what had just happened?

***

"You're moving in with him?"

He was standing in the back yard outside the club sharing a smoke with Hiiro and Naruse, both of them surprised to say the least at the news he was sharing.

"I haven't agreed to it yet," he exhaled, cigarette smoke mixing with their frosty breaths in the cold air.

"But you're considering it, right?" Hiiro was pressing on.

"Well, yeah. Or, I don't know."

Naruse looked skeptical. "How can he turn around just like that so soon? I don't want to see you hurt like that again."

Miya regarded him silently. The truth was he also worried about that. He wasn't good at living with people he was in a relationship with. Or rather, his partners were rarely good at living with him. His personality and habits often clashed with people he was committed to after a while. He didn't want to ruin anything this time. But didn't being committed to each other mean that they would have to deal with challenges like these once in a while? He couldn't deny not having wanted precisely what Miura time and time again presented him with, but he couldn't expect that every single day would bring breakfast in bed and sweet text messages.

"Neither do I," he admitted, "so I don't want to answer him just yet. I can always move in with him at a later time, but…"

"You're always so impatient," Hiiro shook his head. "but if it's right, why shouldn't you go for it?"

It was typical for the redhead to be pushing for something like that. He'd been rushing this relationship from the start. Miya had to admit he was tempted though.

"Maki said the same thing," he shrugged, "but I know what *you* think."

He nudged Naru in the ribs.

"Just looking out for you. If he's right, you're gonna figure it out," Naru calmly replied.

"Yeah."

"Just don't let your feelings run away with you. Try to be rational, and make some agreements you can both meet."

"How are you younger than me?" Miya chuckled, putting out his cigarette with the tip of his shoe, leaning in towards the blond man.

Naruse shrugged, patting his shoulder lightly. "Just looking out for you."

He was grateful to have friends like this—supportive and honest at the same time. There wasn't really anyone else he could talk to about these things. He understood where they were coming from, especially after the recent turmoil he'd gone through. But they'd talked endlessly about it; Miura had apologized over and over, and Miya doubted he'd be hurt in the same way again. He feared it, that was true, but no less than he feared giving up on something that made him feel so entirely whole. Maybe living together could also prove stabilizing for their relationship. Who knew?

His insecurities were driving him crazy, but if the question was whether he *wanted* to try living with the other man or not, the answer was a big, neon '*yes*' glowing towards him. Naruse and Maki were both making good points though; it was probably best to lay down some ground rules, to talk things over in advance and prepare for any potential conflicts that would occur based on their personalities and habits alone.

And while trying to be practical and appearing to be calm on the outside, Miya felt giddy on the inside as he thought about where this might lead. He continued to sleep at Miura's house, picturing what it would be like waking up with him every day, and bubbled with excitement beneath the surface with each date they went on.

He was looking at himself differently as well. When he saw himself in an objective light, compared to the attitude he'd sported earlier, he liked himself better this way. The self that had taken such distance from monogamy had been created from bitter disappointment, while the self that desperately wanted to be loved was merely a product of his own addiction to the feeling itself. This was different. More level.

He was able to balance it out somehow, seeing that he could still be himself the way he wanted while being with someone. Especially as long as that person didn't want to change him into something he wasn't.

He thought that he was way more capable of distinguishing between what was real and what was just a mad crush talking. And at twenty-eight, he wanted to be able to say that he was able to fully commit to someone he loved.

It didn't mean that he'd ever look down on any of his friends for keeping up their lifestyle, or on those who even chose to continue hustling as a form of occupation. It was just that he was at a point in his life where he finally dared to admit wanting something more, something less casual.

And somewhere along the way, he started to realize that it wasn't a hard decision to make at all.

***

While his life more or less consisted of working, going on dates and spending the night at his lover's house, Miya didn't want to be the friend who ditched everyone just because he'd found someone. Making everything come together in a somewhat doable fashion was difficult, but not impossible. First off, he worked so late, it was mostly mornings and Thursday nights that were spent together with Miura. Quality time with his friends could then be done at Maki's and at the club.

But he felt bad about seeing so little of his roommate and finally forced Aki to hang out with him properly for the first time in a while.

It wasn't like he was never home anymore, but it still felt almost nostalgic to be just the two of them in their Higashinada apartment.

They'd picked up snacks and drinks from the local convenience store and ordered take-out.

"Isn't this nice?" he tried, noting that the teenager seemed distraught and quiet, despite them being well into the drinks already.

"Who are you, my mother?" the teen grunted. "Aren't you just trying to make up for feeling guilty?"

"About?"

"Ditching us for that teacher."

Miya snorted. "Hardly. I'm not ditching anyone, and besides, aren't you busy day and night yourself?"

He lifted his beer can and glanced sidelong at Aki, whose only response was gritting his teeth.

"How's Precious?"

"Leave me alone."

Miya sighed. They'd had a big fight a while back. Aki wasn't exactly impressed with Miya's decision to enter an actual relationship, claiming he didn't believe in them, something Miya had challenged. It had resulted in a sour mood between the two of them, and Aki demonstratively leaving the apartment.

Although Miya was curious, he never asked the youth any questions that went too deep. That day he'd crossed a line, and he didn't want to do it again, not unless he was invited. For now, he just wanted to spend some quality time together with his roommate. Despite their age difference, he truly appreciated Aki's company, and he realized he'd probably miss him as well—maybe more than anyone.

"Sorry," he said. "Just checkin'."

"How's... what's his name?"

"Shunsuke?" Miya noticed his cheeks burning, lips curving upwards as he said his name. "He's fine. Told me to say hi."

"Like I even know him," Aki sneered, lifting his glass.

They were already approaching that point where they would start arguing about minor things in their mildly intoxicated states, so he figured he might as well take the plunge. Miya sighed deeply and decided to take certain precautions. He fished out something resembling a cigarette from the coat hanging over the armrest and lit it on one of the scented candles on the table.

He noticed Aki's watchful eyes as he took the first drag and felt himself growing lighter almost immediately.

"I'm sure Teacher-guy *loves* this habit of yours."

Miya exhaled, not bothering to reply. "Want some?"

Silently, Aki reached out and took the joint from him. They rarely smoked like this just the two of them, but it probably wouldn't do much harm.

"Aki, listen..." he finally started, "Shunsuke kinda dropped a bomb on me the other day..."

"Let me guess," Aki cocked an eyebrow, "he wants children, and you're afraid it'll ruin your figure."

"Shut up, you jackass." Miya prodded him hard in the thigh with his leg. Then, retracting his foot, he sat upright on the sofa, regarding the younger man with eyes that were slightly swimming. "He asked me to move in with him."

Aki's face was hard. Expressionless.

"Actually, I haven't answered him yet. But..."

"You're gonna do it, right?" Aki's voice came as a monotonous hum, like it was coming from much further away. "Congrats."

Miya hadn't been looking forward to conveying the news; he knew that a mutual dependence had grown forth between them. He really didn't want to be the one to ruin it, even though...

"You don't have to pretend to be happy for me," he said dryly.

"Who's pretending?" Aki took another drag. He looked tired, not just tipsy. Miya felt a tinge of guilt—not that he had any responsibilities towards Aki, but he still felt bad for not keeping an eye on the boy for a while. Perhaps it really had been wrong to make him cover all those hours.

"I'm gonna talk to him about it. There are plenty of things to agree on before taking a step like that, and even then, we still don't have anywhere to live. So you won't be rid of me yet." He forced a smile.

Although the drugs and alcohol made him feel buzzed and giddy, there was a grave seriousness between them. It was definitely guilt.

"I was just getting used to the thought of you sleeping with only one person, and now this? Are you sure you're okay?" Aki countered. It was hard to tell what he was feeling, even in this state.

"I'm really happy actually," Miya admitted. "I just really want it to work out, so I'm nervous as hell. But then…"

He searched the boy's nutmeg eyes. "I'll really miss stuff like this, you know?"

"Just this?" The raven-haired teen leaned in, placing one hand on Miya's thigh.

"The past is the past, kiddo," he replied with a soft laugh. "But yeah. Maybe. I just… this is right, you know?"

Something crossed Aki's face. Some kind of emotion that was impossible to catch—it was too faint and too brief.

"I'm only saying this because I'm wasted," Aki grumbled. "But… he's lucky to have you. You know that?"

Miya's face lit up into a grin. "Of course!"

The teen smirked. "You and that ego of yours."

They sat for a while, leaning slightly against each other on the couch like so many times before. Aki's hand was still on Miya's thigh—a completely natural gesture.

"You know I love you, right?" Miya broke the silence with a slight tremble in his voice.

"Yet here you are, abandoning me."

"Pft," Miya snorted. "Who's abandoning anyone? For all you

know, this might never work out, and I'll come back to stay with you again. You'll be stuck with me forever."

He wondered if maybe the kid was worried about being on his own. He was young still. It didn't seem like he had much of a network outside of the one he'd created for himself here in Kobe.

"Don't give me nightmares," Aki replied, squeezing his thigh gently. "I can manage the rent on my own though, so in case he kicks you out, I'll leave the room vacant for you. How 'bout that?"

"And if he doesn't, feel free to ask someone to move in." Miya smiled. He purposely didn't hint any further in that direction. Aki didn't answer either. He sat quietly, emptying his drink.

"In any case," Miya continued, "it's not gonna happen until like after Christmas if we decide to go through with it. But I wanted you to know."

"I'm honored."

"I'm gonna stay with you for a while. It's midterm season, so I'm only in the way at Shunsuke's place."

He rambled to cover up what might be evidence of awkwardness, guilt and worry.

Aki didn't seem to be listening all that well. It was getting late, and since they usually slept off the exhaustion from working unreasonable hours on their nights off, maybe he was getting tired. "Can we stay like this though?"

"Wouldn't the bed be better?"

"I don't think Shunsuke would leap with joy at the thought."

Aki sneered again. "Like that's new. But fine, let's stay here then."

Aki allowed Miya to snake his arm around his shoulder and pull him close. They drank. "You know, I'm totally in love with this guy, but he's still just a guy. You guys are my family, so don't worry about him replacing you, 'kay?"

He noticed Aki rolling his eyes. "I think you've had enough," he pointed out. "You're getting sentimental. Just tell me one thing?"

"Mmh?"

A mischievous, teasing grin spread itself across the teen's lips. "You're not saving yourself for marriage, are you?"

"Moron!" Miya nudged him hard, spilling his drink everywhere.

"At least there's *something* left of you." Aki laughed at last, trying to wipe the alcohol off of himself with the sleeve of his shirt. "What's he like then?"

The tension had been lifted. And at least Miya wanted to believe that it was okay between them again. Grinning excitedly, he took a deep drag of the joint and started rambling. "Actually, the other day...."

21. All That Remains

He was lightheaded and hung over when he woke up the next morning with Aki still dozing next to him on the sofa. Every one of his limbs hurt from the awkward position in which he'd fallen asleep. As quietly as he could, he rose on his unsteady legs and headed for the bathroom. He didn't want to wake his roommate up.

Aki was a light sleeper though, so there wasn't really a point in trying to keep quiet. As soon as he shut the bathroom door behind himself and started undressing, he heard the younger man rummaging around in the other room.

He wondered how much longer they would share days like this, and nights like the previous one. It would be strange, leaving the apartment he'd lived in for almost as long as he'd been in Kobe. He turned on the shower and stepped in.

It wasn't like anything would happen right away, so he might as well enjoy the days that were to come and go.

"Aki!" he called out, not entirely sure his voice would carry through the sound of the water and the bathroom door. "Aki! C'me 're!"

"What?" Aki's voice came from the other side of the shower curtain. He heard the water in the sink running and peeked out to see the boy brushing his teeth.

"This was nice, right?"

Aki spat into the sink.

"We should hang out more often. All of us."

"Don't we hang out every night at work?"

"That's different!" Miya reached for the soap. "I'm thinking we could invite everyone over one day; get everyone together and drink till morning."

"As long as I don't have to pay for it." The teen put his toothbrush back.

"Deal." Miya grinned. "Hey, hand me a towel?"

Aki grinned, waving a towel in the air. "Come and get it."

Sighing, Miya stepped out of the shower and grabbed it.

"What would Mr. Boyfriend say to this, huh?"

"Shut up, brat." Miya laughed, wrapping the towel around himself.

He noticed the way the other male was regarding him, with something of a searching look in those unreadable nutmeg orbs of his. "You really are happy, aren't you?"

Perhaps Aki wasn't entirely awake yet, or maybe he was still somewhat intoxicated.

Miya smiled, nodding. "Yeah. I'm very happy."

He didn't care that he was only dressed in a towel and that he was sopping wet when he pulled Aki by the arm, embracing him tightly. "Which is okay you know."

"Yeah, I get it." Aki pushed him away. "Thanks. Now I'm soaked."

"You needed a shower anyway." Miya grinned, leaving the bathroom.

"Thanks, dear!" Aki called after him, his voice lacking any kind of amusement.

***

They had their party, with everyone getting together to celebrate Miya's decision. Although he hadn't talked to the other man about it yet; Miura had been busy with the class's midterms and all kinds of things, and so he hadn't really been available at all.

And somewhere between the nostalgia and the celebrations, Miya heard himself laughing. "If I fuck up, at least it's an excuse to throw a party to make me feel better again!"

Everyone lifted their glasses to that, and they partied till morning.

But as the two of them resumed their dates, Miya knew the time was at hand.

***

He decided that it was time one night when he didn't have to go to work until late, and he'd agreed to come back to Miura's house after they'd been out to eat. Initially he'd planned on bringing it up right away, but somehow his mind had gotten carried away, approximately at the same time as the other man had picked him up and thrown him onto the bed. There was a playful side to him that he only showed when he was completely relaxed, and Miya didn't find it in himself to stop it. So in the end, it had gotten later than expected, and he found himself putting on his make-up in Miura's bathroom to save some time.

He came out once he was done, and their eyes caught each other. It wasn't the first time Miura had seen him like this, but it was the first time he'd applied the make-up and gotten ready for work in the man's presence.

"Shunsuke," he said, glancing at the time. It didn't matter what time it was, he needed to get this off his chest as soon as possible. His voice was firm and clear. "There's something I want to discuss with you."

Miura stood from his chair and came over to him. "What?"

"What you asked me a while back... about living together, remember that?"

The teacher chuckled. "Of course."

"Okay, before we do anything else, I want to say something. And I'm sure you do as well."

Miya knew it sounded like he was about to end their relationship or something and tried to smile, but it fell through. He was nervous.

"I just... I was putting my make-up on, and I'm about to head out to work, and you're finally home, and I'm sure you think this isn't suitable, but... if you want me, this is what you're getting, okay?"

Miura stood quietly before him, appearing calm, blinking a couple of times. A car honked in the street outside.

"I'm almost scared to say this, but I'm really in love with you, and I want this to work out, but it won't unless we're accepting of each other. So I just want to say it right now, that I won't change. I'm not going to quit my job, or stop wearing make-up. I'm probably going to get drunk with my friends and stay out all night. I might be selfish now and then, and maybe even appear fake to the outside world, but this is the real me, and I like to think that this is the person you fell in love with. So... I need you to accept me as I am, and not try to change me just because we're going to be living together as a couple, okay?"

His voice trembled, and his gaze, which had been so sternly fixated at Miura, focusing on keeping eye contact, was slipping towards the floor.

"And in the same way, I won't push you into anything either. But I don't want whatever insecurities you've got to become an obstruction to our relationship. I need you to be open."

He stared down at his feet and then looked up into Miura's face. "Sorry for making all these demands."

"Stop saying you're sorry all the time," Miura said, still looking surprisingly calm. He smiled overbearingly, and Miya wondered when *he* had become the insecure one.

"Didn't I tell you before that you're the most honest person I've ever known? I'd never ask you to change. I fell in love with *you*." He brushed some stray hairs away from Miya's eyes. "Of course we'll face some challenges, but compromising one another out of selfish desires isn't the way to go."

Gripping Miya's chin gently between his thumb and index finger, Miura leaned in and kissed him softly on the lips.

Again, that melting sensation came over Miya. He sighed against the man's lips. "And I don't want to change you either, but there's one thing... You're not out, right?"

"I guess not," the man replied, although they both knew he wasn't out to anyone aside from the people Miya talked to about their relationship. Nobody else knew about them, although his neighbors were probably getting a certain idea by now, even if they'd barely seen Miya around.

"My relationship with my family isn't the best," Miya started, "but I want you to at least talk to yours before we do anything."

He didn't really know why that was important. Maybe to avoid the kind of situation that he'd experienced himself when his parents had unexpectedly turned up on his doorstep, maybe so that he wouldn't have to deal with them himself, or perhaps because he didn't want to experience Miura's disappointment should his family write him off completely because he'd chosen to start living with another man. Even so, it felt like a huge demand to expect from someone else.

"I'll talk to my folks as well, although it's probably pointless," he added. "But I understand if that is way too much to demand so early on."

Miura shook his head. "No," he said. "I already thought about that. I'm done hiding and making up vague excuses. It's time I told them anyway, especially now that I've got you. Just don't expect me to tell the world right away."

Miya shook his head, smiling. "Of course not."

"I'd rather risk everything you know."

"...than?" He needed to hear it, selfish as that might be.

"Rather than losing you again."

Miya burned from the tip of his toes to his earlobes. Wasn't it crazy to say all these things after such a short time? On the other hand, he felt like this was what he'd been waiting for forever.

He pressed himself close to Miura, holding him tightly. "I'm so glad you followed me that time."

"Me too." Miura kissed the top of his head. "But I also have a demand."

"Which is?"

"I want you to stop smoking."

Confused, Miya looked up. Didn't he say that he didn't want to change anything? And in that one confused moment, all kinds of scenarios washed through his head; that perhaps Miura hated the smell of tobacco, that perhaps his skin was suffering or that his breath was bad. He almost started sweating at the thought.

"Smoking is bad for you, you know. I want you to live a long life, after all."

"Oh." He could hear how relieved he sounded and nodded. "I

can try. I'll try, okay?"

"Okay," Miura replied, kissing him again. They broke apart, and the man smiled earnestly at him. "So that was a 'yes' then? You want to live together?"

Miya nodded.

Miura took his hands, led them up to his face and kissed them. "I'm so glad."

Miya's face broke into a wide, happy grin. "Me too!"

He gripped the other man's hands harder, and his heart beat wildly in his chest.

"I'm so happy," he laughed, "but I have to leave you. Work is calling."

His phone was buzzing in his pocket already.

"I'll be waiting."

Their lips met. "I know."

***

When he got in to work that night, he barely managed to get through the door before spilling the news. It was met by a roar of excited congratulations.

Aki chimed in with a playful, "Let's see how long it lasts, shall we?" but everyone seemed genuinely happy. And Miya was sure all the tips he got that night came from his exceptionally good mood. All the same, he was certain he hadn't slept so well in ages as when he crawled into bed next to Miura that night and felt the man's arms wrap around him.

***

The next day, he grit his teeth and took another plunge. He called his parents.

His mother answered. She sounded surprised to hear his voice.

"Satoru! Why are you calling? Are you okay?"

Like he'd only call home if something was wrong. Although it was true that the contact between them had been poor over the last few years.

"I'm fine, Mother. Actually, I'm great. That's kind of why I'm calling." He decided to cut through the chase. "Listen... I've... met someone."

"Oh?"

Was her voice hopeful on the other end? He couldn't tell. Maybe. He swallowed the spiteful remarks he could have made, leaning back in the sofa. He was back at his own apartment—alone.

"Yeah. He's a great guy, and I just wanted you to know that I'm going to move. We're gonna get a place together."

"W-with him?"

He clenched the phone, sighing. He kept calm, forcing himself to breathe and reply in a controlled fashion. "Yes. I guess I'm finally ready to settle down."

She was quiet on the other end.

"We won't be moving yet," he continued. "We're gonna start looking for a new place. So I don't know when it'll be, but I'll forward the address to you when we're settled in."

"Are you calling for money?"

He sighed again. "No. I don't want anything. I just wanted to let you know."

He just wished they'd be happy for him for once.

"Oh. Who is this person?"

"He's a teacher, and he's the sweetest guy ever. Maybe I'll bring him home one day."

That was probably pushing it. Though his mother didn't protest, she didn't answer him either.

"He wants to meet you at least." He didn't know that for certain, but probably. Miura was also going to tell his own parents soon to give them time to adjust. Miya could only hope it would go well.

The awkward silence over the phone continued. "Anyway," Miya fumbled with his phone, "I kinda just wanted to say that. To let you know at least."

"Thank you for telling me."

He longed for more emotion in her voice, any kind of

indication towards how she actually felt. And then he wanted to call her out on her lack of response and remind her that this probably meant she'd *have* to if not acknowledge then at least admit to what he was. Maybe that would be the first step towards not thinking it was the worst thing possible for him to be.

"Does that mean you're finally quitting that job?"

He frowned. "No. He doesn't mind me working at the club, so I'll keep it up. I love my job."

More silence. He sighed for the third time, considering hanging up. And then he remembered. "Mom," he said, dropping the formal speech for the first time in ages. "Actually... I'm really happy. I understand you now; getting to cook for the person I love, getting to see him every day and do the little things that make him smile."

For some reason, he felt tears brimming behind his eyelids. His mother made some kind of sound on the other hand, but it was hard to tell whether she was emotionally provoked by his words or not.

"I'll continue to do my best like this," he smiled. "So if you can, please pass the good news on to the rest of the family."

"I'll tell your father and brother," she replied.

"Thank you." He ignored her monotonous tone. She sounded thoughtful, at least he thought so. "And then... can you say something to Shigeru from me?"

"What?"

"Tell him I love him, okay?"

Regardless of what Shigeru thought of him at this point, he was sure to be embarrassed by a statement like that, but Miya wanted him to know anyway.

"I will." She finally sounded like she was smiling.

"Okay. I need to go now, but I'll keep you posted."

"Thank you for calling, Satoru."

"Bye, Mom."

"Good bye."

She hung up first.

He exhaled shakily, placing the phone on the table in front of him. He didn't really mind her formal tone. He thought that maybe things would change for the better, albeit slowly. At least he was standing up for himself.

He felt different. Like the past months had turned him into something else—someone better. He looked down at his feet, and then lifted his gaze slowly, sweeping it across the living room of the apartment where he'd spent most of his adult life.

He was twenty-eight years old, but he didn't worry about that anymore. He didn't know where he stood with his family, but that was okay. He was happy.

A smile crept over his face.

This was where it all began.

List of Expressions

悟 – Satoru (written with "Enlightenment")
俊介 – Shunsuke (written with "Excellent" and "Concernment")
秋 – Aki (written with "Autumn")
勇気 – Yuuki (written with "Courage")
茂 – Shigeru (written with "Flourishing")

Asahi: beer brand
Aniki: Older brother (respectful form)
Ba-san: Auntie
Conbini: Convenience Store
Dango: Skewered beanpaste balls
Gariben: Geek/studybug
Golden Week: Week of consecutive holidays at the beginning of May
Gyūdon: Beef bowl
Hakama: A type of traditional clothing
Hanami: Cherry blossom viewing
Hime: Princess
Itterashai: Have a safe trip
Izakaya: A type of Japanese drinking establishment which also serves food to accompany the drinks
Jusco: Department store chain
Kushiyaki: Skewered, grilled poultry and non-poultry (vegetables)
Love hotel: Cheap hotels where one can bring partners to have sex
Nee-san: Older sister
Nii-san: Older brother
Obasan: Auntie (formal)
Ohayou: Good Morning

Okaeri: Welcome home!
Omiai: Marriage interview
Otsukaresama!: Good job today!
Pachinko: A type of machine-based gambling
Ramen-ya: Noodlestand
Sensei: Teacher
Soba: Buck-wheat noodles
Sukiyaki: A type of hotpot, usually eaten in winter
Tadaima: I'm home!
Tatami: Traditional flooring
Takoyaki: Fried octopus
Yakitori: Fried chicken
Yukata: Summer kimono

www.ingramcontent.com/pod-product-compliance
Lightning Source LLC
Chambersburg PA
CBHW070556260626
47161CB00002B/621